JACQUELYN MITCHARD

Two If by Sea

SIMON & SCHUSTER

New York   London   Toronto   Sydney   New Delhi

Simon & Schuster
1230 Avenue of the Americas
New York, NY 10020

First Simon & Schuster hardcover edition March 2016

SIMON & SCHUSTER and colophon are registered trademarks of Simon & Schuster, Inc.

For information about special discounts for bulk purchases, please contact Simon & Schuster Special Sales at 1-866-506-1949 or business@simonandschuster.com.

The Simon & Schuster Speakers Bureau can bring authors to your live event. For more information or to book an event contact the Simon & Schuster Speakers Bureau at 1-866-248-3049 or visit our website at www.simonspeakers.com.

Manufactured in the United States of America

1 3 5 7 9 10 8 6 4 2

Library of Congress Cataloging-in-Publication Data
Mitchard, Jacquelyn.
Two if by sea : a novel / Jacquelyn Mitchard.
pages ; cm
I. Title.
PS3563.I7358T985 2016
813'.54—dc23
2015016688

ISBN 978-1-5011-1557-8
ISBN 978-1-5011-1559-2 (ebook)

For Marty

For Susan

Forever

Two If by Sea

ONE

S O MANY THINGS happen when people can't sleep.

It was always hot in Brisbane, but that night was pouty, unsettling. After getting Natalie and her family comfortable in their rooms at the inn, Frank couldn't rest. His leg plagued him. The toll of oppressive weather on that kind of old injury was no old farmer's myth. He rambled around, briefly joining Natalie's brother Brian in the bar on the beach, then painfully mounting the switchbacked decks of wooden stairs that led to a kind of viewing platform just adjacent to the car park, looking out over Bribie Island Beach. Up there, he hoped the signal would be good enough to call home, his home, if home is the place you started. For Frank, that would always be a ramshackle horse farm in south-central Wisconsin—now probably more ramshackle than when he last saw it, three years before. As the *brrrrr* on the other end began, his pulse quickened. He looked up at the sky and thought of all the calls darting through the sea of radio waves tonight, swift as swallows—dutiful, hopeful, wistful, sad.

"Frank?" His sister, Eden, answered, her voice holiday-bright and holiday-brittle, suddenly next to him across nine thousand miles. He was about to ask her to summon his mother to the phone so they could all talk together when he saw it. Without thinking, and without another word to Edie, he let his phone slip into his jeans pocket.

He could not figure out what it was.

He would never remember it as a wave.

Wave was too mere a word.

Although there were hundreds of photos and pieces of film, some shot just at the moment, near this very spot, Frank could look at these and remain curiously unmoved. But should he close his eyes and let himself return, the sick sweats would sweep down his breastbone, a sluice of molten ice. He would hear again the single dog's one mournful howl, and feel the heavy apprehension, something like that moment from his days as a uniform cop when a routine traffic stop went completely to shit and a fist came flying in from nowhere, but monumentally worse. So much worse that it routed even imagination. Many years later, Frank would think, this was his first sight of the thing that would sweep away the center of his life in the minutes after midnight, and, by the time the sun rose, send surging into his arms the seed of his life to come.

Just like that. Like some mythical deity with blind eyes that took and gave unquestioned.

He saw the wave as a gleaming dam, built of stainless steel, standing upright in the misty moonlight, fifty feet tall and extending for half a mile in either direction. Then, as it collapsed in place, it was water, surging lustily forward and drowning every building on the beach, including the Murry Sand Castle Inn, where Frank's pregnant wife and her entire extended family lay asleep. For one breath, Frank saw the inn, its porch strung with merry lanterns, red and gold and green, and in the next breath, he saw everything disappear, every light go out, faster than it was possible to think the words that could describe it.

He shouted, "No!" and stumbled forward to make his way down the high tiers of wooden stairs he had only just ascended.

Hoarse, in the distance, another voice called, "No!" over a cascade of sound—the brittle pop of breaking glass, screams peppering the air like gunshot, and the throaty insistence of the water.

Even as Frank turned, the mud-colored tide was boiling up the stairs and leaping the boardwalk barricade. He plunged forward, trying to wade against it, to find the riser of the wooden steps, but there was nothing; his foot bounced against water; he was soaked to the thigh. Pulling himself up along the top rail of the fence, for he would certainly be able to see something of the inn from there, or at least hear something, he shouted, "Natalie!" There were no voices. No lights except the milky smear from the hotels and office towers far in the distance to his left, like a frill of fallen stars. No sound except the insistent gossip of the water, and he was wet now to his waist. Grateful that he was still at least relatively young and passably fit, Frank hauled himself over the fence. He skip-sprinted across the car park, to their little Morris Mini-Minor. Water was already frothing around the tires. Frank pulled open the door, throwing himself into the seat, fumbling for his keys, quickly gaining the highway.

He stopped again and got out.

He heard a man's voice cry, "Help! Who's there . . . ?" and then again the swallowing silence. Floodwater rocked at the verge of the road; now how many feet above sea level? Of the two of them, Natalie was, pound for pound, by far the stronger, fitter, even tougher. Of the two of them, she was also the more intrepid, the more likely to have found some way to outsmart and elude this cliff of tides. They would find each other, and he did her no service by stalling here, forsaking his own life for no purpose. Natalie would have hated him for that. He floored it, racing inland. Miles sloughed away and he felt rather than saw the dark shapes of other cars congealing around him.

At last, there was nowhere to move, and all the cars had to stop and Frank got out and walked.

Others walked, too.

An old man struggled under the weight of a gray-lipped girl. She was perhaps ten or eleven years old and her sweet, lifeless face had closed in a smile, her nose and eyes pouring saltwater tears. Frank saw a young woman wearing just one shoe. She clutched a bundle of wet clothes, among them a child's small jersey embroidered with cross-stitched Santas. A man Frank's own age sat sobbing near a great blooming evergreen frangipani. Frank avoided their eyes. He thought he might be able to get to a place where he could think, but he only walked farther. He met people hiking toward him, or saw them sitting in their cars, or standing still by the roadside, their hands like the pendulums of broken clocks. After some time, he came upon a large group gathered around a car whose young driver had removed his outsized speakers from the dash. A basso radio voice intoned, "Now you will hear that the tsunami happened because of climate change, friends. You will hear that it struck our coast because of a tropical storm deep in the Pacific. You will hear that this was a random event. But do you believe that? How can any man believe that it was coincidence that water swept into the Sodom of Brisbane on this very hallowed night? Intelligent people will say that we have failed to take care of our earth. But the Lord God Almighty does not care about the climate. He cares about the climate of our souls! As it says in Matthew, 'Therefore keep watch, because you do not know the day or the hour.' And so it has come . . ."

Frank walked around a curve in the road, and the preacher's voice faded to a series of thumps, like the bass notes of a song from a car passing the open window of Frank's childhood bedroom on the farm. A pale vein of light lolled on the horizon.

It would soon be dawn, on Christmas morning.

TWO

Darkness Gave Way to a dreary matte pearl, and Frank noticed that the park where he sat was a cemetery.

Outside of Brisbane, there was so much sheer breadth of land that every dear departed citizen could have had a square mile for a tomb, yet this was one of the streamlined modern kinds of mortuary parks, with flat brass markers, built for economy of space. There were a few benches for lingering, but altogether, it looked more like a game board than a place to greet majestic eternity.

How he'd chosen this small rise, he had no idea. All he knew was that he faced away from the city. Before he looked down, Frank wanted to think logically through the sequence of the night—the family party, the announcement of Natalie's new pregnancy and their sudden decision to move back to the United States, the toasts before hot meat pies and lamingtons, the four huge Donovan brothers socking and slapping him to the point of pain, which was what passed for congratulation in Natalie's big, physically big, and boisterous family. The distress was in stringing together those acutely joyous moments, which even as they happened Frank knew were as perishable as the African iris his mother grew in her little greenhouse, an exquisite buttery bloom that lived only a single day. They filled his head and whirled with the plaintive howl of the dog back there in the darkness, the howl that must have merged with the roar of water—he heard it now with some third ear, booming and sucking.

Natalie!

How could any sensible word or image press through sounds like that?

Someone must have survived.

Nothing down there had survived.

Nothing could have lived through that.

But if he had been craven to leave her to die, was he not more so to abandon all hope of her survival? He had to hope, at least, although it made him feel like the grannies at his mother's church who could stand at the bedside of an eighty-pound ruin barely visible in a tentacled web of ghostly sheets and murmur words of encouragement.

As marriage was a triumph of hope over logic, so must be a husband's belief. His own eyes told him one thing, but he did not have to put all his faith in that one thing. Eyes lied. When he was a rookie, he had learned the nature of eyewitnesses. Eyewitnesses, people with mortgages and diplomas, had seen cougars walking on their hind legs through Grant Park. Eyewitnesses swore that the man in line behind them, a professor from Jamaica with horn-rims and a British accent, had pulled the trigger, when, in fact, the shooter was a ringer for Johnny Cash.

The way back to where Frank had left his car was long, perhaps four miles. He hurried, his breath coming faster, in rhythm with the staccato xylophone hammering of his heart, in the hitching hop-jog that was his only gait faster than a walk. The sun barely up, it was already warm, nearly eighty degrees by the feel of it, the height of Queensland's epic hot season. The palms, restless and dry, rattled above him. Far off, sirens keened, whooped, blended, in a chorus that peaked and fell. He needed to get to his cell phone. Natalie had been an athlete all her life, and was a strong swimmer, with the reflexes of a teenage point guard. Her job had trained her to make instant decisions under enormous stress.

Natalie. As though he were paging through an album, he viewed a deck of her expressions—the gamine and entirely-on-purpose flirtatious glance from under lowered lashes, the opaque concentration in the face of a disastrous injury that verged on a glare, the mirth that opened her lips, passion that clamped them . . . it was not possible that the last time he had seen Natalie was the last time he would see Natalie. Frank remembered police training that taught rookies to stop a sneeze by slamming a fist into their thigh. He did this now, punching his bad leg ferociously to dodge the thrall of tears he had no time to indulge.

It worked.

Frank pictured his mind as a rubber truncheon he could grasp and twist. She could have survived.

Her brother was right; he'd once said Natalie was like an action figure.

He thought of her making bins of things to toss or donate in preparation for their move to the United States, nattering about how she would no longer have to be envious of Brian and Hugh, who'd spent their junior years abroad there and could both do a very passable Brooklyn accent. Like most Australians, Natalie conceived the United States as a series of landmarks arrayed close together: the Statue of Liberty right next to the Grand Canyon, with the Hollywood sign tucked between. She wanted to see everything, all during the first week, with a nursing infant in tow.

Frank almost smiled. She could be looking for him even now.

At that moment, as if in answered prayer, the cell phone rang.

If he hadn't been so physically tired, he'd have made it to the front seat of the serviceable old Mini he'd bought when he moved from Chicago. He'd left the passenger door thrown open. There on the seat were his mobile phone and the wallet he habitually removed from his pocket to stave off the old and scolding pain that fishhooked from lower hip to upper calf. Neither had been touched. The mobile went silent a single second before Frank could grab it.

Fumbling, he depressed the button.

The screen did not light up with the number composed mostly of eights, Natalie's favorite numeral—the number he always saw because he was too lazy to program in her name or photo.

Instead, he saw another familiar number, the origin of seventeen unheard voicemails. He felt crushed, literally stomped. But why should he? How ridiculous to expect Natalie to have a phone, her own phone.

How stupid was he?

His poor family at home. Of course. Eden. Mom. He should listen. He must at least listen.

"Frank!" his sister said. "Call us! Mom is frantic. I am frantic." He thought of the sweet and subdued Christmas Eve at Tenacity, the horse farm in Wisconsin where Frank's mother still lived with Frank's much-younger sister. Eden would be finished now with all but one semester of graduate school. And his grandfather, old Jack Mercy, at ninety-six slipped away into the muck of dementia, how was Jack holding up? Just before he left for Australia, Frank spent the day with Jack, and remembered comparing the old man's gaze to that of a bear he'd once seen—no cunning, no amusement, no plan, only flooding, baffled hunger. Still powerful and rangy after a life spent wrestling horses and throwing bags and bales, Jack had balled his fist and socked Frank's mother, Hope, so hard that she staggered and nearly fell, then threw his food at Hope, his rages seemingly only for her. It worried Frank, but there was no point bringing it up. Hope was just twenty when she married Frank's father, fourteen years her senior. Jack was the only father that Hope had now, since both her parents died in 1960 in the Park Slope air disaster. Whatever he did, Hope loved Jack still, with a foundling passion.

"Please be okay, Frank," Eden said. "Please call us back!"

Frank listened to a previous message.

In that one, an hour earlier, Eden didn't even speak directly to him. She addressed their mother: "He isn't answering. Mom, who should we call? Can we call anybody? It's a disaster area."

The phone chimed yet again. Answer it, Frank thought. Just say a word.

If the situations were reversed, he would have gone mad. All Frank had to do to end their agony, or at least temper it, was to press a button. But he simply could not summon the will. Here, inside this, he had no will to speak to them. At this moment, he was no more than enclosed space, breathing. How to rejoice for his own survival? How even to agree to rejoice for it, for the sake of others?

Go on and call, he thought, and almost pressed the return dial. Then he didn't.

Instead, he thought, he hadn't even told them about the baby. It didn't seem pressing enough to call before Christmas. And Frank was sly. All the Mercy family liked surprises. Perhaps he wouldn't tell them at all and they would show up after the baby's birth, with Natalie already fit again, his mother's first grandchild, a summer babe, just weeks old, in arms. It was a passing thought. Frank had intended, or perhaps intended, to tell them that night—the bow on top of the huge crate of gifts that Natalie had already sent. Every ritual of family was beloved to Natalie, as to all her Donovan tribe, and she reveled so much in her first big run at the hols as an in-law that Frank accused her of having butchered and packaged a wallaby: the box weighed as much as if it had been filled with ore. "But I didn't have the chance last year!" she said. "We'd only just been married. I got them . . . a fruit basket or some daft thing!"

Earlier, Frank had said something about his wife's having spent half the GNP of Australia on Christmas. Natalie's brother Brian, one ale to the good of sense, guffawed.

"No one goes for prezzies more than my sister!" Brian said. "Think of that whenever she says to just give her something simple and ignore it, brother-in-law of mine! You'll have a happy marriage, then. I remember her little, not just counting out what was under the tree but using my mum's sewing tape to measure the parcels to make sure that none of us got bigger than she did!"

The bartender interrupted then, muttering, "More of this bollocks . . ." They all quieted to listen to the curiously electronic voice of the announcer at the Pacific Storm Prediction Centre. Brian was a TV newsman—something of a celebrity in Brisbane—and the barkeep pulled another ale for Brian and asked why everyone got a big stiffie over every tropical depression when they came to nothing.

"It should be called the Watching Tropical Storms Happen Centre," Brian told the bartender. "Not the Prediction Centre. They've never predicted a single damn storm." He sipped his ale. "The tide came way in tonight, though, farther than I've ever seen it here."

"It does that when someone farts in Japan," said the barkeep, and Frank remembered laughing. Laughing! But then, anyone might have laughed. Whoever really believed that the thing you feared most would come to pass? Last night, the barkeep had been getting ready to close when Frank got up to make his call. As Brian rummaged for some bills in his pocket, the bartender had said, "No, no. These rounds are on us, lads. Drink up. I've managed to miss midnight Mass, so I'm happy, but my bride was already plenty pissed I had to work on Christmas Eve. She said the grandkids were desolate. But I think it's she who's desolate because my daughter and her fiancé, two kids and they've finally got engaged, if you please, they went out pubbing."

That man must be dead now, floating open-eyed like a figure in an old *Alice in Wonderland* woodcut, white on gray, with lamps and teacups and tables and chairs and spoons swirling around him. It seemed untrue. Families stumbled into the station house all the time—into the hospital, into the morgue—pleading proximity. *He can't be dead. I just saw him tonight at the bowling alley . . .* and Frank understood the audacity of fate's disregard for logical progression.

Could Brian have lived?

The thatched bar was no more than a couple hundred yards from the little roll of the water's edge. The tsunami would have swallowed that distance. Frank thought of Brian, of his big, affable equine face and mane of sand-white hair, the dark blue Irish Donovan eyes.

Of all of them, only Natalie had brown eyes.

Brian had introduced him to Natalie.

Brian usually hosted a swank event called Everyday Heroes—that year in the ballroom at the Brisbane Riverwalk—and was a friend of Frank's crew chief on the squad of volunteer first responders. Frank had not wanted to go: he was annoyed that he had to buy a sport coat. The tall woman with the thick auburn hair in an unruly pixie cut seemed familiar to him even before the awards were given out, and, as it turned out, she was, at least her face was. At a local high school, Natalie had tripped and disarmed a boy who'd shot two of his classmates, then sat on him while treating one of his victims until teachers took him over. She'd probably saved the life of the girl who was worst hurt, the brachial artery in her shoulder nicked so that she would have bled out in a minute had the Harbor High graduate giving the Career Day speech that day not also been an ER doctor. Since school violence was rare in Australia, and the possession of firearms hardly ubiquitous, the incident was big news for weeks, with many images of a reluctant Natalie, dressed much as she was that night, in the same plain black suit, her only jewelry the fire-opal earrings she loved.

The Natalie he met that night was on her fourth martini and insisted on feeding him three bleu-cheese-stuffed olives soaked in gin. ("I don't like gin," he protested. "I only like vodka martinis!" Natalie had held up a wavering finger. "*Vodka?* Vodka has nothing to do with a discussion about martinis!" she'd scolded him.) At Natalie's insistence that night, they'd never left the hotel. Two months later, they were married.

One Christmas, and then this one. Two anniversaries, one just past. A long trip and a short one. Hardly even the primary constituents of what could be called a marriage.

Frank knew guys, plenty of guys, who, by his age, had been divorced, at least once, a few twice. That was how his disinclination to marry had hardened into a full-fledged position, though he thought of children in the way people think of a winning lottery ticket. Until they met, he had not understood that this was a position a man could maintain only if he were never awestruck by love. The pleasantness of women was leaven in life, but Frank had not ever been in love. Not even near misses. Did this one love matter more in the universe than the love of two teenagers rutting in a car? It didn't, and yet he could not help but feel as though it must, somehow, have deserved a bye. People eaten alive with terminal illness had survived this storm, but not his only wife? He punched his thigh again.

In his adult life, Frank had forced himself to face facts squarely, the better to get hard things underway. He thought suddenly of sitting with families who regaled him with false hopes at the sites of irretrievably ghastly car wrecks, the kind of wrecks in which it was impossible to tell which victim had originally inhabited which car. When he was young, he privately thought those people were foolish.

He would be those people now. A granny. *It's not impossible. Just perhaps. There's always a chance . . .*

Frank got into the car and drove in what he sensed vaguely was the direction of the horse farm just north of Brisbane where he'd worked . . . worked and lived, until he married. But he did not get far. He could not recall which side of the road to drive on, and he didn't care. He would get himself killed; perhaps that was best. No, that was never best. He stopped, and ended up at the cemetery. After he sat for a while on a stone bench, he stood and filled his lungs, then tried to spool out the exhale in a hiss, as he had learned to do after the accident four years ago that had given him, at thirty-eight, his bad leg and his pension.

At the wedding, Brian toasted Natalie and Frank. "Welcome to the family, Frank Mercy. God have mercy on you, because Natalie won't. But she'll give you the most loyal heart in Australia, in the southern hemisphere, and maybe in galaxies we don't know about yet. My baby sister should be an action figure, to tell the truth. I mean, my brother Hugh here's a florist, and Natalie sews people's guts back into their tums after they try to blow them out with rifles. We, her older brothers, are deeply grateful to Nat for beating up on our enemies all our lives and we hope she'll do the same for you and your own five kids. A thousand welcomes to you with your marriage kerchief. May you grow old with goodness and riches." Bawling openly, Natalie two-fisted the heavy wedding bouquet that Hugh had made from white roses and camellias and hit Brian square in the chest. Her smile was incandescent; in memory, unbearable.

Frank began to shiver in the watery sunlight. They called it acute stress disorder now, the revving of the heart, the flushing of the skin, and the narrowing of vision. The emotional sequels were various—detachment, denial, anxiety, the persistent urge to avoid the scene of the event. There. In describing it, he was already experiencing it. If he lay down on this stone bench, he might sleep for six months.

Another car pulled up on the cracked shell road to the cemetery, a man and a woman. She was dressed in bits and pieces of things, a fancy ruffled shirt over sweatpants, a bright shawl and rubber boots. Like Frank, she didn't bother to close the passenger door.

"Man, where are you from?" the woman asked. For a moment, Frank thought of the radio evangelist.

"Brisbane. I live at Carson Place."

"Were you out last night?"

"I was at an inn at Bribie Island. At the beach."

"Have you seen our son?" she asked. She held out a snapshot of a boy around fifteen, astride a motorbike.

Frank studied the photo carefully for a minute or more and finally said, "I'm sorry but I haven't seen him. Where was he?"

"Selling Magnum Mini Moments at a beach stand," the father said. "He was coming home tennish." Moments were gooey little ice cream treats, among them a selection named for the seven deadly sins, Greed, Envy, Lust, Sloth, and, Frank's favorite, Gluttony. "We think he must have stayed for the fireworks." Fireworks were a staple of Australian Christmas, and also of Australian anything else. Aussies used everything from American Thanksgiving to the International Day of the Child as an excuse to set fire to something, to festoon the sky with twinkly, perishing graffiti. "I know he would have beat the storm out, because that didn't come until what? Long after midnight. One in the morning? He's got himself stuck at some gymnasium. James has got a good head on his shoulders. He'll turn up. You can make a good bit of tips holiday nights."

"He should not have worked on Christmas Eve," the mother said. Her eyes roamed corner to corner. "He should have come up to church."

"Shut up," said the man. "You shut up and go to hell while you're after it. It's nothing to do with it."

As the couple made their separate ways to the car, as if alone on parallel moving sidewalks in a terminal that went on forever, Frank pressed the speed dial to the home farm. Eden's answering machine picked up, a minor blessing. Frank would be able to live for a while longer without hearing the reaction to what he had to say. It would be blameless joy. Not that his family didn't care for Natalie. They did. They cared for Natalie, but they adored Frank. If they had to choose who would live and who would die, there would have been no choice.

The message said, "This is Eden Mercy's cell phone, and I'm sorry it's not me in person. How about leaving a message?"

"It's Frank," he said. "Sweetheart, I'll call again. Obviously, I'm alive. Natalie . . . Natalie and her family . . . her brothers and their wives and daughters are missing. Edie, I'll call back. I love you and tell Mom I love her."

Frank went to his car and opened it. There was bottled water in the boot of the car. As if seeing it for the first time, he recognized the first-aid kit and granola bars, all neatly packed in a box that Frank transferred to a horse van when he went to a jumps event, or to deliver or to pick up a horse for the owner of the place he'd worked. He didn't recall ever using it, although he knew that he replenished it once in a while. Distances in Queensland were vast, often parched and heat-blasted, or washed unrecognizable in mud, and habitation was unpredictable. Standing in the road, Frank opened a bottle and downed it. He opened and drank two more, tore open a granola pack, and swallowed it without chewing or tasting.

For a moment, the food centered him.

He walked back to the stone bench and sat down again.

He'd left Brian at the bar at twelve thirty, to stretch his legs after tucking Natalie in. Blissfully languorous, just beginning her fifth month, she'd been too drowsy even to open his gift, so he'd left it at her side, still in its silver wrappings. It came from a gallery in London and was hundreds of years old, a maternal primitive sculpted of thick dull gold with a coil of fire ruby at its center that would hang out of sight beneath Natalie's scrubs, between her breasts. Perhaps she could not have worn it at work. She was too often called on to do minor surgery to wear any jewelry at all, even her earrings. Still, he thought of the primitive mother now floating curved in dark water, to be found in five hundred years and presented by another bemused fellow to another abundant bride, and of the man who had forged it once, to commemorate the majesty of the commonplace miracle.

"I might like to maybe take some time off," Natalie said one morning, after they'd been snorkeling, after they demolished enough Eggs Benedict to feed four and made love in a way that left nothing else to do except sleep.

"Research?" he'd said.

"Social research, Yank. Say you have a kid. You'd want him to have every-thing, right? Like a stay-home mommy for a year? Like dual citizenship?"

Frank said, "Well, a theoretical kid? We haven't ironed out the kid business. I'm not pushing you for kids. I am forty, after all."

"So am I. I need to get some of these genes passed on. So this kid, it will be theoretical, but only for about the next six months," Natalie said, drawing out every word, preening, as a woman who'd made life had a right to do, as though she had been crowned a serene highness. Two weeks later, they saw the ul-trasound picture, his son's assertive penis and cunning alien leer. Pictur-ing that moment, their astounded faces, how they gripped each other's hands, Frank tumbled from the bench. He grasped his knees and puked in the mud beside the shell path.

The cell phone rang.

It was the chief of volunteer firefighters in his sector, outside the city, alerting him to a voice page from the State Emergency Service. He ig-nored it, pressing the button to power the phone off. Before he could, it rang again. Frank touched the speaker.

"Goddamn it, Frank Mercy, if you aren't answering this phone, you'd best be dead," the woman said.

His chief of volunteers was a hard woman, who had no idea where he was or what had happened. He also knew that she would have called him anyway and would find him somehow, as she had when he was two hours home from his honeymoon. Frank threw the phone to the ground near the car. It kept on ringing.

Fifteen times.

Twenty times.

Thirty.

THREE

FIVE HOURS LATER, in sweltering heat before noon, his back and flanks sweat-soaked under his duffel coat, Frank stood in the back of a patrol boat with two college kids, raw rookies, a young woman and a young man so terrified and clumsy they were more likely to brain each other with the eight-foot blunt-end body hooks than they were to pull anyone to safety. Still, even a raw volunteer was better than nothing. Not much better. The floodwaters still rose. Helicopters crowded each other like fat-bodied dragonflies darting at the many stranded in places the cutters couldn't go. As the Brisbane River burst its banks, whatever resembled a cogent plan of rescue was abandoned in favor of desperate duck and drag efforts on the part of every crew in every kind of conveyance, from cutter to rowboat.

There was no time to search.

A search would need to wait until they could pull out families they could see. There were plenty of people stranded on top of their cars or clinging to their gutters. So far, Frank and the crew in the patrol boat had hauled ten survivors up to waiting transport to Our Lady Help of Christians, where Natalie had been chief of emergency services. One family, a grandmother and two children, were floating on a hollow-core door. They brought each group to at least some dryish area nearby the hospital. Each time he glanced up, Frank could see small figures in blue drab, Country Guard, hastily erecting tents that they filled with cots and blankets and first-aid supplies. Most of the people they found were at least able to walk the last block to the hospital under their own steam— but a few were in shock, and others had serious lacerations or fractures. For them, Frank and one of the college kids unrolled the Easy Evac stretcher and hustled to the bottom of the hill where paramedic teams parked in lines exchanged their stretchers for Frank's empty one. When one bus pulled away, it was replaced by another: Frank saw the names stenciled on the sides—*Rockhampton, Cairns, Wollogong.*

The medics must have driven all night.

As soon as Frank and the rookies finished depositing a group, they ran back and threw themselves into the boat, the driver opening the throttle before they could sit down. The closer they came to the river, the more often they saw what appeared to be a shred of forfeit future. Impossibly, a Christmas tree, still lighted and fully decked out, beamed up at them from a depth of three meters. With the porch and front wall of their house ripped off, a family sat with their feet in the water, watching the television. A woman, hip-deep, was taking down her wash. A stiffened cow, a big black dog, and chickens. Frank had not thought of chickens drowning, for they could fly. And then there were the floaters, looking like duffels. The rookie girl—Frank thought her name was Cassie or Cathy—cried, each time, "I hope it isn't someone!"

Not once or twice but six times thus far, it was.

When that happened, the pilot, a man Frank knew slightly, threw down a buoy, as dignity seemed to demand.

Two of the dead were old men, one a woman Frank's mother's age; another was a teenage girl. They were wedged between bridge pillars, bobbing in cars like aquarium fish or hung up on the cornices of roofs. In the time it would take to dislodge and move them, others would die. The pilot turned up the boat's radio. Emergency Services Medal Radio transmissions warned residents not to stop for food or petrol but to leave the city in an orderly and calm manner, despite every road being jammed with cars like pegs in holes. The south stadium and commuter railway station were filled to capacity with refugees from submerged streets.

Every block or so, they had to slow to make their way around an inflatable or a rowboat, or the intact debris of a house ripped off its stump. Trees so large that a full-grown man could climb them tumbled past.

All of them were drowsy with fatigue and hyperarousal.

The sight of a young couple, perhaps twenty years old, wearing life jackets, open-eyed and livid, but still clasped together, snapped the teen volunteer like a matchstick.

"How can they be dead?" she said. "They're floating! They've got to be just unconscious."

"They're dead, honey," Frank said. "Try to take some deep breaths." With the pole, Frank towed the pair of sweethearts to higher ground and got out to tuck a numbered blanket over them.

As he scissored a single long step back over the boat's side, the girl said, "Did you even check for a pulse? How did they die? What if they are alive?" Frank thought, but did not say, that the couple were upended long enough to breathe too much water. He could see the muddy smudges around their nostrils.

"They're not alive," Frank said. "You'd know. You're a first responder."

"This isn't rescue," she said, rubbing at her forehead with her hands, quivering between a tantrum and tears. "I came to rescue. We're just dragging for the dead."

To allow her the privacy to calm down, Frank asked the boat pilot, "Where do you live?"

"Down there," the man told him. "A few kee from here. There's no way to get to it."

"Tough."

"My wife and the boys are with her mother. Something to be said for divorce." He shook his head and said, "But you lived on the river."

"We lived on the river," Frank said.

"Did Natalie have her night off? Was she at home?"

"Not at home. But yes. She was at the beach. A Christmas party."

"I'm sincerely sorry for your loss, Frank."

"Thank you," Frank said. Nothing ever meant so little that was meant to mean so much. Dozens of times, pierced by their inadequacy, Frank had said the same words. He never had enough stamina to explain. During his life, Frank met people who said "it was never talked about" (whatever "it" was). He found this kind of people unbearably precious, more self-important in their magnificent silence than the ones who repeated their experiences in endless and lugubrious detail. Now he identified with the silent ones. He might never speak this, his own unspeakable. He fully understood how those people spent their lives unable ever to speak of the war, the crash, the fire.

"It doesn't do to think about it," the pilot said then.

"No."

The girl volunteer turned to Frank and said, "His mother and father are missing."

"Look sharp," the pilot called to them, as if to distract the others from considering a presumption of grief on his behalf. He nearly heeled the boat, rounding the corner of Queen Street and Myer: Frank saw the green-forked sign protruding a foot above foaming brown water and remembered stopping there on the way to pick Natalie up from work. Some kind of boxy microbus was hitched on its side, half buried in muck. "I saw movement in there. Purposeful movement."

At the same moment, the girl moaned, "There are kids in there. Oh please, please, please no."

Frank could see the level of the water rising inside the van, nearly keeping pace with the flood tide. One of the kids was bigger, maybe six or seven, kneeling on the passenger seat, his arms and upper torso above water. The other two were nearly submerged. A girl? No, it was a woman. The woman tipped the smaller kid's face up to the roof, as though pointing out a constellation, while the water lapped their shoulders. Both children were boys, or at least both had short, thatched blond hair, their square chins and bulk suggesting Dutch or German. They were nothing like the woman, who was tiny. Indonesian, Frank thought. Mother? Nanny? From a distance, Frank could see the older boy hammering at the side window, his mouth stretched wide in . . . this surprised

Frank . . . a smile. As the boat sidled nearer and their eyes linked, Frank saw a drowsy peace descend. The kid was thinking, Here come the Marines.

"We can get them out of there," Frank said.

"Whatever we do will shift that thing," said the boat pilot. "There's nowhere at all to stand."

"Well, there has to be something down there. They're hung up on something," said Frank. "We can stand on that." Frank jumped over the side. He tried to see the vertical plane under his feet. It seemed to be the roof of a second car, slick but firmly lodged. The pilot cut the motor, and immediately the boat began to drift down toward the valley basin. Frank said, "Come on. You need to be out here with me."

To the boy rookie volunteer, the pilot said, "Here, idle this, there's a mate." As the boat pilot unhooked the Jaws of Life, the rookie boy scrambled over the back of the seat and expertly set the boat against the tide, the motor burbling, while the girl, her concentration sudden as a shot of sedative, steadied herself with her thighs against the hull and leveled the rescue hook. If they could make any opening, there would be a chance to snag them. The current was unexpectedly vehement, and Frank needed a pitched intensity to keep himself standing. His perceptions slowed to the rhythmic song of his breath. Never hurry, his first partner had told him, twenty years ago. The mistake you make going too fast will cancel out any good you do. He could see the older kid mouthing, *Help*. Frank crouched, giving the pilot room to attack the hood of the van with the spreader. Slowly, the man opened the jaws, prying the roof from the door pillar, and as he did, the older kid began to wriggle toward the gap. The pilot shouted, "Stay still, son. Almost there. Easy does the trick." The rookie girl primed the blunt loop of the hook, sliding it closer to the woman and child in the driver's seat as Frank prepared to haul the older kid free. Frank had a handful of the boy's soaked shirt in one hand when the kid shrank back. "It's okay," Frank said. Still, the bigger boy scrambled out of Frank's grasp. "Son! No!"

"Take him first," the kid said quietly. Again, he smiled. Frank thought,

What kind of kid smiles as a flood closes around his throat? The boy said, "He's little. Please. He's important, too. He's very important."

"We'll get him. I promise. You're closer."

"Take him first," the older child said clearly, visibly shivering. "Hurry. He's important. He's my brother." The woman leaned forward to the margins of the seat belt harness, holding the little kid by his shoulders, then the strap of his backpack. For an instant, the little one tottered beyond the reach of her hands, and Frank was not sure he'd snagged the child or only the pack. In his arms, the child had the deceiving insubstance of a kitten. Frank sat back against the current and turned to hand him to the girl in the rescue boat.

Then, from the corner of his consciousness, Frank glimpsed a solid cloud, a muddy cumulonimbus. He hesitated, despite his custom of reacting, even now, in the moment to anything that looked out of place. He couldn't trust his own eyes. But it was real; it was coming, another river of dread, another flood. Frank hurled himself onto his back in the bottom of the boat, the child pressed against his chest. The boat pilot grunted in pain as he struck his neck on the gunwale, the jaws shoved against his chest like a jackhammer in reverse.

The girl rookie shrieked, "Get them! Get them! No! No way!" Frank and the pilot hauled themselves to their knees.

The inland tsunami pushed the van farther back with a metal moan. Frank threw the little boy to the rookies and lunged toward the open side door, fighting to grab for purchase as the car beneath shifted. "Give me a hand," he said. "I can't hold this!" The older brother and the mom were clinging to the welded feet of the front seat. Frank let go of the door and dove in, pulling the bigger child loose. Then the van swept from its fragile perch. Frank felt his right wrist wrench. He clung to the older brother with his left hand. The boat pilot scrambled across the bottom of the boat. Then the van spun and hit the bigger kid broadside, ripping him from Frank's grasp. Frank shucked his coat, ready to plunge in and chase the truck. But it gamboled away before Frank could haul his arms out of his mac.

The rescue boat pilot said, "No, Frank. It's no use."

In the time it took him to speak, the van was borne away, hideously fast and slight in the current. They watched it heel over, the wheels spinning in the air. Then there was nothing at all but the turbid brown surface. Onlookers cried from the top of the hill, the street to the hospital, "Look there!"

"You're the navy," a woman shrilled. "Go get them!"

"She drove off the edge of the high road up there! That woman in the purple van!" an old man shouted. "She drove right off the road like a suicide. People stopped to look!"

The first woman screamed, "Harry! You're blind as well as daft. She was scared, you fat stupid old bastard! Didn't you see that big black limo that was after her? Bumped right into the back of that caravan of hers. She was pushed off the road, she was. There's no doubt about it. That big black car was giving it a flogging. I saw it with my own eyes."

"Do you need help?" the rookie boy called to the old couple.

"Nah," the woman called. "My daughter's coming in her boat now. For Harry, my husband here, and me. We're fine until then. But thanks."

Frank struggled to his feet. The girl handed the little boy to him. The child had not stirred, and if he had not felt the faint surge of his breath, Frank might have shaken him to start respirations. Huge-eyed and slight, his head like a daisy on a stalk, the child looked up. Frank parted the canvas lapels of his jacket and tucked the child inside, as he would have done with a puppy, and the child nestled in. By the time they got to the ER entrance, Frank was certain that they had lost him. With the child against his chest, Frank began to cry, the only occasion since the day his father died that he knew for certain that he had cried, although there must have been other times. He opened his coat and surrendered the small body to a nurse.

The boy had fallen asleep. He looked back at Frank and held out his arms. He struggled until the nurse set him on his feet.

Frank reached out with the hand of the wrist that was not swollen and held the boy's fingers as he followed him down the hall.

FOUR

THE DOCTOR WHO put tape on Frank's wrist had known Natalie since school days.

"One thing you don't want to do is to give up," said the man, who'd been born in Hong Kong. "Certainly not on Natalie Donovan."

"I won't. Although it's hard. I saw it happen."

She must be dead, Frank thought. He glanced down at the little boy. Had the child spoken?

"I treated a man this morning who had been sitting on one of the lampposts outside the theater since it happened. The police went right past him and assumed he was safe, until this morning. And he is safe. He has some infection, but eventually his legs and feet will heal. I don't know what to say," the doctor told Frank. "Certainly, I would not give up on Natalie Donovan."

Finally, Frank said, "I'll try not to."

The child sat at Frank's feet, quietly winding surgical tape around his right shoe. His shoes were small Converse high-tops, a bright orange through the thick brown mud stains.

"He's fine," the doctor said. "Isn't he? A bit damp and dirty. You were married before Natalie? He's a lovely kid."

Frank said, "He's not . . ." and then added, suddenly, "He is my nephew. One of Natalie's brother's boys." Why did he lie? Frank had no idea. In his time, he'd rescued twenty kids from circumstances fully as dire. He liked children, at least better than he liked adults. They seemed comic, as a group, but he never had a particular feeling for one child. And yet now he couldn't take his eyes off the little boy from the flood—despite his own distress, Frank was fascinated by everything the child did. This was undoubtedly a subconscious reaction to having, in a sense, just lost his own son.

His own son. The only child he would ever have. Now the child he would never have. The floor canted.

"Would you like some tea?" the doctor said. "You look shattered."

"Sure," said Frank, for the first time fully grasping the Anglo-Celtic avidity for the solace of any hot beverage. Where most doctors would keep samples of enticing drugs, this one had an electric kettle, mugs, sugars, and a wooden box of teas. He handed Frank a steaming mug.

"Natalie was sort of a legend," the man said. "She made doctoring like space exploration. We would hear of her exploits in emergency. Fearless. She was fearless."

Frank set down his cup.

Had she been fearless when she woke in dark water, without Frank beside her, clutching her belly, trying to break the surface? Had it been so fast . . . ? Frank picked up and drank the tea in a single gulp, his eyes smarting at the pain. He could feel little flags of flesh unfurl from the roof of his mouth. The doctor said, "You'll want to let it cool . . . well."

The doctor pulled a packet of gum from a drawer and handed it to the little boy, who accepted it with an amazing and trustful grin.

"You'll look after Uncle, won't you?" the doctor said.

The boy stood and slid the gum packet into the rucksack, which was very small and also pale orange, with a soccer ball decaled on it in silver. Carefully lifting the doctor's outsized silver pen and a prescription pad from his metal desk, the boy drew a line, along which he carefully drew an intersecting arrow facing up and to the right, then one up and to the left, finally holding out the finished product, which was no more than an inch long, as if this explained everything. What did it mean? Was it some sort of writing?

Had that little woman, the mother, been Japanese?

She had not been Japanese.

And this was not Japanese, or anything else.

When the doctor nodded, the child delicately lifted his two small hands and swung them in a small arc in front of his chest, back, forth, back, describing in the air the same angle as the lines he drew. Frank thought, He's trying to behave. Behave? What? Had the child spoken? Frank said, "He's shy. Now, especially."

Frank led the little boy down the stairs and out the door. They walked a quarter of a mile down the street to a big makeshift auditorium, a square block of canvas tent with the Red Cross flag on a high pole, visible even to the ships at sea. The line was halfway down the street. Frank took out a couple of the Vicodin given him by the doctor and bit down. He had a prescription for more of it, and just where would he find the nearest operating pharmacy? Some wily entrepreneur was selling lemonade and stuffed pita. Frank bought two of each and he and the boy stood in the line, munching on some sort of fried vegetable stuff with yogurt as a sauce. The child had a good appetite. Gradually, the line of the hopeful, dirty, deranged, sleepless, and damned shortened. In a moment, Frank would be able to present the child to the caretakers, where he belonged. Finally, they came to the front of the line, and a sweating volunteer fixed on them—exhausted but desperately good-natured. And Frank looked down at the child and thought crazy shit he hadn't thought since he was writing poems during night school lectures with the goal of toppling girls into his bed. This child was his pulse . . . he was Frank's. No one else could have him. Nothing could change this. Frank took out his mobile, although it hadn't rung. "Of course!" he said loudly. "Yes. Great. Be right there." He nodded to the volunteer. "Found his dad! All's well. Thanks anyhow."

Later, after what seemed many hours, but could not have been, for it was still early afternoon, Frank ended up at the entrance to the place he'd lived and worked until he met Natalie. He glanced up at the scrollwork arch that spelled out *Tura Farms*.

He stopped, reluctant to drive into what he supposed had been the only other home he'd ever known, except for his own farm in Wisconsin. He didn't count the series of anonymous apartments he'd barely inhabited around Chicago, places where he'd never so much as made a meal. He'd never settled down, never come close to it, despite how much he loved Chicago and his job. He moved every year. In one of his (very brief, very few) therapy sessions after his accident, the police psychiatrist had basically kept her shoe planted on Frank's chest until he admitted that he kept everything temporary on purpose. He had been waiting. It once seemed possible that he might fall enough in love with a woman that she would install him like an appliance in her own life. In anticipation of that unlikely event (made more unlikely by dating women to whom he felt about as attached as he might have felt to a very good TV show), Frank didn't want to become overly fond of a certain neighborhood.

"Or a china pattern?" the psychiatrist asked him.

"Things like that, sure. Fabric or leather for your sofa. Whatever it might be. I just wanted to stay flexible and keep my options open."

"I would say you accomplished that," she told him.

Frank hadn't expected to become attached to the farm's owners, Tura and Cedric Bellingham, although he probably should have advised Tura of that before she began setting a place for him each night at their table—just as she did for their adored nephew, Miles. At those dinners, listening to Tura's discourse on her upcoming exams for her volunteer paramedic certification, her views on cheese as a binge food, and her gratitude toward Helen Mirren for making it safe for middle-aged women to be considered babes ("Middle-aged if you're hoping to live to be a hundred and twenty-five," Cedric commented quietly), and working beside Cedric, watching the man's vast and unassuming skill with animals, Frank tumbled unawares into the kind of affection he had felt for no one except his own mother and his father, dead since Frank was seventeen.

So he sat. When he pressed the button, the gates would swing open and he would have to find out if anyone in Cedric and Tura's family was lost; he would have to divulge Natalie's death, and everything else about this astounding, harrowing day. He sat thinking of the first day he'd come to Tura Farms, hesitating at this same gate, just seven months after he'd spent thirty days in the hospital, two weeks in a rehab facility, and a solid summer in the rack at the house where he'd grown up.

All those months, his leg was suspended, long enough for ivy to have twined around the pulley, and he took handfuls of pills and watched everything from *Masterpiece Theatre* to Swedish porn, his laptop strapped to an aluminum stand and propped on his stomach. Finally, before starting in on a series of documentaries assembled by his mother, a high school librarian, despair at his state of weakness caught him. His thoughts turned mortal, and snaked out toward the future, which he realized, quite suddenly, was his to have or have not as he chose. If he took too many of these pills, not even his mother would know it was by choice. Pills were a messy choice, though, Frank thought, and he would have to wait until he was able-bodied enough to get to his gun, and by then, given that it was only his leg and not his mind that was maimed, he might no longer want to do anything so dramatic. Still, his life would always be neatly sliced into two eras, one before and after a single blunt moment.

On a rainy, cold spring night, when Frank was two days past twenty and a block from his house, he spotted an older guy struggling to change a tire. Frank would have stopped even if he didn't have time, but he had time. He was planning a leisurely hot shower and a fast nap before a late dinner with a woman he was seeing, and had two hours of grace. The old man's car was in a bad spot, invisible until a motorist pulled out of a long downhill curve. Parking his own car safely in front of the guy's, Frank showed him his badge and they set to work. No more than three minutes later, a seventeen-year-old with a brand-new license cut the curve too fast and crushed Frank's right leg with such an impact that surgeons had to extract a quarter that had been in Frank's pocket from the muscle of his thigh. It shouldn't have meant that he was finished as police, but it had. He was unable even to sit for long enough to hold a desk job, unable to stand for the work of a shift, so he got full disability. He also got all sorts of combat dollars and payouts from insurance policies he'd forgotten that he ever had, and a fat check from the family of the kid who'd been driving the car that hit him. Frank kept returning the check, and the family kept sending it back to him, desperate with gratitude because Frank refused to ruin a good kid's life with some foolish charge of aggravated vehicular assault. Finally, Frank kept the money.

Then, there was nothing to do but heal and face a future washed all to shades of dun.

He had loved being police: he had wanted to be police all his life. All little boys do, and Frank, simply put, never stopped. His mother cherished the idea of Frank as a professor of literature; his father publicly endorsed that wish, but hoped that Frank would grow into the love of breeding and training horses for the highest levels of competition on their own home farm, the place that Frank's grandfather had christened Tenacity. Frank liked horses well enough, and admired his family's work, but on his own would probably never even have trained a beagle to fetch. Certain that he didn't want the latter, Frank compromised and tried the former. As it turned out, he loved college, and the immersion in books, but after a semester, he dropped out to enter the police academy for no reason other than he wanted to do both, and one couldn't wait. For his mother, his work then became a source of alternating distress and chagrin, as Hope was certain that Frank would end up grievously hurt— as he had. Even for him, the job was not without its drawbacks, chief among them the bloodlust that some of his fellow officers openly displayed. When he finally trained for and joined the thirty other mounted officers in Chicago, two of his worlds folded together, and he was so content that he never even wanted to take his vacation days.

He loved caring for his partner, the big dark gray Morgan, a retired carriage racer named Tarmac. He loved it even when he worked almost every summer holiday, well into the night, his partner's massive flanks and nerveless bulk sidling up to hysterical concert crowds. He loved being able to go where squad cars couldn't. He loved cutting through lots to run a punk down and seeing the big man cower and throw his weapon away at the sight of Tarmac's flaring nostrils. He hated being the one to spot nine-year-old Suzie Shepard's lime-green sweatshirt where her killer had thrown her, in a culvert not far off the bridle path in the forest preserve. He didn't even mind the silly stuff—like the way that mounted police had their pictures taken in parades more often than Miss America. The extraordinary pleasure of unexpected usefulness never went away.

Then, it all went away.

After the accident, ranks of brother and sister cops came bringing pizza they ended up eating themselves, doughnuts they ended up eating themselves, and candy they ended up eating themselves, as well as true-crime books, funny tee shirts, fishing poles, a huge aloe vera plant, and cases of beer. His sergeant, a man the size of an offensive tackle, taught Frank to knit. His first partner on patrol, Elena, organized a Sunday-night poker game at the hospital. Just before he moved to rehab, the detective Frank had been dating on and off for a couple of years came to visit as well, although Frank hadn't reached out to her. She visited, twice, and the very air in the room seemed to shrink with the awkwardness between them. Frank opened the card she brought to the second visit, and out tumbled a note, asking if their time was up. Frank set the small vellum note on his stainless-steel tray, and studied the worms of puckered flesh that banded his leg and considered how this detective, a smart, sturdy southside Irish girl, who now starred every night in Frank's drug-stoked erotic dreams. He finally admitted that what he longed for was not this woman, but a woman, an extraordinary and good woman who would put up with a diffident guy with a bum leg, a fondness for nineteenth-century British novels, and an aversion to sports and amusements of any kind except the archaic diversions of equestrian show jumping, a sport for little girls who read Pony Club books. Trying to force this woman into that space, given that neither of them to this point had the candle to take the next step, would be like trimming pieces of a puzzle to make them fit.

When the friends thinned out, Frank spent the enforced solitude and inactivity in deciding what to do with at least some of the money. Over his mother's vigorous protests, he hired a contractor to remodel the kitchen and library of the farmhouse at Tenacity, adding a full first-floor bath and a brand-new twenty-year roof. When his sister told him that the old machine barn was so tumbledown as to be calamitous, Frank installed a new one, and a big arena, although he wasn't sure he'd ever live there again and his mother needed a new arena like she needed another nostril. For good measure, he retooled the inside of the big barn, adding four new stalls and a commodious and well-equipped bunkhouse with a double bath for the teachers and grooms his mother didn't employ. When he was finished with all that, there was still a shit-boat of money left over, and then Frank had no idea what to do with what promised to be a fairly long life, and with what was certainly too much money for a cop whose career had been distinguished by little glory and no corruption.

It was in watching one of the slew of neglected documentaries that he happened upon Cedric Bellingham.

Not in personality, but in early achievement, Cedric Bellingham reminded Frank of Jack Mercy, his own grandfather, whose second horse had taken Olympic silver. Cedric's Gentle Griffin had taken Olympic silver in the eighties, and years afterward, the great-grandson of that horse, called The Quiet Man, a gold. Cedric had trained both of them, ten and thirty years before, respectively. Cedric rode Gentle Griffin himself, until the riding part of his life was snipped off by a leg injury not very different from Frank's own. Unloading some feed, Cedric had fallen from a truck bed, just the wrong way.

They traded a few emails.

Next came a phone call.

Frank didn't want to be a trainer like Cedric, but thought that it might be fun to be around one—horses being all he knew except police work.

Completing college would have been attractive if, once he was on his feet, Frank could have even remotely considered the prospect of a sedentary way of life. Not only Frank's background, but his willingness to work for almost nothing except bed and board was the big attraction for Cedric, who was cheap except where it came to horses. It didn't hurt that Frank was the heir to men who'd trained ranked horses for riders from all over the world. Frank wanted to assure himself that the Cedric he encountered would be at least a vestige of the man in the documentary, not some bitchy old martinet soured by his past glories and present difficulties. But vocally at least, Cedric was as vigorous as a man half his age, more vigorous than the current version of Frank Mercy, and without a single bleat of self-pity. As unfamiliar and odd as Queensland seemed in every astonishing detail, from its deserts to its rainforests to its bizarre fauna, it couldn't have been different enough from the Midwestern United States to satisfy Frank, who wished he could relocate to the moon.

"What do you think of Australia?" he asked Hope one night as his mother worked on mending the spines of some books. Frank had finished the excruciating series of contortions that were supposed to increase his mobility and flexibility—and probably had, since he could now move like a spry eighty-year-old, a step up from the four-wheeled walker just retired.

"I always wanted to live in England," Hope said. "Like the Brontës."

"I might move to Australia," Frank said. "Not anything like the Brontës. And not forever. Just . . . for a while."

"Why?"

"It seems like a place a guy could get lost."

Hope's face crumpled. She was so certain that Frank's disability had pushed him to the ledge of life that she'd succeeded in making him wonder if he actually *was* still itching to put a bullet in the back of his neck. With no thought at all for how foppishly Edwardian it would have looked to an outsider, Frank got up and awkwardly knelt next to Hope's chair. "I'm not going to end up wearing dreadlocks and ranting in the outback, Mom. And I'm not going to leave you forever." Looking away from him, Hope lightly touched Frank's hair.

He said goodbye to someone he loved, who counted on him. Now he would say goodbye again. It was bright clear to Frank that he would not stay, equally clear that Cedric and Tura, who needed him, too, would feel the loss keenly.

Frank passed through the gates and under the arch, considering as he did that unless they were extraordinarily lucky, Cedric and Tura would mourn tonight, just as Frank would. Their daughter, Kate, had been singing last night, somewhere down the same beach from the Murry Sand Castle Inn. Frank hoped to Christ that Kate Bellingham had finished at midnight and hurried to join her parents far up in the town of Barry, where Tura's old mother lived.

Instead of opening the door to their house, he knocked.

Kate Bellingham opened the door. She grabbed Frank around the neck. "Where were you? Where is Natalie?" She stood back when she saw Frank's face. "Have you heard anything, Frank? Is Natalie lost? Surely there's a chance?"

In a low, measured voice meant to convey a calm that he certainly did not feel, Frank said, "I don't think so. All her brothers and their wives and kids were there, too, on the beach at the Murry Sand Castle. I'm glad to see you, Kate."

"I left the place I had the singing job, with my boyfriend. It was eleven. He's religious. We went to church up the road here and picked Granny up then, but we ended up coming back here. The news isn't all good for our family, Frank."

Tura Bellingham came down the back staircase, carrying a pile of folded blankets, which she let fall to the floor in a heap when she saw Frank. "Thank God you're here. You're not even wet. I'm just bringing these blankets down to the church. Kate will do it now. They're full, sleeping bags every inch of the school and the community hall, as everywhere. Frank, tell us. How did you make it? Where is Natalie? Is she out there in the car?"

"Natalie was asleep when the wave hit," Frank said. "Natalie's whole family, her brothers and their kids and her father, they were asleep. I wasn't there because I got up to call my mother and have a beer with Natalie's brother. Today, I just thought I would come out and check on the horses. And you, of course."

Natalie's mother had died a few years before, struck down by flu.

That was all of them.

Tura shook her head, casting her eyes down away from Frank. "Natalie," she said. "I don't know what this means, this force of the world turned on innocents. Nothing, I expect."

"You're probably right. Nothing."

"Ceddie!" Tura called. "It's Frank come! He's alive."

Frank heard the scrape of a chair shoved across the planks above and Cedric came pounding slowly down.

"Frank, there you are!" he said, the Yorkshire vowels still broth in his mouth, although Cedric hadn't seen the moors for longer than Frank had been alive. "You're here and so is our Kate."

Frank said nothing, but nodded and gave Cedric his hand to shake. In Cedric's bluff good humor, there was the hollow clap of an exception. Someone was missing. Cedric's nephew, Miles, everything but a son to the old man, was not there. Frank decided not to mention Miles until someone else did.

There were bound to be rescuers lost, too, and Frank would need to go back out.

"There's a child there," Tura said then, uncertainly.

Now Frank would have to explain what he couldn't explain even to himself.

"Yes," Frank told her, gently leading the little boy into the room from the Bellinghams' enclosed mudroom, still surprised by the confident strength of the white, tiny hand that wound around his thick thumb. For the first time, Frank noticed that his hair was blond, a strange almost milky color, his lashes nearly invisible against his deeply tanned cheeks.

"Who is that?" Tura asked.

"We pulled him out of a van this morning. His . . ." Frank stopped. He had been about to tell Tura how the child's mother and older brother had been swept to their deaths before the firefighters' horrified eyes. But the kid hadn't yet spoken. Shock, or he didn't understand English, or was hearing impaired. At the mammoth tent, Frank had found some dry clothes only a size or so too big and helped the boy into them, horrified by the child's tiny, trusting willingness, thanking Christ he wasn't some kind of soft-fingered, candy-bearing monster pervert. They would be abroad on Christmas Day, the child stealers, looking for bargains, little peaches to keep or kill or sell. That was why the boy was still with Frank, or at least this was what Frank conjectured. He'd intended to leave him with the first decent minder he met, and yet he had not left him with the first one, the volunteer at the gym, who was just that kind—everything that could go right if you were a native of Brisbane, jolly, smart, comforting, primed. "I don't know why I brought him, Tura. I just did. It seemed right. He needs someone to look out for him while I go back out for a while to try to help out," Frank said. Tura knew he was a volunteer first responder, who, one weekend a month, helped out with small urgencies and prepared for just this, the impossible full-scale emergency. "I have to see to Natalie and her family, too."

"Of course, he can be here," Tura said. Cedric's phone rang.

"My sister," the old man said, apologetically. "Our Miles is still missing." Miles had been expected at Kuranda, where the family presumed he'd gone with his girlfriend. No one had called Cedric's sister. No one at all. Frank heard Cedric murmuring about phone service interrupted and early days yet. Then he turned back to Frank. "Could be he'll turn up. You did, didn't you?"

"What if our Miles is gone for good?" Tura said, her eyes filling.

The child had let go of Frank's hand and approached Tura, who sat down and, without seeming to think, took him onto her lap. "Get out some biscuits and cheese, Kate, before you go, and put on a kettle so we can give Frank his tea."

"No need," Frank said. "I had some. I drank it too hot." He remembered then that Natalie could not eat, or nourish their baby son, curled inside her. He wanted to be alone, and to be free to scream and kneel and keen. He had to go back to the rescue crew. How had he forgotten? Even for an instant? His very thoughts were slowing to a drip.

"You'll want a cup," said Tura. "What's happened to your wrist?"

"Nothing," Frank said, unwinding the bandage. "A bruise." The wrist was fat and blue. "Maybe some ice for this." The boy had begun to eat the wafers and cheese, taking small bites. Frank sat down and waited for his tea, in the strangely quiet kitchen inside a reconstructed universe.

FIVE

FRANK WOKE WITH a shriek, embarrassed. He had been asleep in the boat when the new man driving it nudged him. The fellow told him to head off to wherever he would sleep the rest of the night. The bright dial on the man's watch indicated that it was four in the morning.

Frank said, "I'm good still."

"I know. You're fine. But you need to be back later tomorrow. There are people trapped we haven't seen yet." The man must have been up all night: his skin had that telltale patina of Queensland sweat and dust dried and reapplied. Yet he seemed as alert and relaxed as if they were fishing. The rookie girl had been replaced, although the boy still hung in. The boat made widening circles, heading in the direction of pale faces that swam into the light or shouts at first faint and then urgent. They had spotted more bodies. The pilot steered the boat over to a man so young and robust-looking that he must have been knocked unconscious to have drowned. Leaning out, Frank stuck a numbered pinny on his chest, as they did with two old women and two teenage girls, whose chic shoulder bags still festooned their tanned shoulders. Those bags would have had ID in them, Frank thought, and cursed himself for a fuckwit for not trying to anchor those children before they sank—for if their parents were alive . . . They brought the living, a bedraggled man sobbing for his wife but clinging to his son who clung to their collie dog, as well as an American woman with her sister and the sister's boyfriend. They left

37

behind two grannies, who refused to leave their cats. Frank remembered that people in New Orleans had died after the hurricane because they would not leave behind their pets.

"There's too much to do," Frank muttered.

"The chief said you lost your wife. You need a rest and a meal at least. She said to call you off."

Dropped at the makeshift levee near a huge car park that remained above water, Frank got back into his car. He reclined the seat and somehow, his leg awkwardly outstretched in a futile attempt at elevating it, he must have fallen asleep again. When he opened his eyes, it was to a watery sunlight. He turned the key. At the same moment, his phone lighted. Along with another list of phone calls from his mother, the unidentified caller had tried again. Impatient, his leg run through with a soldering iron from sitting cramped in the rescue motorboat and then this tiny car, Frank punched the return dial.

"Frank?" said Brian Donovan. Frank couldn't speak. The voice was indeed his brother-in-law's. Frank had heard it last on Christmas Eve, but dozens of times before he even knew Brian, when Brian read the news on MAT21, the Brisbane iteration of the national public channel. Ten times or more throughout his and Natalie's brief courtship and the year of their marriage, they'd done some small thing with Brian and his wife, although Brian was older, in his fifties, mad for football, everything Frank was not—but still a good and comical man. "Frank Mercy?" It was just past nine on Boxing Day, the day in Australia when people visited relatives they didn't like as much. Frank liked Brian very much.

Now Frank found his voice and said, "Brian! You're alive."

"Just. I was still down in the bar and we were swept out, the bartender and me, up onto the roof of some broadcast tower. We hung there for hours."

"Where are you now?"

"My leg is broken and my shoulder. I'm in hospital."

"Natalie, Brian," Frank said. "I know what I saw, but you might . . ."

There was a reason Frank Mercy had lived, and saved the boy. It was fair dinkum for Natalie's life.

"No, Frank. The only hope is for my Adair, but her . . . her things were found. Her shoes. And her backpack. And my brother Hugh and his wife, Mairead, have not been found."

"All the rest?"

"That's right."

"Brian."

"They have me doped up. Can you even understand me? I feel like I'm speaking from inside a balloon . . ."

"I understand you just fine," said Frank.

"All the rest. They were found. My wife and Kelly. And Da. My brothers. I'm on the fourth floor and they've taken me down to identify the bodies. You'll want to see our Natalie. Frank, Jesus God."

Frank said, "Yes."

Silently, opening the door to shield him so no one could see, Frank threw up there on the dirty blacktop. Let me cry, he thought, the grief a dry wedge thrust thick end up from his chest. He threw up once more, all the day's food, a disgusting greasy pile, and still he retched, like an old drunk. Tears were at least pure. Tears, he heard from his sister, dissolved the wedge; they had hormones of grief in them that were released by the crying. Brian had actually seen her, seen Natalie. It seemed indecent, that he had seen Frank's own dead wife.

But she had been Brian's sister long before.

Frank wanted the ring he had put on Natalie's hand. It had been his mother's. He wanted to keep that ring close for however long there would be for him. He wanted a lock of Natalie's dark hair.

He wanted his wife and his life.

Brian had been talking the whole time that Frank was cupping the mic of the phone to muffle the sound of his heaving. What a giant of a man Frank had turned out to be, he thought. His self-pity was so huge he could not console a man who had just lost his whole family. "It's the girls, Frank. My wife . . . was a woman, and she'd had a life. But they never had a life. They never rode a motorbike or drove a car. They never slept a night away from home except at girlfriends', or flew in a plane. They'll never know what it is to be in love. They never saw a world outside Brisbane. At least they didn't know what happened. Losing a child, you can't endure it."

Frank said, "Of course," and thought, It must be. "I'm so very sorry, Brian." It occurred to him then. "How did you think to call me?"

"They brought me a newspaper. Your photo was on the front, standing in a boat, holding a little child's body. Didn't you know that? Did the child live? If I hadn't known you, I wouldn't have been sure, your face was half hidden by the fold of that yellow anorak. But it was obvious to me that it was you."

Frank said, "That child did live. We didn't save his mother or his brother."

"Our Natalie would be proud, then. Proud you didn't give up. That's what she would have done, gone out to try to help." Brian asked then, "What will you be wanting for a funeral?"

"I don't know if Natalie would want that," Frank said.

"She would. She would want to be mourned extravagantly. But I thought, perhaps, all with a single stone. They will all be together."

"That is fine, Brian. Whatever you want. Whatever it will cost. Rest now. I'll be along soon. Tomorrow, if that's okay."

Oh Christ, the Irish, Frank thought. Brian was correct, however inconveniently, about what Natalie would think of him. Natalie would have sneered and cursed him for a sissy for even once thinking of driving his own car off the road and so disgracing her. She would have scorned him if he hadn't gone straight back to business. And if he had been the one who had died, Natalie would have grieved him and outlived him because she loved life as a philosophical choice.

Frank drove to the hospital.

He knew that Brian Donovan was there, in his bed and banged up, but that visit could wait. He took the elevator to the morgue and did the thing he had done with hundreds of people—who had sometimes fallen to their knees and screamed and sometimes clutched Frank's arm, but most often looked up at him as though to ask how it could be that they were on the other side of a glass picture window looking at the composed faces of their wives, or husbands or children or brothers. The bright, antiseptic smell meant to mask malodorous death stung his eyes.

Frank looked at Natalie, her broad shoulders covered by a blanket and the light straps of her summer nightgown. Her tussocky short reddish hair had dried and wound its way into the curls she hated and fought to restrain. Her face was only pale, without a mark, her lips still a ruddy brick, her eyes slightly less than closed, as though she might at any moment open them. Frank asked the morgue attendant, "May I go to my wife?"

"No," she said. "I'm sorry."

"Natalie wasn't sick. She drowned," Frank said, reflexively showing his volunteer first responder's ID.

"It's not a forensic matter, sir," said the young woman. "It's a matter of possible contagion."

"May I have my wife's wedding band?"

"No," said the woman. "I'm sorry." Then she glanced around her and said, "Yes. Of course you can. I'm sorry for being such a bitch." Pulling on gloves and a paper mask, she pressed the button to open the automatic door with her hip. Frank watched as she lifted Natalie's hand, and it was then he caught a glimpse of the livor mortis, the purplish flesh of her arms and back. Humans usually drowned facedown, their legs and arms dangling, their extremities displaying this grotesquerie of gravity, then, as time passed, the swelling came that made them floaters. Natalie had clearly lain on her back, alone, on some surface, for a time after her death. Frank closed his eyes and squeezed his temples as if he could press out the indelible film of Christmas Eve, as though that could be accomplished short of his own senility or death. His mouth was filthy. His emptied stomach writhed for more food. How could his body still want?

He thought of Natalie naked beside him on the floor of their living room. She'd told him to pretend that they owned a fireplace, but had pushed open the screen door to invite the sound of the river, because she loved sex outside—on a beach without even a blanket over or under them, on the hood of her car. She called it "home porn."

"What brings this up?" Frank said. "I married a doctor. I want a linen suit. I want an Odyssey dive watch." This was an ongoing joke. In reality, they had so little clothing that their closet looked like the "after" picture in a magazine story about organization. Between them, unlike any other man and woman on earth, Natalie and Frank could easily share a closet that was six feet wide and eighteen inches deep. Frank called it a look-in instead of a walk-in. Of the women in his life, including the few he had spent enough time with to see what they wore when they weren't wearing it, he had never known one who had only five pairs of shoes. Frank had five pairs of shoes. Natalie had seven. She joked that they should send to Paris for cheese because they had nothing to spend their money on.

One night, just after she told him about the baby, chiding him for not guessing, for thinking she was simply getting fat, she said, "We once talked about living at your ranch for a while. Don't you want to live there always? You wanted to train your own horses sometime. I would like living with your family." Frank thought, On the same land. But in our own big house, about a mile away from the rest of them.

He said, *"Natalie, it's not a ranch. You're imagining a sheep station in one of those places here that has fourteen syllables and ends in . . . 'gong.' Or an American TV show. You don't have to take a Rover and camp out in a tent to do the chores. You can walk across Tenacity in thirty minutes. It's a little horse-boarding outfit with a couple of chickens and a cow and a great big white farmhouse like a thousand others, too big for just my mother and my old grandfather and my sister. It's not as far as the eye can see. It's eighty acres, twenty rented to a farmer to plant in alfalfa for the horses."*

"Sounds grand. I've only ever lived on a street."

"You don't like horses. It's unsanitary and there are flies."

"I've cleaned maggots out of wounds, Mercy. I've put maggots on necrotic tissue to eat the dead flesh. I treated a baby whose father—"

Frank said, "Okay! You're the queen of tough."

"Don't forget again," she said. "Or you'll pay for it."

She looked anything but tough now. She was tiny and forlorn, a dirty broken doll. He finally began to cry, shocked when it made a noise, snot running down his chin. Eden was wrong. The crying hurt worse than the dry wedge. Frank thought he might suffocate.

The morgue attendant had returned and was standing quietly outside the door. She wiped down her wrists and the ring with hand sanitizer, snapping off her gloves, pulling off her bonnet and mask. She placed the ring inside a plastic glove and knotted the glove. Frank slipped it into his pocket. He wiped his face with the backs of his hands. The woman pulled off several wet wipes and handed them to Frank. She asked him if she could now close the curtain. Frank said yes, she could. She asked, "Will you want Dr. Donovan to be removed to a facility nearby here? I'm afraid the choices are very limited for the next while. We don't know how long."

"Natalie's brother is alive. His wife and children died. They were all at Murry Sand Castle Inn, as was my wife. The rest of her family died also. He is hospitalized here. His name is Donovan, too . . ."

"Yes, he was here yesterday. Brian, the news guy. I recognized him. But I knew Dr. Donovan. I admired her. We will all feel her loss personally."

"Thank you. I'll see to it," said Frank, immediately forgetting what he had promised to see to. He left.

On the road back to Tura Farms, he pulled off at a farm track. He might kick in the side of the car, but his leg would rebel. He couldn't pound the steering wheel: he'd sprained his tiny wrist, after all. And why wreck the car? Yet something must happen. The one hundred and thirty pounds of flesh on the table back there was his own family, his wife, his son. Back out on the road, Frank thought, perhaps Kate Bellingham would mind the child until they could find proper channels for someone nice to adopt him or take him into foster care. Maybe even Cedric and Tura would look after him, fostering the little kid informally, at least for a while. Was Tura up to that? The child couldn't be more than three. Frank parked nearest the house, counting the cars. The truck, Tura's old Volvo station wagon, Kate's newer Audi. No sign of Miles's old super-stock Chevy, which the kid, for some reason, adored. It was possible to tear up the road around Tura. No one ever bothered with traffic stops in Queensland, unless you happened to be driving on the wrong side with a bighorn sheep in the passenger seat and then it was only to inquire how the sheep liked the view. It was one of the things Frank had liked best about Australia.

The child nearly knocked Frank off his feet. He had come from no-where, now clad in antique denim overalls and a red shirt with kanga-roos all up the arms. Like a cub, the child climbed Frank, resting his head on Frank's shoulder with a clinging softness and strength. Frank laid a hand on the boy's back and felt the silent, regular throb of his heart. Carefully, he carried him into the kitchen, not bothering to knock.

"You've a friend," Tura said. "He's been out running all day."

"How old do you think he is?"

"Three and a bit. He's small but he can take good care of himself. The toilet and so forth. I had a deal of work to keep him out of the stable. Ev-erywhere Cedric went, he went, and mimicking the way Cedric walks. Kate was laughing and Cedric, too." With a sharp stitch of fear, Frank imagined the kid slashed by Glory Bee's hooves as she performed her daily martial-arts routine.

"You didn't let him in by Glory Bee?"

"Good God, no, Frank. Cedric throws that horse's food over the wall and leaves her."

What would become of Glory Bee when Frank left?

Cedric would sell her for the glue if he had to.

Frank would hate that. Glory Bee was the only horse he had ever truly cherished. As much as she hated Cedric, she loved Frank in her way.

Unlike the men of his family before him, Frank had no special feel-ing for animals. Horses were big, odd, and generally dumb. They did not feel about people the way people felt about them. Only in training

Tarmac for the force in Chicago, and in moments with Glory Bee, had Frank experienced the lyric properties of man and horse, the ones his father insisted were just south of sorcery. Tarmac would have done anything Frank asked, and had, more than once, wading into harm's way with the implacable grandeur of a warhorse on a Roman fresco. Tarmac, however, had literally been that, a warhorse, not like Glory Bee, a finely strung fluty thing meant for the airs above the ground. Tarmac demonstrated no more feeling for Frank, personally, than a car would have shown. In fact, during his first months at Tura Farms, Frank had done grunt work and stayed away from training. The old man finally combusted, taking the piss out of Frank for what he called "false pride."

"If you can't be the trainer your grandfather was, you'll take your bat home, that it?" Cedric roared.

"Not even a little!" Frank, who was not given to roaring, roared back. "I've spent more than thirty years trying not to follow in their footsteps."

"Then pack your kit," Cedric said. "I won't work around a dosser who says he's Jack Mercy's grandson." Frank did pack his kit, and left for a week. When he returned, there were no words between him and Cedric: Frank simply moved into the bunkhouse and put his back into it, humbly emulating Cedric's nephew Miles, fifteen years Frank's junior and an incarnate centaur. He learned the language of the outsized, glossy beasts, who didn't know they could kill anything they chose and cringed from a fallen leaf like kindergarten girls at a picnic. He learned that he did have what Cedric called a sense, that he never had to speak sharply, or above a normal tone of voice; the horses listened. They seemed to wait for him.

No one was more shocked when one of Frank's riders placed high up in All Australia. He was stuck, then—train or emigrate. He trained.

The horses, properly speaking, were all Tura's: they came on airplanes from the working breeding farm in Yorkshire where Tura had grown up, where she had met Cedric and his family. She'd come out to Australia with her mother and all her earthly goods, as Cedric and his sister had done. If Cedric vexed her, she reminded him that all his bluster and skill were nothing without her mounts, and that she could always leave him and go back to her own place. Every year, with Kate, Tura did go back, for a visit, and every year, she returned to dusty Queensland longing visibly for the haphazard heather and the imperial purple-ink cloud banks massed on the hills of her rocky moorland home and the unretouched goodwill of those who lived there. Increasingly, Tura spoke of going back—now not just to infuriate Cedric but as a woman yearning homeward as the evening light grew shorter. To Frank, who'd never been to Yorkshire, or to England at all, she issued an open invitation to go and spend time at Stone Pastures.

Glory Bee was one of five foals born out there the first year Frank lived at the farm. She was ravishing, with, Tura claimed, not a single white hair on her coaly hide, a dynasty horse whose only flaw was her temperament. She looked like a great jumper, and moved like one, unless anyone came near her. Even then, it would have been possible, just, to make a great broodmare of her, had it been possible to convince anyone that it would be possible to touch, much less ride, one of Glory Bee's offspring. Frank adored her, although every morning he had to start with her anew, as she pitched and plunged and pawed, her eyes rolling, more white than brown, foam in drifts at the corners of her mouth. He sometimes imagined he could hear Glory Bee's thoughts, and that there was an implicit apology in her resistance. This isn't personal, she seemed to be telling Frank as she strained and strived, this is how I'm wired.

Cedric would not go near Glory Bee, not even to feed her. The sire, a big red Dutch Warmblood, a steeplechase horse called Say Amen, had the same exquisite gait, height, musculature, natural ability, and the same personality—according to Cedric, who'd been back to Yorkshire exactly twice in thirty years, that of a serial killer. Cedric, who had recently trained the great young stallion Airborne, and now made more than a good living from Airborne's progeny, and he hoped Frank could train Glory Bee. If Glory Bee could medal reasonably, she could go out to auction. Frank, who loved their battles, couldn't bear to think even of that.

But he couldn't stay.

"I've made something to eat, Frank, nothing really, some pasta and beans." Tura was a horrifying cook. Still, Frank sat and ate, with a grim will, as though he was trying to medal in food consumption, beside the child who silently and politely spooned up everything in his small bowl. "The clothes belonged to Miles. Ceddie's sister kept some here for him, so many years ago. I'm as bad a housekeeper as there is to still have them." Frank glanced up. "No word about our Miles." Tura pressed her lips together and went on. "The lad doesn't say a word. But I know he hears what I say. He hears the telephone."

Frank shrugged. "Maybe he never could talk. Some kids can't."

"He does a funny thing with his hands." Tura held her hands out before her and swung both of them, once, left and right.

"I know," Frank said. "Do you think that's autism?"

"Frank, for heaven's sake, no. It's a sign. It's speech of some kind. Sign language."

"I've never been around a kid, Tura. How would I know?"

Cedric banged in at the door, meticulously sluicing off his mucking boots in the foundation that sloped down from the slop sink, slapping his gloves and his duster. Frank stepped behind him and pushed the door open. The day was cooler, but still thick with the promised punishment of withheld rain. Tura said, "I've told the boy he wants a sleep. He doesn't seem to agree."

"You can lie down," Frank told the child. "For just a little while. Just here. You don't have to go in the bed. On the sofa." The boy held up his begrimed hands and Frank lifted him to wash him off at the kitchen tap. Frank had lifted newborn lambs that weighed more. After he'd covered him with a blanket, Frank came back and sat down with the Bellinghams. "I've seen Natalie's brother. He survived. And I've seen Natalie." There was a beat of silence. Then another beat.

"Natalie," Tura said.

"Yes," said Frank. "I wouldn't say she suffered." He hadn't let himself think about it. Drowning was not the easy death people liked to imagine. There was a great deal of air in the submerged body. It took time and the body fought.

Lethal injection, he thought; now, that was a good death.

"She was a lovely girl," Cedric said. "Will you still go back to the States now, Frank? The way you and Natalie talked about?"

Frank said, "Yes." He added, "Later. I have to . . . I don't know what you do."

"Call your agent," Cedric said. "Ask the funeral fellow. There are forms."

Cedric meant that Frank should call his lawyer. Frank didn't have one. A real-estate lawyer had signed papers when they bought the condo.

The telephone rang. No one moved. It rang three times and stopped, no message given. It rang again. Finally, Tura got up and answered, on the fourth ring. Plainly as if the telephone had been a bullhorn, her face said that Miles Bellingham had been found dead. Tura listened, punctuating her nodding with murmurs of "Oh, my dear . . ." and "Of course, anything . . ." She gestured to Cedric, who shook his head severely. Finally, she put the phone down.

"Right," Cedric said, and wheeled, clumsily vaulting the stairs two at a time.

"He's said we'll stop," Tura said. "If Miles died." She sat down heavily. "It's too much, really, Frank. It's too much to take in. I think we will go home, finally. We will."

"Miles was a great kid," Frank said. "I'm so sorry for your loss."

"It's more than that," Tura said. "We loved him dearly. Moira's life won't ever be real again. He was her only, her bonny boy. And for Cedric, without him, and might I say also, without you, none of this will mean a thing. We wanted a bucket of land when we came here, land as far as you could see, on the cheap. Now a smaller place, I think. Something quiet."

"It's a farm as well, in England. And horses."

"But a different thing," Tura said. "A world you can manage. We should travel, though. Before we go back to Yorkshire. We should go to the States. I've never been."

"You always have a place there. With me."

"I'm afraid to think of there being another day, and doing the same things, making the tea, putting a roast in the oven." There were few times in anyone's life when it was ever possible for one person to say he knew what another person was feeling. But Frank knew exactly what Tura meant, about the horror of witness embedded in the urgent banalities of ordinary life.

Frank said, "It feels . . ."—he would only say this to Tura—"like pieces coming loose."

Tura nodded. "I'd run if I could. I'd run from all this. Wednesday and Thursday and then sometime, next year, another Christmas Eve. I would go home now, but what about Kate? And what about my mum? This is Kate's home, her friends, all she knows, and my mother lives for her church." Frank glanced at the presents heaped on a table. Randomly, Tura began pulling out and unwrapping them. "Here," she said. "That was to be for you, in any case." She gave Frank a waterproof pullover and a sweater, and a few pairs of jeans reinforced at the inner thigh, the kind riders wore, a heavy diving watch, an Omni, just the kind Frank had play-begged for from his doctor wife, and a barometer for the wall, because Frank, like all farm-raised people, was foolish about weather. An irony now. Tura kept going. Black corduroy slacks with a hem, a fine brown leather jacket, a linen shirt and vest. Frank understood that these last ones had been for Miles, and accepted them, kissing Tura on the cheek. He was broader across the chest than Miles, but about the same height. Natalie liked him to dress well and keep his hair cut shorter than he was used to. After leaving the force, he enjoyed letting his hair curl around his collar. She called him a hippie.

Their son would have had dark hair.

None of Natalie's brothers was bald, and Frank's hair was still a thick brown tightly curled pelt. Frank had suggested they call their son Donovan. Natalie said that was madness, but he caught her smiling.

His wife and his son.

"You have nothing but what you're standing up in," Tura said. Frank had forgotten. It seemed that his memory would be like old Jack's, a series of events closed off like the windows on an Advent calendar, each one a surprise to him when he glimpsed it again.

They both turned as they heard Cedric making his way down the stairs. Existence narrowed to a commonplace. Cedric, despite his lame leg perhaps the fittest man Frank had ever known, had done just what it said in paperback novels, and aged twenty years in thirty minutes. The very flesh of his face was looser and a paunch had appeared, as well as an old man's stoop. He crossed the room to the alcove where the boy lay flung out in sleep, and straightened his limbs and pulled the gaudy afghan up around the thin shoulders. It was impossible not to think of the motions of tucking this child in as meant for the younger Miles, for Miles's long rest. As though he was alone in the room, Cedric brushed the little boy's hair off his face with the tips of two fingers. Then he stood up and faced Frank.

"I've been thinking while I did the stalls up. Now I'm sure. I'm done here. I take it you'll want Glory, that savage bitch."

"I don't know what will become of my life now, Cedric. She's four. She can be a great mare. Maybe Grand Prix. With a few years of good work, maybe less, you could get plenty for her at auction, and if she settles down, and I think she will, she could be bred and her foals—"

"I would like you to have her," Cedric said, suddenly absorbed in a fly spot on the window across the room, which he quickly addressed with one of his massive handkerchiefs. "I didn't ask you to give me money for her. I would like you to have her, as your own."

"What do you mean, Cedric?"

"Start your life over a bit."

"It's too soon to think of that."

But Natalie had said as much. *You'll want to train your own horses . . .*

"Train a jumper and a rider for what America has that passes for an equestrian world team. It can't compensate. I'm not suggesting anything like that."

"For Natalie?"

"No, rather I would like you to do it for Natalie, for Miles. For me."

"It's a wonderful thought, but that's not how you are."

"How am I now, Frank? Will you be the one to say that Natalie's life was meaningless because a great bloody monstrous wave knocked her out of the world?"

"Of course not. She is dead, and so is your Miles," Frank said. He had not meant for it to be so harsh. But it was harsh. What kind of twaddle was this, about doing it for Natalie? "Nothing I do from now on has anything to do with Natalie."

"Are you so sure?" Cedric asked, a ghost of his customary bluster under the challenge.

"What about this lad?" Tura said. "He's just a child of three. Where will he go?"

"I thought perhaps here, until I could figure out a home for him," Frank said.

"Authorities and social welfare? It will take years," Tura said. "This isn't New York, Frank. It's Queensland. Mind that. He's quite the lad, really. He's seen a great deal in these days. And there he was, out chasing the cats."

"He's a child. They don't understand," Frank said.

"And we do, then," Cedric said, turning back from the window, squaring his shoulders and looking around him in a way that got his wife up and scurrying to put the kettle on.

That there's nothing to understand, Frank thought. Only that, at the end of the day, there's nothing at all to understand.

"The child needs a proper life," Cedric said.

"I'm not responsible—" Frank began.

"Then why didn't you let him drown? Leave off pitying yourself, Frank. It doesn't look good on you." Cedric was his old self for a moment, frosty and blunt. "The lad chases the cats because it's his choice to present himself alive." Cedric reached for the Driza-Bone that Miles had left on its customary peg and then threw it, hard, at the door. "Not all this 'go slow now, easy does.' That's horse bollocks. We're alive for the time we get. I sound like an effing card for the old nutters' home." Cedric left the room and Tura and Frank could hear him thumping back up the stairs to his study.

"It's the boy putting him in mind of Miles."

Frank said, "Sure."

"But it's the boy, too."

"What do you mean?"

"I have no idea," Tura said, mechanically washing up a handful of cress at the sink, selecting some thin bread for toast, and slowly slicing away the crusts. Frank had no idea why all Brits didn't weigh four hundred pounds. They stopped chewing only to sleep. "When I was on the phone just now, I thought of the boy. I thought it would be good to have grandchildren one day. And I don't want to be a grandmother."

"I thought all women did."

"It's the end of your time as a woman, Frank," Tura said. "It's becoming a sort of sofa, not a woman. The end of being all the center of attention. I love Kate, and yet I admit I was happy that I had her in my forties, because it would be longer before I was redundant, if you will." Tura sliced a cucumber thin and took a carton of salad cream from the fridge. She tapped the knife on the thick butcher-block table. "It was just in that moment that I understood why people are all on about being grandparents, and how natural it would be for them to come here in their time, and how this place wouldn't be such a man's place now, and me its only dame, as Yanks say. It would be the grandparents' house. But it won't be this house. It will be somewhere else."

Frank could say nothing. Tura was a fine-looking woman late in her sixties, and knew it, and took care to stay fit, sashaying around in high-waisted Katharine Hepburn slacks and soft, man-tailored shirts and boots. She didn't tend toward philosophy, and Cedric treated her like the Queen of the Silver Dollar. Tura set a plate of sandwiches on the table and whisked the cold teapot away before Frank could pour out anything wet. Drama had the same net effect as a stakeout on a summer night. He longed for a pitcher of ice water, a shower, and a long private piss. But Tura wasn't finished. "I was singing to him before. You know, Frank, my name is after the old Irish song 'Tura Lura Lura.' When I stopped, he tapped me on the arm, sharpish. I know he hears."

"Maybe he's scared out of it. Now I think of it, his brother said he was special."

"Special?"

"In America, that means the kid's got problems. Retarded. Something. They call them special."

This, Frank now remembered, was not what his brother had said at all. He had said the boy was important. The brother was just a good boy. Frank would have been the same if it had been his little sister. Life was not a statement of choice in the fucking good earth or whatever Cedric had said. Life was random as a pair of dice with ten sides.

"He can be here as long as you need, of course, Frank. We're happy to have him. Until you've arranged for your way home."

"What about Kate?" Frank nodded toward the boy.

Tura snorted. "To keep the child? Kate? That stupid sod she's with will never marry her. She's got her bloomers all up over him, now they've 'gone through' so much together." Tura made phantom quote marks in the air with her fingers. Tura was a brick. How could she be ironic the day Miles was lost? How could Frank think it? Was this what you did? Trip over your life and have a cucumber sandwich? None of them was making sense. "Our Kate's almost glad they weathered the tsunami in church together. Romantic." She stopped. "I'm awfully sorry, Frank. I meant no harm in that."

"No offense taken, Tura," Frank said. "I'll go have a look at Glory Bee."

"Wait and have a cup." Tura got up and began to clear off the dishes, and, as Frank watched in astonishment, began throwing the crockery away rather than scraping the beans into the trash.

"Tura?" he said.

She glanced at him.

"You're throwing your dishes away. Do you want to do that?"

Tura almost laughed. "Look at me!" she said. The little boy, who was now awake, smiled, and did a funny thing with his hands: sweep, sweep. Tura said then, "Frank, I don't want to be on about this. It's a day we need to be ready for mourning in our house. I like to think of the child with you. Perhaps I mean you with him."

"Tura, you know that if I did that, and I can't do that, it would be kidnapping a child."

Tura was at her desk by then, her large binder open before her, pen in hand.

"Kidnapping?" she said. "That would only be a legal thing, surely?"

There you go, Frank thought, she's nuts. Perhaps she'd always been nuts. Frank threw down his tea and, in two bites, ate four of Tura's cress-and-cream sandwiches, then walked out toward the stable. Halfway, he thought he might faint. A black band strapped his eyes. He sat down in the dust. What did Glory Bee matter? It was mad that the world had literally gone under and here Frank was on his way to check the swollen ankle of a fractious filly. Glory Bee had banged her hock badly during her murderous ballet on the morning before he left.

As he approached, he thought Glory Bee looked a bit sulky. She was huge, eighteen hands, and muscled like a wrestler. Black as her soul, Cedric said. Nothing wrong with Glory Bee that a mallet to the temple couldn't cure, he said. Glory Bee nickered softly and rolled her eyes. I'm not up to you today, lass, he thought. You'll be staying in that box.

Just outside her stall, Frank sat on a tack chest and tried to think through the angles. If he left in two weeks, could he host . . . host a funeral, do up papers, and find care for the boy? Could he leave in less? A week? This baked land was nothing to him anymore. The airport was already open. Planes were bringing in supplies, medicine, doctors, relief workers, and press, but what would they be taking out? He hadn't even considered an airline. He had to replace his passport, if he had SCUBA gear to dive down to the U.S. embassy, which was underwater on Porter Court, in the neighborhood where he and Natalie lived. His crew chief would expect him back tonight, but that . . . well, there were enough crews out there. Everyone would want to say he or she had been part of the rescue of the Christmas Eve Tsunami.

Kidnapping? Only a legal thing, surely.

Frank thought, then, of Charley Wilder.

Charley could help.

He'd met Charley, a Texan, a few months after his injury. Charley happened to be in Madison with his wife, Annie, who also was a lawyer, at some sort of legal-aid convention. They'd ended up sitting back to back in a Cajun joint where Frank was supposed to meet a buddy who had to beg off at the last minute. Normally, Frank would have cut up and eaten his water glass before tapping a stranger on the back like a life-insurance salesman. But he heard them talking with their friends, or colleagues, about going to Australia, specifically to Brisbane, to help resolve issues of domestic same-gender partnerships in the most freewheeling, and yet sometimes numbingly conservative, nation on earth.

"Funny thing," Frank said when Charley turned around. "I'm moving to Brisbane."

"What's over there for you?" Charley asked.

"Horses," Frank said. "I'm going to work for a guy who trains Grand Prix jumpers."

Charley had the usual male human reaction. "Why?"

Frank had a prepared rejoinder. "Somebody has to," he said.

Charley was leaving with his family the following month. They'd rented out their two-hundred-year-old grandly restored home in San Antonio's King William neighborhood and were going full bore, with their two grammar-school-age sons. They'd visited back and forth since he arrived.

Would Charley and Annie take the boy? They had two sons and they were softhearted liberals. It was a good idea. It was a very good idea.

Frank got up and stumbled over his own feet, on the way over to Glory's stall. As he stood watching the mare snuffle through her manger, he became aware of a small sound, like that sound from the trunk so long ago, like birds singing. He realized then he'd been hearing it the whole time.

What the hell.

Frank stepped into the empty stall next to Glory Bee.

He looked down.

His very skin grew tight, from his hips to his hairline.

The boy was sitting in the straw, literally under the mare. He was rubbing the place her hock was sore. He was singing. He was humming a little song. Frank's breath caught on the exhale. Don't let him move. If Frank so much as touched Glory Bee at this moment, she'd go off like a firecracker. A horse was not a gorilla. A horse would not care that this was a vulnerable young mammal and she should suspend her murderous kicks for the nonce. This kid was dead. There was no way to get him out.

Noticing Frank, the boy stood up. Frank thought his bowels would dissolve. The boy walked over to the side of the stall and held up his arms. Glory Bee gazed at Frank with a look that plainly said, What can you do? Then she put her nose down and nudged the boy. Slowly, like the progress of a glacier, Frank reached in, grabbed one of the boy's arms, and pulled him out. Glory nickered softly and went back to her manger of hay. Frank had sweated through his shirt. Sweat was running down his legs. He had to remind himself to breathe.

"That horse could hurt you very, very badly. You must never go in there again. You must never go near a horse again, ever, unless I am with you. I'll teach you when it's okay." The little boy nodded, with a replete sigh. "Do you understand? Never again. Horses are very good, but they can hurt boys." Frank set the boy down. He opened the hasp and gingerly stepped into the stall beside the huge black filly. Quietly chomping, she quivered in pleasure as Frank scratched her neck in long, slow strokes. He stepped out and locked the door.

Frank had picked the child up to carry him back to the house before his head began to shout simultaneous bulletins about what he had just seen happen, in Glory Bee's stall . . . and more importantly, what he had just said to the little boy whose name no one knew.

He sat down on a stone bench, with the boy on his lap, and held him close, and he watched the sun dip until it splashed orange on the horizon and the darkness was like a firm line drawn.

SIX

THE DOORS OF the elevator opened, and Natalie put out her hand, favoring Frank with a big, conspiratorial smile as they paused to step in. She was all dressed up in what she called her dancing clothes—short red sheath with sparkling threads and four-inch heels that made her taller than he was. Because of the instruments she used in the ER, she rarely wore her wedding ring, but tonight, the heart's-blood ruby flanked by diamonds sparkled on her hand. She whispered that she wished there weren't other partygoers behind them. "It's twenty-seven floors. We could ride it twice. Do you need more than that? Some men do . . ." Frank stood back to let Natalie pass. She took one step, and then dropped out of sight.

Frank leaped forward, grabbing the doorsills.

Where there was supposed to be a floor was boiling water. The elevator shaft was filled nearly to the level of the floor with boiling water.

His heart banged like a dryer filled with tennis shoes. Frank reached out but the heat shoved him back. He shouted, "Natalie!"

And he woke.

No one had noticed: the airplane cabin was in turmoil, track lights flickering, images on the individual TV screens just so much fractured ice.

"What's going on?" Frank called to the flight attendant scurrying past.

She held up one finger, rolling her eyes toward the cockpit.

In seats in front of Frank, the copilots who were off shift threw down their blankets and sprang to their feet.

Then the microphone came to life with its throaty absence of sound.

"No need for panic, folks," the pilot drawled. Why did all airline pilots, even this Qantas pilot, seem to draw their accents from a childhood in southern Virginia? "That sound you heard was lightning just barely glancing off one of the wings of this big Airbus A380 aircraft. Now, these airplanes are made to withstand this kind of weather interference, usually with no more than a scorch mark. The lightning engineers protect the electrical system, and metals just conduct that current right through the wing and back into the atmosphere. You heard some homemade thunder there, folks. But, as you see, your entertainment has resumed, and we're just fine, passing over the Hawaiian Islands right at this moment. The last time a plane crashed because of a thunderstorm was way back in the Vietnam War. I'm sorry you were all startled. But settle back now, and enjoy a snack or a beverage on us. In five hours, we'll touch down in Seattle."

The storm still bullied and blustered around the windows, and, suddenly back in himself, Frank raised the seat to check on the little boy, who'd been asleep next to him the last he saw.

The child was gone.

His bum leg burning, as it had for ten hours in the clubby rotisserie of business class, Frank vaulted awkwardly into the aisle. He nearly toppled a tiny, pretty cabin attendant. Her tag read *Francie*. A doll's name. And she looked like a doll, like a pocket person, supremely slim and clean.

"My little boy," he said. "Did you see a child, blond, three or four years old?"

Three or four years old? Some father he was.

"Oh, Ian! He's our best friend," the woman said. "Don't worry. We had him belted in a seat during the weather event."

Ian?

Yes, Ian. That was the name on the child's passport. But the passport

was in Frank's backpack. The manifest. Of course. They knew everyone's name.

Ian. One day, Frank had begun calling the silent, sunny child Ian. He
didn't know why he called him "Ian" rather than "Henry" or "Paul"; it
just seemed right.

Now Frank tried to move and clenched. An awl of pain bored into his
eye socket, vying with the pain in his leg.

He was out of reach of the painkillers he sometimes needed for his leg
and needed urgently now for his wrist—the thing about a sprain hurting
worse than a break entirely true. If he had the bottle, he'd have taken an
overdose. Instead, he grabbed and drank three cups of water, three of a
dozen or so he'd had since getting on the airplane. His mouth was as dry
as the flap of an envelope. He'd had to go to the bathroom four times.
With the combined tension over his wrist and his leg and his omnipres-
ent fear about the kid, he should have had himself catheterized.

The last familiar face he'd seen before the airport in Australia was
Brian Donovan's. Brian was back in the hospital, his leg healing poorly,
requiring surgery. Frank brought him a stack of novels and, this had
been a wrench, one of only three pictures Frank had left from his wedding. The one he gave Brian was of Natalie in a basket chair made of
brawny brotherly arms, all five of them laughing as wildly as dogs
without horses. Brian's eyes spilled over, and Frank at first thought to
apologize for upsetting him, until he realized that Brian was made of
tears—and would be for some time to come. Brian's leg was suspended
in a sling. Without stopping to wonder why, Frank kissed his brother-in-
law's forehead. Brian cried harder. Ian came to the bedside and, with the
hospital pen, drew that funny little line with arrows pointing right, then
left. "This is the little boy from the flood," Brian said.

"He has someone in America who'll be his family," Frank said. "I'm
taking him there for them." Well, his mother and sister would be Ian's
family.

"I'm going to do a documentary film," Brian said. "To honor my family. So far as I can tell, this is the largest single loss of life in one family

from one disaster, ever, in history. I'm going to do it as soon as I get out of hospital."

"Do you think that's a good idea?" Frank asked. He was horrified. It would be good, and end up being aired all over the globe. "Do you think it will be good for you?"

"I do. I think it will be healing."

"You should wait awhile and see how you feel, Brian."

Brian clutched Frank's arm. "Do come back, Frank." It was a sorry state when you had to rely on a brother-in-law, Frank thought, to be the only proof that your family had ever existed, apart from an ancient auntie in Sydney. But just that must be what Brian was thinking, right now. Frank was all Brian had left.

"I will," Frank said, knowing even then he would never set foot on this continent again. "I'll be in touch."

Going through security an hour later, Frank was sure that he was as close as he would ever come to some kind of cardiopulmonary event. Even on the job, faced with three or four amphetamine-torqued adolescents the size of a family of yetis, Frank had never been so scared. He watched his own hands shaking as he laid the blue-jacketed passports on the podium. The gate, A-2, was just beyond the security checkpoint, twenty feet away.

Peering at his passport with a penlight, the uniform said, "Are you repatriating? Child born here?"

Eyes popping, throat coated with suede, Frank croaked, "Yes. Bereavement. My wife died in the storm."

"Who was your wife?"

Fuck, Frank thought. It was over. "I say, who was your wife, sir? Did you hear me?"

Frank said, "Yes. Of course. I'm sorry. My wife was Dr. Natalie Donovan. She was chief of emergency services at Our Lady Help of Christians."

"I thought I recognized you."

Oh, sweet Christ! Fuck!

"From the newspaper," the fellow said. "The photograph, holding a child. You're the fireman, the one went right out Christmas morning, with your own wife lost. And you an American." Frank's mind slapped shut, a freezer door, sealed and cold. "Davy!" the uniform bellowed. Everyone in line sprang to alert, keen as hunting dogs for sordid news. "Here's the Yank went out rescuing people after his own wife died, the volunteer fireman. Frank Mercy."

Yank. In the paper!

Jesus!

How had he forgotten that picture, now the size of a roadside billboard in his mind? The one Natalie's brother Brian spotted from his hospital bed?

Frank smiled like a stroke victim, pulling muscles into place one by one. He managed to croak out the word "Yes."

"Going home now, with your boy?"

"He has dual citizenship," Frank said. "Yes. Mom was Aussie."

"Good for you."

"Say, how did you know my name? It wasn't in the newspaper."

"No, but it's right here on your passport," the man said, rolling his eyes a little. "Now, I figured you had to be the man that my little brother Dicken told me about. Same name. Dicken's on the volunteers. He was with you in the boat. He was all over the Yank that pulled the little boy from the van. About the same age as your lad, wasn't he? That boy?"

Dicken. The kid on the rescue crew. The boy rookie.

Frank tried to show his teeth in a genial way. Stripping his lips back from his teeth was like trying to start a stuck tape roll. He nodded. What if the kid chose this moment to speak for the first time, to scream, to struggle away from him and cry out for his mother? He knew that the kid thought about the swamped van: every night, Ian came into Frank's bed. Every night, he woke to Ian crying in his sleep and saw him put his small arms up over his face.

"Sorry, Yank," said the uniform. "Good luck to you now. You, too, lad."

And they passed through.

What came next was even stranger, and more harrowing.

As they approached their gate, Frank saw the man, a slim young light-haired guy with tortoiseshell spectacles, hands in his pockets, lounging against a pole just outside the melee of travelers at gate A-2. There was nothing about the man to suggest in any sense that he was a wrong guy, and yet Frank's every instinct shrieked that he was indeed a wrong guy and that, moreover, he was here in the Qantas gate because of Frank. Unlike everyone else, surging forward as if to escape ten thousand zombies storming the terminal, this fellow took his ease as he dreamily watched the crowd. He carried no ticket or passport, no book or food, not even the smallest piece of hand luggage. Grabbing Ian, Frank ducked behind a deserted podium and set down his long duffel bag. He took out his silk windbreaker and several of the electronic board books Kate Bellingham had given him. "You stay right here," he told Ian. "Don't move. I'm going to find some chairs for us and it's okay if you sleep a little. I'll watch you." Ian lay down, and Frank draped the windbreaker over him. As if the windbreaker were a magician's cloak, Ian, entranced, let his eyes close. Frank slipped Ian's orange backpack under the little boy's head for a pillow, and laid his hands on the child, willing him to rest. Then he stood up stiffly and made a show of finding a seat thirty feet away. Making himself behave slowly and with fuss, as an inexperienced traveler might, he painstakingly opened his novel, searching for the place, twitchily shifting on the molded plastic seat, finally settling back. He felt rather than saw the man slip into the seat next to him. Frank looked up. The young man's pale eyes met Frank's, and he smiled, with a kind of lazy wink.

"You're an American," he said. Frank nodded. The slender man said, "Me, too. Time to go home, huh?"

"Probably," said Frank. "I'm not sure my wife would agree."

"She's not American?"

From the rind of his peripheral vision, Frank had spotted a woman in her thirties battling two little girls, the smaller one still in diapers. He lifted his chin toward the woman and the little girls, who were reaching around their mother to whack each other with the sandals they'd taken off. Please, Frank thought, don't let her husband come.

"Oh, your wife?" the man said. Frank knew accents. The man had none, so far as he could tell. His voice was as pure as Wisconsin tap water.

"I can't get enough peace to read a page," Frank said, and his mind bellowed, *Don't let her husband come. Don't let Ian wake up. Don't let her husband come. Don't let Ian wake up.* Frank opened his book again, with an ostentatious sigh. When he glanced up, the man in the tortoiseshell glasses had moved on. As Frank watched, he strolled through the aisles of seats in the gate, and then stopped again. He exchanged pleasantries with another man. Another man on his own. Another man aged about forty, with brown hair and a medium build. The typeface of the novel wavered before Frank's eyes as if he was trying to read through moving water. He looked up again, scanning the gate, when, just at that moment, Ian came running. Frank stood up, glancing around him, wildly, sweat exploding from his chest, his tee shirt as soaked as it had ever been after a five-mile run, back when he could run. The man was nowhere to be seen. Frank retrieved his duffel, then took Ian into the bathroom, where he washed himself as best he could with wadded paper towels, but ended up removing his undershirt, balling it up, and simply wearing his long-sleeved button-down over his skin.

Time crawled toward five p.m. Frank watched the faces in the boarding area. Finally, he and Ian boarded the plane.

When the big aircraft was fully boarded, using Ian's supposed restlessness as an excuse, Frank quickly walked the aisles with the child, scanning for anyone who even vaguely resembled the slight young guy with the tortoiseshell glasses. But there was no one at all. By the time they took their seats in business class, there was Patrick Walsh, a kid of twenty or so who'd turned up at Tura Farms just a few weeks before, looking for a meal and a place to sleep. Patrick said he could work; Cedric was in no shape, and Frank was mostly gone running through those parts of Brisbane that had electrical power, rustling up legal and illegal paperwork, from Natalie's life-insurance forms to Ian's forged passport, which had cost Frank a thousand dollars. To everyone, he'd given Brian Donovan's address instead of his own at Tenacity Farms in Wisconsin. Brian would forward whatever was Frank's, including any more paperwork, or he wouldn't. Frank didn't care. He glanced over at Patrick. He'd forgotten all about Patrick over the past hour, but was glad of him now. With Patrick there, Tura Farms stayed crisp as a tuxedo shirt. Patrick knew horses, and he knew how to get things finished. Patrick was competent, clean and quiet, even though he sat down methodically on the side of his bed every night, reading library books on everything from extinct birds to Francis F. Kennedy, and steadily drinking brandy until he was cross-eyed.

Ten days earlier, with Cedric's consent, Frank asked Patrick if he would like an adventure, to go with him to the United States to get Glory Bee settled down at his home farm, at good pay, enough to bum around a bit before heading back. "How far is your place from Hollywood?" Patrick asked.

"Not as far as you can go, but almost. A good five-hour flight, maybe three days' drive straight through."

"But a fellow could do it."

"Sure."

"I don't mind," Patrick said.

Frank was relieved, but also rueful: a part of him had hoped Cedric might take to Patrick and go on with the work of the farm once he got his mind around the death of Miles. But Cedric was quick to send Airborne back to England. Cedric then sold his driving team, and, last of all, his own fond Saddlebred, Welly. The other four fillies were yearlings, and Cedric said they'd go for the glue if needed. At this, Frank saw Patrick wince. Although his burr identified him as an Irishman, in one of perhaps five sentences he'd spoken the whole time at Tura Farms, Patrick said he'd spent time around Liverpool. That, his ease with the horses, and his size—for he was a miniature human, a hundred pounds, if that, with feet no longer than Frank's opened hand—told Frank the young man once was a jockey of some kind. Once, Frank overheard him say something to a feed dealer about wrecking his back in a crash in a pack, and that meant a bottleneck of horses. Another time, Patrick got up and left the room with a muttered curse when Cedric turned on the TV for a moment to watch a jumps race at Aintree, the home of the Grand National Steeplechase, a race that a colt of Airborne's was favored to win. Evidently, Patrick had a history there, and not a good one. And evidently, he shared Cedric's bias. To the extent that he cared about anything, since Miles's death, Cedric was appalled that Airborne's foal, Sky Pilot, was a jumps racer. He watched the race in horrified fascination, as any decent horseman would. It sickened Cedric that the sport went on in the country where he lived, at least in southern Australia and Victoria, touted at Warrnambool. It was outlawed elsewhere.

What had happened to Patrick, that luckless day in the pack? He wasn't saying. Frank had seen Patrick grimace and knead his back, but youth was also on his side. Most days, he scaled ladders and walked up canted roofs with the agility of a howler monkey. Now he shrugged at Frank, clearly asking if he thought Glory Bee was okay. She had boarded, Patrick said, reasonably calmly for an animal that was, the young Irish said, "daft at her best." Now how would she be?

Jesus Christ, what a piece of work he was, Frank thought, looking back on the last two weeks—the scurrying and prodding, the obeisances and formalities, the rude time-lapsed dismantling of a life. What if the goddamn plane crashed in this pounding storm and Frank had plucked this child from the flood and from his own land (and possibly his own people, somewhere) only to treat him to a dreadful, horrifying, conscious death?

"We're going to be serving some food in a few minutes," said the flight attendant, interrupting Frank's reverie of distress. It was Francie, Ian's new best friend. "Will he eat steak? We can bring him a hotdog."

"He'll eat anything," Frank said, proud (proud?) that this was true. Perhaps Ian's family had been chefs. Perhaps they had been beggars who ate out of restaurant dumpsters. Either way, the boy was happy to eat anything from fish and chips to eggplant Parmesan.

"He'll have steak, then, won't you, mate?"

As Ian nodded, several of the other flight attendants gathered around again, like so many sleek waterbirds in their black uniforms with slashes of pink and orange.

"Later on, we'll play Go Fish, Ian," said one of the younger flight attendants, a guy, who was still pale about the lips—assurances about "lightning engineers" notwithstanding. He still didn't look entirely sure he wanted to be on this dark highway in the sky. Frank watched as the boy put down his drawing pad and touched the man on the shoulder, and how the young man's shoulders visibly unpleated.

There it was again.

Kidnapping? Surely, that's just a legal thing.

What was it?

If he'd doubted the kid's effect on Cedric and Tura, he'd seen it plainly with his lawyer friend Charley, who wanted no part of black-market passports until he shook hands with Ian, and who then helped Frank obtain one anyway. Once or twice, Frank could have put it down to Ian's waifish charm, a kid being little and cute and alone and blond as a dandelion. But it had happened with Glory Bee. Little and cute and charming didn't count with a horse.

Patrick was now motioning urgently to Frank, who realized he was thinking slowly, woozy from the cocktail of ibuprofen, prescription pain-killer, and Benadryl he'd stuffed down in order to try to sleep in his pod. He must have heard the boom of the lightning slash with the inturned ear of sleep, at the moment in his dream when Natalie stepped into the steep shaft of boiling water.

Settle down, he lectured himself. Breathe.

Lightning veined the clouds outside the window again, and Frank thought of his grandmother saying, "The bad ones are struck by light-ning . . ." which was no more than another ladle of Irish fantasy. If light-ning really struck down bad-deed doers, the prison guards at the big maximum-security prison at Joliet would report each morning for work with shovels and dumpsters to dispose of the previous night's crispy corpses.

The kid didn't seem fazed at all.

Glory Bee, Frank thought then.

His senses switched on, one by one. Fear had heightened all the body smells in the cabin, as it will, from cologne to digestive disruptions. The flight attendants were carrying around cups of water and tea and a few ice packs. Francie handed Ian a tiny box of chocolates.

"He's doing just great," Frank said to the woman, and watched as Ian abstractedly touched the sleeve of every flight attendant who passed. He is being careful to spread it, Frank thought. What the hell was he seeing?

He told the kid, "You stay here. Unless you need to go to the bathroom? I do." If everyone else was having the same reaction to the lightning strike as Frank was, the bathroom should be a hellhole. He thanked again the last-minute purchase of business-class seats. High-priced shit was still shit, but there would be less of it.

When Frank came back, after using a dozen tiny, antiseptic towels to bathe his face, he stretched, massaged his leg, and took the drawing pad Ian was holding up for him to see. There was Glory Bee's dark face, the slabs of her cheeks skillfully sketched, her lashed, side-seeing eyes flicked forward. It was primitive, but clearly sketched by someone who could see things the way artists see things.

"Who made that?" Frank said.

The boy's face said clearly that he had. How could a kid three years old draw like that? The doctor put him at just three and a half, maybe not quite, and Frank, saying he was the boy's uncle, the kid's parents having been victims of the flood, gave him an arbitrary birthday.

How did the real Glory Bee look right now? She would not just be shivering and shaking, as was her custom, but fighting with all her considerable might. She would snap her leg.

Frank's father had told him how, back in 1960, before Frank was born, the great Olympic jumping horse Markham had to be shot just for this reason, when he went berserk, probably because he couldn't tolerate the confinement of the quarters on the flight to the games in Rome.

Planes were better now.

Horses, however, hadn't changed much.

Frank didn't like to think about how much he'd paid to get Glory Bee on the airplane in the first place. The passage had cost him the equivalent of what a good used car (a very good used car) would have cost in Madison, and the whole setup had a shaky ad hoc feeling (not unlike everything else about Frank's current cosmology) that would never have passed muster in the absence of the natural disaster. Valuable horses usually were transported overseas on specially fitted-out cargo planes, or even on freighters, with experienced handlers paid for the purpose—not in makeshift stalls ordered from veterinary catalogues in Sydney. Frank knew better than to watch Glory Bee loaded: the sight would have wrung out his guts. Crates and kennels were fine for dogs and cats, and perhaps even smaller exotic creatures, but not for livestock.

Patrick had a tagged, approved syringe of light sedative in his backpack. There were several loaded rifles on board, and Frank assumed one was down in the hold, for such situations and other situations he didn't like to think about. Had anyone ever shot a hole in the wall of an airplane? He could tell, just from their posture and their shoes, that at least four of the passengers were police, which made him feel alternately comforted and queasy.

"Guys, excuse me," he said to the resting pilots, who had just tucked into a full-fledged meal. "I have a request. I need to see if my horse is okay." The pilots were demolishing steaks so uniform in shape that they looked to have been stamped out of a kind of colloid. "I know you probably don't usually let people do this. She's a champion, and she's valuable. She could die unless we sedate her." Frank saw the shrug in both guys' eyes. "You don't usually have lightning strike the aircraft either."

"You brought your horse?" one of the pilots asked. He was an American.

"I train horses. We're going back home to Wisconsin. Now, sure, horses normally travel on specially fitted planes—" Frank stopped. The pilot clearly could not care less. So far, no one single part of this was a lie, although lies were now Frank's medium. He swam in lies, and drank them.

"I grew up in Wisconsin," said the other pilot, and Frank knew he was in. "Whereabouts are you from?"

"Outside Madison, near Spring Green. My grandfather started the farm. He's still there. Ninety-six years old."

"I'm from Rhinelander. Up north. I'll show you," the Wisconsin pilot said, then noticed the child. "I can't take responsibility for the kid going in the hold. Francie will watch him."

"He won't leave my side," Frank said. "His mother died on Christmas Day. And my groom has to come, too." Frank nodded to Patrick, who was at his side in a breath.

Later, Frank hoped to Christ it wouldn't become a legend, what happened down there. If he prayed, he would have prayed that no one would take it on himself to talk to a TV station about the human-interest angle of the time lightning struck Flight 500.

In the same way people assume that hospitals are clean and schools are safe, Frank had assumed, despite having watched cargo handlers throw luggage into the guts of airplanes with the same care and skill as garbage collectors, that the holds of planes were at least somewhat orderly. He could not have pictured how much of a formless, planless mess the cargo hold of a plane really was. With this system, no one's baggage should ever arrive or get matched to the people who hopefully checked it. Nothing should ever remain unbroken. Suitcases and trunks and boxes were strewn across the floor, in no order, not on shelves or set between stanchions or grids, simply tossed in piles on the floor of a bare, dark, metal cavity. The pilot turned on a dim light. It was not a track light, but a single pair of bulbs, like something in a cellar. Frank could see more then . . . of the same. Among that welter of boxes and duffels were kennels and crates that held animals, but not in any sequestered place. Some kennels sat all wonky on top of the suitcases; some had slipped off and lay on their sides or even on the grated fronts that were supposed to allow animals to see. To get to any one crate or kennel, anyone would have had to tunnel through or clamber over the luggage. Large animals, it seemed, were against the sides. Wedged on the far back curve was cargo—goods of some kind, Frank assumed, although what sort of exports were leaving Brisbane right now? It must be household furniture of people like him, getting out of Dodge. Big metal containers were stacked at the far end of the plane's belly and secured by straps. Fortunately, there did not seem to be much cargo, but the airplane was full, and the luggage was piled ten high in places, and on the tops of some of those piles, Frank could see pet crates.

"That sucks," the pilot said, moving to take down the few kennels teetering on the highest piles. Eyes peered from kennels wedged in the middle of heavy pyramids of luggage. The stink alone could have killed people—shit and piss and vomit. How had it been before the lightning hit? Frank was willing to bet not good. At least it was relatively warm; and, according to the behavior of his ears, the pressure was the same as the cabin. It was louder, though, infinitely louder, as though the sound of the engines was magnified, when, in reality, it simply was not blocked.

From somewhere outside the circumference of the light's halo, he could hear Glory Bee, shrieking and plunging, her hooves clattering the floor and sides of the flimsy stall. He could hear the rasp and split of wood.

"Do you have a flashlight?" Frank asked the pilot.

By the focused beam of a medium-sized Maglite, like his own when he was on the job, Frank took a few steps deeper in and saw Glory Bee. She couldn't get all the way up on her back legs—she was cross-tied and wore a tie-down—but she was certainly about to kill herself and anyone who got near her. Those straps wouldn't hold forever. Patrick, looking ever more the size of a twelve-year-old, stepped forward, his young and somehow Wizard-of-Oz shrunken voice desperate, chanting, "Steady on, girl. Just steady now." To Frank he said, "I don't blame her. When we ran into something . . . I thought I'd shit myself, actually. Sure that we were crashing."

"You heard what they said," Frank said. "Lightning hit a wing. Not much."

"Enough for me, Frank. I never was on a plane. If I get near her now, it's my death."

"She's like this. It was a chance bringing her."

Sweat foamed her neck and sides. Her eyes were blue-white with terror and rage. She strained, her whinny a pure and unceasing scream. He would be surprised if even he, who could always gentle her, could get close enough to give her a shot.

A score of dogs howled, and Frank spotted the muscled blackness of some kind of big, caged thing. A panther? And another . . . a tiger? The boom of the big cats' roars seemed to come from inside his chest. The sides of a tall Plexiglas terrarium with two feet of wire at the top were befouled by big flying foxes.

They were in some kind of nightmare ark.

Who shipped a bat?

Frank remembered now: the big park zoo in Brisbane was drowned; how the navy got out what animals they could, to send them places, in-country and across the world, where they could be looked after. These must be some of them. All this chaos, the exigency of the flood.

He would have to kill Glory Bee.

In his hubris, he had brought the gorgeous filly onto the plane as a thousand pounds of exquisite horse who, even if she could never conquer her anxiety enough to perform, would throw beautiful babies one day. In humility, he would see Glory Bee taken off as a thousand pounds of meat. Now he was a widower with a stolen child and a crazy horse that would have to be shot.

Of course, until *he* died, Frank would remember the flash of Ian's red sweater as he broke away and ran to Glory Bee. Time went over to a recording, unplugged and slowing down, down, down to a guttural groan. The pilot took down a rifle, and, as if reconsidering, handed it to the groom. Patrick put it up to his shoulder.

Frank stepped forward and said, "Wait."

The boy had to jump back after the first time he touched Glory Bee's leg through the wide-spaced metal bars and wooden slats of the makeshift stall Frank had purchased for the passage. She was roaring, cantering in place. But the second time Ian touched her, she stopped, and if she were a woman, Frank believed he would have seen her stand there, sobbing. He exhaled. As the groom and the pilot watched, not sure how to move or what to say, Ian came back and reached up for Frank's thumb.

Together, slowly, they circled the hold, the pilot following them, Frank waiting while the kid climbed over bags or slid across them on his butt.

Ian squatted to pet each of the dogs that nosed up against the doors of their crates, and then, afterward, lay down. When a kennel was out of reach, the boy waited patiently until one of the adults set it on the floor or lifted him. There must have been twenty dogs, and ten cats. The boy put his hand on each of them. A huge, bat-eared cat continued hissing, but then backed away balefully, silencing herself in a ball on a high shelf in her elaborate cage, which had been thrown sideways, scattering her foul-smelling food. Ian then made a break for some kind of huge crate Frank couldn't see well enough to know what the contents were. As the boy approached, a Frisbee-sized palm came up—great, pale, and weary. Ian laid his hand on it. Frank squinted. He saw smudges of bronze fur. It was an ape, an orangutan who, unfurled, would be about the height of a regulation basketball hoop. Ian stayed a long while with the orangutan, shrugging his shoulders, shaking his head, wiggling one of his fingers, which, of course, the ape did in return, entirely with human affect. Not one word came from Ian's lips. Then, with a whirl and a skip, he headed for the tiger's cage.

"Not there," Frank said sharply, and Ian stopped. The animal snarled with impossibly loud and princely assurance.

Farther down, they saw a llama in a crate, and Frank knew they were nasty, spitting, stinking beasts, but he nodded when Ian sent him an asking look. What could Frank do? The hold, which had been a cacophony, like a killing floor in some Texas slaughterhouse, was now largely quiet, except for the big predators—and how great was that, their being right in there with horses and llamas? Glory Bee didn't know that the *tiger* she smelled was in a cage! The animals began making ordinary sounds, shuf-fling, chewing, stirring restively, but not with hysteria.

What kind of nitwit would put an orangutan on a jet to . . . he peered closer at a series of oversized, numbered labels—the Brookfield Zoologi-cal Park? But what choice was there? Those animals had no home at all anymore. He looked back. The ape wasn't alone in his crate, Frank now noticed: there was another with it, smaller, peering straight back into Frank's eyes with solemn regard. He supposed that whoever had done it knew the ape had not ever seen an Indonesian forest and preferred the ape to live.

What kind of man would take a child who wasn't his own nine thou-sand miles across the world?

Painfully bending his legs, Frank beckoned to Ian. The little face was pale, almost blurred with exhaustion. Whatever he's doing, it takes it out of him, Frank thought, hoisting Ian over one shoulder.

"Fucking saint," said the groom. "What was that about?"

"He's good with animals," said Frank. Turning to the pilot, he added, "Don't say anything. About what you saw."

"I won't," the pilot said, messing with his cell phone. So much for phones screwing up those delicate navigational systems. "I'd get in the soup . . ."

"For what?" Frank said sharply.

"Bringing a kid down here . . ."

Frank and Patrick exchanged glances. The pilot astonishingly, remark-ably, had noticed nothing at all.

"I won't say anything. One cheesehead to another," Frank said. He thought his heart would burst and he would die.

The pilot said, "Go, Badgers."

They ate afterward, the flight attendants handing out extra chow and chocolates. The boy ate enormous amounts of food, politely. He con-sumed his steak, with the vegetables and bread, before the cake, as a kid should, and then ate Frank's bread rolls and cake as well. Then Ian sighed, as though seventeen-hour flights were something he did on most weekends, and, covering himself with one of the fuzzy blankets, went instantly and deeply to sleep.

Frank could not sleep anymore. In Seattle, they would have a layover, four hours. He would call his mother, and Eden, to make sure they understood when he was coming. Eden had needed to arrange the three-day quarantine for Glory Bee before they could bring her to Tenacity. The facility was somewhere north of O'Hare. Arlington Heights? Patrick would stay with the horse, putting up at a hotel—nicer, Frank bet, than any other he'd ever slept in—and then driving her up when the exam for communicable diseases was completed. Did Patrick have a driver's license? Frank had no idea. He was lucky that it was only three days: the Australian quarantine was two weeks.

Now, home approaching, he had to think.

He had to think, as he had not in this month of nonstop motion.

He had not told his mother or his sister that he was bringing home a child. Frank rationalized that, until the last days, he hadn't been sure, really sure, that he would go through with it.

He had tried to stop himself.

He had meant to plead with Charley and his wife to take the child in until someone could find him a good home.

He couldn't do it.

He was stunned that he could not.

Even after the plan was in motion, Frank intended to pull the plug. He went on convincing himself that all the things he'd asked Charley to do were only a last-ditch measure, that something would turn up before Frank ever left Brisbane. He'd even called the city's Bureau of Human Services, but when the operator asked him to wait briefly until she could locate the right person to help him, he put the phone down.

Frank had emailed photographs of the horse, and of Natalie's makeshift memorial, which would later be replaced with a family headstone, and of the devastation where their condominium once was. He had not quite decided what he would tell them, although he was sometimes sure he would say that Ian was the child of one of Natalie's dead brothers, perhaps Hugh. Hugh's wife had been married before. She might have had a child. No one could question that. Depending on when someone got around to it, if ever—Frank was counting on *if never*—Charley Wilder might certainly never practice law again, and he might go to prison.

In the best-case scenario, these acts had long shadows.

Undoubtedly, somehow, even Eden and his mother had seen the photo of Frank on the front page of the *Telegraph*. They were librarians, for God's sake. Finding out information was what they did. At least the caption hadn't used Frank's name.

During the nights at Tura Farms after he'd visited Charley Wilder, Frank lay awake, alternately torturing himself with images of Natalie in her casket and images of himself in prison. Kidnapping? There was also a false passport and a false birth certificate, all of these good for more years inside.

Before he could decide what to confide in anyone else, he had to be able to be sure he was telling himself the truth. And he didn't know what that was. When the child curled up next to him in the bedroom that had been Kate's, he put his arm around Ian and tried to reason out if what he had done was an artifact of his grief or an act above the law.

There were no acts above the law.

All police knew it. Kids went back to their parents, even if their parents were unspeakable turds, because the law said that a minor child belonged with, if not to, the custodial parent. One or two times, Frank had to follow through on some criminally stupid situation in which that parent had less self-discipline than a feral cat, in which the kid would certainly have been better off with the other parent, or adoptive parents, or no parents at all.

The next-to-last day came. Then the last day came.

Night upon night, Frank Mercy considered how, until this point, he'd based his life nearly entirely on logic and also on law. Even marrying Natalie was a choice born of incandescent love, but also logic. Frank didn't expect to meet his match, but when he did, it was time to have a family. He did not bring it up with Natalie, only hoped that she'd feel as he did. At forty, he was grown, nearly overgrown. Natalie was strong, self-reliant, a professional woman who wouldn't want to completely domesticate him. She didn't want a four-over-four with a garden. She would want to ramble, family in tow, and would thrive with Frank or without him. He was not so sure he could thrive without her. He had not counted on the completeness of his surrender.

And certainly, he hadn't counted on what he felt about the child. The child was a small stranger, and yet what Frank felt was the pilot light of the full-blown flame he had felt for Natalie, the same sense of steward-ship in miniature. Since he hadn't yet grieved for Natalie, beyond a few spasms and a few sleepless nights, everything else that came after could have this result. He might be an emotional snowball, picking up debris, heft, and contour as it swept downhill. Shock and grief, followed close upon by the power of being a half-assed savior, brewed up a recipe for rebound attachments. From what little he'd learned in college psychol-ogy classes, he knew that children grieved backward, their sense of loss growing in direct proportion to the time the loved person was missing from their lives. He didn't even know about Ian's family. Sunny as he seemed, the boy was clearly afraid. As much as he sounded like that dreaded granny, Cedric was right. Ian had given Frank a purpose in life.

Quotidian concerns about Ian occupied him, forcing Natalie quicker into history. Still, he would always be that man who had loved Natalie. He would waken on holidays, especially Christmas, and on the October day they had married, and the life that he had, in those moments, would be Natalie's alone. There would never be another wife.

October 4, he realized now. They chose ten-four, so, Natalie joked, Frank, a cop, would never forget it. And as he would never forget it, he had chosen that day for Ian's birthday.

SEVEN

WHO HAVE WE . . . HERE?" Eden said, when she finally let go of Frank's neck and stood back to make sure he was really here, and really alive. "Did you escort a child for somebody?"

"I did," Frank said. "This is Ian."

"Hi, Ian," Frank's sister said uncertainly. Her fiancé, Marty, grinned at Ian and waved. Ian waved back.

Because Ian didn't speak—or at least, didn't yet speak—Frank found himself sometimes forgetting to speak directly to him. He tried to be mindful of it, and so now he turned to Ian and said, "Ian, this is my sister, Eden. This is Marty. Eden and Marty are getting married." Ian jumped behind Frank and refused to look out.

"Where's Mom?" Frank said.

"Whose kid is that?"

"Where's Mom?"

"Mom's at home, crying, and cooking everything in the world," Eden said, her eyes going wide in a parody of surprise as Patrick lifted his silver pocket flask, had a nip, and then turned to the marked door of the bathroom behind the baggage claim. "Who's that?" Eden asked.

"He works for me," Frank said. "I think."

"You think?" said Eden. "You don't know?"

Patrick emerged just minutes later, smelling of wintergreen instead of horse sweat, wearing a blue chambray shirt and fresh jeans. Eden

78

was maybe five six, like Natalie. Patrick had to look up at her. Frank saw Eden recalibrate to accommodate the fact that Patrick was a grown man of an eleven-year-old child's height and weight.

"Patrick Walsh," he said, offering his hand. "I work for your guv. Your brother, that is."

"Hi," Eden said uncertainly. "Welcome to America." She had not expected a little man and a little kid to accompany the prodigal brother—only a big horse. Turning back to Frank, she said again, "Whose kid is that?"

"Well, he's my kid," Frank said. "I'm his . . ." Father? Jesus Christ. "Guardian. Actually, this happened suddenly. I adopted him. A family member. His parents died . . ."

All humans were family.

"You're lying," said Eden. She'd known Frank too long. "Whose kid is that?"

"He's really mine. Now. One of the brothers' wives was married before." Each of these essential facts was singly true. "I can't explain any more now, Edie. I'm worn out and I want to go home."

"Why didn't Brian Donovan take him? The news guy?"

"He barely knew this kid either. And Brian's got some complicated injuries and he lost not just his wife but his entire family. It would be the way it would be for you if not only Marty died, but Mom and I, too." Eden nodded ruefully, accepting, and Frank pressed his advantage. "I won't ever be able to explain what it was like there. Or why he ended up here with me. It was the right thing, though."

"I didn't say it wasn't the right thing." To Ian, Eden said, "Come out if you want any presents later." Ian knew better than to ignore that. "Well, I'm your auntie Edie. Did you bring your horse?" The child nodded, and with a deep, shaky breath, he summoned himself to take Eden's hand. Eden blushed. "That's good. Because we brought a trailer for her to ride home in. She's a girl, right?"

Ian nodded.

"And you right in the back with the horse."

"Don't say it. He would," Frank said. Turning to Marty, he reached out and squeezed his future brother-in-law's shoulder. "Still in gradual school, man?"

"It's very gradual," Marty said. "I don't want to actually be a psychiatrist. What do you think I am, nuts?"

Eden began to cry. She leaned against Frank in an attitude of yielding that was entirely unlike her compact, keen, businesslike self. "I can't tell you how hard it was for us to wait until we knew that plane was in the air."

"You, too, Marty?" Frank said.

"I wept like a baby," Marty answered, then added, "Frank, a joke is beyond even me. It was hard to look at those videos of that place and picture someone in your family there. Maybe we imagined it was worse than it was. But it looked like hell."

"It didn't look worse than it was. It was like hell."

"Frank, we're so sorry about Natalie," Eden said. "We loved her. We would have loved her more."

Frank could only glance away. The thought of being here without Natalie was as new as having loved her. It was not durable. He had grown used to being a husband in small increments, sometimes glancing at himself in mirrors and mouthing the words *my wife*. When the idea of himself as a husband was ordinary at last, it was over. This scene should have been happening months from now, and everyone alight over newborn Donovan Mercy in Nat's capable arms.

Frank longed to see his mother. His one fat suitcase circled the carousel, as did Patrick's comically battered leather case, and the Glenlivet Scotch duffel bag that contained the three outfits Tura had found for Ian.

"He didn't come with much . . ." said Eden.

"He's not a plastic play set," Frank told her, sharper than he meant. "Everything he had was gone. Everything I had was gone. It was only a miracle I had my passport in my briefcase with my medical cards, and that it was in my car. I have no idea when I put it there."

"Don't bite," Eden said. "You know what I just noticed?"

"What?"

"No one has a winter coat. It's ten degrees out there. What did you plan on covering up with?"

Frank had remembered a horse blanket for Glory Bee. The cold. Another surprise fact he forgot that he knew. "I came from a place where the median temperature was in the eighties. If I have a winter coat, it's at the farm."

Eyeballing sizes, they decided that Marty would go to the big-box store at the first exit north and get coats and gloves for all of them. Marty did, bringing back the same blue down jacket for the two men and a red snowsuit for Ian, who was fascinated. On a plane he might have been . . . Frank had the sense that it hadn't been Ian's first flight, but he might never have experienced cold. Marty also brought back a car seat, surprising them all.

"I'm a physician," Marty intoned. "It's my responsibility to make sure this child is properly restrained." Frank's jaw tightened. He'd driven all over Brisbane with Ian in the backseat of the Mini without the first thought of a car seat. Marty said, "He's nowhere near sixty pounds. This one converts into a booster for when he gets bigger. By then, we'll probably need it, huh, Edie?" The knit cap that Marty brought for Frank was a Hello Kitty hat with pink bobbles that Frank happily pulled on over his wiry brown hair. Ian was delighted.

Eden said, "You have a wild look and a two-day beard. With that hat, you could be a child molester."

Thankfully, they'd brought both the farm truck, with the trailer that Patrick would use to take Glory Bee to the equine disease control center, and the eight-seater Suburban van stenciled with the name of Tenacity Farms. Working quickly, they all filled the van's wayback to bursting with the suitcases and some boxes that held a few things of Natalie's from her office, including an album of their wedding pictures, and Frank's oldest training tools, the tack pieces that had been his father's. There were a few more boxes and a big crate Frank had shipped that would arrive later—or maybe never. There was his life, Frank thought, contained in a four-by-three-foot space, the life he had thought, for a short while, would fill up the world and brim over. He lowered the hatchback.

They all drove around to the loading area outside a metal-pole barn, where animals were kept until they were claimed.

The sedative had worn off, and Frank recognized Glory Bee's angry, high-pitched whickering. She was still tethered to the stanchions that formed the travel stall around her, but pulling back with all her might, her muscles bunching under her gleaming black hide.

Frank heard Eden's sharp intake of breath.

"Oh! She's beautiful," his sister said. Frank could easily forget that Eden, the computer research whiz, was a horse farmer's daughter. "Make sure that he . . . Ian! Don't go near her now."

"He'll be fine," Frank said as Ian stroked Glory Bee's leg, and made that funny little motion with his hands that seemed to be his default in times of stress—right, left, as if his little hands were paintbrushes.

"You're awfully casual about his safety," Eden reproved Frank.

"He's got a way with animals."

"No animal is trustworthy, Frank. Jack always taught us that."

"How is Jack?" Frank asked. Eden compressed her lips and shook her head.

With half a shot of sedative in her, Glory Bee went placidly into the trailer and turned to her bag of grain. They all prepared to set off on their journeys.

"See you in a few days, guv," Patrick said.

"Do you even know how to get there? Do you even know how to drive on the right side of the road?"

"It's only a frontage road from the airport," Marty said. "I programmed it in. Patrick can follow us there."

"I'll practice driving on the odd side while I'm here," Patrick said. "Should be something a person can do. Tourists do, when they come to Ireland."

"When was the last time you drove?"

Patrick laughed and used his thumb to flip two Life Savers candies off the roll. "I've a lousy memory for dates. Some months, though."

Probably twenty or thirty, Frank thought.

"Got my GPS. I ordered it last week," said Patrick.

"Leave the people in the town some of their brandy," Frank told him. Pat grinned and left.

The rest of them got back into the van, Eden and Frank first taking turns threading and securing the car seat, which seemed to be built with the complexity of a lunar module. "I'm so glad you're home," Eden said as they tucked Ian in. The child was already asleep on the backseat, and hardly stirred when Frank snapped on the harness.

"You just don't want to muck out the stalls."

"Frank, how can you joke?"

"I don't know," Frank said. "I don't know how not to. For twenty years, it was what you did when the worst got even worse."

"How long are you going to stay?"

"I don't know how long. I don't have plans."

"For a while, then?"

"Do you guys mind?"

"Of course not. It's a big house . . . there's plenty for all of us. Frank, it's your home, too! I wouldn't mind if Marty and I lived in a trailer."

"I would," Marty said.

"Well, I don't mind living at home. I have to figure out what I'm going to do, and I have enough to live on."

"I hope we'll have our own house soon," Eden said.

Marty said, "Define soon."

"Then Mom will be on her own."

"She'd probably like that," Frank said.

"I'm not so sure."

Frank fell asleep for a while, his head pillowed on a clean horse blanket he found in the backseat. Under the surface of his slumber, he could hear Marty and Eden's companionable murmur, the slight rise and fall of their conversation against the blat of the radio. When he awakened, they had crossed the border from Illinois into Wisconsin.

"Wow," Frank said. "I zonked out."

Eden said, "You should sleep for weeks. How are you even walking? I mean at all? I couldn't live through losing Marty that way." As imperceptibly as a child grows an inch, the landscape began to change, the slurry of rubbled parking lots shoved up against apartment sprawls and strip malls giving way to stretches of snowfield, some dotted with a smudge of trees clubbed around a plain house with straight-up walls of red brick or whitewashed clapboard.

"You do, though. There are moments when it's all too bright and loud or beautiful. Then you catch yourself just living, noticing a sunset, happy to be in a soft bed. And you hate yourself . . ."

"I can't imagine it." Eden sighed. "Marty, do you want to drive for a while?"

He said, "Sure. There's that highway plaza in a couple of miles. Pull off."

"You can't imagine," Frank said, after a moment. "I saw her, and I kept thinking I could wake her up."

"You saw her? Oh, Frank. Of course you would, at the funeral. Or, was it like that?"

"I saw her at the hospital. And before the . . . burial. She wasn't, well, disfigured. She looked like Natalie."

"Why did you tell us not to come, Frank? My only brother. My only sister-in-law. We should have been there with you. All this would have been easier."

"It was dangerous there."

"That doesn't matter," Eden said.

"What they tell you is true. I thought, there was such chaos, it could have been someone else. Even now, I expect her to turn up. I pick up the phone to call her twice a day." Frank stopped. "I don't want to talk about Natalie now." He put his warm arm against the glass, polishing a porthole in the fog on the side window the way he had as a child. "What's going on at home? It's been a long time."

Eden admitted that it had been hard, working her job at the library, finishing her master's, trying to help their mother with Jack—worse every day mentally and sound as an oak plank physically—and keeping up with the ten horses they boarded.

They pulled off to change seats. Ian slept on, not even flinching when the door slammed.

"What about your man here?" Frank said.

"I'm the Jewish stableman," Marty answered. But Marty was in medical school. How much time could he realistically spend on a farm that was always a mess at best? At least it was paid for. Frank's mother, Hope, often said that if she had to be widowed, she was glad it happened fast, in a freak explosion at the grain co-op where Francis Mercy worked a few days a week. She was glad because Francis never had to be sick. He never had to face waking up and seeing that death had taken a step closer to the door. The big insurance settlement meant that Hope did not have to sell the farm and move Eden to an apartment in Madison. There was a sum set aside for Frank and for Eden, and Hope didn't have to work, although she acted as though the high school library would be gone in a frenzy of book combustion if she took a sick day.

It was more than twenty years ago, now. Frank had been in his first year of college and Eden in first grade, but to Frank it seemed a lifetime. He could hear his father's voice, but no longer summon up his face.

"You have kids come to help," he said to Eden.

"One girl," Eden said. "I tried five boys. It's not like I couldn't pay them. Something, at least. But you can't pay enough. Because they don't really do anything."

Frank could imagine Patrick preening.

Patrick would see to Tenacity and its tenants . . . Hollywood might have to wait. Like most jockeys Frank had known, Patrick would have been a gypsy, and like most of them, he seemed adept at other physical things, like acrobatics and tumbling. Maybe Patrick wasn't interested in gawping at movie stars. Maybe he wanted to be a stunt man. He'd probably read about that kind of world, on one of the many nights when Patrick plowed steadily through a book and a bottle. Frank didn't even know if Patrick had a family. He didn't speak of them. Patrick probably would not leave Wisconsin for a while, possibly a long while. That was good; it would help Frank manage the jaw-dropping prospect of slipping back into the life that was never really his, as an adult, in any case. It would be his now, though. Tenacity Farms was at least something he could put out his hand and touch, that would not give way. It was Eden's as well as Frank's, but Eden wouldn't want any part of it after she and Marty were married in the spring.

Married, Frank thought suddenly. Eden? Of course, she was now, what? Thirty? Thirty-one? To Frank, Eden still seemed like a child.

And to their mother, Frank was sure that even he was still a child.

He longed to see his mother more now than at any other time in his life, except for the days Hope spent at the University of Wisconsin Hospital after Eden's complex birth, when Frank was eleven. At the wedding, Natalie said, "You have a crush on your mother." She said it with the same sweet and sour fusion that tinctured Hope's voice once when she described Frank as emotionally retarded. It was probably true. What cause had he to assume the mantle of a man in full? He played with guns and horses. They said most people truly didn't grow up, until they had a child.

Another little door opened.

Frank had never told Eden and Hope about the baby. The thought of Natalie standing on the table and shouting out their joy made his hands shake. His bad leg ignited.

Leaning forward, he urged the car ahead. The three hours from the airport seemed far longer than the twenty hours from Brisbane.

Ian splashed languidly in the oversized claw-footed tub that was the centerpiece of the new upstairs bathroom. But when Hope tried to lay him down in bed alone, the boy made it clear that he would not go to sleep until he was assured that Frank would be beside him. Like a small businessman, Ian cast his eyes upward and pointed at the other side of the demulcent queen-sized bed that took up most of the smallest of the five bedrooms in the farmhouse. He pointed to his hand, asking for paper, and drew that funny little thing, the arrows along the horizontal line—right, left.

"I'll be up in a moment," Frank said. "I want to talk to . . . to Grandma."

Ian eye-rolled and Frank laughed.

"He doesn't believe you."

"I really will come," Frank said.

In the big living room, paneled with logs from the maples that fell for the gourmet kitchen, Frank told his mother about the storm, the flood, and the rescue. He told her about the hillside at Tura Farms—unused land that Cedric and Brian worked with a local priest to have set aside and summarily consecrated. On the morning after the funeral, although the crowd would have been huge if Frank had allowed it, only a few doctors came from Our Lady Help of Christians, as well as Natalie's brother and Frank's crew chief. They stood with Frank and Tura and Cedric under a hastily thrown-up tent, in, impossibly, another swizzle of rain. Natalie's father Jamie's favorite song was, of course, "Waltzing Matilda," and a friend of Natalie's, a young intern who'd studied violin at conservatory, played that, and then the lullaby "Tura Lura Lura," like the name of Frank's employer. The late Mrs. Donovan had sung that song to lay down her babies. With people practically on their knees in tears, Brian ended the short ceremony by repeating a part of the Yeats poem about the entry into heaven of a fiddler from Dooney.

At this, Hope smiled, got up and took a volume down from her banks of curved bookshelves, and read, " 'When we come at the end of time, to Peter sitting in state, he will smile on the three old spirits, but call me first through the gate. For the good are always the merry, save by an evil chance, and the merry love the fiddle, and the merry love to dance.' "

"She was merry," Frank said. "I don't know how she ended up with me."

"Oh, Frank. You were what she wanted. She lit up when she talked about you. She lit up when anyone talked about you. You were the great love to her. It's unbearable."

"Mom," Frank said. "Natalie was expecting a baby. By the time we came here, we'd have had a son." Hope gripped his arm. Frank almost resented it then—how much more it hurt Hope than it seemed to have before. Perhaps he only imagined that. Frank kneeled beside the arm of her chair and let his mother put her cool hand on the back of his neck.

"I know you're more than grown up, but all this makes me feel terribly protective of you, Frank. This is way, way too much. My poor boy."

"You didn't know how much fun we had. I didn't want her to go to work. I was like this high school boy. I wanted her to come and watch me train horses so I could show off. Do you know what that's like?"

Hope said, "Not that exactly. Your dad was older."

"I thought we were just getting started . . ." The dry wedge formed in Frank's throat. "We had a whole life to know, and then, when we knew everything, to enjoy it together growing old."

"That much I do know."

"You do. Yes, you do, Mom."

"The little boy . . ."

"Mairead, Hugh's wife, was married before. Brian Donovan was in no shape to take care of him."

"I see. Tell me how it was, Frank. About everything. Work backwards. Nothing ever got worse from talking about it." It was one of Hope's axioms, like "many hands make light work," or "discretion is the greater part of valor," "lie down with dogs, get up with fleas," or (Frank's favorite) "a day without sunshine can be very restful."

So Frank sat back on the floor and traced patterns in the old Oriental carpet, and told Hope how recovery workers quickly found the bodies of Brian's wife and daughters, and her brothers and their families. He described the Mass for all of them on December 27, at Brisbane's Cathedral of St. Stephen. He was lucky to be able to schedule the Mass at all. Funerals were being booked like two-for-one holiday cruises. He pleaded what was by then a rare flirtation with the truth: he had to go back to the United States very soon, and, as his home was destroyed, he had nowhere to live with his little boy. Like everyone else in Brisbane, it seemed, the priest knew both Natalie and Brian. Natalie had been the first doctor to see Father Lawrence Boynton in the ER when he broke his ankle in a fall on the way home from his own brother's late-in-life ordination; his brother had raised a family and buried a wife before becoming a priest.

Frank went with Brian and Tura. Cedric stayed home with the little boy. It was the cathedral's name day, the Feast of St. Stephen, celebrated anciently in Ireland by children carrying a stuffed toy of a wren from door to door to beg for pocket change—supposedly for the poor bird's funeral. The church was bedecked in purple and red and set about with holly bushes. Clerestory windows laid gold bars of late afternoon sunlight over the grand, horrible carnival of fifteen caskets of Australian camphor laurel, an extravagant waste of a beautiful hardwood that no one could help but forgive, next to the huge framed image of all of them, made by a beach photographer the day before Christmas Eve. Natalie's family was buried in the same festive, silly clothes they wore in the photo, the guys in identical shirts with great, blue Parramatta flowers on them, Natalie and her mother and the girls in plain blue sundresses. That fact alone loomed surreal: it had been such a short time that Frank could remember how they all smelled— the little girls' grapefruit shampoo and lemon butter from the shrimp lunch they'd all had in midafternoon. The big family photograph, with smaller copies for everyone made by Brian's office staff, was the only representation of Hugh and his wife, Mairead, whose bodies still had not been found. Just twelve hours before the funeral, Brian's daughter Adair was found in the wreckage of the hotel, her badly battered body identified from her dental records. Brian had seemed ready to accept the solace of the Mass with a fragile peace. He'd covered enough "miracles" that he'd still kept a slender thread of one wrapped around his finger for Adair. The discovery demolished him. Frank had to push

Brian in a wheelchair—for he would go right back to the hospital—and Brian slumped to one side, as though he'd had a stroke as well as broken his leg. Adair had just had her purple braces put on. The purple cost more, and she'd written her daddy a letter, thanking him. She was almost thirteen.

Natalie's obituary was on the front page of the newspaper—the Donovans' the greatest loss of life in one family from this catastrophe or perhaps any catastrophe. They would all slumber together under one piece of dark gray granite with a rood of Australian copper. Although at the end, Frank felt oppressed rather than uplifted by the great press of the Donovans' Catholicism, and even Brian stared vacantly at the repeated promises of the world to come. Frank's comfort came from Cedric and Tura's offer of that hilltop, Frank told Hope, knowing that a part of Natalie lay under ground he'd walked on and ridden on and loved—even though it was only expedient, because the largest Brisbane Catholic cemetery was flooded.

"It was selfish, to want her buried there. For I thought, even then, why would I want to live there? Look at it every day? Coming back was what we planned to do, Natalie and I, in time for Edie's wedding." His mother nodded. "And then, I decided it would be better for him, here. For Ian."

Hope laid the book down and said, "I know."

"I didn't even think of what to do with our apartment. Insurance and so forth. Brian said he would find a lawyer to sort it out."

"You can deal with it from here."

"I just wanted to get home," Frank said. He paused, then said, "You should know this, though. The little boy isn't any relation to the Donovans, Mom."

"What do you mean?" Hope raised her two hands and pressed her palms together. "What are you telling me, Frank?"

Frank told her then, in unsparing detail, about his decision to bring the child home with him, entirely against the laws of any country and good sense, and, strangely, his own will—although nothing would have changed his choice now. Finally, he told her about the hold of the airplane, and all the animals. Hope sat silent for a long while, five minutes.

"So much has happened to you. You've just lost your wife," his mother said. "And your unborn son. You're not yourself."

"That didn't make it right! But somehow, I don't think there's somebody out there looking for him. He had to have a father of his own. Everyone has a father."

Hope nodded, her face composed. "If there was a father who was alive, you might think he'd have seen that picture of you in the paper. Wouldn't he? It ran everywhere. Germany. Japan. All over the world."

"You couldn't recognize the child from that picture. You could see his orange sneakers. And just a corner of his face."

"You would know if it was your child, Frank. Then again, I'm not sure that a month is enough for someone to come forward."

"I didn't want anybody to come forward! I dragged Charley into it, too." Briefly, he told Hope about how he had gone to Charley in the early days, with Ian by his side.

"You could tell Charley didn't like it. But you could tell he didn't hate it either. He's a straight-up guy. And he would have taken Ian. But I wouldn't give him up."

Hope went back into the kitchen for more coffee and returned, sitting down in a double-sized chair closer to Frank. She always drank coffee, the high-test kind of coffee, all day and through the evening, like religion, and she slept exactly eight hours each night without getting up at all. She closed her eyes in the dark and opened them in the dark, just before six, and had all her life. Even as a child, Frank was an indifferent sleeper, who envied his friends' ability to fall into small comas even on the bus home from school. When he asked Hope her secret, she said it was because her soul was just, and Frank, in his reverence for her, never thought of this as ironic. "So, how did your friend Charley manage to come up with a passport?" she asked. "Especially at such a chaotic time."

"I think anybody can do it, maybe especially in a chaotic time. It's shady, of course. Lawyers know people like police know people. They just don't talk to those people. The birth certificate calls him Ian Smith Donovan, in the name of one of Natalie's dead brothers. The other papers call him Ian Smith Donovan Mercy. The birth year is right. I didn't want to know too much. But, Mom, I know enough!"

"Maybe this man wanted to give you some way to deny it . . ."

"There's no way to deny it."

"I think I hear him," Hope said. "Let me go up and check." She sprinted up the stairs, with more alacrity and bounce than Frank could have done, and Frank sat back, using his hand as a forceps on his temples to ease the tension that perched between his eyes. He still found it difficult to believe that he had done what he had done.

He recalled the live power lines of tension that whipsawed the air between him and Charley as he sat in his library, looking at Frank, then at Ian, his face first grave, then concerned, then amused, then resigned. Without talking about why they were doing it, the two men took their places at laptops and began searching the databases for missing children. In Brisbane and the surrounding area alone, there were thirty alerts for children under the age of eighteen—one of them Natalie's niece. None of them was a blond male child about three years old. Frank next moved on to the six provinces, turning up a wild number of missing teenagers, hundreds of them between the ages of fifteen and seventeen. The numbers of missing children under the age of twelve dropped sharply. Excluding the cold cases, there were a few dozen, and not a single one a child of Ian's age or description. After an hour's search, with a last look at Ian, Charley told Frank he would call Frank in a few days.

"Does he cry out in his sleep?" Hope said, returning from the bedrooms upstairs and taking her place in the big chair.

"He does sometimes."

"It scared me. I was going to pick him up, but he never woke."

"I want to wake him up and tell him we're here, and nothing can hurt him. But I don't want to disturb him either," said Frank.

"You were talking about you and Charley."

Frank told his mother about the search of the databases for missing children, and how few turned up, none like Ian.

"How can that be? In a whole country?"

"That whole country has a population not much larger than the New York metropolitan area, Mom."

"Maybe the father or mother was hurt. What if he's in the hospital? I suppose, in that way, you could think of it as being a foster-care arrangement until you can find the father. You can take him back."

"Take him back to Brisbane? Maybe. I don't want to. Say he has a father. If he is out there, he's looking for his child. But, Mom, I know there's a different story to this," Frank said. "I was a cop for twenty years. You have a sense of things."

"I don't want to push you, Frank. But think of what you're saying. This doesn't make sense. I know how you did it, but why did you do it?" Hope's face creased. With a sigh that showed how tired she was—and this terrified Frank—she pincered her own temples, just as Frank had done. He didn't think of his mother as having an age. As Eden said, Hope had cooked everything, a great kettle of obscenely caloric creamy potato and leek soup, turkey with stuffing, braised beets with bleu cheese, two kinds of pie, and a tart.

"You and Natalie were expecting a baby boy. Then, here was this little boy."

"No, it wasn't that . . ."

"It's not myself I'm thinking about. Having him here. Any culpability I might have. He's fine. A great little kid. But he had to come from someplace. Even if his mother died, and his brother, that poor little boy, he has other people . . ."

"He has no other people."

"You should talk to somebody, Frank."

"You mean a lawyer, here in the States?"

"I mean a therapist," Hope said, "I mean a psychiatrist. This isn't the way you talk. Ian's fast asleep. I want to do some reading and go to bed myself. This has been quite a day. I have to help Jack get to bed first."

"I'll do it," Frank said. His grandfather had his own apartment, two rooms and a small bath, at the back of the house. Frank had added them thoughtfully, so that Jack had a big picture window and his own entrance that led directly to the older barn, the one Jack had built himself, where they still boarded several horses. Having him on his own helped his mother, or so Frank believed. In his addled fury, Jack routinely treated Hope like a servant and sometimes went off his nut and smacked her with the old shillelagh he'd bought forty years ago in Ireland. But he could still read fluently, and did, for hours at a time, almost to the exclusion of everything else. He could still shower himself, and even shave, although he'd shrunk to the size of a seventh grader. He hadn't known Frank at all and seemed wary of Eden and Marty.

"He won't let you," Hope said. "We could pay for nurses. We've tried. He's like your horse." She stood up.

"I'll help you at least," Frank said.

"You don't have to."

"I want to."

"Another time. You must be worn out, with all this. He's not your responsibility," Hope said.

"He's not your father."

"He's Francis's father. He loved me as a daughter," Hope said. "I'm used to it." In one of her weekly letters, Hope said she put up with Jack because there were moments when Jack's glance betrayed how deeply shamed he was.

"It's too hard for you now, Mom."

Although Hope put on her lipstick and swooped up her long hair before she ever came downstairs in the morning, Frank never thought she looked artificial, or as though she was trying to cover up her age. Now he thought, She's seventy-two. He had never asked his mother why she and his dad had married when she was twenty-one, only to wait for ten years to have a child. Perhaps they hadn't. Perhaps no child had come until Frank, and then so many years between him and Eden. Back then, people didn't talk about such things.

"Well, it might have been getting to be too much for me," said Hope. "Now it won't be. I have you around. Are you planning on buying a house of your own?"

Shocked, Frank said, "I wasn't. Not now. I can, though. I thought we'd stay here, for a while at least."

Hope smiled, relieved. "Good. I missed you. You'd better go see to . . . Ian."

"What?"

"What you said about what happened in the airplane, Frank. It could be . . . the strain. It's really difficult for me . . ."

"To believe that. I know. But I saw what I saw. Patrick saw it, too. And I saw it before."

"I think you're under a great deal of pressure."

"You think I'm crazy."

"I don't think you would ever knowingly do anything that was wrong. I don't think you're lying."

"He does it all the time, Mom. Do you think I'm saying he's supernatural or something? Like he has superpowers?"

"What you're describing doesn't exist, Frank. It would be like faith healing."

"No, it's nothing like that."

"That's what you're describing."

Frank thought back to the odd, boxy, maroon van where he had first seen Ian, trapped. "His brother said to take him first. He said he was important."

"He probably said it was important. How could you remember exact words at a moment like that?"

"Mom! For twenty years, I listened for people to say things like, 'She wasn't dead. When I put her in the car, she wasn't dead.' People who were out of their minds. I learned to listen no matter how involved I was. That's what the bigger kid said."

A fierce, throaty bellowing issued through the lower hall. "That's Jack," his mother said. "I give him some hot milk and something to eat about now." They headed past the fireplace, into an ell that led to Jack's rooms.

"Does he talk to you? Jack?"

"He doesn't *talk* at all. He hasn't talked for years. Since right before you left. Not a word. Just sounds. Crying or rage."

Unaccountably, for Hope said he never did this, Jack had pissed himself. The wood floor next to the tapestry chair gleamed under an amber pool. Together, they urged the old man toward the bathroom, although he could walk under his own steam, balanced and surprisingly strong. Suddenly he shook Frank's hand off his arm and jabbed him, hard, intentionally, in the ribs, with one knotty fist. "Don't, Jack. It's your grandson, it's Frank." The ancient old man drew back and struck Frank on the shoulder. Frank rubbed the place. It hurt.

"Get something to clean that up," Hope said. "I'll help him. I'm glad you're not squeamish."

Frank passed Ian without seeing him. Ian was standing in the doorway, probably keyed up, past exhaustion, on some plane of nerves that kept his feet moving when the rest of him was inanimate.

"Put that down," Hope said, and Frank looked back. Jack had raised his walking stick.

Ian darted past Frank and, gathering himself visibly, stood facing Jack with his fists on his hips. Jack sat down heavily, on the pile of towels Hope had slipped into the chair. The shillelagh slid out of his hand and its clublike head struck the floor. Ian's hands moved—right, left.

In a voice that sounded of old gears, Jack said, "Who are you, son?"

Hope clutched the pile of clean towels she'd taken from the closet. She said, "Well."

EIGHT

FRANK LEANED AGAINST the tailgate of his mother's old pickup truck and watched the horses come, smudges in the mist, down the lane from the big barn to the small pasture. His father had stood in this lane, and so had his grandfather. Frank wondered if they had been so tired, and, an hour after the sun came up, so hungry and dirty as he was today. As he had come to expect, the little paint mare, one of the boarders, bit everything she could in her urgency to break into the line. He whistled at her, one sharp blast, and she paid no attention. Finally one of the two thoroughbreds aimed a kick at her hip. The paint was unfazed, and bared her teeth. Frank had to check this behavior, and he would. Not today.

He pulled on the wrist warmers his mother had knitted for him and lowered his watch cap over the sunglasses he wore even before daybreak. Patrick made fun of the sunglasses, but they were a twenty-year habit. On the job, Frank was naked without something covering his eyes. He wore Jims, the only sunglasses he ever found that could correct his vision, which was sharp but could fool him at dusk, when the earth's wildings woke, looked around them, and decided without plan to take what they wanted. It was piercingly cold, but the old men at the feed store insisted that the wind was a thaw wind. Frank hoped they were right in this, as in so much else.

This morning, he would take Ian to the Growing Room, a preschool in the center of town.

The mayhem of school kids pinged in his belly, where the big bowl of oatmeal he'd eaten an hour ago might as well have been no more than a sip of water.

Being a child of seven or nine or ten had scared the hell out of Frank.

He had been strong, and athletic, but he never relaxed among other boys, who had no stops and no funnel on their vicious energy. He played with the little schoolyard thugs, who switched allegiances by the hour, freely pounding away on the one they'd defended as a best friend before lunch. He played sports and excelled, and tried hard every day to make sure he never got on anyone's bad side because he was certain that the kids he knew would kill him if they could get away with it and sleep tight afterward. He went to their birthday parties and bought them the toy weapons they wanted. None of them was really a bad boy. He didn't know people who'd turned out to be criminals: if they had, they chiseled loans or cheated on taxes. They were ordinary, voracious kids—boys with blocky heads who came to school on Mondays in Green Bay Packers jerseys, having smudged black streaks under their eyes in anticipation of that night's game.

It was because of these boys, not because of any sort of lust for authority, that Frank grew up certain he would be a cop. Only with some kind of order did he see how he could live in such a terrifying world.

Now he saw Hope watching Ian constantly. Hope knew everything. Frank had believed that as a child, and believed it now. If Hope believed in what they now called "the Ian effect," then, if it wasn't real, at least they would share the same hallucination.

When would Ian break? When would he crack like an egg that spilled hot rage? So far, Ian was only a gentle kid, too curious, and needy as a duckling when it came to Frank's presence. When he was overtired, Ian balked, went boneless, and made Frank haul him up the stairs. Even while Frank was doing that, though, he could tell that Ian didn't really disagree with going to bed; it was a ritual protest on behalf of all children. Told sternly to stay in his bed in the small room that adjoined Frank's room, he cried for ninety minutes straight, until Eden came down the hall from their room, picked him up, and tossed him in Frank's bed, with an oath about some people needing "to actually work."

Once, he deliberately dumped a full bowl of fruit on the floor because Hope put maple syrup on it. Once, he threw one of Frank's old metal Hot Wheels cars at a light fixture and shattered the bowl, showering milky shards down on the people around the dinner table. He then sat in a closet for ninety minutes and wrote a laborious letter of nonsense whorls and curlicues, signed with the inch-long line and the arrows.

More often, Ian was never bored, and grateful for everything.

Where had such a child come from, in this century?

A few days after they arrived, Hope and Frank went to Target with Ian and let him pick out his kit, a wardrobe from the skin out. Ian selected jeans in every color and plaid shirts with snaps. There were not enough colors to have one of each, so he had doubles of the bright blue and bright orange, still so stiff that when Ian put them on, he looked like he was wearing a box. He changed four or five times a day, and wouldn't allow Hope to wash them, or even take them out of the little trunk at the foot of the bed that had once held Frank's toy cars. Periodically, Ian laid all his clothes on the bed and mixed and matched them. His favorite, worn three days running, was the pair of orange jeans with an orange-and-blue shirt. His other cherished item of apparel was a deerstalker hat that belonged to Grandfather Jack and, when he could get it away from him, Jack's shillelagh.

Jack didn't smile, but seemed to regard Ian with more than casual interest when Ian put on the hat, the pants, and a necktie that Hope had found in a big basket of fabric scraps. Frank once saw Ian tap Jack's knee twice. Jack tapped Ian's knee twice. Ian tapped Jack's knee six times. Jack did the same thing. They were, Frank saw, playing.

"He's strange about possessions."

"Maybe he didn't have many," said Hope.

"But he's funny. Obsessive."

"He eats nicely. He doesn't count pieces of food or get upset when we change his routine. He cleans up after himself. He's extraordinary with people." She meant ancient Jack. She further insisted that "the Ian effect" did not pertain to her.

"He does what I tell him to do."

"How do you know?" Frank teased her.

"There's no reason for him to try to get his way with me. You may be right about this . . . ability, but it seems to me that he's just a remarkably charming boy."

Then, one day in the dullest stretch of what Wisconsinites fatuously referred to as early spring, Frank saw a huge blue truck making its way up the driveway. He didn't pay much attention. Hope had been talking about their need for a bigger washing machine and dryer. The truck remained quite a while, forcing Patrick to drive the pickup into the gully to get around it. When he came inside with Patrick to shower before dinner, Frank could see the moony blue glow from the living room, and, once inside, he was aghast. Curved in along one whole wall, as a bay window would have curved out, supported by pillars of stainless steel as incongruous in the big farmhouse living room as a fire escape, was an aquarium that was twelve feet long and four feet tall. Corals nested brightly in corners and Frank recognized from his and Natalie's diving trips a squadron of military-blue Achilles tang, a spiny red lion-fish, clown triggers, a miniature grouper, and translucent sea horses that floated among fronds of delicate green and violet vegetation. He turned to his mother, speechless, more surprised than if she had planted a forest of sequoias behind the house while he was working up at the barn. Hope smiled at him indulgently. On the big boat-shaped oak table was more candy than Frank had seen outside a store—the really evil-colored stuff that looked like individual toxins, ropes of licorice, yards of dots, Pixy Stix taller than Ian, peanut-butter cups as big around as Frank's palm.

"Are we having a theme party?" Frank finally said. "Or am I at the wrong house?"

"Oh, you mean the fish tank," said Hope. "It's just a fish tank."

"If that's just a fish tank, then the Sears Tower is just an office building." Frank began to remove the top layers of shirts for the laundry. "Why . . . how did you get something like that? And what did it cost?"

"Oh, I don't know. Setting it up cost more than the tank. They have whole companies that set up aquariums, can you imagine?"

"Why, though?"

"It's pretty. It livens up the place. It's very educational. These creatures are native to the ocean where he grew up."

"He, being Ian?"

"Yes. I got a sort of grouping of leather furniture—"

"A grouping?"

"So that we could sit around it and read and look at it. And feel the serenity. That's why they put these in dentists' offices, you know . . ."

Frank regarded the candy, some variations of which he hadn't seen since he was eleven. "And all this must be fish food, Mom . . ." To Ian, who was all but out of sight, matching the bowls and lids of the Tupperware and putting them away in lower cabinets—"his job," as Hope had told him—Frank said, "So, son, is all this yours?"

Ian stood up, and, to his credit, gave Frank a blinding smile, as if to say, *A bit of all right, huh?*

"You made Grandma do this. You're not supposed to make Grandma get things you like."

"But he didn't, Frank," Hope protested.

"But he did, Mom." Frank gestured at the room, which now resembled a combination country inn and South Beach nightclub. "Next it will be a litter of puppies and a miniature motorcycle. And now you have to admit it. You went to Madison to look for a nice serviceable large-capacity Maytag and you brought home the Great Barrier Reef. Admit it. You don't run for the penny candy on your own."

Hope poured herself a cup of old coffee, splashed a little milk in it, and added a few ice cubes.

"Frank," she said. "I do like that aquarium, and I honestly thought it was my idea."

"I'm sure it was . . . at least after a while."

Ian needed school. But he couldn't talk. So Frank was avoiding preschool. Wasn't it just too soon? On the other hand, didn't Ian need compatriots (no, Frank's instincts roared, he was perfect as he was!)? That night, Frank read Ian a book about a little bunny who'd run away from his mother. He turned himself into a mountain, into a fish in a stream, and a crocus in a hidden garden—all to hide from his mother. At the end of the rather sweet story, Ian kept tracing the picture of the mother bunny climbing the mountain to bring down her errant son. Frank knew he was thinking about parents who followed children anywhere—from home to danger and back.

Frank said, "You know, I can find people. That's what police do sometimes. If you were lost, I could find you. And I would find you. I would never let you be lost."

Ian got up and pulled down his drawing pad. He opened the aluminum box of forty-eight colored pencils he kept sharpened and arranged carefully by gradations of shade. After a few minutes, he showed what he'd drawn to Frank. It was a mature, if primitive, drawing, the face of a boy who might have been Ian a few years older, except he had brown eyes, a mitered chin, and longer, darker blond hair. "It's your brother."

Ian nodded.

He smiled.

He waited for Frank to tell him that he would soon climb mountains and cross rivers and search in gardens until he found a boy who'd been dead for months.

"Honey, I don't think I can find him. I think his body swallowed too much water. I don't think his body could get better, just like my wife, Natalie."

Then Ian shook his head violently. He lifted one hand like a crocodile puppet, and then snapped the fingers closed, plainly telling Frank to shut his mouth.

Was there, after all, any wonder that Ian was hoping that his brother was alive and Frank could bring him home? Frank lay down next to Ian in the twilight, remembering himself as a child in this very room, huddled under a delicious thickness of quilts that never seemed to be enough, reaching with his toes for the hot water bottle that Hope customarily gave him. The present was so hard that Frank was grateful he couldn't see the future. He put his arm around Ian and fell asleep.

The next morning, Ian got hurt.

Since Frank hadn't decided about school, he still kept Ian with him most of the time while he worked, figuring that a child who's survived a tsunami should have some credit at the happenstance prevention bank. Any experienced father—farmer, idiot—would have known that a farm is the most dangerous of all workplaces, a minefield of accidents literally waiting to happen, and that having someone there to look after Ian and Jack was only baseline prudent.

It was a Monday, and though Hope would be ready to look after him in the summer, this last term she was working long hours every day, training a new media specialist—the modern name for librarians, as libraries were now "media centers" and books apparently were "media." Her pension earned twice over, Hope Mercy was finally retiring from the high school, after forty years.

Fetes and observances were planned.

With this and the wedding on the horizon, Frank should have waited for summer to start trying to mend the various messes and malfunctions at Tenacity. He should have attended to urgent things, like putting Ian on his medical insurance and getting Ian a Social Security card. But one dawn rolled as every repair uncovered another set of problems and tasks, and the mind under his mind was able to find a little study in which to think while his muscles were busy. That had always been Frank's way. There was money to hire someone to do the work, but there wasn't so much of it that Frank and Patrick couldn't make do. Activity led to practical considerations, but idleness bred speculative thought like burdock. Frank needed practicality. Concentrating on here and now was a struggle. Then and someday sang like sirens. Whenever he was alone and short of exhausted, his mind began to plow. What if the father came? What if Charley repented of his foolishness? What if Ian remembered everything and produced his family's phone number? He didn't want to remember Natalie's drained, inert face, or Brian's anguished mourning, all those identical Donovan coffins, or the purple minivan tumbling away with Ian's older brother inside, or anything else.

At least when he fell into bed these winter nights, he was spent. He'd never worked harder—not at Tura Farms, not on the job. No sooner did he lie down and surrender to the sounds of the house going to sleep around him, the doors snapping shut, lights flicking off, shades pulled with a swoosh, the heat clattering to life, than he went out, and no sooner did he go out than he woke before it was light when Hope snapped on the hall light and walked past his door on the way down to the kitchen.

That same morning, Hope said, "Do you think he'll stay with me in summer? Go with me and do the things I do? I don't think he will. He wants to be out there with you. He wants to be with you every minute."

Frank said, "I'll make sure he does."

Then it was too late.

Frank wasn't watching. There was so much to be done. Everything in the big barn was falling down, and when the big pasture bloomed in spring, there would be a whole new set of problems because, even under snow, he could tell it was a welter of burdock, mallow, poison ivy, and thistles as big around as broom handles. Weeds didn't really matter, but Frank hated weeds. The higher pasture would have been better for exercise; it was flatter, bigger, and drained well. But something big had taken out about sixty feet of fence in two places at some point, and neither his sister nor his mother claimed to know what it was, although Frank suspected Marty with a tractor. The family horses were healthy, but not for long. Eden's quarter horse, Saratoga, was just eight, but had ballooned to the girth of an oil drum from more than adequate food and inadequate exercise. Hope was an accomplished rider, and rode her big Clydesdale mare, Bobbie Champion, to visit neighbors the way other women might drive a car; she sometimes even rode her horse to school, although this created too much of a sensation to be practical. In summer, she harnessed Bobbie to her big-wheeled pony cart and went to and from town and the farmers' market. But now Bobbie needed the farrier and the door on her big stall hung off its hinges. Bobbie could have walked out anytime she wanted and gotten on the road to Madison although she never moved. Still, anything broken was dangerous. Frank put Glory Bee in the sturdiest of the boxes, but she succeeded in leaning out slats after the first two days. Forty days of work and more before the place was even safe, Frank thought. It was not safe. Ian would have been safer in a housing project on the west side of Chicago.

That day, it was so cold that he and Patrick were encumbered by thick Carhartt overalls and gloves. Frank had forgotten the raw misery of a Wisconsin February.

"Sweet fucking Jesus, guv, how would you bear it ever?" Patrick said. "Filthy fucking cold."

"You don't get used to it," Frank said.

At least, inside the big barn, they were out of the wind.

"What did you do before?" Patrick asked. "When you lived in the States."

"Police," Frank said. "Mounted police. In Chicago."

"Did you like that?"

"I liked it. Now that I look back, I loved it. It was the best thing I ever did."

"Stopped out, though?"

"I got in an accident."

"On horseback?" Patrick was suddenly still, steeped in attentiveness, and it was fearful to think of him remembering the screams of the horses, the curses of riders, the clatter of stiles and crisping of smashed foliage that attended a fall in a jumps race. For pure unluckiness, such an accident felt like a house fire.

"No. I got hit by a car in the rain. I had been covering for a regular traffic cop."

"Whyn't be a detective? Or some big toff like that?"

"Detectives in Chicago are just regular police, not commanders. They work on major crimes, murder and big robberies. I liked working with the horses," Frank said. "I liked how people saw the horses. Police show up and everybody hates you. Firefighters show up, and everybody cheers. Hooray! Here come the Marines! I was police, but that's how people reacted to the horses. They respected them."

"Your own horse?"

"No. He was a donated horse, Tarmac, a Standardbred. Dark gray. Like asphalt. A funny color. They started to train him as a harness racer . . . would you call that a carriage racer? It didn't work out." Frank finished the interior patch of a three-foot-round hole in the roof of the barn, over an unoccupied box stall. The shingling would have to wait for better weather. "What about you? Did you always want to ride?"

"I didn't want to do it when I did it," said Patrick. "I hated it. I just had the knack. I was the youngest of six boys, ten kids altogether. I was for a priest. I graduated with honors from seminary and had a scholarship to college." Frank knew better than to ask what changed, as some kind of pain shimmered, then melted like mist. Patrick wiped away nothing on his mouth with the back of his glove and said, "Bastards." Frank wasn't sure if Patrick meant the moldy, studded boards they'd just thrown down or whoever had driven him from the steeple to the dangerous thunder of a steeplechase.

That was when Ian screamed.

Frank leaped down five rungs of the ladder, staggering on his bad leg. Ian had stepped on one of those curled roof boards studded with rusty roofing nails Frank had thrown down. Blood pooled where the tender rind of his pink heel was pierced in two places, right through the sole. Everything he'd heard about horses and metal and tetanus flooded Frank's brain. Taking Ian in his arms, he judged where the big veins were, and knew he should pull out the nails. He pulled them out, ignoring the child's screams as he wet a towel with hot water and pressed it to the small foot.

Summoned, Hope was back in five minutes. She drove to the emergency room while Ian wept (loudly; he *did* have quite a voice) and clung to Frank's neck.

The tetanus shot was ferocious, as was cleaning the wounds, which went deep, because Ian had been running. If she hadn't known Hope since high school, the doctor looked as though she would have liked to report Frank.

"That's not a child-friendly environment," the doctor said.

"It's his home, and I have to teach him to be careful there."

"You can't really teach a three-year-old kid to watch his feet every minute, Mr. Mercy."

"I know. It's my fault. I feel awful about it."

Hope and Frank took Ian to the achingly expensive tourist-grandmother toy store in town and bought him hundreds of dollars' worth of Legos. For two days, whenever Ian gently disengaged himself from Frank to play with his new toys, it was Frank, not Ian, who seemed emptied out, bereft. Devoutly he wished Ian did not have superpowers, because he could not discern what Ian was eliciting from him, and what Frank really felt on his own.

The following week, Frank took Ian to school. Just before he went inside, Frank realized he had no idea what to say.

"He doesn't talk," Frank told the teacher, after telling Ian that it was okay to go over and play with the blocks. "He talked before the tsunami, but not since then."

"That's hard," the teacher said. "For you and for us."

For her? Frank thought. Had she not heard the word *tsunami*, or was that not common lingo every day on Center Street in Spring Green, Wisconsin? He had to remind himself that this was the nature of teachers, a kaleidoscope with a very narrow lens. His leg began to drum.

He said, "Well, at least he won't be disruptive."

The teacher said, "We do teach kids who have handicaps." A little girl sat in the corner with a grubby doll tightly clamped between her feet, twisting a strand of her hair and rocking metronomically. "Has he had his hearing tested?"

Frank said, "He doesn't have a hearing deficit. We think it's a result of trauma."

"But does he have a history of ear infections?"

"No."

"It's not always easy to tell. Some children form scar tissue without parents ever knowing. Their hearing is then like this." The young woman with her ingenuous clusters of hair ribbons stuffed both index fingers into her ears. Frank wanted to stomp on her foot. "Has he had a hearing test since you've been here?"

"No, but doctors in Australia know about hearing," Frank said.

"Doctors at the University of Wisconsin specialize in children who have hearing loss at the upper and lower ends of the spectrum."

"I would guess this was the result of emotional trauma."

"What kinds of emotional trauma?"

"Besides seeing most of his family die in a flood on Christmas morning?"

"Yes, besides that. Were there other kinds of abuse?"

"No! Isn't that enough?" Frank said.

"We're set up to handle only a small range of differences . . ."

"He's not as different as that little girl in the corner is. I don't know if he's going to grow up gay or allergic to cashews . . ."

"What other allergies does he have?"

"He isn't allergic to anything I know of." Frank glanced over at Ian, who carefully bared his teeth in a monster face and put up claws, waggling his head back and forth. Frank laughed. "Do you have some papers I should look at? I'm sure his pediatrician can fill out the forms you need, too."

"We have two open spaces in this class. But we would need the full tuition for the semester that started in January."

"Okay. That's fine. Why?"

"Well, he needs all the same things as if he was starting school in January. School supplies, an art cart, tissues, a sturdy backpack . . ."

"I see. You supply all that?"

"No, those things are supplied by the parent."

"So . . . I don't mind paying, but what am I . . ."

"Paying for? It's more demanding of our staff expertise with individual child development to mainstream a student with learning problems coming in midterm. We'll have to wait and see," said the teacher with the cherubic face and satanic soul, as though preschool was something mysterious and arcane, like the Electoral College. "If you can get those papers back to us by next week?" Proudly, Ian held up a paper on which he had written all of his letters, capitals and lower case, and his name, IANMRCY.

"Did Dad teach you this?" the teacher asked, and Ian nodded. Frank had no idea that Ian could write those letters. Ian gave her the paper, and did his small motion—right, left. The sabertooth preschool warden melted. She knelt and hugged him. "Welcome to school, Ian."

"You made her do that," Frank said. Ian chuckled soundlessly. "And you've been holding out on me. Where did you learn to write letters?" Big, elaborate grin and shrug. "You think you're smart?" Frank tickled Ian so hard that the whole car seat shook.

The following week, loaded down comically with ten pounds of school supplies, Ian joined his class. When Frank left, Ian's hug was urgent, tenacious, but the other kids were eyeing him closely, and after a moment, Ian straightened his shoulders and gave Frank a cheerful salute, his eyes overbright. As Frank turned away, he thought, Good boy. And he thought, Well, I can do this. For the first time since Natalie's death, and since Ian came to him, he could see a clear path. If nothing else went awry, he could walk that path. Putting the invisible house of his life in place had taken months of human effort. Knocking it awry was but the work of a moment for the gods, and nothing would ever be the same.

"Kate Bellingham called," Hope told Frank as he swung down from the truck on that bright, unseasonably tender Monday morning.

"Cedric and Tura's Kate?"

Through her nose, Hope chuffed in the exasperated way that women all over the world were, at that moment, doing in response to men who needed to verbally verify the obvious. "She needs you to call her back."

"That's fine. It's what, ten at night there. It must be Cedric. I'm sure he's sick. A stroke or something. I hope it's not worse than that."

Hope's uncharacteristically pale face went still, her gaze dark and fixed. "I think it is even worse than that, Frank. Something in that girl's voice was dire."

"I'm going to grab a bite of breakfast first, Mom. You used to say, bad news always keeps."

"Don't quote me to my own face, Frank," Hope said. "I'm not psychic but I heard it in her voice. Call now."

The pad on which she'd written the number of Tura Farms was propped against the phone. Gingerly, Frank lifted the receiver. He knew that Cedric must be ill . . . and hoped he was alive, but he didn't want to know the details. The *brrrr* of the telephone on the other end was interrupted on the first ring.

"Frank," Kate said. No greeting. No brisk hello.

"Yes."

"This is Kate Bellingham. Now Kate Piper. I got married."

"That's wonderful, Kate." He paused. "I had actually heard about this. I spoke to your dad ten days ago and he said congratulations were in order . . ."

"Mum and Dad are dead, Frank."

If he had heard a message of death in his life, he'd heard two hundred, and they seemed to be his personal coin in recent times. Still, he sat down hard at the frilly little table where Hope did her "telephoning," always with a list, and a pen for notes, as formal as a Jane Austen matron. Squeezed into the desk's embrace, he felt like a toad on a velvet pillow. "Kate, I am so sorry for your loss. I . . . I hate this."

"Thank you."

"How can this be? Both of them? May I ask, was there a . . . fire? Or did they wreck the car?"

"Frank, they were murdered." Kate began to cry, a hoarse, harsh caw. "They died last night. Sometime after midnight. It's difficult to tell. The weather is warm. The police have been here all day. And I somehow forgot that you didn't know. I forgot that you didn't already *know*, until just now!" Kate began to cry louder. The phone was muffled as it dropped, and then passed from hand to hand.

Finally, a sharpish, prim young woman's voice spoke up. "Mr. Mercy? This is Detective Inspector Rosemary O'Connell."

"Hello, ma'am."

"You were acquainted with the Bellinghams."

"Very well. I lived at Tura Farms for nearly three years."

"Of course it would be best if you were here . . ." Not for me, Frank thought. Not with you. "But perhaps you can help us answer a few questions."

"I'll do anything I can. The Bellinghams are, well, they were, very dear to me. But may I ask, first, was this a personal killing? Or a robbery that went wrong? A home invasion?"

"I'd like to ask the questions at this point, if I may. This is a new investigation. I can't share it at that level of detail even if I knew it."

"I'm sorry. Old habits."

"Katherine Piper told me you had been a police officer." Kate, married to the bounder Tura had said so long ago would never put a ring on her hand. It was good she was married, now having to withstand such rough weather. "Mr. Mercy, this is a very upsetting business, and mine should be the apology. I will say that the Bellinghams appear to have been asleep, or at least in bed, when someone entered their home. There were tire marks down by the gate, many kinds, and no footprints in the house at all . . ." Frank thought, Then they were pros. But why? "No sign of forced entry."

"They leave it open. They don't lock."

"Kate wasn't sure. As you can imagine, she's distraught. She doesn't come out here every day."

"How did she find out about the murder?" Frank said.

"There were three text messages in quick sequence to Kate's mobile phone. All the same words. 'Go look after your parents.' The mobile that the messages came from was a disposable. It hasn't been found."

"Sure."

"She wasn't sure about the precise arrangement of her parents' things either. Did they keep valuables? That you observed?"

"Cedric had a converted cabinet next to the refrigerator. It looked like an ordinary cabinet door, the kind where you might keep food in cans . . . er, tins, or vitamins. They did keep tins in there, and a spice rack, I think. But there was a safe in the back, behind the tins, a big cavity where they kept their papers, and Cedric had an old dueling pistol, that didn't work, the horses' papers . . ."

"Yes."

"I think they also kept some cash there."

DCI O'Connell said, "I will tell you this in confidence. All that is still there. More than ten thousand in cash. And what appear to be antique coins. The safe was closed, although the tins of food were removed. There seems to be nothing missing of any value. The odd thing is what was indeed missing."

"What?"

"Well, there were photos. Those are gone. They were hung on the wall, all in identical frames." Frank saw them now, Tura's wall of photos, in scrolly, expensive brass frames. He was there, in the old high-ceilinged timbered Queenslander kitchen, the welcome night breeze ruffling off the hills, the red crackle of a winter sunset announcing a perfect winter night in July. He could see Tura as he had seen her dozens of times, her hair in wisps from the elaborate Edwardian confection she rolled each morning before she came downstairs, a style that Hope, when she met Tura at Frank's wedding, called a "Gibson girl." Dressed for a movie set rather than a dusty pitch, she would be cheerfully whipping up some mess featuring perfectly good sausages ruined by one of her preternaturally bad sauces, slicing the thick bread, brewing the sweet strong tea. Cedric's eyes sought her out as he banged in at the vestibule door, the pipe with nothing in it clenched in his strong, square teeth; he'd be wearing a flannel shirt and his leather cap, despite it being seventy degrees. Frank wanted to weep.

Gone, all gone, the entirety of his world on the other side of the world—Natalie gone, and now Ceddie and Tura gone, a ruthless tide.

"There were photos of Mr. Bellingham's horses, including one that Kate says is now yours . . ." DCI O'Connell was saying, and, suddenly, Frank's hands chilled around the phone receiver. "And she seems to think there was also a picture of the whole group of you, also taken before you left. All those photos are gone. And the guest bedroom was torn apart, with a fury, children's old clothes scattered all over, the mattress tipped off the bed. Same thing with the bedroom in the farmhand's cottage. But that's all. Not another thing disturbed. Why would you think this would happen, Mr. Mercy?"

The tock of the clock on his mother's wall grew louder, a small hammer against Frank's brain. He said, "I have a copy of that same photo. It's here in my room. It was taken up on the hill where there is a grave and a big gum tree. My wife, Dr. Natalie Donovan, died in the tsunami, and she's buried there with most of her family."

Ian had been in that photo.

"Oy, Westbridge," O'Connell said to someone else, evidently in the room. "You take Mrs. Piper up and show her the albums. See if she can pick out a face, anyone who did work here for a short time. Anyone at all," O'Connell said, evidently speaking to another cop. Then she continued. "It was a nasty business. An execution. Their throats were cut. No weapon. No trail of blood."

Pros, Frank thought again. They leave no marks. Frank touched his cheek. The skin of his face had gone cold and stiff.

"I would like to give you my number if you can think of anyone, anyone at all, who might have had a grudge against the Bellinghams, for any reason."

Frank said, "I only knew them for three years, but in that time, I can tell you now that there was no one. They were not only well liked, but beloved."

Rosemary O'Connell said, "Not by everyone."

Frank wanted to shout, This had nothing to do with Tura or Cedric!

Saying so would help nothing, though, and no one would ever be arrested for murdering the Bellinghams, this much Frank knew for certain. He asked to speak to Kate again, and when she came back on the line, he murmured his intention to book right away to come out for the funeral, his muscles tensing as he willed her to refuse him.

"Thank you, Frank, but I'm not going to do that. Mum and Dad weren't religious, and the way things happened, it would be too awful to drag it out. As it is, we have reporters buzzing around us all day. We just hope the publicity will smoke out whoever did this, and the law will be all over him. It had to be a mistake, didn't it, Frank? They were looking for someone else, and my poor parents just got in their way?"

Frank said, "I'm sure you're right, Kate." Hope reached out and squeezed Frank's shoulder, her face crumpled with concern. Bright sun burst in at the windows. "This didn't have anything to do with your parents and the good lives they led."

There were ways to kill people and other ways to kill people. A bullet in the back of the skull was swift and painless, its sound a negligible concern at a place as far from the closest neighboring ranch as Rhode Island was from Manhattan. Cutting a throat was not only cruel, it was meant to be a message of terror to those who survived. The texts to Kate were meant to be a message as well: she had not looked after her parents. Whoever had come in the night to break Cedric and Tura's sleep with a harsher sleep had not come looking for valuables but for information about the American man they'd had the sad fortune to employ, then to know and love as a surrogate son. They had come because Frank had something they wanted, in the person of a miraculous child. Were the killers part of Ian's rightful family, simply trying to claim him back? Frank's intuition told him no, something else was going on. He didn't understand what it was.

He would have been willing to bet that the old couple, one as gentle and stern as the other, refused to offer up one word about Frank or Ian— even when promised that one word would save them.

They would have known even that their refusal was in vain.

Frank knew it, too.

*   *   *

A thick envelope containing a photocopy of a land deed arrived just three weeks later with a long letter from Kate. The wills had been read. Cedric had his own will. Tura had hers. They had one together, also, and the joint will was recent, just months old.

> Dear Frank,
>
> I didn't know you well, but I do know that Mum and Dad loved you as a son. Hence you will understand that they wanted to remember you in their will. Enclosed you will find the nature of their remembrance, which may puzzle you. It did puzzle me. But Mum and Dad had their own ways, of course.
>
> It has been a very hard time.
>
> Dad's leg bothered him more than it did once, but he had years left in him, and Mum was as strong as houses. The police think the fellow must have wanted the frames or something, because they were handmade, very expensive, from a local coppersmith. This has been a long time of tragedy. First Miles and your wife and her family, now my parents. Life presses down upon me with its brutality. Fen and I will have a child in the next few months, and I'm afraid to bring a child into this world. I wish my parents could have seen their first grandchild, a little girl.

The letter continued.

Kate was selling the swath of dry, hilly, yet somehow verdant land that had been Tura Farms. Forty of the best acres had been platted out for a house that she would one day build. That land included two acres of hilltop comprising the consecrated ground where Cedric and Tura now lay with the Donovans—and where several dozen other plots would be ruled off for family.

Frank thought of the morning of the tsunami, the radio preacher's voice blasting out the warning, "For you do not know the day nor the hour."

The rest of Tura Farms was slated to go to a "nice" developer. It made Frank wince to think of what *nice* meant in this context, one-acre houses on one-acre parcels, side by side on the hills where Tura and Cedric's horses had lifted their heads to the wind.

There were also bequests of money, in trust, because Tura, who saw to the books, had been frugal and canny with cash. Here began the puzzles, according to Kate, who hastened to point out she felt no rancor about any of these choices. Tura and Cedric had left the portion that would have gone to Miles, more than twenty thousand pounds, to Frank—who would have instantly refused it except it was in trust for Ian Smith Donovan Mercy.

In her own testament, Tura had left Frank her own home, the breeding farm called Stone Pastures, that included a five-bedroom stone house in Yorkshire, with two housekeeping wings, each with another bedroom and bath, and a carriage building and some eighty acres of hillocky moorland fields, near a small village called Stead. Kate explained that it was still in the name given Tura when she was born, Kathleen Tura Claidy. Kate assured Frank that her mother's instructions carefully pointed out that the farm manager, like his father and his grandfather before him, was a very astute breeder, but that Frank might want to choose his own. A separate addendum laid out the manager's salary, his schedule of bonuses and what would prompt one, with funds set aside for five years for that purpose. In a handwritten note, Tura pointed out that the caretaker regularly saw to the swallows on the roof and kept the gutters and lawns up, and that the place was cleaned once a month down to the linens, should Frank wish to visit, as Tura was sure he would. She gave Frank all this with her abundant love and the wry hope that Frank would be seventy when he signed the papers receiving Stone Pastures as his own.

Kate had found and copied for him some old photos from Tura's girlhood.

It was these that made Frank pinch the inner corners of his eyes.

In the photos, Tura would have been younger than Kate was now, soft and round, not plump but certainly not the slender wintry madonna she had become by the time Frank knew her. As a young woman, Tura had not been so fashionable as the older version—just an ordinary, neat, compact country girl, her hair long and dark and glossy in the black-and-white photos. In one photo, she held a little child's hand, and, with her other hand, was waving to someone, standing in tussocky flowering grass that came up to her knees. This was, Frank supposed, the purple heather so hallowed in Brontë novels. Below Tura was a drive that looked to be made of crushed stone and a house exactly like a Monopoly building, two stories of straight-up stone walls, windows like long, doleful eyes flanking a red door of a nose. Newer wings, built later, a lighter brick, ran away to either side. Crooked rows of handmade stiles climbed gentle mountain clefts above the house, and sheep grazed like clouds on the ground. Here and there was a low stone wall and an outbuilding with a sloped roof made of something thick, like slate.

Another photo showed Tura with a young soldier who resembled her. A brother? A cousin? His shoulders were thrown back, his young lips compressed in a stiff, manly smile, hair a pale, vulnerable brush cut. Tura had turned her head and the wind had blown her own hair across her face, but Frank could see that she had been smiling. In a third photo, she was on horseback, wearing short boots and a summer dress and holding the reins low on her thighs. The tough little mare—the regal curve of its neck signaling Arabian blood, the long legs something else, as well—gathered under the saddle pad like a bundle of springs.

Frank knew, but Kate also explained that the farm had belonged entirely to Tura, not to Cedric. It had been hers and her much older brother's, but the brother sold his portion to Tura when he moved to the United States. Tura had lived there on her own into her thirties, until she met Cedric and sold him four foals, one of which grew up to be his greatest horse, The Quiet Man. Then they were partners. Marriage was inevitable.

Tura apparently made her own will shortly after Frank married Natalie, and had not amended it. Her reasons were her own. The legal process by which Frank could claim the farm was described in an enclosed note from an attorney. Two last pages were color copies of photos on plain white paper—raw earth with grass just sprouting like new hair over a low, curved stone that said *Bellingham* and, below that, *Cedric Arthur* and some dates, and *Kathleen Tura Claidy* with some dates. Cedric had been eighty-two. The quote, from Shakespeare, was "I will not jump with common spirits."

The stone sat side by side with the much larger monument, shining bright pink in the light of what Frank quickly calculated would have been late afternoon. It read only *DONOVAN.*

For a moment, he saw Natalie as he had first seen her, opening her mouth the way an adult feeds a baby, prompting him to accept the gin-soaked stuffed olive.

Why had Tura left Frank a farm so far from Brisbane—so far from the United States? Kate could think of no practical reason; she said as much in the letter. *Mum did as she would do, Frank. Perhaps she thought you would find something there*, Kate wrote. *You should go to see it.*

Someday, Frank thought, he would. But he could not imagine it now. He lay down on the couch and dropped into a sleep thick as those stone roof slabs. When he woke, by the sun, it was late afternoon, and he almost screamed: someone was supposed to pick Ian up at preschool, hours earlier. But Ian was there, quietly building Lego bridges that arched like flying buttresses up to the gates of the castles inside the huge aquarium. They rested there, with one end against the glass, as if waiting for fish to walk.

NINE

I'VE GOT A customer for you," Marty told Frank one night a few weeks later as he heaved himself to his feet and began to pass out the dinner plates. Marty's eyes swam with exhaustion. School would end soon, and though his internship at the University of Wisconsin was secure, he thought endlessly about residency, about choosing a program that would determine where he and Eden would live for the next four years.

"Why don't you worry about this after, say, your wedding?" Frank suggested. "After your final exams?" One would follow the other, in rapid succession, a month from now.

Marty ignored him. "Let me tell you about this client."

Frank said, "I'm going to relax with the young dude here and watch Animal Planet."

Holding up a restraining hand, Marty tucked into the chili like a man who wanted to drown his sorrows. Then he said, "Look, I have to tell you. Or she'll kill me. You'll like her. She's a rare case."

Frank waited, knowing Marty would go on, no matter what he said, although whatever Marty said, Frank would refuse to do it. Since Cedric and Tura died, he had no stomach for new plans, and his head ached as if watchfulness was a cap two sizes too small.

"She's my professor. She's taking a year off to train for something. Maybe the Olympics. Actually, she's taking two years off if she makes the team, and she seems sure that she will."

"What's she a professor of?"

"Botany," Marty said. "No! She's a psychiatrist, obviously."

"Is she delusional? Is that common? Because if you get to the age she must be and you haven't realized a dream in the Olympics, that's pretty far out of sight."

"No, she's young. Edie's age. Kind of young. She . . . you know . . ." Marty made the universal hand sign of the inverse humpback *C* moving along the table to signify jumping horses. "What you do."

"I meant does she do all-around dressage and so forth, or just jumpers?"

"In-a-ring type jumping, judging from the pictures on her wall. She's very good. Tops."

"I'm not set up to train, pal. That's a whole business of its own."

"Wouldn't you like to do that, though?"

You'll train your own horses, he heard the vanished say.

"Someday. I might. But right now I have the farm to get fixed up, and Ian—"

"She's going to come over anyhow, to see the place, and she's invited to the wedding," Marty said. "She moved here two years ago from North Carolina and she just moved her horse. She's not happy with where he is."

Under the table, Ian was methodically kicking Frank in his bad leg, waiting peevishly for a response. As it turned out, Ian loved school and, despite his muteness, was a hit with the other kids. The only downside to school was that Ian threw himself into it like a cyclone: he fell apart every day around four, and never got any traction until the weekend, when he slept twelve hours straight both nights. Waving to Marty, Frank pointed at Ian and said, "No TV tonight, buddy. You're out of here." He draped Ian over his shoulder, and Ian began to pinch the back of Frank's head, digging his nails in. Frank tried to see it as a sign of how much the boy trusted him, but it hurt so much he wanted to drop Ian on his face. He would not later remember what he said to Marty.

As it turned out, he didn't meet Claudia Campo until a couple of hours after he'd walked Eden down the aisle.

The wedding morning came up a bold, blue, late-May day and Frank was stunned as he lifted out his morning clothes, which had shown up in the one crate that actually did arrive, by the bruise of emotions. His suit was folded in broad sheets of tissue paper, next to Natalie's wedding dress. He thought of the last time he'd put the suit on, which also was the only time.

Natalie saying, "Well, your eyes are too deep in your head, but you're pretty when you smile, teeth like one of those horses of yours. And if you wear trousers like that every day, I'll be your genie . . ." Natalie, in her crown of white rosebuds, at the top of the aisle, shaking off her father's arm and kicking off her white pumps to run down the aisle to him.

Frank pressed the heels of his hands against his eyes, then took Natalie's wedding ring out of the child's china mug where he kept it, and warmed it in his palm. Under the clothes lay the slim album. Natalie must have had it in her office to show to friends. She had asked that all the photos be sepia tinted, so they would never look outdated. Now Frank turned to the one of him laughing, arms linked with Cedric on one side in his ancient frock coat and Tura on the other, in a floor-length pale suit. They gazed at Frank with pride. Gently, he laid the album back in the box.

Later, at the ceremony itself, those memories tucked away with the ring, he was brought up short by even older sentiments. He gazed in astonishment at his mother's straight-backed, fading beauty, and at Eden, the chubby, bookish baby, now a slim tulip of vanilla satin. A lone guitarist played Hope's favorite song, "Stardust," which had been played at her own wedding. The couple took their simple vows under a huge catalpa tree, where a traditional chuppah stood. Hope's priest and Marty's mother's rabbi bestowed the mostly extraneous Judeo-Christian blessings. Marty stomped a lightbulb wrapped in a white handkerchief and Eden tossed her bouquet, which landed at the feet of a friend's six-year-old daughter. Taking hands, they walked proudly into the arms of their families. Everywhere, there were splashes of Eden and Marty's humor: the roses, irises, and the lady trumpet lilies that Hope said were called Pretty Woman were displayed in big zinc feed buckets. Behind the wedding canopy, they'd set up a makeshift altar, a two-tiered jump with *TENACITY* painted on it in thick bold letters. Instead of hiring a photographer, except for two or three formal portraits, they'd handed each guest, even the babies, an upscale disposable camera. A long water trough invited guests to "Dump Your Snaps Here When You Leave," while an email guest book promised a selection of the choicest shots to everyone who signed up.

After the new-minted couple greeted the guests, everyone sat down at one of the long trestle tables on a hilltop patio to drink Spotted Cow Ale and eat picnic food—hamburgers and hotdogs and chicken kebabs passed among vats of potato salad and baked beans. The bridal dessert was almost as tall as Eden, a tower of crenellated carrot cake cauled in a hive of fly netting, with rubber horses that Ian clearly coveted racing around each layer.

Frank had jotted down ideas for the toast he would make as surrogate father of the bride. But when he stood, he said, instead, "I've never seen you two even be rude to each other. You guys have perfect sympathy, or at least you have the class to let everyone think you do. It seems like bad luck to wish you good luck. I can't believe that Eden is grown up. What I really can't believe is that you two won't be coming home tonight."

"It's okay, Frank. We'll be home tomorrow night," Marty said.

Although they were spending their wedding night at a pricey bed-and-breakfast inn in Madison, their honeymoon was not set until July: they were going for a month to Australia, the tickets long since purchased. Brisbane was no longer on the itinerary. Their wedding-night treat was a gift from Frank, who had known the innkeepers since a night in Chicago a decade before when he had saved their then-teenage son from a robbery and a bad beating or worse. Several times over the years, visiting his mother, he'd opted to stay at the expansive lakeside mansion, where one whole floor with three luxe bedrooms was the honeymoon suite.

After the couple was drawn away to change for the dance—driven by Hope in the pony cart, with its canopy of blooms—there came a lull. Patrick took off to feed the horses. Hope phoned to say she was going to lie down for an hour, leaving Frank to greet an endless stream of people he hadn't seen in ten years, if ever. Finally, in a cabin on the grounds cleaned up for the purpose, Frank changed into black pants and a cream-colored silk shirt Natalie had given him. He tried in vain to coax Ian out of his tuxedo, which he realized he would be buying tomorrow from Salvatore Rose Formal Wear.

The woman was standing alone near a circle of stone benches when Frank came out, and he noticed immediately that she was standing with no apparent expectation of any kind of reward or amusement or any sort of busyness—thinking, gazing around her, a skill Frank did not himself possess.

When she saw Frank, she said, "I'm Claudia Campo, Marty Fisher's friend. And I know you're Frank."

"Hello," Frank said. "You're the rider."

"That's what I want to talk to you about. Not today, of course. There are enough splendors today. But could we talk, sometime?" The woman didn't look as though she expected an answer in the negative. Frank wondered how old she was. Younger than he was, maybe Eden's age or a little older, thirty-three, thirty-five, she was the kind of expensive dark blonde who had been told all her life that she was beautiful. A few lines around her lips said she'd become impatient with hearing that and wanted to move on to other things. Her eyes were big and brown and the makeup that emphasized them was cursory. She wore loose and drapey wide-legged black pants and a sleeveless coat. No necklace, no purse, Frank noticed. The only other woman Frank had known who never bothered with a necklace or a purse was his wife, although Natalie was vain in other ways.

"Sure," Frank said. "Someday." But the woman had shifted her attention to Ian.

She held out her hand, and Ian took it.

"I'm Claudia," she said. "Hello."

Ian said, "Hi."

Heat that had nothing to do with the growing mugginess of the blue May evening flooded Frank's face. Miles off in a cloudless sky, lightning winked.

"Are you okay?" said Claudia.

"I'm fine," said Frank, sitting down on one of the benches. He asked Ian, "What did you say?"

"I said hi to her," Ian told him. Although this was impossible, Frank recognized Ian's light voice with his drawn-out, nasally Aussie vowels. The boy added, "I want those horses, please."

"He hasn't ever talked," Frank said to Claudia.

"I know."

"Marty told you?"

"Marty said you adopted him after his parents were killed and that you never heard him speak."

"Could I have those horses?" Ian said. It took Frank a moment to figure out that Ian didn't mean living horses; he meant the little rubber racing horses on the wedding cake.

"Yes, after they cut the cake."

"Can I go find the grandma?" Ian said.

"Not now. She's having a nap."

"Then, can I go play with Patrick?" Ian said.

"No."

"Do I have to sit here?"

Frank surveyed the flat ground near the vast renovated antique barn. A deejay had pulled up, and his crew was carting sections of dance floor and speakers into the barn no more than twenty yards away. "You can go watch them." Ian grinned. Then Frank said, "Wait a minute. Can't you tell how surprised I am? Could you talk always?"

Ian stared at the ground.

"Could you always talk?"

"Yes."

"Did you ever talk?"

"I talk to the horses. And I talk at night. I talk to Sally."

A drinking pal of Patrick's, who lived with his grandparents just down the road from Tenacity, had given Patrick a border collie called Sally. Even Frank had to admit that she had terrific manners, although she loped nearly constantly and ate the rest of the time. Sally was a good dog, and a farm needed a dog, and she adored Ian extravagantly. She never barked unless an unfamiliar car approached, and then she whined, nervously, for about two minutes before anyone else heard its approach. Under Sally's unwavering gaze, the little paint filly no longer bit the other horses. She let Farmer Frank be his bemused self.

"Okay," Frank said. "Well, you can go now. Look at me and yell when you get there."

"I will." Ian ran off. Another little boy just slightly bigger seemed to have been waiting and fell into step with him.

Frank turned to the woman called Claudia. "Can you explain that?"

"Because I'm a doctor? Not really."

"I thought we were going to have to get him a computer with a voice synthesizer when he got old enough to type. Do you have a professional opinion?"

"Sometimes stuff like that just happens."

"That's your professional opinion? Stuff happens?"

"Well, my professional opinion and my personal opinion are the same. Sometimes stuff like that just happens. I'm glad it happened for a good reason, and I mean by that a positive reason. Maybe he didn't have a good enough reason to talk until now."

"But what's the reason now?"

"You would have to ask him, and he wouldn't be able to tell you in a way that would make sense, I don't think. It was the right time for him."

Frank laughed. "Do you think it's good?"

"It's pretty great. How could it be bad?"

"The world falls open for him and me. I hope that's a good thing."

"There's no going back."

"I can ask him how he thinks about things now." Frank thought, I can ask him who his real parents are, and if that woman in the van was his mother. But if, more likely, they're still alive, and have a million acres of cattle land in the vast Northern Territory, and their own airplane, then I have to bring him back, which means going to prison for life, with my pal Charley.

Come down off the ledge, Frank scolded himself. Ian was not yet four. His real parents' names would be "Mummy" and "Daddy." If Ian's living parents were jackaroos and he longed for them, Ian would not act the way he did. Even Frank, whose sum total of hours with a kid he could count on both hands before Christmas Day, knew that. I could lose him, Frank thought. No. How could he lose Ian? He's mine, Frank thought. And then, He's not mine. He belongs to someone else. He's someone else's boy. I was only ever supposed to protect him from getting caught in the tidal pull of the human flood that came after the real flood, just until I found the people he really belonged to.

So why didn't you look for them?

"I wouldn't expect big ponderings from him. He's a little guy," said Claudia. "You knew his family?"

"Only slightly." For about ninety seconds. "Anything at all would be big." Frank's guts squeezed, in sync with his temples. Like the deepest throat of a cello, a note of despair opened.

"You seem to already know how he thinks about things," Claudia said, then stopped. "If I had to guess, I would say he wanted those rubber horses on the cake more than anything else in the world. Kids, they think differently. If something's too big for them to think about, they won't think about that. But a small thing to us gets really big to them."

"Do you want a drink?" Frank asked. "I'm buying."

Marty Fisher's mother and father had brought out the champagne. It was now on ice in wheelbarrows—a good use for wheelbarrows, Frank observed. Marty's college-age twin sisters were dancing silently to music piped through their earbuds.

"That's an iconic twenty-first-century sight," Claudia said as the girls swirled and gyrated on the grass in their ballet flats, to the tune of apparent silence. "I'll bet they were IVF twins. You think?"

Frank had no idea what the woman was talking about. He stared at her. A drink might help . . . or do nothing. He wanted to take Ian and go home to Tenacity and lock the doors. But it was Eden's wedding day; and he was just a father, so everyone thought, a new and somewhat tragic father whose own story, thankfully, did not bear much examination. He should sound normal. So he concentrated on what he would have said if his mind hadn't been a damaged boat heeling around his skull.

Frank said, "Marty and Eden hired a string quartet for now and for the ceremony, but they called this morning. One of them had a headache. I don't know if you're from Madison, but . . . you know, he had a headache."

Claudia said, "I'm from there now. I know exactly what you mean."

"They were hired six months ago. And he had . . . a headache."

"You'd think there would be a violinist standing by."

"I liked the guitar, though. That is my mother's favorite song," Frank said.

"I think it must be everyone's mother's favorite song."

Claudia smiled in a big, unaffected way at odds with her precise but somehow Mediterranean prettiness. Frank fought to relax. His leg and his wrist now pounded with every pulse of his heart.

"Is it the shock of him talking?" Claudia asked. "You're sweating."

"I guess it is. I thought that would happen, some quiet way, or some huge, dramatic way, years from now. I don't know why I thought that." Frank wished the sun would fall already and he could stop squinting, feeling untented without his ever-present sunglasses, which Eden forbade him to wear today. He would call Patrick and ask him to bring back his sunglasses, but there Patrick was, his hair still wet from the shower, flirting with one of Marty's sisters. The girl must be eighteen. Frank hoped she was twenty. Ah, well. "I hurt my wrist not long ago. It acts up sometimes."

"I've got some aspirin," Claudia said, and reached into her pocket.

"You fall off a horse enough and some things just don't get their lube back. So I'm always packing acetylsalicylic acid."

A blue-jeaned bartender offered them flutes of champagne. Claudia was thoughtful and pleasant: Frank tried to smile, despite the enormous net drag of grief stirred up by the wedding day. On a day this bright, he'd promised a future with Natalie. And now, there was joy that Ian might finally be able to articulate both his process and his provenance, and so his future, which wouldn't include Frank. He needed a psychiatrist. Here was a psychiatrist. Why didn't he just talk about it?

If he did that, he'd need a psychiatrist and a lawyer, too.

"I'm a widower," he said.

"I know," the woman replied.

"And this is a wedding."

"I see. Everybody feels all sorts of mixed-up stuff at a wedding, sadness and loss along with joy. Even if they're not widowers."

"And Ian talked."

"Well, he's not going to tell you why. Maybe in twenty years."

What if he didn't know Ian in twenty years? What should he say to this woman that wouldn't entail ornamenting the tunic of lies he wore? He smiled again.

Hope was back, her gray silk replaced with a long flowered skirt and ruffled vest. From across the long verge of grass, she shrugged at Ian, who was jabbering to everyone, dancing with a collective of little girls and big girls, like a heron in a spasm. Hope motioned Frank over. Now in thunderous pain, Frank extended his arm and he and Claudia walked over to the dance floor.

"I don't know what to say," Hope told Frank. She turned to Claudia. "Hello, I'm Hope Mercy, Eden's mom. I'm sorry we didn't get to meet earlier."

"I'm from the groom's side of the aisle. I was one of Marty Fisher's supervising professors. I'm Claudia Campo." Claudia extended her hand and took Hope's. "I'm trying to talk Frank here into helping me and my horse train for the World Cup, and maybe the Olympics. What do you think of that?"

"I think that if you could talk him into it, you wouldn't find anyone within a thousand miles, maybe more, who could do that better. I'm also sure there's no way you could talk him into it." Hope turned and nodded at Ian. "The disco king over there has taken our lives over a bit."

"I'm going to have to try to grab a dance with Mr. Ian tonight. But I haven't given up yet. I know from Marty that your husband trained some remarkable champions."

"He did, and Jack, that's Frank's grandfather, trained Midsummer Night's Dream . . ."

"The horse that won the gold for the 1952 Olympic team. I know. And also Rough Magic, the great mare who fell at the end of a perfect round."

"I'm impressed," said Hope. "She wasn't disqualified, but she was hurt, and no one ever got on her back again. She made some beautiful babies for DuPree Farms. They bought her from Jack, right there. On the spot."

"Babies like Twelfth Night. I know all about it. My own horse, Prospero, is descended from Twelfth Night. So, you see, it absolutely has to be Frank Mercy who trains this horse. And this rider. Well, along with my other coach. He has shelves of international trophies. But I trust my gut."

"Well," said Hope. "You make a compelling case."

"Except I don't do that work," said Frank. "I haven't trained anybody for much of anything yet. I don't have a gift."

"I heard you did. In Australia?"

"Some. In Australia. But here, I'm just a farmer, ma'am. Those days are over. If they aren't over, they haven't started yet. Now, I hate to spoil this particular midsummer night's dream, but if I'm going to dance with the bride tonight, I really have to go home and get something stronger than aspirin for my leg, Mom. You'll take over with Ian, right? Claudia, please excuse me. Maybe it's that the storm is coming, but my leg is now killing me," Frank said, grateful that the wrist no longer ached. "The storm and old age, of course."

"Well, yes, you're spry for a senior citizen. Do you have some hydro-codone back there?"

"I do."

"Well, at least don't take it until you get back to Hilltop here. How far away is Tenacity Farms?"

"Five minutes, really," Frank said.

"Well, why don't I go with you? I've been wanting to see it. Marty said you might have room, at least, to board Prospero. You can take your medication and be ready to dance with the bride, and I'll drive us back."

Frank laughed, and the laugh exploded the wedge in his chest into a fine mist. "I'm driving a pickup truck from the farm. I had to drive the trailer, too, with my mother's horse, Bobbie, in it."

"Is the trailer still on the truck?"

"No."

"I'm fine with driving a truck. I am a rider. And I am a single woman. I drive my truck with Pro in it all over. In fact, I drove it all the way from North Carolina when I came to Madison." Claudia, obviously knowing how to do it, switched on the high beams behind her brown eyes and let the thickness of blond hair flip forward. She was used to getting what she wanted. "Please, let me come. Marty has told me so much about the farm. Even if you won't train my horse and me."

"That's fine," Frank said evenly, working hard to avoid seeing his mother's eye roll. He hoped nobody could tell that he was going through life in a robotic state—since planning was beyond him. Every night, he lay down to read to Ian, and then planned to connect the dots. Then it was dawn. He was too spent to decide anything. He knew this was by design. He knew it had to stop.

Claudia opened the door to the cab.

"Do you need a hand?" Frank said as Claudia gathered her long pants up in a fist over smooth-calved and tight-muscled rider's legs.

"I'm just fine," she said.

Just as Frank was about to turn the key, he heard Ian calling, and saw the boy tearing across the parking lot in a way that put a knot in Frank's throat.

"Doesn't seem to want to be too far away from you," said Claudia.

"Not that much," Frank said. He scooped Ian up, clutching him against his chest. In his ruined, muddy tuxedo, the boy smelled of burned grass. How could Frank have even considered leaving Ian behind, even for five minutes, on the day he first spoke? Disengaging the airbags, Frank buckled Ian into his car seat between him and Claudia. They rode in silence for a minute or two before both of them noticed that Ian was asleep. Frank said, "I'll grab some clean clothes for him. No reason to wake him."

When they swung into the long driveway, it was not quite dark, and Frank felt it right away.

There was no sound, but somehow, a disturbance: then he heard Sally, or another dog, barking, far off. He put the truck in park and opened the door, slowly. "Stay here for a moment," he told Claudia. "I think someone's messing around up there. My grandfather is ninety-six, and he and the day helper are there. She's a young girl, Filipino, and she doesn't know much English. She probably has the TV on loud."

Frank began walking away from the house, out toward the big pasture, so that he could walk down toward the barn unseen. Then he turned back and spun the lock on the box behind the cab. "Paranoid farmers," he said as he lifted out his old service shotgun, the Remington pump-action twelve-gauge he'd kitted out for himself more than twenty years ago. Although he'd never fired it except in practice, he believed that the simple sound of that gun loading, and the sight of his big horse, Tarmac, bearing down on a punk with steam streaming from his nostrils like a preview of the Apocalypse, were more effective than any dozen warning shots from his Glock. Limping by then, Frank covered the half mile down the road up onto the slight ridge in a few minutes. He could see the unfamiliar double trailer parked at the barn's open door. Then he stood amazed as he saw the kid from down the road, who'd given them the dog Patrick called Sally, coming out of the barn holding one end of a long rope. And then Frank heard mayhem. He began to run, as best he could.

Somehow, the kid had managed to get a halter on Glory Bee, but she was straining and cantering in place, pawing at him with one hoof, hauling him along at the end of the snap rope. The guy was holding on as if the horse was a rogue sail in a storm.

"Stop!" Frank yelled. The kid looked straight at him. Dropping the rope, he let Glory Bee take off at a dead run, and fumbled in his pocket for what Frank could vaguely see was some kind of shitty little no-name automatic the kid would use to blow an ugly hole in Frank and in his own already fucked-up life. Frank loaded his shotgun, that deadly cash-register sound, and prepared to walk down the hill toward the kid. How old was he? Twenty-one? Twenty? He was shaking so hard he had to grip one hand with the other in the parody of a military crouch. Unbelievably, he took aim at Frank. "Put it down!" Frank yelled again.

"No, you! You put yours down! Get out of my way! I'll kill you! All I want is the horse! Move now!" The guy was screaming. He kept looking down at the gun and shaking it, poking at it, and then, in the next moment, remembering his life-and-death confrontation, furrowing his brow and turning back to Frank. When he looked away, his absorption in the gun was so complete, reminding Frank of the way Ian concentrated on his Legos, that Frank was sure that if he rushed him, he could knock him off balance.

Frank was about to move, when, out of the corner of his eye, he saw something that trapped his breath. Holding the rope, Glory Bee following him, Ian was making his way back to the barn. In the shrieking silence, the kid turned the gun on Ian. "Stop!" the young man yelled. "I'll shoot you."

The kid went into his stupid crouch again. Ian kept walking. Then he stopped, dropped the rope, and, so quickly Frank wasn't sure he saw it, swung his two hands, left, right. He said, "Be *nice*. Please."

The kid with the gun seemed to glower, and to somehow grow bigger. Frank didn't want to fire the first kill shot of his life, but before he could, the kid threw his gun down and sank to the ground, sobbing. "I'm sorry," he said. "I'm sorry."

One shoe off, Claudia came stumbling into the drive.

"I couldn't catch him," she said. "I was standing on the running board, trying to see you, trying to get service on my phone to call 911, and he just slipped out."

"It's okay," Frank said. Frank jerked the big kid to his feet. "Do you have shit for brains? You pointed a gun at a little boy?"

"It's not loaded," the kid said. "It's just some gun a guy gave me in Milwaukee. I don't even know what size bullets go in it." He was a pale, soft-looking kid, his hair-sprouted belly lapping over a cinched belt and jeans. His faded blue tee shirt read *I Live in My Own World. They Like Me Here.* Frank picked up the gun. Not only was it not loaded, it didn't have any kind of trigger.

"So you have a death wish, too. You pointed a fucking *broken* gun with no bullets at a guy with a loaded shotgun and at a three-year-old kid."

"I was going to take her to the auction in Des Moines. The horse. I owe a guy money. I don't have anything left to sell. I can't rob my grandpa. He's old . . ."

"Jesus Christ," said Frank. "How decent of you. What's your name?"

"Clay. Clay Bannock."

"Your dad is Cal Bannock."

"My grandfather."

To Claudia, then, Frank said, "Do you mind just helping me for a moment? Please help Ian put Glory Bee out in the pasture. Can you? I don't think he can close the latch by himself. She'll go with him, but I don't know if she'll go with you . . ."

"She'll go with me," Claudia said, and reached for Glory Bee. Already overexcited, the horse began to strain backward, then went up. Claudia cried, "Ian, no!"

The child simply moved back until Glory Bee came down, and then approached her, with a whisper and a touch. As if a sedative had poured through her, Glory Bee dropped her head for a mouthful of May sweet grass before obediently following Ian into the paddock.

"I'm sorry?" Claudia, confused, said to Frank. "What . . . ?"

"No, it's nothing you did. She's probably scared and she's always way too high-strung." Claudia followed Ian to the pasture, where the child unclipped the lead from her bridle and handed it to Claudia, who looped it around her elbow and hand. Frank depressed a button on his phone and said harshly to Patrick, "This is urgent. Get here fast." He tied the big kid's feet with the halter rope and his hands with some baling twine, then pushed him down so he was sitting on a square bale.

While Claudia washed up in the first-floor bath, Frank found his painkillers, took two, and helped Ian change out of his tuxedo into jeans and a fresh shirt.

"I don't want to leave my horses," Ian said. Frank was confused for a moment, and then watched as Ian carefully removed twenty sticky rubber racers from the pockets of the defunct formal wear. "He had a gun."

"He did."

"He didn't want to shoot people."

"Maybe not."

"Were you going to kill him?"

"Of course not."

"Were you really going to kill him, Dad?"

Frank's arms prickled. He had not misheard Ian. Dad. He wanted to take off his own clothes and put on his oldest clean sweats and lie down in the dark.

Dad.

Instead he said, "If he tried to hurt you, yes, Ian."

Who was Ian's real father, that he could call Frank *Dad*? On the first day he could talk?

The aide taking care of Frank's grandfather hadn't noticed anything. Jack was already asleep, and she was hunched over a deep bowl of french fries, so engrossed in a consummately violent war film that she wouldn't have noticed if a real war broke out in the kitchen. She waved to Frank and Ian.

Then Patrick burst through the door, one of his small, potent fists clasped around the fat kid's bicep. The kid's feet were still hobbled and his face was smeared with snot and blood.

"I swear on my mother, Frank," Patrick said.

"I know that. Did you tell him about Glory Bee?"

"I told him about Glory Bee and that she was worth a lot. He hung about, Frank. We had a drink. But I swear to you . . ." The big kid's nose was broken. Ian held up a dishtowel, which the Bannock kid, for some reason, took and pressed against his nose and jaw.

"It's just the same legally as if he tried to shoot my . . . son. He could be dead now, your friend. He could be dead, easy." He turned to the kid. "How old are you?"

"Eighteen," said the kid. He looked older, stuffed and bloated with drinking.

"He's even an underage drunk, Patrick. Well played."

Patrick looked away. As the pain of his headache began to recede, Frank's vision cleared, and he appreciated Patrick's laconic manner. One more word, and he would forget whatever instinct was propelling him toward an impulse of charity.

"Don't blame Pat. He's a nice guy," the kid said. "I got to know Pat because of the pictures I was supposed to take."

Frank said, "Pictures?"

"I met the girl on Twitter. His daughter? The guy from New York who's buying the farm?"

"No one's buying this farm."

"Her father paid me to take pictures. Five hundred bucks. I just really thought I would come over when you guys weren't here because I wouldn't get in the way. I was just going to take the pictures because she said her father was trying to figure out if they were going to knock this house down or fix it up and try to sell it—"

"What in the hell are you talking about? You don't even have the right farm. This farm isn't even for sale," Frank said.

"It is. They sent me a picture of the farm. 'Course I knew it. This guy is some big deal in real estate. He's going to build a hundred houses here. But the girl. We got to talking . . ." Cal said, and blushed. "She liked me. I told her about my music. I play guitar. She sent me pictures . . . you know . . . of her. And they wired me the money. It was a lot of money."

"For these . . . pictures?" Claudia said. "That you didn't even take yet? Didn't you think that was strange?"

"No . . . because the girl and I had a relationship. We've been talking a long time. Two weeks. Three weeks." Snuffling, the Bannock kid went on, "Then I got here and I remembered the horse, and I just went back for our trailer. I'm really sorry, man." Without prompting, he fished in the back pocket of his half-staff jeans and pulled out a disposable camera. He threw it to Frank. "You can have the pictures. That's the only roll."

Simultaneous wires of information told Frank that the fat kid wasn't lying, but that what he was saying was also not the truth. Clay Bannock didn't know the truth.

"What did she tell you about her father? The guy who's supposedly buying my farm?"

"The builder. He wanted to see where all the bedrooms and bathrooms were, and how the barns were set up—"

"You went into our house?"

The kid cringed. "I didn't touch anything. I swear to God. Nobody locks their doors around here . . ."

"Patrick, do you know anything about this?"

Patrick murmured in the negative.

If wishing could make it so, Frank would have stood alone in the graveled circle in front of the farmhouse, seining the summer light through the lens of memory. He would never have gone to Brisbane. He would never have met Natalie. He would never have put on his rescue coat and set in motion this tumbrel that never stopped, only changed course, and rolled forward.

"Take your truck and get out of here," Frank said. "I'll speak to your grandfather tomorrow. If I don't turn you in tomorrow and get you charged as an adult with felony assault and armed robbery, it will be because your grandfather knew my dad and he tells me you're in an inpatient program for alcoholism, starting Monday. Otherwise, you'll spend the next ten years with people who'll see your ass as a pillow park. Do you understand me?" The kid nodded. "Put your grandfather's number in my phone and label it." The kid did. "Go on. Now. Get off my farm."

When the room was quiet, Patrick said, "I'll see to packing my things."

"That's foolish, Patrick. It's not anything you did. Just find Sally . . ."

"She's under the porch. I guess she was scared."

"Some watchdog. I have to get back to my sister's wedding. This is over now. Let's forget it." Frank peered at the disappearing flash of the trailer rounding the bend on Sun Valley Road. "What do you think he meant?"

"I think some guys think everything is for sale. I knew a guy who lived like that. His cars. His house. He would say, everything is for sale," Patrick said. "I think maybe some fellow got the wrong impression."

"I think someone is after Ian."

"Too right, guv. I do as well," Patrick said miserably. Claudia said nothing until she and Frank were back in the truck, Ian in his car seat. "And here I was worried that you'd fall asleep at the wheel. I had no idea it was going to be the gunfight at the O.K. Corral."

"I can't believe this. It's a nightmare I can't wake up from."

"You handled it well."

"I don't know that I did. It was a mess. And I know better. I was in law enforcement for twenty years," Frank said. "It's like I have combat fatigue. I can't think straight."

"Marty said you'd been in an accident in the line of duty."

Frank shrugged. "Not hardly. I got hit by a car."

"You saved lives other times."

"I doubt that, unless it was sending some idiot to prison for ten years of his life so he would have to wait longer to breed little criminals. I do know I thought that this was Disney Farm, USA, though. It's been a long time since I lived here. Patrick said we needed to get motion sensors. I was thinking, crazy. Now maybe we need razor wire."

He glanced over at Claudia and saw how fixedly she was looking at the little boy, and, with an electric surge along his forearms, he knew what she was thinking. After quieting a colossal plunging, high-kicking horse, a forty-pound child had quietly told an adrenaline-pumped ado-lescent with nothing to lose to "Be nice," and put down his fake gun—a gun Ian didn't know was fake. "So, you saw what Ian did. I think he just assumes most people want to do the right thing. And he's, well, he's good with animals."

Claudia said, "Is that what you really think?"

Frank said, "Not really." In a few sentences, against his better judg-ment and almost against his will, Frank told her about Ian's effect on his mother, and the animals in the hold of the airplane, and about Cedric and Tura's deaths—everything short of how Ian had come into his life.

"Marty said he's a relative of your late wife."

"Yes, indirectly . . ." They are both human, Frank said to himself.

"What did other people in the family say?"

"Nothing. Not to me," Frank told her. "I would imagine it's some-thing no one talks about."

Claudia then sat quietly until Frank pulled the truck into the parking lot at Hilltop. Necklaces of paper lanterns swung like festive plums from poles and eaves at the opening to the converted barn that was now used as a banquet hall. She didn't say a word for so long Frank thought she would simply get out of the truck, get into her own car, and drive away.

When she did speak, it was to say, "I met someone who could do that once before."

"Was it part of some study?"

"No. I was in college."

"Where?"

"She lives in North Carolina, not far from where I grew up. We moved to the south when I was twelve. I was born not very far from here, north of Chicago. Then later, my father was a professor of anatomy at Duke. My sisters and I went there. This woman was probably in her thirties then. I thought of her as old. She's probably fifty now."

"How did you meet her?"

"Well, she was the aunt of a professor of mine. This professor took an interest in me. I was going to medical school, and I was interested in neurology then, the physical part of the mind, and mostly in the vestiges of instinct in human beings. This professor, she took me up there, a few times. I don't want you to get the impression that the woman was some kind of hillbilly mystic . . ."

"I don't think that."

"Her name was Julia. Julia Madrigal. Isn't that lovely? Everyone knew Mrs. Madrigal. Sounds like 'magical.' She did a great deal of good. She taught school. There were kids whose parents abused them, and people who hit their wives. There were kids like that guy back at your farm."

Frank glanced at Ian, who had seen the lanterns, and, impeded by the pockets stuffed with rubber horses, was struggling to get out of his car seat. "Ian, here. You can go ahead and find Aunt Eden."

Gratefully, Ian said, "Okay."

They watched him, a small dark hullock moving against the mounds of faraway clouds and hills, disappearing with a bounce into the sweet orange glow of the barn's open bay. They could hear the music, an old Eagles song.

"So, she worked with the parents and those others," Frank said.

"She didn't need to work with them. She was just with them. The way Ian was with that guy at the barn," said Claudia.

"Did you want to study her?"

"Of course I did. My professor did, too. But she wouldn't allow that. She told us that she had always been this way, and helped people do the things they should do and that they probably really wanted to do anyhow. She didn't want anyone outside the county to know about it."

Frank admitted to himself then that this was why he had let the fat, drunken kid go home to his grandfather's farm when he deserved to be in the back of a cruiser on the way to the Sauk County Jail. He admitted that he didn't want to answer questions, to draw even more attention, and his aversion was a wall in front of his common sense. The ranks of those who knew about the Ian effect were swelling, and if people didn't want Ian for their use, then certainly they would want him under their lens.

"Do you want me to talk to Ian?" Claudia said. "At least, you want to know if this troubles him."

"I don't know," Frank said. "Do you think it troubles him?"

"Maybe now that he is talking, he could talk about what it's like. That makes people feel better, to talk about what things are like for them."

"I'll help you and the horse," Frank said.

"You don't have to. I wouldn't tell anyone about Ian. I'm not like that. I'm offering to talk to him because he's little and you can't help but care about him."

Frank said, "I think you misunderstand. It's not a quid pro quo. I assumed you wouldn't tell anyone about Ian." Frank got out and opened Claudia's door. "I'll try to help, although I'm not really at all like my dad."

"Don't take me on if you really don't want to."

He put out his arms and Claudia let herself be lifted down. Frank felt a stirring, like a memory, at the spring of the warm flesh under her light coat, and was surprised.

"I do," he said. "I can try. I've done this with horses way more than people. And not really at your level. My dad was the master. Better than my grandfather, who was a legend. In Australia, I was starting to get good at it, but I'm not at all an Olympic coach . . ."

"You could be."

"No, I couldn't be, because that would have had to have started a long time ago. You, you still have events to go through . . ."

"Quite a few. I've taken a year off. A second year if I make the national team. I'll be ready if I qualify for Sydney."

"Sydney? Seriously? They're going to be there again?"

"The summer games. Sydney. Australia."

No fucking way was he ever going to fucking Sydney. Even if her horse was Pegasus.

"Well, you should find a real coach," Frank said.

"I have one. He comes up from Chicago. I knew about you from Marty. Then I heard you were coming back, so I spoke to Marty."

"I can help," Frank said. "Maybe. I'm reluctant. What I can do is give it a try. Once. If your real coach doesn't mind."

"When I was twenty-two, I almost got there. But I didn't. I got hurt. The orthopedists said I'd never ride again. So I went to medical school . . ."

"What happened?"

Claudia said, "I broke my neck."

"Oh. Are you sound now?"

"Yes. I got better. Like how you got hurt, it wasn't glamorous. It was a stupid error. I wouldn't risk ending up paralyzed. This is my last chance." She lifted her hair off the back of her neck. Frank saw that she was young, and only seemed rather than looked older. She said, "I'm curious. Would you have changed your mind if this hadn't happened?"

"I don't know. I might have. But it goes without saying that I'm grateful. And of course, I'd like you to look at Ian, not formally, but . . ."

"I get it," said Claudia. "Well, it's been quite a day. Are you going to tell your sister?"

"Maybe someday."

"Ready for the dance?"

"Sure."

"But what?"

Frank told her, "I don't know what to do."

"Anyone can dance," Claudia said, a smile exploding with dimples and creases.

"I can dance," Frank said.

"What, then?"

"I meant, I don't know what to do about Ian. Or what to make of my life."

Claudia said, "If today was a taste of it, I wouldn't either."

TEN

YOU'RE GOING TO have a hard time getting a clean run at that speed," Frank called out. "I'd rather you ride a careful course and avoid taking a rail, Claudia."

She laughed. "I like to go fast, and so does Pro."

Frank sighed. It was an early summer afternoon, sulky with rain to come, his fifth session with Claudia. She was the most stylish rider he'd even seen, astride the prettiest and most ungainly horse. Prospero was a big, red, fancy ten-year-old Hanoverian stallion with a sweet streak. Standing still, he looked like the proverbial million bucks. In motion, none of his legs seemed connected to his body. He was like a horse marionette manipulated by a child. When he cantered, he was all tossing and extra motion, even with a tie-down in place, and he looked so slow that Frank could scarcely believe the times he recorded on his stopwatch. When Prospero approached in that jerky all-over-the-place way, Frank held his breath. Almost every time, he thought Prospero would refuse, and then, instead, he sailed over fairly high verticals with inches to spare, his leap anything but classic—a sort of goat jump with a crazy feint at the end, almost like an air kick. Sometimes, the air kick knocked a rail, but never, not once, dislodged one. Fortunately, the way horses looked when they jumped didn't matter at all in show jumping classes of the kind Claudia would need on her march to the Olympics, an absurd, sweet dream at best. The fastest clear run won. Prospero could jump backward

142

if he went smoothly over all the jumps in the right order. He could make all the noise he wanted, and bang the rails until they shuddered in their cups, so long as he didn't knock them out. Still, watching Claudia's patrician carriage on top of that lumbering creature drove Frank nuts.

Claudia had raised Prospero and trained him, too, with the help of a college coach and then two esteemed professionals. It could have been a murderous combination, like a codependent couple. It was not, but Claudia had an inflated faith in her own flexibility. Now she pulled up and brought Prospero to the center, where Frank stood. She slid off, with one hand automatically soothing the horse's glistening neck.

"Pro is a really tidy horse, Frank," Claudia argued. "You see how much room he has."

"Until he bonks a stile . . . that is, a pole." Frank sometimes caught himself using the quasi-Brit Australian terms. "He's not a tidy horse, Claudia. He's a lummox that can jump like the cow over the moon."

"But those are just touches. I think I can go for the time and trust him not to take any rails. If I don't win this class, I won't even get near the Olympic trials. I have to take chances."

"I'm not saying that you shouldn't take chances later. Later, you will have to take chances. Today, right now, I would rather you be conservative, Claudia."

"Conservative? I am being conservative."

"It's a hot day. Go slower. You said you would do what I say. I thought you'd agreed to do what I say?"

"I am doing what you say," Claudia insisted. "And you said you're not a real coach." Frank realized that it wouldn't have occurred to Claudia that she refused on principle to do anything that wasn't her own idea. Woe betide the man who married this woman. Maybe she was already married, for all Frank knew. Maybe she left her husband in a closet when she went to work, like a broom. Maybe she wasn't even into marriage . . . or men, for that matter.

"Frank?" Claudia said. "Frank!"

"What?" He blushed, having been caught imagining Claudia brandishing a riding crop over the prostrate form of a woman wearing only thigh-high leather boots. He laughed and said, "You're going to take him all out no matter what I tell you."

"I'll try to pull up a little."

"Good. But really try. A class like the Mistingay is your perfect event. We don't know the order, but you're already coming in under the qualifying time for the final three . . ."

Ian squeezed through the fence and came running, skinning past Prospero's back legs to rub his belly. Claudia had to visibly stop herself from calling out for Ian to look out. He was so little, these horses so big and excitable. Since the night of Edie's wedding, "the Ian effect" had not been much in evidence. Many children were deft around animals. Frank saw Claudia watching Ian, and imagined her thinking, Am I seeing anything extraordinary? He didn't discuss it with her. Claudia, he decided, would have to speak first.

"Helmet," Claudia said to Ian, and Ian zoomed off again, returning with his riding helmet, the size of a melon on his little head. As Frank and Claudia discussed strategy for the Mistingay Medley, a very formal, old A-level event in Chicago sponsored by some soft-drink heiress, Ian set up his mounting stool, scaled Prospero like a tree, settled on the smaller, flatter jumps saddle, and began circling the ring in a posting trot. Patient and sedate by nature, Prospero responded sweetly, but the big stallion must have felt as though he was being ridden by a talking monkey. Frank had taught Ian to hold the reins properly, but the horse's ears seemed to flick in response to Ian's cheerful monologue—*Do you like hotdogs, Pro? You would if you tried them. Do you like chocolate, Pro? Do you like chocolate cake best of all? Do you like crisps? You would if you tried them. But they'd make you fat, I bet. I like crisps. They don't make me fat because I can fly. Can you fly? I know you can. I saw you fly!* If Prospero had been a cat, he would have purred. Even Claudia didn't soothe her mount so easefully.

"Look at him," Claudia said. "He's three. I rode a pony when I was three. Not very well either."

"I absolutely could not ride like that when I was three, or ten, and I grew up on a horse farm." Breezily, Ian urged Prospero into a slow canter, which worried Frank a little because Ian's legs were so short that he used the saddle straps as makeshift stirrups. Ian needed his own saddle. Frank would make the call tomorrow. He also should get Ian his own horse. He would make that call today. Glory Bee was more than eighteen hands tall—not that a fall off a short horse was any more or less hard on a child than a fall off a tall horse. Most often, Ian rode with Frank's own childhood saddle. It was functional, but still too big. Frank had used it from age eight to about twelve, before he got an adult saddle, but after he switched over from riding bareback with a rope halter. Though he ate more than Frank—ate more in fact, not pound for pound—Ian still weighed about as much as an armful of thistles.

Claudia said suddenly, "Do you think he can do this because he's telling the horses how to be good?"

Frank waited to see if Claudia would say more. When she didn't, he answered, "I think he's a natural rider. Maybe he had some experience with horses before. The Ian effect probably helps, though."

"Is that what you call it?"

"Never out loud before, but sure, I suppose I do."

"Do you think he does it deliberately, or it just happens to people and creatures around him?"

"I know he does it deliberately, the little hand thing. But I think it just happens, too."

"The little hand thing . . . I think I almost recognize it," Claudia said. "I don't know from where. I can't remember."

Frank pictured a concentric ring of circles spreading out from a single pulse—relatives, friends, teachers, pets, wild horses, orangutans. Why not Cape buffalo? Disarmament summits? Divorce mediations? Prison riots? Forcibly, Frank folded his mind back to manageable size. Ian trotted past them. Did doing what he did make Ian happy? How would it feel to know for certain that you could make people be good? Why wouldn't it make you happy? You would feel powerful, but at the same time, peaceful and protected, at the top of the food chain. What if police could do this? No one would ever need a handgun the size of a cannon. The volatility of people, the particular terror of Frank's own youth, was already husked away for Ian. From everything Frank had ever heard about giftedness, from a supernatural grace at being a shortstop to a voice that spanned five octaves, such blessings were inevitably mixed. Yet there seemed to be no downside to Ian's way of being.

"Bring him to me now," Claudia said, smiling, her face shiny with sweat.

Ian said, "No way!"

"Yes. I get to ride now. Pro has to practice. Remember, we have to be polite."

"Can I get Glory Bee?"

Half exasperated, Frank said, "Sure." Ian surely knew he was a major force. Little as he was, he was well aware of the privileges he could command. Even Frank, who knew what was going on, couldn't resist the boy. Around the child, Glory Bee wouldn't kick or bite Prospero. But Frank could tell from her demeanor that Glory Bee didn't like Prospero. She didn't like any other horse. Although an impatient equine sneer had replaced her homicidal glare, Glory Bee was still Glory Bee. The irascible part of her personality was all the personality she had. She was in thrall to Ian. She behaved for Frank. She only put up with Patrick, although judging by the changes in the jumps Patrick had built, Glory Bee was coming along quickly. Thanks to Ian, Glory Bee might actually experience her destiny. Ian jogging around yelling or humming was better for him than sitting inside watching the computer play Ping-Pong with aliens. It was better for the horses. Most competition horses had been raised around adults who weren't big talkers—for whom horses, not people, were the warm-blooded credential. World Cup A-level events could be sedate affairs and tedious, the announcer's stagy whispers reminiscent of old-time golf tournaments. Once, at the Australian Show Jumping Championships, a baby's cry shook the great horse Tanzania so fully that he stopped in the middle of a parallel oxer and refused to budge, even when Brian Mahoney whacked him on the rear end. Ultimately, Mahoney had to lead the horse out of the stadium, and Tanzania stopped a second time when the same baby cried out. The crowd was so indignant on Mahoney's behalf that Frank feared for the innocent mom and her child.

Jealous as he was of Patrick's incarnate aptitude for coaxing the best out of horses, an aptitude that Frank never possessed, he found himself looking forward to the work with Claudia. The small needs of the farm receded. In a burst of largesse, he hired a crew of Amishmen who piled out of the back of a truck driven by an outsider and put the roofs and fences and stalls in order in two ten-hour hives of holy carpentry. It was better work than Frank could have done himself in an uninterrupted month. Lesson learned. He was sharpening the skill he supposed he did have that the Amishmen didn't; and they had set him free to do it.

As Claudia took her seat again, Frank noticed that her pants were baggy. She was getting thinner. A tall woman, five eight or so, she now weighed no more than a hundred and twenty pounds. From years of police work, Frank could guess weights as ably as any carnie. She looked more angular than womanly, and tired, her brow pleated against the late-day sun.

"Claudia, don't worry. Worrying about this isn't going to help. Let's stop for today. A rest helps put everything to rights." He sounded like Tura. For a moment, he was swept back to the farm kitchen, Tura setting out a bowl of pasta the consistency of papier-mâché, and Cedric, who with Tura was always the soul of politeness, finally putting his fork down, telling his wife, "Darling, I would rather eat my shoe . . ." Frank thought of the last time that the Bellinghams sat at their old table on a hot night. Did they know that this was the last time? Did they gaze at each other, and ignore the harsh voices?

Claudia spoke up then. "Frank, I'm thirty-three. I've waited so long for this."

Frank shook his head forcibly, scattering the ghosts. "But you're very talented, and you're very close. The more we're on the same page, the closer you get."

"I think we are! You're just so held in."

"Today I am. In Chicago, I won't be."

"But Pro's strength is that sensitivity, those fast turns. I have to go all out right now so he knows that's what we expect."

"He'll listen to your hands when the time comes. Let's try to make this a smooth, clear round with the jumps configured this way and no touches. And next time we'll build on speed."

Claudia said, "Fine."

She set off again, light and relaxed in her seat, walking Prospero to the center before she took off in the complex series of jumps on the course Frank moved each time.

In a show canter, twelve steps was the standard for horse and rider to build to a jump; if he set up a line with half of that, Prospero and Claudia had to adjust dramatically. She always could, and simply the sight of her hands in motion was enough for her horse. Today, he added height and width so that the verticals were seven feet and four inches, higher than any legal course would ask, and an oxer with a seven-foot spread. Frank had made a water jump by nailing a tarp to a rectangle of two-by-fours, then filling it with an inch of water. Today he drew that makeshift pool away so that Prospero would have to soar beyond thirteen feet to land with his back feet solidly on the far side. He tapped every other fence, but rocketed over the false wall as though it wasn't there, and cleared the water like a man might jump over a stream no wider than a kitchen sink.

"I'm going to try again, and make sure he does a really clear round," Claudia said. The second time, they did just that, and Frank applauded.

Just as he did, he saw the car ease into the driveway. If he hadn't been looking at Claudia, he wouldn't have seen it. The car was nondescript, big and black, with tinted windows. It kept coming, slowly, raising no dust, to within three hundred yards, then two hundred. Then it stopped.

Two men got out. Both wore suits—the kind of odd, boxy-tailored suits that, in Frank's experience, turned out to be very expensive. Before one of them could adjust the flap of his blue suit jacket over his hip, there sparked a fiery particle of light. A gun. Automatically, Frank reached behind him for his own gun, to the place inside the belt behind his hip, where it hadn't been for years and wasn't now. Frank turned and went into the barn to unlock the shotgun. He brought it out as Claudia sat, immobile, Prospero's tail flicking at flies the only motion in the world. Lifting it to his shoulder, he pointed it at the broader man, the driver's chest. If the guy was forty yards away, and had some fancy big-assed hand cannon, he could murder Frank like a dog. They stood there, this way, for a long time. Frank knew that both of them saw him raise the shotgun. Then, to his horror, Frank felt Ian take hold of the back of his jacket. One of the men waved at Frank. He called out something, some kind of greeting in a voice thickly grottoed with guttural sounds. Then the thickset driver got back into the car, and, after a pause, so did the other man, and the car pulled away.

Frank glanced down at Ian. He was shaping his small fingers at chest level again, as if pantomiming spectacles.

Claudia slid down from her saddle, dropping Pro's reins on the ground.

"Hey, Ian," she said. "Where's Glory Bee?"

"Patrick said wait a minute, and then those bad guys came." He shrugged.

Claudia said, "Oh. They were bad guys?"

"Yes, but maybe it's a minute now." Ian whirled and took off at a run.

"Who were those guys?" Claudia said to Frank. "You don't point a gun at everybody who comes over, do you?"

"No. But I pointed a gun at them."

Claudia said, "Wait. Wait." She sat down on the mounting stool and covered her eyes with her hands. "I know what Ian was doing now."

"Now?"

"Just then. It was speech. That was American Sign Language. That was the language I studied in college."

"What does it mean?"

Claudia held up one hand and turned her back, jogging outside the ring to her car. When she came back, she was studying the screen of her cell phone. "There's a website . . ." she said. The sun was broiling the meat of his neck, dazzling his eyes, making him blind and slow. Suddenly Claudia looked up at him.

"It means 'behave,'" Claudia said. "'Be nice.'"

Frank said, "Sure. That makes sense." He carried the gun back to its locked rack. When he came out, Claudia was stroking Prospero's crest, under his mane, with hungry hands. He said, "How would you write that?"

"You don't write it," Claudia said. "That's the whole point."

"But if you did write it?"

"In books, they make drawings of two hands pointing to the right and then to the left, once or twice. They show the direction with little arrows."

ELEVEN

ON THE MORNING of the competition, as Frank and Claudia loaded Prospero and Glory Bee, Ian hopped down the steps, his backpack carefully stuffed with what appeared to be most of his clothing and a large box of cereal. Hope followed Ian, wearing a frown of annoyance unusual for a summer morning. For Hope, a summer morning was as close as she ever expected to get to heaven: the prospect of a day in her pony cart, filling the cart with good food and her head with good talk from her friends, was a tonic she waited for during the entire school year. In her first summer of retirement, and perhaps with Ian's company—although she would not admit how much she looked forward to the time she spent with him—Hope was grown younger. From Eden and Marty, just last week, had come welcome news. There would be a grandchild, or, as they were graceful enough to refer to it, "another" grandchild, not long after Christmas—a plan that simple arithmetic proved had apparently been in place for some time.

"Did you tell him he was going?" Hope said.

"I didn't tell him that he was going."

"Did you tell him he was not going?"

"I didn't tell him he wasn't going either."

"Nice," Hope and Claudia said together.

"Are you scared of a little kid?" said Hope.

Frank said, "Scared? No. It just didn't come up."

He was scared. He didn't want to leave Ian here, at the whim of . . . whoever showed up, with only an older lady and the occasional presence of Marty and Eden. He also didn't want to disappoint Ian in any way: Ian had known too much disappointment. He also knew that Ian, denied, would either drive Frank nuts by some mechanism Frank couldn't imagine, or, and Frank could imagine this, turn away from him.

"Ian, you can't come this time. I'll be busy with Claudia and Pro, and Patrick will be busy with Glory Bee. Next time, you can come." He could hear Ian about to say it . . . *Be nice. Please.*

Instead Ian walked past Frank, crawled up onto the running board of the truck, and buckled himself into his car seat.

"Honey, you can't go," Frank said, the endearment on his lips again surprising him. "You can't come this time. You have to get out."

When Ian would not allow Frank to unbuckle his car seat, Frank quickly but gently pulled the whole seat out of the truck and set it on the ground. He laid one arm across Ian's small chest until he could extract him from the seat.

Be nice, be nice. Could it work if you knew? Well, this was the template. How could you discipline a kid who could push your decisions around like game pieces?

Hope came down and took Ian's hand. "Let's go get Bobbie Champion hitched up to the pony cart," she said.

"No," Ian said. "You go on if you want to."

"You need to come with me, Ian," said Hope.

"I need to not come with you."

"You do need to come with me."

In response, Ian fell flat on his back, as if someone had chopped him down. He was in seconds full into a massive, sobbing tantrum. He pulled at his hair and screamed. He kicked the car seat and his backpack. He took off his shoes and threw them at Frank. Frank started toward Ian, to carry him into the house, but Claudia put a hand on his arm.

"Let him work it out," she said.

"I don't want him to go! I don't want him to go, I don't want him to go, I don't want him to go! I can't stand it! I don't want Dad to go, I don't want him to go. Get it?"

"He'll be back after tomorrow night. Early in the morning on Sunday. We'll go to the market, and then we'll go swimming at Willy's pond if you want. Allison has strawberries, and she has new kittens."

"I don't want him to go! I don't want him to go, I don't want my dad to go!"

When Hope finally tired of it, she let Ian lie on the baked ground in front of the front door, rolling in the dust sobbing until he looked like some kind of archaeological relic. She went into the house and began to grind the beans for her second full pot of coffee of the day.

"Mom! Are you just going to leave him here?"

"He'll come in when he's ready," Hope said through the window.

"He'll run after the truck."

"You just gave him that idea, Frank."

"Well, what's your plan, then, Mom?"

"Bring him inside and I'll see to him. He'll settle down as soon as you're out of sight."

Frank scooped up Ian, who by then lay limp, shuddering and giving out the occasional elaborate bronchial gust. As Frank carried him inside, Ian said, "I don't want you to go, I really don't want you to go, get it? Dad? And Pro doesn't want to go with you either."

"He does want to go. He wants to be in the show."

"No," said Ian. "He's sick. I hate you."

"Okay."

"I said I want to go! Listen to me. Be nice. Are you crazy or something?"

Patrick tried not to laugh but ended up spitting his coffee. "So are you mad, Frank?" Patrick said. "Are you daft?"

"Stay out of it," Frank said. "Mostly, I take you everywhere I go. But I can't take you all the time."

"Well, okay. I hate you. Maybe you'll die."

"Ian!" Hope said.

Frank said, "I don't think I will. I'm pretty sure I won't. I'll be back Sunday morning for sure."

The phone rang then. Frank, wet at the armpits, quickly told his mother, "I'm not here. Even if it's the president."

Fanning out her elegant hands with their small tombstones of pale polish, Hope said, "You seem to have the impression I'm your secretary, Frank."

The call went over to the machine, and Frank heard Brian Donovan say, "Ah, Frank, I was so hoping to catch you . . ." He snatched up the phone.

"Brian! You caught me. I'm just on my way out of town."

Brian had finished his documentary. The brass had called it heartbreaking, stunning, authentic, worthy of the Kirk Dunred Durning Prize, Aussies' equivalent of an Emmy. It would air for the first time next Friday and several other times throughout the coming month. "I've sent you a DVD, Frank. There's a scene that one of my dad's mates took at your wedding, when you and Nat were doing the twist. Just ten seconds. It's so funny. I cried so hard I couldn't see."

Frank wanted to cry, too.

"I'm glad you did it, Brian," Frank said. All he could think, in the face of this good man's tribute, was that the fucking photo would now have a name attached. All that was missing was his address and his email. Want the golden child? Or perhaps the kidnapper? *X* marks the spot! Frank could smell himself, rank as old cooking oil. If he didn't get out of this house now, he never would.

As they rattled the trailers down the drive from Tenacity, turned left, and hit the state highway in a convoy, Frank called Hope twice. As his mother predicted, by the time the horse trailers were out of sight, Ian was marching around in striped cargo shorts, wearing rubber boots, his deerstalker cap, thumping the ground with Jack's shillelagh, and insisting that they have steak with the strawberry shortcake. Hope added that she thought Frank was doing a great job and would have been a great father.

The past tense stung.

Frank turned to Claudia and said, "I hate to leave him upset like that . . ." but Claudia was already staring ahead, seeing the course in her mind, and murmured that Ian would be fine.

How did she know? What did she care? She wasn't a parent.

Neither was he, Frank thought then.

They drove straight through. Frank was forced to listen to talk radio because Claudia's sole conversation consisted of "No, thanks . . ." (when offered coffee) and "I think I-90 the whole way . . ." (when Frank guessed aloud about the fastest route to Lakefront Coliseum).

Although Claudia's class wouldn't be held for five hours, she was eager to walk the course. The order of jumps was posted on the gate, well in advance of locking in the course, but no one was to be admitted until two hours before the event. That was a generous amount of time, Frank said. His father once told him that riders were lucky to be able to walk the course at all, and often got no more than thirty minutes: being able to think through a course for a rider was as important as being able to think through a dance combination for somebody at a Broadway audition.

"They're so high," Claudia said.

"No higher than what you're used to. They're just fancier, more substantial. Don't let that get inside your head."

After getting the horses settled, Patrick, who would ride Glory Bee as a novice horse and team in the same class, came out as well, thoughtfully wandering the outside of the fenced area a single time, hardly seeming to look. Claudia appeared very small and wilted. "Do you want to go to the hotel and rest?" Frank asked her.

"I guess," she said. "But I'll check on Pro first. I'm going to braid his mane."

"Right now?"

"Sure."

"Don't bother. Do it tomorrow."

The temperature of the day was killing, and Frank hoped that the judges would dispense with the requisite jacket and let the riders compete in white breeches and polo shirts—or else, he feared, some of them would be slipping off their horses. At least one always fainted. It had been twice as nasty in Australia.

Claudia's room was across the hall from Frank's, and neither of them asked where Patrick was staying, although Frank had put up the money. Patrick seemed to have a brother, or a brother and a sister, or an uncle, in Chicago, and he either was or was not going to see them or him that night; it was difficult to tell. As soon as he got in his room, Frank fell backward on the bed, and immediately his sweating went over to shivering. Covered up by the stiff sheets, he nearly slept a dozen times and was finally so miserable that he got up and took a lukewarm shower. Then it was time to go back to the arena.

The advanced jumps was the last event of the day. Inside, he and Claudia and Patrick walked the course in silence.

It was done up, as these things sometimes were, on a theme—this one of a European summer. One of the verticals was paid for by Euro Disney. A rather demure Minnie in fishnets and flats, and Mickey in a beret, flanked an approximation of the Eiffel Tower in the middle, a choice that Frank thought nearly made it a joker, because the phony point of the tower, although no higher than the rest of the jump, drew the eye. Jokers, unpainted fences with two plain downward-sloping wings, like slats, on either side, were deceptive because they had no filler. Horses could see color, especially orange and blue, and those rustic jumps were difficult for them to judge. He pointed out the possible hazard of the Parisian vertical to Claudia, who nodded silently, deep in concentration or nerves. It was a very high obstacle.

One of the fences was bedecked in fake wildflowers—meant by the designers hired by Lancaster's, a British auction house, to look like an English country hedgerow. A triple combination was three modest oxers, each painted to look like an Italian gondola, complete with gondoliers and musical notes, advertising Ponte Vecchio Pizza. One of the offset oxers was commissioned by Bavaria Brewers. A simple set of ascending poles with the higher in back, it looked massive because it was built with the sawn ends of real beer barrels between the poles, and the poles were flanked by two double-high racks of beer barrels, lovingly scrolled in with the rich gold-and-green leaf-and-nymph pattern of the brewery.

End-to-end, it was the size of a bus.

They studied each of the fifteen, looking for places that would need a diagonal approach, an especially fast corner, or that might pose optical problems—which was difficult to discern from the eye height of a human being. With a fresh pouring of sweat that had nothing to do with the heat, and the heat was thick as a wet cloth at four in the afternoon, Frank started to consider all this trouble and preparation balanced like an egg on the card pyramid on the foundation of ten training sessions with an ex-cop who had trained precisely nine jumpers and riders. At least Claudia had come into this event with earned points.

Patrick had not. Frank had paid a ridiculous amount, tens of thousands of dollars, to enter an advanced event with a crazy five-year-old horse, ridden by a drunken jockey whose own experience was in murderous steeplechase races. How much of the application had Patrick faked, drawing on obscure international events that never happened? How much of that was Frank as the owner responsible for? He wanted to lie down on the grass under the bleachers.

Claudia peered at the order of the jumps, which was drawn on the map on the gate. They included three "Liverpools," so named for their similarity to the water jump called Becher's Brook on the course where the Grand National was run. It was undoubtedly a tricky jump, but Frank thought more jockeys were in error than horses for falling at Becher's. Horses didn't know that it had the reputation of the maze with the Minotaur. People did. For all his ungainliness, Pro was a brave horse with a big stride, fearless. And Claudia was also fearless.

As she began to walk off, Frank caught her arm. "Think about the approach, not just the speed."

"I know," she said.

Impulsively, Frank kissed her on the forehead.

Just as impulsively, he got into his truck and went back to the hotel. He showered and lay on the bed. Then he took out his cell phone and called Hope.

What kind of coach couldn't bear to watch his own rider? And his own horse competing? I have fears enough for all of them, Frank thought.

"Are you coming home in the morning?" Ian said.

"No, Sunday morning. I told you that, buddy."

Then Hope was on the phone. "He says you told him you were coming tomorrow for dinner."

"I didn't, Mom!"

"He's fine," she said.

"Is he really fine?"

"He is, just not . . ."

"Not?"

"Not happy."

Frank wasn't happy without him either, and thought, I should have brought him. Here I am, sitting on a bed. What would it matter if there were cartoons on the TV? A few minutes later, though, Frank fell asleep, first groping to turn the phone to vibrate, then laying a rolled towel over his eyes. The crazy dream voice said to him, *I'm so tired of waiting. I'm tired. Let me come home.* There was a memory that the phone had gone off, but when he sat up, in the dark, it was to a persistent banging on the door.

Swinging his feet over, he opened the door.

Claudia stood in the hall in bare feet and an oversized robe. Her hair was wet, and she was crying.

Frank said, "Are you hurt?" Obviously, she wasn't hurt. "Did Prospero go down?"

"He refused."

"Claudia! Did he have a stomachache?"

"He has a broken bone near his fetlock."

Thinking of the great thoroughbred Barbaro, his leg shattered in the Preakness, but probably, actually, factually, years before in training, of the surgeries and rehab that ended in a heartbreaking euthanasia a month later, Frank said, "One bone? Or more than one?"

"The vet took a preliminary X-ray. He said one."

"What do you want to do?"

"Pro's on the way to the University of Illinois Veterinary Hospital in Champaign. The vet found me a medical escort. I'm going to go in the morning. I have to rent a car."

"Why didn't you go with Pro now?"

"I wanted to tell you myself about Glory Bee."

"We lost her," Frank said, straightening, forgetting to breathe.

"She took fifth," said Claudia. The field was eighty.

"Where's Patrick?" Frank had to struggle to quench his own excitement and joy in the face of her grief.

"He was drunk last time I saw him, in the bar and grill called Steel Pier. I made sure he had the name of the hotel in his pocket and money for a cab."

"Okay."

"I raised Pro from a weanling," Claudia said, her voice harsh with misery. "This is a career ender. I know that. I don't know if Pro can be saved, but if he can, he'll be loved and cared for at stud. You would let him stand at Tenacity, wouldn't you?"

"Of course," Frank said. There was something else.

"Now I don't have a horse."

"You should rest. We'll see what happens."

Frank reached out to grasp Claudia's shoulders and she leaned into his arms, and, surprising himself, he kissed her, his hands closing around her rump, lean under the worn terrycloth, drawing her to him, conscious of, and then embarrassed by, the insistent hardness bowing out the crotch of his sweatpants. "An excess of comfort," Frank said. "I apologize, Claudia. I'm only human."

"Me, too," Claudia said. She glanced up at Frank. "Could I come in?"

"Sure."

"Could we make love?"

TWELVE

FRANK THOUGHT THE floor shifted, but it was he who swayed. What a sissy he was.

He'd just kissed a beautiful woman. Why did he feel like he was about to piss himself?

He said then, "Why?"

"Nobody ever asked me why before." Claudia attempted to smile, but the smile broke up into pieces of grimace. Now he'd embarrassed her, and she was already sad.

She put her powerful, smaller hands on Frank's, drawing them to her cheeks, her neck, her breasts. "Don't you feel anything?"

Frank said, "Lots of things."

Not all of them were good.

He made a stab at opening the knot on Claudia's robe, and then sighed.

"Sighing? Is this hard labor? Should I help you with the belt?" Claudia glanced up at Frank and he nodded. She was certainly the more fit. Her rider's hips and thighs were muscled, harder than his own, and her hands were cold, but the rest of her skin was hot under the robe's thin fabric.

What the hell was the matter with him?

"Am I being presumptuous?"

"No. I don't know. But that doesn't bother me. I like people to just say the thing, whatever it is. I'm just not sure that I'm . . ."

"Ready? Because of your wife."

"Probably."

"You seem ready." Claudia nodded at the bulge in Frank's pants.

"That's physical."

"I wasn't asking you to marry me."

They both laughed.

Frank said, "I'm also not very promiscuous."

"Nor am I. In fact, my last . . . well, affair, and it hardly merits the term, was eighteen months ago."

"What happened?"

"He was a practicing anesthesiologist who was always short of money. That meant gambling to me. Or maybe worse, although I never saw any evidence of worse."

"That's complex. I'm just a gimpy ex-cop with a broken-down farm. So why me? Why tonight? Consolation?"

"No. Friendship and lust."

"You're attracted to me?" You fucking half-wit, Frank's brain was bellowing.

Claudia shrugged. "I don't think I'd be standing here otherwise. And I don't think I've ever been challenged in this way either, and I'm trying to find it refreshing. You're a good kisser. You're a good father. You're brave."

Quietly and before he could repent it, Frank nudged one index finger inside the knot and finally, with some trouble, loosened it. Claudia had tied it hard, and she had strong hands, so it wasn't the work of a moment. When he finished, the robe hung straight, Claudia's olive skin naked from neck to feet, the space plain between the soft swellings of her breasts, just beginning to lose their girlish tilt, the small rise of her belly with its pale evidence of a summer two-piece, down to the lush light brown curls between her legs. Her skin was unbroken by a blemish. He could not help a rueful reflection on the thick grid of scars that crosshatched his leg. He slid his thumbs from her square chin, along her neck, feeling the pulse banging away there, grazing the outer edge of her breasts, circling the nipples. "What are your feelings?"

"I want to laugh because of you saying that, because you're a psychiatrist. But I don't think this is the moment for laughter."

"Yup," Claudia said.

"I'm a widower. Not for a year yet."

"A year is a long time. You feel you'd be cheating on Natalie?"

"Not at all. I think it's more that . . . I'm your coach."

"You mean, if I did have a horse? What if you were coaching your sister? Or your wife? What if it was your son? Would you be able to be straight with them? You think you couldn't be honest with me after this?"

"There hasn't been any this yet. But more to the point, Claudia, you're standing naked in the hall. Come in here." Clutching the robe, she reached behind her and brought out a bottle of wine that had been sitting on the floor.

"This was for celebration. For when Pro covered himself in glory." Tears shimmered in Claudia's eyes.

"Do you usually bring condoms for celebration, too? Like, to a dinner party?" His was a dumb joke. But she smiled.

"Well, you don't know how crazy dinner parties get in Madison. *La vida loca.*" She said, "Didn't you think of me this way?"

Frank stopped to consider. "Yes. No. Of course. You're gorgeous. But I never thought of us having sex. Correction. Of me having sex. With anybody. Except maybe myself."

"You're a young man."

"Not since last Christmas."

Claudia got up and searched for the long ends of the robe belt, but didn't tie it.

"Don't feel you've made yourself foolish," Frank said. "For coming here."

"I don't."

"I hope you can forgive me bringing up Natalie. You're like her. You're like her and you would have liked her. She was a hardheaded doctor."

"Do you want some wine?" Claudia asked. Frank said he did, and

Claudia, still unsettlingly half clothed, found round hotel tumblers, expertly popped the cork, and poured the champagne. Frank noted approvingly that it was Roederer, which Natalie, who liked her wine, insisted on for their wedding. "How am I like her?"

"Natalie was athletic. She was bold, the way you're bold. She fancied herself a drinker but got drunk quickly."

"Me, too."

"And me."

Claudia drained her glass and set it down. "I am tired. I will return to my maiden's bed for a few hours before I go to the clinic and see about Prospero. No hard feelings."

"None."

A knock came at the door. "Mike and Minky's," said a voice.

"Stripper?" Claudia asked.

"Worse. Ladies' clothing." Motioning for quiet, Frank answered, and, standing in the doorway, chose one of two boxes proffered. He said, "I paid on the phone."

Claudia wanted to see what was in the box, but Frank demurred. "Come on!" she said. "Is it drugs?"

He opened the box to reveal a long ocean-gray cashmere sweater with the hint of a rolled collar. Confused, Claudia said, "I don't . . . Is it yours?"

"For my mom. There's this boutique here, called Mike and Minky's. Hope loves the clothes because they're usually from Italy. So I bring her something."

"Just from here? Or anyplace you go?"

"I guess anyplace," Frank said. "I got used to getting her things from here when I lived here. Christmas, Mother's Day, just for nothing, because she works so hard. I know. A bit much." Frank glanced down, abashed.

"Don't be embarrassed. That's sweet. And in good taste."

She got up to leave, and as she did, Frank's longing for her scent, like oranges and cloves, as well as the delights he knew could come, nearly strangled him. At the last moment, he said, more in a growl than he meant, "Look, Claudia, please stay. I'm some kind of idiot. Of course I want you. I have a bum leg, so I can't carry you to this bed, which they seem to have short-sheeted, but if you come over here, I'll try to make us both happy."

So she let the robe drop, and lay down, stretching her arms up over her head to pull his head to her. Her mouth tasted of the wine, and that same tincture of cloves he'd smelled. In his arms, Claudia, tall and assured, felt smaller, her rib cage bowed, as some people's were, and her legs frankly thin, topped by those overdeveloped thighs, like renderings of Demeter. He lifted her breasts, gently rolling the nipples between his hands, which, he now noticed, were as hard as hooves. His mouth must have been soft, for when he suckled her, he heard Claudia first sigh, then draw in her breath sharply.

"Let me," she said. She helped him out of his sweats, and his shirt, and they faced each other naked. "We've never kissed before. And here we are."

"I'm shy," he said. "Everybody says you feel like a kid. It's a cliché, but you really do."

"Oh, me, too. I wish we still had clothes on and were stuck on the seat of the truck. Hurry up and kiss me."

Frank kissed her and she put the hook of her smooth calf around his leg. No matter what else he was doing—anywhere and anytime, for these past months—whatever else he was concentrating on, Ian was there, too, present as another personality. Claudia's touch forced even Ian out of his mind. He didn't want to explode like an eighteen-year-old, so he tried to think of Prospero and the likely laminitis that would ensue if they could heal the break . . . When he attempted to slide down Claudia's belly to taste her, she said, "No, no. Can't do that. I'm prissy. That's for later. For next time."

He felt the same way.

"Is there something we can do that you do like?" he asked, suppressing a gasp. Her thumbs were stroking his hipbones, her strong hands massaging his cock as though it were a newborn rabbit, a touch so delicate and firm he wanted her to stop, go faster, maintain that touch forever.

"Well, I ride horses," she said finally.

Frank pulled Claudia astride him, and she descended with aching deliberation. She said, "Be slow." Be *slow*? he thought. "It's been a while for me, too," she explained. "It's not like hospital TV shows. We're not screwing away in abandoned supply closets." Frank supported her with his hands around her waist, and she with her hands on his shoulders, and, wanting to push deep into her but obliged to wait, he followed her into a shy rhythm that had his hairline beaded in sweat. He could feel Claudia gathering, shuddering. "Wait," she said. "Wait. Wait. I forgot the condom. I have to get it." Frank wanted to murder the inventor of prophylactics. Claudia slipped off him, leaving him awkward and exposed. He quickly used his toes to shed his socks; what a rube. Then she was back, and the thing was on and the transient awful foreignness quickly swallowed by her heat. She was down all along his length, her breast brushing his mouth, her hands urging him deeper.

"Oh please, please," he said. "Oh, Claudia. How did we get in this position?"

"In the world or this bed?"

"In the world."

"Oh, just shut up for now. Make me come a hundred times, okay?"

"Not on this ride," Frank said, breathless. "I don't think I'm in for endurance."

He rolled her over onto her back and sucked in his breath as she raised her legs to clamp his waist with her thighs. "Did I hurt you . . . ?"

"One of the uncounted benefits of riding is a strong seat. That was just amazement."

Then there was a soft rap at the door.

"Ignore it," Claudia said. "This is too sweet. Just be here with me now. Even if it's the fire department."

Frank called, "Come back later!"

"'S Pat!" a voice called. "I need you now, Frank."

"I'm getting out of the, uh, shower. I'll come right over."

"Wait here," Patrick said, and they heard him sit down, hard.

Frank groaned. They stopped.

"He won't leave."

"And he won't notice, the shape he's in. But I will."

"Okay," Frank said, moving slowly, feeling way too familiar for how unfamiliar all this was. Claudia put her hand over his mouth and, pulling a corner of the pillow across her own mouth, she whimpered out as she clasped Frank to her, bore down hard on his shoulders, and with her orgasm, forced him to give up his own. For a moment, Frank thought of Glory Bee in flight over a triple combination. He hadn't jumped a horse since the time that Tarmac, his Morgan, gathered himself and took a five-rail fence when they were chasing down a couple of fire starters in a forest preserve. It had only happened a single time, but the sensation was the way he imagined flying when he dreamed of flying—one animal, aloft in a soundless tranquility, like the line from the Koran his father had scrawled once on a desk blotter, "And thou shalt fly without wings, and conquer without sword."

That was like this.

"Well, thanks. What if I had let you leave? God, I'm glad I didn't let you leave, Claudia," Frank said.

"Speaking of God, big points from me for not calling out to God while we were having sex. I hate that," Claudia whispered, stifling giggles as she kicked the robe under the bed and ran for the bathroom. Frank was shocked at the realization that he hadn't considered her having sex with anyone else, ever. Now Claudia was inventorying him against a phalanx of Nordic Ivy League rowers who supplicated Jesus.

He remembered Patrick.

If there really was a God, Patrick would be passed out on the floor. But, although he fell into the room when Frank opened the door, Patrick was wide awake.

"And you slept all this while," Patrick said.

"I didn't sleep the whole time. But I don't like to watch a competition. It gets on my nerves."

"So you wouldn't know."

"That . . ."

"She's fifth in the field, Frank, going into tomorrow! Her a filly, well, not a filly, but a young mare, and half the age of most, and a tenth of the training. She's like Red Rum, or Milton, like your Ruffian . . . She could be better than all of them . . ."

"That's down to you, Patrick."

"That's down to the horse." He turned to leave. "I just wanted you to know. I have to get my sleep. I need sleep."

"You need to lay off the sauce is what you need."

"I had a drink."

"Or six."

"Three, on my mother's name."

"Do you have a mother, Patrick?"

"I do not, not since a child. But I have a father, the dirtiest old fir in Sligo. And a sister in Sligo, God love her, called Pen."

"You don't talk about her."

"She's my twin," Patrick said, as if that explained it. "She's got three little ones and her husband a bastard after my own da."

"Of course," Frank said, hearing water run in the bathroom and elaborately glancing out into the hall, so that it seemed the water was coming from another room, while Patrick followed his gaze. "I'll come tomorrow. I wasn't really asleep. I did some reading."

"Did she tell you?"

"Claudia? Yes."

"At least Prospero didn't go ahead and try to do the round."

Lowering his voice, in clear understanding that Patrick would be as doleful as possible about Prospero's chances, particularly in his cups, Frank asked, "How bad did it look?"

"He wasn't even lame. If it's a fracture higher up and not clean through, he could live well. I've seen horses healed carry the blind. Children."

Nodding, Frank said, "You did well. Exceptionally well, Pat."

"Thank you, guv."

Frank had no sooner closed the door than Claudia emerged, stereotypical as a college girl in Frank's shirt. But the door hadn't latched and Patrick was in again, and already saying, "I should sleep. But first, I need to go back over and see to Glory Bee, give her a rubdown, unless you want to. Claudia. Hello there."

"Hello, Patrick. Uh, hi. I was just stopping by. You'll excuse me. I have to get the rental car now. It should be here by now."

"It's after ten," Frank said.

"I want to go look after Pro."

"You said you'd go in the morning."

"You wouldn't, and neither would I."

"Do you want me to come with you?"

With a modest maidenly crouch, Claudia retrieved and slipped into her robe.

"You can't," she said. "Your horse could be jumping for a ribbon tomorrow."

"She is right, Frank," said Patrick. "Hello, Claudia."

"You said that, Patrick."

"It's a four-hour drive. I went to school in Champaign," Frank said. "Patrick, I'll go over and see to Glory Bee. You get some sleep. Claudia, are you sure you don't want me to come?"

"I'm a very good driver." Claudia said to Patrick, "You look better than when I saw you last. You're standing up." Patrick glanced at his black boots. "I'll leave my suitcase with you, Frank, and just take my bag with a couple of things. I don't know for sure how long I'll be gone. It depends on Pro's . . . hopes." Claudia made a wide loop around Patrick and left.

Desperate for a topic, Frank said then, "Why was she fifth? Glory Bee? Why wasn't she out of it altogether? Or first?"

Fortunately, spirits had loosened Patrick's tongue and he gave what amounted, for him, to a valedictory speech.

"She knocked out a pole. It was a clear round otherwise. I didn't drive her as fast as I could have. I didn't know how much of a chance I could take. I don't like to think of getting hurt either. The water . . . she didn't even notice it. She could have done it again twice, and half again as fast. Horse like that . . . Frank, she could do anything."

"Don't bitch it," Frank said, an old sliver of his father's superstition pinning him between the shoulder blades. He didn't know anyone who worked with horses who wasn't deeply superstitious, whatever other belief system or lack of it went on in that person's life.

"Wise," Patrick said, as if insanity-as-gospel meant perfect sense.

A few minutes after Patrick left, there was another knock. Frank had just struggled into his jeans and shirt. Claudia was back, her face washed clean, wearing jeans and a denim jacket. Frank pulled her to him and kissed her throat, swiftly undoing her jeans and sliding her up onto the edge of the laminate bureau.

"No time," she said. "I'm sorry." She hopped down and walked a few steps away.

"I know," Frank told her. "I have to see to Glory Bee before she's stiff anyhow. I'm sure Pat rubbed her down, but I'm not satisfied it was well enough."

Claudia said, "Sure. By the look of him at the Steel Pier, I would say you have cause to wonder."

Frank said, "What were you doing at the Steel Pier?"

"Having a whiskey. Not like Patrick. Prospero was hurt and I couldn't do anything for him, and it got to me. I was shaken."

"So you went in a bar and ordered a whiskey by yourself?"

"Yes, Frank. Girls do. Would you have said this before tonight?"

Frank told her, "I don't know."

"I'm not a lady."

"I think you are."

"I'm not, though. I'm a jock. I'm a doc. I'm a jock doc." Claudia crossed back to his side and stood on her toes to kiss him goodbye. Then, in an afterthought, she kicked off her pants, slipped up onto the long console, and, looking up at him from under her eyelids, offered him the condom packet while slowly opening her legs.

"Not being a lady," she said.

"Not called for at a moment like this." They did it clothed, standing there.

Later Claudia said, "I didn't mean to start a thing."

"Serves you right. Whiskey-swilling cowgirl."

"That's what everybody says."

Frank watched as Claudia made her way down the hall, wondering all the while why he didn't just walk down with her, as an ordinary person should. He thought that the elevator had probably already come and gone when he called, "Wait! Claudia!"

From a distance, he heard her call, "What?"

"Come back here for a moment if you can?" She did, impatient, wary, her keys whirling on her finger. "Sit down for a moment."

"Frank, don't get agitated. Don't think I expect you to be my boyfriend now."

"That's the problem, see."

"Why?"

"I think I want you to expect that. I want you to hope for the best between us. Do you think that the best between us is only one night?"

"I'm okay if it is," Claudia said, twirling her keys briskly.

"But I'm not," Frank said.

Claudia let her keys go still and then said, "Oh."

"So what do you think the best between us can be?"

"I guess I think it can be . . . I don't know. The very best? Maybe you have nasty habits. Like you pick your teeth."

"Maybe you do."

"Maybe you don't," she said. "Maybe if I did, I'd change."

"Maybe you don't have to."

"I can be awful," Claudia said. "I can be an awful, stuck-up, snobby know-it-all bitch!"

"Is that a warning?"

"No. It's a description. I'm just telling you."

"Okay. I'm not afraid."

"And if you ever lie to me about anything, I'll leave you. Even if it seems like a little nothing. Of course, you don't have to tell me everything. But if it affects me, us, there can be no secrets."

Oh, Frank thought, oh no.

"Well," he said, making his slow way from one supercharged precipice to the next, even higher, willing himself to keep going and not to look down, aware that he'd never before been the one who did all the talking—that every woman who came before, including Natalie, had done all that, for both of them. "I don't know how this story goes. I'm not saying that we're in love. What I'm saying is, I'm a sentimental guy."

Claudia came into Frank's arms. He held her, and kissed the top of her head.

THIRTEEN

WHEN SHE WAS GONE, Frank swung into the truck and zipped over to the coliseum barn, where he showed a couple of tiers of security his credentials. Considering the millions of dollars in horseflesh sleeping or rustling back there, he appreciated more than one checkpoint. He was surprised to see a girl who looked to be twelve or thirteen outside Glory Bee's box stall.

"Hey!" he called. "That's my horse."

Smoothly, the young woman—the closer he got, the more she looked like a young woman and less like a child, although she was no taller than five-feet-nothing at the most—held out her hand.

"I'm Linnet," she said. "Like the bird? Patrick paid me to sit up with her and let me help rub her down. She's fantastic. I think Patrick was tired when he came back around."

"I think Patrick was drunk."

"That, too," Linnet said smoothly as Frank stroked Glory Bee's neck, marveling at the mostly durable change in her, as though she'd had her brain removed and replaced with the temperament center of another horse.

"So she's had a good rubdown . . ."

"And her dinner. A light dinner."

"Are you here for juniors?"

"I was, back when I was a kid."

"What do you do now?" Frank meant, What do you do now at Grand Prix events, but the girl had a different answer.

"I'm in jockey school."

"You're in jockey school?"

"College."

"There's a college for being a jockey?"

"Yes, a regular college sports program. There are only a few, but I'm in one."

"Where?"

"Indiana. The big one is Chris McCarron's school in Kentucky, but this is a good school. Trevor Caven runs it."

"That's something I never would have believed," Frank said. "Jockey school. I thought you just did that."

"Well, I guess you once just did being a doctor. But not very well."

"Huh. I'll go back and call it a night, then. Are you okay?"

"I'm fine. I'm twenty. I know I don't look it. I can take care of myself. And there are big guys out there with guns. Not that I would need their help."

"Then you won't mind my saying you should stay away from Patrick."

"I do mind," Linnet said. "He's not a bad person. You think the drinking is all there is to it. But my father drinks like that, and he also has no talents."

"You don't know Patrick."

"I do. He's been down to our school."

"Patrick? For what?"

"He did a series of lectures on two weekends a couple of months ago about avoiding common injuries. He knows Trevor."

"*Patrick* did a series of lectures?"

She might as well have told Frank he'd said Mass.

"He's very thoughtful about it."

Frank stopped. She was right. Patrick had a good heart and a keen mind; he treated Glory Bee like a duchess and Ian like a little brother. The response to jockeys as lecherous little creatures who drank to avoid eating and tried to skewer every woman past puberty was an easy shot. "I'll apologize, then."

"I might come to see your farm one day."

"That would be good. Do better. You let me know if you . . . Do jockey school students need summer jobs?"

The girl beamed. Her skin was parchment white, with freckles, and she was almost plain until she smiled. The smile recalibrated everything. No wonder Patrick was smitten.

She said, "This one does. Do you have full-time help?"

"Well, Professor Patrick lives and works at Tenacity. But early summer is hard. We put up hay and we're going to have my . . . a friend's horse there, healing . . ."

"Prospero. Yes."

"If he makes it, and we still board a few. Do you like work?"

"I've been working since I was ten."

"So you must like it."

"I'd rather have wealthy patrons of racing buy villas and hot cars for me, but yes, for now I do like it."

Back at the hotel, Frank fell asleep for a few hours to what seemed like one endless *Law & Order* episode, but was probably, in fact, four or five, to wake sweating from a dream he didn't recall until he had finished the cold toast and coffee he'd nearly kicked across the hall—having forgotten he'd ordered them the night before. He brought the tray back in, knocking over Claudia's suitcase that was just inside the door. Suddenly deciding that he and Patrick would drive home tonight no matter when the event finished, he humped all the luggage down to the bell stand. It was while standing there, folding claim tickets into his wallet, that he realized that he'd dreamed again of elevator doors opening, but that this time first Natalie and then Claudia and then Patrick were stepping in, only to reach up to him from boiling water while he held back from all of them, clutching Ian in his arms. His phone pinged with a message. Claudia had written, *Pro is resting on a suspended bed. They pinned a fracture, right hind leg fibula. The doctor says his tempera-*

ment is on his side because he won't fight confinement as he heals. Transport will bring him home next week. I'll wait and drive back. I thought about you all night. C.C.

CeeCee.

Her initials formed a natural nickname. Someone would have called her that in high school. He wondered what, and who, Claudia had done in high school. It was unseemly even for him to wonder about it. She was not his. He had thought of her, too, last night, nearly torturously replaying their sex to a groaning schoolboy conclusion while Sam Waterston snappishly reminded a mopey ADA of the moral fiats behind his oaths. And then he had slept, and dreamed her into his particular hell.

He texted back, *Me, too. Good for Pro. Patrick will baby him. Try not to worry.*

Frank got into the car. As he pulled out carefully onto the frontage road, he heard someone say plainly, *I want Ian. Can you bring me?* It was a voice, but not a voice, the same crazy head-talk he'd heard just a few days earlier. Ian couldn't do what Frank could only think of as mental telegraphing—although Frank could not be sure of anything anymore, since he'd been sure that Ian could not speak. Perhaps it was Ian, saying in his small child's way that he wanted Frank.

On the way to the coliseum, he called his mother three times, and once he could have sworn that Ian picked up, and then, whether from anger or silliness, left the landline off the hook, hidden someplace Hope wouldn't find it. Frank had to call his mother's cell phone to attempt to reach her and was peeved when her message said, *Hope Mercy here. Please leave us a message and we really will get right back to you.* Who had a name like Hope Mercy? She sounded like a health conglomerate. Frank thought of wireless minutes as costly as uranium rolling up, because his mother, not quite altogether keen on the idea of cell phones, often left hers behind when she was out in the garden or driving around in her pony cart. He thought of Glory Bee possibly—well, impossibly—taking away honors and points from an event that she had no business being in at all. And he thought of Claudia, and what he might now mean to a woman he didn't even know, and what she might now mean to him, and what any of that meant to Ian, and Ian's presumed assumed identity, and of Patrick's comic appraisal of all he could see of Claudia from beneath Frank's shirt, which had been plenty, and why was Patrick to blame; he was a man, even if he had an inseam twenty-six inches long.

Then he heard the voice again. *Do you hear me? I'm not dead. God-damn dub!*

Could Ian do this, too? Was he being haunted? Did he have a brain tumor?

Frank had to pull over to rummage in the glove box for his trusty painkiller (he would end up a junkie, drifting pleadingly from doctor to doctor wearing a false lumbar belt and a quivering smile) when lightning flashes from the corners of his eyes threatened a four-eleven alarm headache. The walk to the open stadium was at least a mile once he parked: Patrick had parked the trailer and van by the stables and cabbed it in luxury. When Frank got out of the air-conditioned truck, he nearly swooned. It was easily a hundred in the shade. That wouldn't bother his cantankerous Aussie girl, but it might kill other horses. And it could easily kill spectators who were elderly, hatless, or simply sane, because, with the earlier and junior classes, these events were longer than bad marriages.

Why was he here?

Frank turned around and wandered back to the stables. His head was pounding through a full Vicodin . . . without it, he'd probably have needed to be hospitalized. His head hurt as though somebody had kicked him while he was unconscious. He'd never had a headache like this.

Hiya, said the phantom voice. *Hiya! Fireman!*

And though he got injured, he never got sick . . . or sick enough. In twenty years on the job, he had never once called in sick. He had *been* sick, dog sick, with bronchitis, a sprained ankle, cuts, bruises, concussions, sinus infections, scratched corneas, broken ribs, pinched nerves, even food poisoning, and a cracked kneecap when Tarmac, sage horse that he was, prudently stopped at a dumpster but let Frank continue his trajectory through space. He'd probably transmitted upper respiratory distress to whole neighborhoods, not to mention tiers of the Cook County Jail and ranks of the court system. But he had never called in sick, and after fifteen years, he had decided that even if he went thirty, he never would; it had become a dare, a challenge, like never being divorced or married, like never having eaten a hotdog or gotten a parking ticket. But he would have called in sick to his very life, not only his job, today, if only to take four painkillers and stop the tennis in his head.

He should not have slept with Claudia.

He wanted to see Claudia.

Ian would hate him.

A boy needed a mother.

Double fault! A mother? On the basis of one night and two lush couplings? With someone who was a psychiatrist and suspect for that fact alone? A boy who needed a mother was a boy of your own who didn't already have a mother and not, instead, your own unknowing victim of a felony. Frank wanted to see Ian. Hope would approve of Claudia. Fault! Approve of Claudia for what? Eventually, Frank found the Steel Pier, where Patrick (and Claudia) had imbibed the previous night—a small, crisp, pubby little place nestled against the outside perimeter of the coliseum complex. He ordered a grilled Swiss and tomato to go and two cold Cokes in go-cups. He ate the sandwich on an ornate iron bench in the street, a bench surrounded by a nine-by-five rectangle of brutalized turf studded with a few plump rusty evergreens, one nearly obscuring a sign identifying the little space as Kerri Waldo Creativity Park.

A "toasted cheese" sandwich was his mother's remedy for anything, and so it proved. The headache still crouched in the shadows of his brain, but sheathed its claws. His phone pinged. It wasn't a call, but a picture of Ian, sent by Hope. Even before he saw the picture of Ian, wearing swim trunks, goggles, and Frank's muck boots, he saw that somehow, it was three in the afternoon. The final was at four.

Goddamn wally.

What?

Hop-skipping in his parody of a run, he went to find Glory Bee.

Either Patrick was very unforthcoming with his skills or he'd met a woman in Linnet who hadn't minded sharing hers, for Glory Bee's mane was plaited in flat braids and her black coat shined glossy. With what was, for her, uncharacteristic calm, she was idly dragging Linnet around in a way that made the small girl look like a big doll. Frank took the halter rope from Linnet, so assaulted by heat she looked as though she'd been swimming, soaked through with Glory Bee's sweat and her own. Glory Bee stood relatively quietly for Frank, the sweat in thick suds on her own neck. Patrick appeared from wherever it was he appeared from. He looked to have stepped out of a magazine ad, his white trousers and polo shirt blindingly clean, his boots mirror-polished, and his black gloves fitted like his own skin. To Patrick's immense credit, he only nodded, sliding not a single glance at Frank that would have betrayed any hint of mirth or lewdness connected with his encounter with Claudia last night in the hotel. In fact, Patrick said fewer words even than his customary four or five. Clearly, he, too, for different reasons, was a fist of nerve endings all firing at will.

They walked to the arena in silence.

The order of jumps was posted. To Frank, it looked like the kind of chopstick drawings Ian made on table napkins and called his "algebra." But he walked the course with Patrick, and noticed that everything that made him want to throw up his hands—a triple combination with a six-foot spread in the middle and what looked like a single canter stride for the horse between the three jumps, far short of the three given to test their mettle, and wildly short of the six strides a horse usually loped gathering up for a jump; and a simple single pole decorated with flowers that hid a three-foot-thick wall papered over with what was meant to look like cottage stone, sheer death on a cracker—seemed to calm Patrick. They then walked the jump-off course, which would determine the winner, four jumps in the fastest time. Frank left the arena with no idea where any of the jumps were at all. Patrick went back to claim Glory Bee from two stout stable hands who were holding her down with all their might; he gave Frank a nod and set about wiping down Glory Bee's flanks and neck before fitting her with the tiny close-contact saddle.

"There are still people she doesn't like," Patrick said. "She doesn't like a rough hand. She likes that little girl, though."

"The student jockey."

"Yeah. She's a solid girl."

"Good," said Frank. He gave Patrick a thumbs-up and left him to it.

There was, Frank noticed, an owners' box. But he'd left his credentials in the truck. He doubted if he could make it to the parking lot and back in time, and was scanning the bleachers for something he could climb to without murdering his leg, when someone said, "Frank Mercy?" Frank nearly jumped the five-foot height of one of the jumps obstacles himself, without benefit of a run-up.

The old man approaching him with his hand extended seemed familiar, in the way high school photos of movie stars suggest the current edition of the person.

Frank said, "Hello. I'm Frank, yes."

"I'm Stuart McCartney," the man said. He might as well have been Paul McCartney. "You're exactly like your dad. You don't remember, but your father trained my horse and coached me. Fiorello and I were on the United States team in 1980."

"You competed in the Olympics?"

"There weren't any. The United States boycotted the Olympics in 1980. Russians invaded Afghanistan . . ." And on the old man went, finally asking, "Did you come to just look on?"

"I have a horse in this."

"Which?"

"Her name is Glory Bee."

"Ah!" said Stuart McCartney. "That would be the tall black. The mare. She was going for a clear round until some half-wit kid in the stands popped a balloon. She kicked a pole down on the last jump."

No wonder Patrick got hammered, having tasted one bright bite of a miracle. Frank's phone pinged, twice, and then twice again. Finally, although he hated it when other people did this, he took the phone out, and, with an apologetic gesture, glanced at the screen. It read, *Pro doing well. Me, too. GB? XO C.* The next message said, *Dad, Dad, Daddy, Daddy, Daddy, Ian. He wanted to type this, love, Mom.*

Frank's throat tightened.

"Does your mother still own Tenacity?"

"Yes, she does." Surprising himself, he said, "With me."

"Are you going to sit here with the owners?"

Frank stood. Someone handed him a pale ale and a bottle of water. He drank both in three swallows. He wouldn't need his credential cards, at least. He could go through this torture without portfolio.

At her draw, Glory Bee entered the ring grapevining sideways like a dressage horse. Patrick patiently walked her once around in a tiny circle. She stood, twitching in every muscle. Patrick sat her with a magnificent stillness. Frank thought of people who considered jumping, even stadium events, a cruel torture, when horses would act much the same way if they were wild, fighting to outrun and best each other, in the nature of all herd animals. Frank put on his sunglasses and pulled his hat down low. If it wouldn't have drawn attention, he would have pulled his shirt over his head, too.

In two minutes and fourteen seconds, it was over. A pure round, clean as the sole of a bride's shoe. Glory Bee's hoof never came within six inches of a pole. He watched as Patrick thoughtfully stroked her neck. Most of the others who did a clear round slapped their horses in companionable exultation. Horses hated being slapped. They wanted the feeling along their necks they had as colts, when their mothers licked their necks.

His holy admiration for Patrick soothed Frank's own nerves finally and brought him straight down from all the places he'd been—with Claudia, and with Ian—to the feel of the rounded metal chair back under his hands, still hot enough to sear a scallop even though the owners' box was now in shadow.

Discreet lights came up.

The crew arranged the jumps, adding height to the critical few for the jump-off.

Five horses formed up.

Glory Bee went first. She went angelically, as though she were insubstantial instead of a creature that could kick down a garage with thirty minutes of concentrated hysteria. With each loft, Patrick lay on her neck, unmoving, as though he were painted on her. Other riders of ordinary size plumped into their seats as the horse plunged on landing. Patrick's muscles were apparently much like split oak, because you could see sunlight between his ass and the saddle even when Glory Bee cantered. With a start, Frank realized Glory Bee wore no martingale on her bridle, no strap to hold her head loosely, but down. If she threw her head up, she would break Patrick's nose or worse. The sweltering crowd roused itself, waving programs and straw hats to cheer her. Patrick touched the brim of his cap, so quickly it was almost unnoticeable. Frank thought, Classy, Patrick. The other riders, all men, favored each other with stoic, military nods.

The second horse knocked a pole off its sockets. The third did a beautiful clear round, but so slowly it looked as though the big gray Warmblood was running in surf, finishing an unimaginable six seconds behind Glory Bee's time.

The fourth horse was willful and fast, completing a clean round.

Glory Bee won by only half a second.

In tradition, Patrick would have ridden Glory Bee twice around, pumping the air. But he was off, on the ground, quietly, with his arms around her neck.

Frank wanted to cry. He wanted to clamber over the stadium wall and run to both of them. If she could repeat what she had done here, she was a century horse. Maybe even an Olympian. He cursed himself for a coward for not using his phone to video the jump-off. His mother would be amazed. Cedric would . . . Cedric.

"Did anyone catch that on video?" he asked. One man waved at Frank. "That's my horse. Do you think you could send it to 608-555-5568?"

Frank wrote the number down on a trampled program and passed it to the man. He then smoothed the remainder of the dusty program over his knee.

Glory Bee. Tenacity Farms. Spring Green, Wisconsin.

If Frank had a regret, it was only for Patrick. Like the old man, his Olympics might end here. Patrick beamed up at Frank, a broad parade wave. It was too unfair. And yet Patrick had only begun. He would have his own mount in the future, if he chose to go that way. Frank thought of what Cedric would say: horse and rider had scope, the brew of natural talent, physical capability, a horse's conformation and spirit in one. A small word that encompassed so much.

Not unlike the word *love*.

Claudia had her horse.

FOURTEEN

HOLDING A COUPLE of green glow sticks, Ian was dancing around in the driveway, with Sally the dog leaping beside him, when Frank pulled in. It was after nine o'clock. What was Ian doing up? And yet, when he saw Ian, the surface tension Frank had not realized was right across his chest burst and he relaxed back into his own, his safe world. Swinging himself out of the truck, swinging Ian high in the air, Frank said, "Guess what, you little kid?"

"Guess what you brought me?"

Frank had brought him a full formal equestrian outfit in his size—or what Frank hoped was his size—and a big sitting pillow in the shape of a black horse with a blue ribbon sewn around its neck, something Ian could loll upon while watching his fish, at least forty of whom had names—from "Grace Amazing" to "Feller" to "Pimple."

On their way out to meet friends for a midnight film-fest movie, Eden and Marty came down the steps, Marty delicately escorting his bride.

Frank tried again. "Guess what happened."

Eden said, "What? Something bad? Where's Claudia?"

Frank explained about Prospero's foot. Marty said, "She's out of it, then. This whole dream Dr. Campo had is kaput."

"Maybe not," Frank said, and watched with a pang as Patrick unloaded Glory Bee and stalked away to the barn. "You won't believe this, but Glory Bee won it. She won it all!"

"Frank!" Eden breathed. "You trained a champion."

"*Patrick* trained a champion. It could be only the one time, too, of course. She might never equal this ride. But Glory Bee looked great."

Marty said suddenly, "But . . . you want Claudia to ride Glory Bee. Why?"

Where had this come from? Marty stared at Frank. He was good at subtext.

Frank said, "That's her dream. You said so yourself. It's her last chance, and Pat's what, twenty-two? He's got a whole career ahead of him, here or in Australia."

Eden said, "Pat's the man without a country."

"It's hard, though," Marty said. "Pat did the work. He should ride the horse."

"Pat is good," said Ian. "And don't forget, I should have my present?"

Eden gave Frank a congratulatory smooch, and they got into their car. As they left, Eden called to him. "Beware, Frank. There be dragons in there. I don't know if Mr. Peabody"—she nodded at Ian—"gave her a hard time this weekend. But she hasn't said two words since yesterday."

Frank came into the kitchen. "Mom, Glory Bee won the Mistingay. How do you like that?"

Hope's silence was as loud as a diatribe. She sat at the table, which, except for her full pot of coffee and her cup, was immaculate of so much as a pencil, plate, or piece of paper. This was upper-echelon consternation, possibly fury. With the same set of emotions across his gullet, Frank's father would have blown himself out by now, with a staccato of *what-the, in-the-name-of, what-the-hell-were-you* . . . that always used to remind Frank of the old-time actor Eddie Albert. This was the way Hope had behaved when eighteen-year-old Frank, the son of a widow, bragged with foolish bravado about having achieved the highest possible score on the police academy qualifying test.

Frank finally said, "You seem out of sorts. To say the least."

Hope finished her cup of coffee and poured another. Frank had no idea how his mother didn't spend her whole night cleaning the house in the dark, her eyes as wide as a lemur. Finally, she said, "Ian could have been killed today."

"Did he get in another accident, Mom? Was it bad? He looked okay just now . . ."

"The reason he's not in bed is because I just haven't had the strength to put him to bed. I've just been able to sit here. I can't believe that I saw what I saw, and how much it frightened me. So I've just been sitting here."

Frank sat down, and got up again, filling his glass from the tap, abruptly so thirsty it seemed his body had forgotten to inform him of the half marathon he'd just hobbled. The dream voice whined, *I'm tired of this. This is so boring!* Though he'd learned to ignore the voice, which he thought of as Ian's other voice, Frank wondered if Ian was unbeknownst either a medium or a ventriloquist . . . or if Frank was finally and emphatically experiencing aural hallucinations under stress.

"What happened, Mom?"

"He could have been killed, but that's really not factual. He should have been killed and anyone else might have been killed. I know Ian isn't invulnerable, Frank. He gets sore throats. He steps on nails—"

"What happened?"

They had been at a McDonald's.

"Don't tell my dad we ate here," Ian urged Hope.

"You're not supposed to tell *me*. Your dad eats anything!"

Ian was rapturously consuming two number fours, and Hope a plain cheeseburger with black coffee. She remembered the appetite of a kid whose ankles seemed more substantial than his calves, a pallor that nearly scattered light, the clusters of paprika freckles over the bridge of his nose and cheeks the only evidence that this child, who spent all day outside, ever saw the sun. It was then that Hope became aware of two men hassling each other in the way men will, in a booth at the back of the restaurant. She turned half toward them, not wanting them to notice her staring, but to see if she knew either one of them, since half the young men (and not-so-young men and women) in town had writhed or skated through their term-paper research in Mrs. Mercy's library.

She didn't recognize either of these two at first.

They were farmers or construction workers, with hands rough-dried as stumps, past the point that immersion in a bucket of hand lotion could ever have silkened them. Between them sat a woman who was no more than twenty-five. Hope knew that it was uncharitable and unworthy of her, but she had a certain reaction to the appearance of a woman like this: the girl had dyed her hair to the texture and color of dried grass, presumably to effect an improvement. Unable to stop herself, Hope wondered what they thought when they consulted their mirrors every morning. Were they happy? Did they think, Now, that's the look I was going for? How could any previous hair have been less attractive? Hope colored her own hair expensively, with a few strands of its original brown through the sides and back, and attractive silvering waves around her face, neither denying age nor permitting it liberties. When she saw girls like this girl, she felt the way she had about teachers at school who spent six hundred dollars on leather boots but didn't get their teeth straightened.

Frank had, by this time, consumed four glasses of water, and thought he might go mad if his mother didn't get to the point. It was a trait he could have forgiven had it been a sign of the meandering discursiveness of age; but Hope had been like this all her life. Much as she admired writers of lean prose, she had never been able to tell a story in anything but the most upholstered fashion. She was the Mozart of anecdotes.

The two men seemed at first to be engaging in some kind of rough-cut verbal horseplay, but then, and fast, it turned ugly. Soon one, then the other, was on his feet, and the girl with ruined hair eventually began to remonstrate with both of them to cut it out, get over it, that it was ancient history, just finish eating.

The first clear sentence Hope heard was, "I will if that rancid sonofabitch admits he did it. But he ain't never admitted he did it. He keeps saying it happened, like it was some kind of goddamn lunar eclipse or something . . ."

"Which is why if I'd done it, I'd have said I did it. Why wouldn't I? What am I scared of, you?"

"You fucking ought to be scared of me, you done it."

"Listen, Larry, if I did do it, I'm so absolutely not at all scared of you that I'd do it again right now. But I didn't do it."

And then the guy Hope later called the Astronomer got up and threw a cup of ice in the face of the man who hadn't done whatever it was, and that guy leaped to his feet and shoved the Astronomer, the girl now actively with her hands on both of them, pushing them apart as they slapped her hands away.

"Look," Ian said. "I have this whole fries. No ketchup."

"There's kids in here!" called a fat young man with the crisp white shirt that identified him as some sort of management. He put both hands on the counter and hoisted himself halfway over. "You either sit down or get out of my store!"

For a moment, it looked as though both the Astronomer and Larry would forgive their mutual grievance and whale on the graduate of McDonald's University, but the chubby young man said, "You take one step at me, and I'm calling the cops. A.J., I don't care if you got a hundred brothers and all of them are seven feet tall. I will do it."

While the Astronomer was eyeballing the manager, Larry threw a punch. It wasn't a hard blow, but it connected with the Astronomer's substantial gut and he whirled and backhanded Larry across the jaw.

"You asshole coward, can't get a woman on your own."

"You couldn't do nothing with her if you had her, your pecker ain't long enough to poke past that belly. Lot of Bud in there, ain't no running back no more, are you?"

"Why don't you say that again while I'm looking right at you instead of behind my back?" The Astronomer grabbed a fistful of Larry's shirt and pushed him hard against a stack of trays, which flew out over the floor like a stack of cards, and the manager yelled, "Okay, I'm doing it now! I'm calling the cops."

Half dragged, half pushed by the girl, the two battlers went outside to the parking lot, and, as Hope finally got up to get a little paper cup filled with ketchup for Ian, she noticed that the thirty or forty patrons were beginning to gather at the windows to see what they could see.

"A. J. McCarron never had any sense, and what he had, the war beat it out of him. I don't care if they're separated and she's doing a lap dance, she's still another man's wife, and if that's not how they do it in Madison, that's how they do it here."

A woman murmured, "She doesn't exactly look like she's worth going to jail for."

"She did once. She had some drugs back a while ago, but that girl was a cheerleader for the Badgers. College girl. The whole thing."

"You think they'll cool off now," the woman said. It wasn't a question.

"Look! Hell no!" the man shouted, and Hope peered out the floor-to-ceiling windows. Unbelievably, the two men were about to kill each other in the parking lot, in front of the restaurant patrons and ten ladies in pedicure flip-flops who'd come out of the nail salon next door. From each of their company trucks, each guy grabbed a weapon. Larry took the first swipe, with an eighteen-pound hammer, aiming straight for the Astronomer's head. He may not have been a running back anymore, but his reflexes were intact; he hopped up on the running board of his truck and came at Larry with something that looked to Hope like an ice ax. He threw that, then he grabbed up a huge scythe that glimmered evilly in the sun.

He swung, and got Larry in the elbow with the flat of the scythe. Two of the pedi-women opened the door. "Call the cops!" one of them shrieked.

Larry struck back, landing a hard blow on the other man's shoulder with the hammer. Hope heard the injured man shriek. The girl who had been with them leaped around them like a terrier.

"That's enough!" the girl screamed. "That's enough!"

But the Astronomer kept coming, slashing at Larry, who jumped back a few inches every time the blade flickered closer. "You messed with the wrong man this time, you lowlife piece of shit. Next time she comes to see you, it'll be in the ICU!" He took the hammer in two hands and raised it over his head.

One of the older women at the windows shouted, "Where are the police? The police station is two blocks from here! And oh my God, one of them has a little kid with him."

Hope carried the ketchup back to the table, hoping Ian's own curiosity wouldn't get the best of him. Other kids were standing on the molded plastic seats along the widows, and a couple, to her horror, were yelling, "Cut him! Cut him!" She was counting on Ian's love for forbidden fries to keep him cemented to his seat.

He wasn't in his seat.

Hope glanced at the crowd around the windows. Ian wasn't with them.

She cried out, "Ian!" No one even glanced her way. She screamed, "Ian! *Ian!*"

She did not put two and two together, she told Frank.

She ran toward the bathroom, where Ian loved to go, in any public place, to soak paper towels, make them into balls, and try to stick them on the ceiling. Then the same woman who'd asked at large for the police said, "The guy with the hammer just almost hit that little kid!"

"Dear God! That little kid is trying to grab that sword!"

And there was Ian.

He was almost to the space between the two men, who were thrashing furiously, with fists and tools, their faces empurpled with rage and new bruises, blood coursing freely from a wound on the forehead of the man who was not Larry. One good blow and one of those guys would be dead. Hope's skin tightened and she opened her mouth to stop this, to shout, to shout and make this stop, but she couldn't speak and she couldn't move. She watched her dream self burst through the doors, throwing her own body between the combatants, but all she did in reality was drop the ketchup and take a single, unsteady step.

Ian's back was to her.

She could not see Ian's mouth moving, or his hands moving.

She could see only those big war weapons splitting the air.

Ian reached up and touched Larry. Larry swung—and then, needing all his body weight to interrupt the descent of the big hammer—stopped it two inches from Ian's head.

"I'm going to faint," the manager said. "I have to sit down."

Ian swung his hands, rocking them, back and forth.

"What's he doing?" one of the pedi-women asked.

"It's some kind of talking. He's deaf and he's talking to them. My daughter-in-law can do that talk."

"He stopped them. That child . . ."

"No, it's one of their own kids, is all," a male spectator said firmly.

Larry burst into tears and dropped to his knees on the pavement next to Ian, clutching Ian in his arms. "I'm so sorry!" he called out.

The other man bent down, too, heaving for breath, his hands on his thighs. When he got his breath, the Astronomer tossed his ax and scythe into the back of his truck and smiled at Ian, reaching past him to give Larry the Hammer sort of a good-natured clap on the shoulder. The lethal boil went flat, stopped as if the stop button on a projector was pressed.

"Whose kid is this?" Larry yelled.

"It's not their kid!" the manager said. "Is he from TV or something?"

Hope had finally forced her feet to move.

"That's my grandson!" she called, her voice a cackle of breath. "Leave him alone."

"He's fine, ma'am," the Astronomer said. "There, kiddo. Go on by your granny. You probably scared her coming out here. My buddy and me, we were just being pigheaded. Didn't come to nothing. I better get back to work. Now Dudley Do-Right in there is calling the police?"

"He fainted! But I'll call the police myself! You could have killed my grandson. You both deserve to be arrested." Hope, Frank knew, rarely lost her composure; it was her secret weapon, and the gale force of her agitation had shocked even her. Closer now, she studied the man they'd called Larry, who'd gotten to his feet. "You're Luke Cerniak. You're Emily's son."

"Yes, Mrs. Mercy." For some reason, the young man removed his cap and held it in his two hands. "I'm sorry."

"You were in honors classes! You went to college!"

"It's my company," the man said, pointing to the name Cerniak & Sons Custom Cement on the truck. "I do well."

"Then what's the meaning of this? And why were they calling you Larry?"

"I changed my name. 'Luke' sounded too much like an old man."

Hope said, "You fool." Larry wiped his eyes.

Hope said to Frank, "I felt like Alice in Wonderland. I had no idea what was going on. I just grabbed Ian's hand and got in the car and I passed the police car coming the other way, and I'm sure fifty people recognized me and saw what happened."

"They didn't understand what happened," Frank said.

"They did. They said the words. 'That little kid stopped it.' They said he was from TV."

"No, they remember the fight," Frank said. "They remember the drama." He hoped this was true. He *hoped*. He knew it was not. His scalp tightened. Who were the guys in the suits? Who sent the fat horse thief to take pictures? What would happen if Channel 3 Eye on Wisconsin pulled up the drive? If Katie or Terry or Mike or Matt just wanted to let people know about a little boy making a big impression, and it went national, and then viral . . . That pilot was from Wisconsin. Frank imagined him looking up from his Wisconsin wife, for Frank imagined that all transoceanic pilots had insane sex lives, and saying, "I know that little kid. He talked to the animals!" Sweat rolled down Frank's cheek.

Hope refilled her cup. Ian ran past with Sally, up the stairs to his room. "Go to bed, Ian," Hope and Frank called, halfheartedly. A few minutes later, Ian, now wearing a cape made from a bath towel, ran down the stairs and out the door again.

Hope said, "He's all right. He can go to bed later. So, Frank, it isn't just getting people to buy him candy. What if that had been Camp David, Frank? What if those two guys had been Mahmoud Abbas and Binyamin Netanyahu . . ."

"Are those guys still . . . ?"

"Frank, that's not the point. What if it had been the leader of South Korea and North Korea, whoever they are, now or in the future, or any generals in Somalia, and Ian could tell them to be good? What will people want from him in the future? What do they already want from him?"

Frank said, "I think about it all the time. I keep coming back to how it would be okay, somehow. He wouldn't have been given this if—"

"Oh, Frank, that's just stupid. There are violin prodigies who end up in mental institutions! Maybe if he had . . . bodyguards and was . . . a Rhodes Scholar. He's not even four! He weighs about as much as the dog!"

Thoughts of Claudia's muscled legs gathering him to her, of Glory Bee's strong legs bunching before the water jump, Claudia's sweetness, Glory Bee's stunning prowess, Patrick's stoic skill, the little jockey Patrick fancied—all those thoughts swirled in Frank's mind, like ingredients in a hot dish first flamed then peppered. One spoonful would be too much. He had to sleep first. Hailing Ian, Frank stumbled upstairs, leaving the trophy on the table, falling on the bed thinking of all the ablutions he had neglected.

The third-to-last thought he had before he dropped out of consciousness, aware of a button pressing into his cheek but too spent even to adjust so that he would not have a bruise in the morning, was of Claudia.

Where was she now?

What was she to him now?

Frank decided to let Claudia figure that out.

The next-to-last thought he had was about the Ian effect on the rumble in the McDonald's parking lot. If it meant what Hope thought it meant—global speculations that Frank had acknowledged long ago—he would have to make a plan. He would have to do what men do, to gather up the things that were his and make them safe, in a fortress with only one way in, and Frank standing guard.

They used to play cards on Friday nights when he was a cop. It was serious. No one dared miss short of a funeral, an immediate-family funeral. No Texas Hold 'Em either. Real poker. He remembered the crumpled look on the face of an Italian guy who felt sure that he had the cards, but *knew* for certain that he had a fierce Italian wife. *All in*, the guy would say, his face scaffolded between hope and despair.

Hope had identified herself as Ian's grandmother. She was all in. Frank was all in.

Then there might need to be a fortress. The last thought he had was of the rough breeding farm in the Yorkshire hills that he had never seen.

FIFTEEN

"THAT'S A VERY good picture," Claudia said. "That picture really looks like a man. Most guys your age just draw a stick figure with hands that are too big, but your guy has a neck, and look how his neck goes right into his shoulders and his arms are the right length compared to his body."

Claudia spent more time at the farm. It seemed entirely natural. Every time she talked with Ian, Frank was more impressed by the way she did it. Calling a preschool child a "guy" automatically inducted him into the paradise of men. She didn't stop with "Good job!" but explained in specific ways to Ian what was remarkable about his drawing (and it was remarkable). Although Ian seemed largely indifferent to a number concept of any kind, his facility with drawing and reading was fierce for his age. Claudia went on: "So now I'm curious. Who is that?"

Ian flicked an eyelid, a wink or a grimace, but didn't look up. He went on drawing, carefully fitting out his man with boots that hit just below the knee, then tooled the leather with triangles. He said nothing, but reached for a darker brown crayon. This also happened every time Claudia sat with him, now a total of four times.

"Who's that?" Claudia asked again. "Is that your dad?" After he painstakingly colored in the darker brown of the boot that framed the lighter diamonds, Ian nodded. "Is that your dad now or your dad who was your father before the big storm?" Ian indicated Frank, who was sitting at the

194

kitchen table, ostensibly reading a newspaper and drinking a cup of coffee, but actually watching. "What's he doing?"

"He's looking at Grandma. You can't see her, but she's outside the barn putting Bobbie Champion on the pony cart."

"Okay. Why isn't Dad helping her?"

Ian laughed. "Grandma says he makes her be like an old lady."

"Well, Dad probably just likes to do things for her."

Ian shrugged and then smiled.

"I know you're happy. Do you think about your dad from before? Or your brother? It's okay to think about them, even if it doesn't make you happy."

Ian shrugged. Visibly, he drew away from Claudia, not in a way that could be measured in inches, but as though he had opened a book he now hastily closed. Claudia had explained to Frank that children's grief behavior was different. She described it as "taking bites." Little children, who didn't have the large vocabulary necessary for ritual mourning, were sad in small "bites," but then rushed away to play. For this reason, people used to believe that children's natural resiliency healed them sooner. Anything but, Claudia said. Kids just didn't always look the way we think people look when they've suffered a tremendous loss.

"It's good that Dad now knew him, and he knew your mom, too."

Ian shook his head, glancing at Frank. "He did not know my dad before. Only bad guys knew my dad before."

"He did know your dad, not very long."

"When we lived in Etry Castle?" Ian said. "My dad now didn't come there. They would kill him if he came there." Listening, Frank was appalled—not only at how close Claudia was tailgating the truth, but at the cold calm with which Ian described the certainty of mayhem as an ordinary part of his little life.

"Were they bad guys like in cartoons?" Claudia smiled. "With robber masks?"

"No," said Ian. "They wore normal clothes, but they were . . ." He rapped on the table three times. "Real. Bad. Guys. Like the ones who came to our house. " Ian turned one of his hands into a pistol and fired. "My brother said he saw them where he is."

"Your brother? Your brother . . . we think your brother was so hurt in the storm that he died, Ian. All of us are sad about that. Where was he this other time?"

"I mean, today."

"Oh, well, okay." She paused. "I like to pretend I'm not sad sometimes when I really am. You might be really sad about your brother."

Claudia shifted, and began to draw her own picture. From the table, Frank saw a woman take shape, a drawing not as good, really, as Ian's. "This is my mother. My mother died, and I miss her."

"I'm sorry she died," Ian said suddenly. This was the most conversation he'd had with Claudia since he'd asked for the plastic horses at Eden's wedding. "What died her?"

"She had strep throat, a bad sore throat, and that is the kind of disease that most people get better from, but she did not get better because she didn't know that she had it so very badly as she did. This was seven years ago, and I was almost grown up, but I was very, very sad and so were my sisters."

"What are their names?"

"Rebecca and Miranda."

"What was your mother's name?"

"Mary Ann."

"I had a dad who died like your mother. Well, Collie had him. I don't remember him."

Ian drew a square-faced boy with a mop of blond hair. Claudia asked, "Is that your brother?"

Ian nodded at the paper. Then he looked up at Claudia with a half smile and an arched eyebrow that said plainly, This conversation is over.

Claudia stood up and poured herself a cup of coffee, lightly kissing Frank on the side of the head, which made Frank want to pull her down on his lap or else slap her away the way Glory Bee slapped a fly with her tail. It wasn't as though Natalie had even been Ian's mother: still, every time Claudia made some perfectly ordinary display of affection in Ian's presence, Frank felt as though he was cheating not only on Natalie, but on the kid. What would a psychiatrist say? And what would a psychiatrist say about Frank's web of lies, Claudia asking if Frank didn't have any wedding pictures with Ian's real parents in them, Frank saying those were all lost in the flood, Claudia saying couldn't Brian Donovan get hold of some of them, Frank saying he didn't like to impose on Brian's grief . . .

"Frank, what's going on? You knew Ian's family. What does he mean?"

Desperately, Frank shrugged, the universal gesture that was supposed to mean, *Kids? Who knows?* He displaced another shovel load of lies. The only person to whom he couldn't lie was Ian.

"She's your girlfriend," Ian said of Claudia.

"Yes, but we're not married."

"I know that."

"And we're not getting married."

"Okay. For sure?"

"I don't know," Frank said helplessly. "It doesn't have anything to do with you being here, with me and Grandma. Or your room or anything." After weeks of negotiation, Ian had agreed to sleep in his own bed, although he would not *go* to sleep in his own bed unless Frank or Hope read four books. One night, exhausted, Frank got fed up and read three, and Ian didn't protest. But at six the next morning, when Frank got up to see to the horses, he looked in on Ian, who was wide-awake in his bed, the stack of books still beside him. Wordlessly, the child got up with Frank, straightened his blanket, put on his boots, drank the milk with a splash of coffee and three spoons of sugar he had every morning, and followed Frank outside. Frank knew that Ian had not gone to sleep, and Ian knew that Frank knew.

Ian said now, "Why would Claudia want my room?"

"That's what I'm saying. Don't be afraid of that."

"I'm not afraid."

Of course she didn't want his room. Frank's hands were big and his cheeks swollen hot, a great idiot staring down at an attorney less than forty inches tall.

Ian left, but then returned.

"Would you leave?" he asked. "For her?"

Frank had to physically restrain himself from clutching at Ian.

"I would never leave," Frank said. "For anyone."

Ian vanished.

It was only a question. Ian, thankfully, now had friends, and no longer felt the need to be Frank's shadow, at least all the time. He went bowling—bowling was his passion—and on what Frank learned to call playdates, the modern equivalent of what Frank used to call "playing over." His favorite friends were unregenerate hellions, Henry, Oliver, and Abe, triplets whose forty-six-year-old mother had the look of someone who'd just regained consciousness and didn't remember the nature of her injuries. She wore clothing even Frank knew was expensive, but so haphazardly that she looked like a scarecrow.

One Saturday, she dropped Ian off—while Oliver, Henry, and Abe howled like coonhounds from the backseat of their big SUV.

"Thanks for having him," Frank said. He'd been building new stalls and was filthy. "I'm sorry. I must stink."

"You're fine," the woman said seriously. "You know, Frank, Ian is unusual."

Frank froze.

"My boys are what you would call incorrigible. I say this as a loving mother. There are days that I think Abe will hit Oliver and actually disable him. I am no match for them. But when they're around Ian, they settle down. They play board games they've never touched instead of breaking the furniture over each other's backs. They wash their hands after they use the toilet. They're nice. What do you feed him? Do you want to board him out?"

Frank felt saliva at the corners of his lips. Jesus Christ, he was drooling. As though he were folding a piece of linty gum he found in his pocket, he made a show of removing his striped glove, glancing down to unwrap the gum, and composing his face. "Oh, his mom taught him manners," Frank said.

"It's more than that. He's like . . . a good influence."

Frank couldn't get Ian into the house fast enough. Oliver and Henry were throwing empty soda-pop cans out of the car windows.

It was full summer then, but for a brief period the heat suddenly withdrew, a cloth whisked away from a table. Everyone took a long breath. That cool time was a foretaste of fall. Wisconsin was like a young woman with gray hair at her temples; you never got a chance to forget that winter was only briefly on hiatus.

Claudia had put in her bid and been accepted to Hiram Jacoby's legendary weeklong clinic in northern Kentucky—a dozen riders and "their pets," as Jacoby put it, including some promising newcomers and some veterans like Claudia. Among these high-point scorers were certainly at least some of the United States Equestrian Team members-to-be, and the team for the summer Olympics in Sydney. Jacoby traditionally arranged a sit-down with each of the riders to give counsel on the projected goals and plans. Jacoby had known Frank's father, and was interested in Claudia's protégée status at Tenacity. If Claudia couldn't sit Glory Bee like paint on a rocking horse—as Patrick had—she was more willing than Patrick to take chances. Frank knew that she would learn more from Hiram in a week than she would from him in a year.

Patrick was now fully on board with Claudia's dream, and spoke of returning to England the following summer to sort out his life before attempting to become a permanent resident of the United States. After that, he would want to raise and train his own colt—preferably one Glory Bee threw after her retirement in a few years. As was only right, he had taken over coaching Claudia on Glory Bee, and was making good money because of it. Frank suspected that Patrick would pay a visit to the jockey school in Indiana while Claudia was at the clinic. Frank might have welcomed the chance to see Hiram Jacoby, whom he hadn't met since he was a child traveling with his father.

Frank welcomed the break. He needed their absence to think, and he was not a fast thinker.

He knew perfectly well how to name his feelings for Claudia, and had there been no Natalie, or, perhaps especially, no Ian, Frank might have known what to do with them. But there had been a Natalie. Frank had wanted all the things Claudia now seemed to want with him, but he had wanted them with Natalie. Claudia wanted children, her career as a teacher and a counselor, and a stable home life that would not, after this period, include competitive jumpers. She was certainly in love, and he supposed he was as well, his experience of love being limited to once and Ian. Frank didn't know if he could want those things again.

Really, though, what *did* love mean? He didn't want to be away from Claudia. They argued more than they agreed and they could argue about anything. Last night, it had been Dickens: Claudia had grown up on his stories and called him the great reformer, who would never let fat complacent Brits forget that the poor were always with them. Frank countered that if Dickens wasn't really a racist, he certainly was a cultural chauvinist.

"He was on the side of everyone in theory," Frank said. "In real life, he didn't like anyone who didn't look like him."

"He thought everyone could reach higher than his rank in life."

"He thought the best thing that could happen to any fuzzy-wuzzy was to go through some kind of tea strainer until he at least looked like an English gentleman, or sounded like one."

"What's a fuzzy-wuzzy?" Claudia asked.

"A person who wasn't European living in England. Someone from Southeast Asia. A black person. And Fagin . . . well, kids in eighth grade know about the 'Jew' in *Oliver Twist* . . ."

"Fuzzy-wuzzy? Who's a racist?"

"You mean me?" Frank said. "Give me a break. I was a cop."

"Cops are some of the most virulent racists and I sure don't see many people of color in your life," she said, biting off the words.

"Well, I just met a black woman in Madison I'm interested in dating," Frank said. "I'm sure that psychiatrist school is loaded with people of color. Lots of them are psychiatrists." Claudia lobbed her shoe at his head. "Anyway, you're patronizing me. You're pretending to be interested in British literature. Whereas I would never pretend to be interested in crazy people." He repented that because Claudia had on the elbow-length rubber gloves she used to apply poultices to Pro's back legs. The next thing she threw, with good aim, was a turd.

They had fun. Not in the same one-of-the-guys way he and Natalie had . . . but they had fun. The sex they had still astonished him. His cock stirred if Claudia so much as reached inside her shirt to delicately untwist a bra strap. He came to visit her during the day at the lakeside condo in Madison that was basically one big room with four walls of windows framing an enthralling lake view, four strips of bookshelves crammed both horizontally and vertically, and a gigantic bed with about twelve pillows. Claudia had sex like she rode, as though this would be the last time and she didn't care if it killed her. When she finally let him put his mouth on her, she gently taught him to flatten his tongue to give her the best pleasure. She loved sitting atop him, and hated doing it with him behind her, and told him it felt lousy to women. Grown people, he and Claudia, lay on a blanket in the back of his truck, parked on the wooden bridge over Sandman Creek. Being naked outside was like being rich, Claudia said, sounding just like Natalie. He loved her mind, under her blond cap of feathery hair, as much as her body. Her head was filled with antic recipes for discussion, for discourse, for dinner. He thought of her hands—her strong and spatulate hands that seemed grafted onto her slight self from the model of an Italian peasant woman—on Glory Bee's shining neck, on Ian's milky, knobbly spine, on Frank's own neck with its humiliating farmer's tan, and he felt safer every day.

At his house, Claudia fell easily into a routine of asking Hope to teach her things, pitching in when Hope was armed with an immersion blender the size of a small rifle, "putting up" tomatoes, tomato soup, tomato salsa, tomato relish, tomato sauce—a fetish from her newlywed days and no longer any kind of economic necessity. Claudia said the jewelly jars of produce made her feel satisfied in the same way riding did—a job of substance and shape. Though Hope was ironic about almost everyone, and well aware that, as Natalie had said, Frank had a "crush" on his mother and a wise woman would honor that, she was still not immune to Claudia's robust cheer, at right angles from what one might expect of a professor of psychiatry. And Ian liked her. He liked everyone, but he liked Claudia more. They had private jokes; he called her "Cloudy." She called him "Eeny."

"You're different," Eden said to her brother. "You just smiled."

"I smile all the time."

"No," she said. "You don't."

Frank smiled again. "You look healthy, too, Eden. Well fed. Your wedding dress wouldn't fit you now."

"But I'm still fit," Eden said, slugging Frank hard. "And you can't hit me back because of my delicate condition."

Like some vaudeville character, missing only an oily mustache, Frank's new brother-in-law took this as a cue to sidle up to Frank and ask, "So, with Claudia Campo. Is it a match? You're not getting any younger, Frank. Psychological studies show that guys who were happily married get remarried right away. I'm only saying."

"If I were going to do anything, I would be sure to rely on psychological studies before I did it, Marty. I can't date a doctor anyhow. I only finished a year of college and that in night school. She wouldn't have me."

"Maybe she likes those rustic types who aren't cerebral."

"I'll introduce her to some, then. We're friends, and she's good to Ian," Frank said to Marty. "Her dreams are about the horses."

This wasn't inaccurate. Claudia was hardly the type to follow Frank around with stars in her eyes and sighs on her lips. She was nearly always busy. Be careful what you wish for, Frank thought, for you will surely get it. Although on sabbatical, Claudia seemed to have a hundred friends who needed tending and a zest for daylong events with names like "Digging Your Grave with Your Teeth: The Link between Childhood Obesity and Factitious Disorder" and "Depersonalization Disorder: Out of Body Politics." She trucked Prospero to therapy every week in Madison so he could swim in a pool half the size of a football stadium, and joined her friends for weekends in Chicago and New York, to shop and go to the theater. Why wasn't she more obsessed with him? Frank wondered. The solace was his time alone with Ian. When Claudia wasn't around, Frank didn't always insist that Ian patter off to his bed. He pulled Ian's compact furnace of a body close to him, and when he wakened, Ian had not moved.

Finally, Claudia left for Kentucky, trailering Glory Bee, with Patrick riding shotgun. Frank didn't hear from her, and worried. Old acquaintance aside, Jacoby wouldn't be sentimental when it came to fielding a national team. But when Claudia hopped out of the truck, she was lit from within. Jacoby as much as promised he would try to throw his word behind her team hopes—which would mean her leaving eventually, to go to train with the rest, with a *real* coach. As much as he'd hoped for this moment, Frank was surprised that he was aggrieved. Gravely, Claudia thanked Ian for looking after Prospero. She said there was a surprise for him in the truck.

It was his own saddle, the duty that Frank had neglected for months. Point, Claudia.

Inelegantly, he asked, "Who made it? Elves?"

"There were a few there that Mr. Jacoby already had," Claudia told Frank. "I bought one."

"It probably won't fit," Frank said, hating himself.

"You can try it on Saratoga," Claudia said. "Eden's horse."

"No. I want to ride Glory Bee," Ian said.

"Glory Bee's working with me now on being a horse, a great show jumper. You can ride her in a few years."

"*Years?*"

"And we can get you a horse of your own," Frank said. So there. A horse was better than a saddle any day. They went criminally cheap at the auction in Baraboo. A college girl would sell a horse like used luggage, simply because she'd graduated. A pretty little horse couldn't pull a plow, and often, those horses went unsold, to a heartbreaking fate.

"When can we get this horse? Tonight?" Ian said. He was sitting on the saddle in the grass with his feet angled out to each side.

"Pretty soon," Frank said. "I can go to the auction in a couple of weeks."

"*A couple of weeks?*"

"What do you want, Ian? Not everything happens in one day."

"A horse now," Ian said. "I have a saddle! You have horses. I need my own horse."

Frank sighed. "How about lunch first?"

They went in, and Ian ate his peanut-butter-and-potato-chips on toast, with carrot sticks. Frank wanted a nap when coffee failed to restore him. So Claudia asked Ian if he'd like to draw. Frank didn't mistake the slight hitch of tension. He felt it himself. He wanted to complain, What, *now*? Even Ian knew that drawing was code for Claudia's gentle brand of therapy.

"I'm only drawing one picture," he said.

"One is good. What is it? What's it going to be?"

"A boa."

"A snake?"

"No, the kind you wear. I want to get one," said Ian. Frank could not suppress his laughter: Marty routinely insisted that Ian was headed for a career in musical theater. "No, I changed my mind," Ian said then. "I'm going to draw where I lived before." Frank stood at the sink, unable to move.

"Where did you live?"

"Etry Castle," Ian said quietly, coloring furiously, the green thickness of waxy crayon darker and darker, like slime in a floor drain. "I told you five times."

"Etry *Castle*? Wow," Claudia said, warning Frank with her eyes not to react. "Are you sure you can draw that?"

Ian shook his head. "I can, but decided I don't really want to draw it after all."

"Is your mother still there?"

"Nope."

"Where is she?"

"She's dead, too. Like your mom."

Ian went back to drawing big circles filled in with hexagons of color, like kaleidoscopes or stained-glass windows. Frank struggled to control his breathing. After a while, Claudia said, "I'm sorry that your mother died. What, ah, died her?"

"Some guys. Some bad guys. She took some medicine that died her. I don't remember."

Frank took a long step, but at a warning look from Claudia went back to the sink and ran water into his coffee cup, then began to dispose of the grounds in the pot.

"What's this, Frank?" Claudia said, suddenly behind him, her voice no more than a breath. "His parents were Natalie's relatives. They died in the tsunami. What does he mean?"

"I have no idea," Frank told her. He found plates in the drainer that were already clean and began to rinse them, too. He really did have no idea, he consoled himself. Until he had to jerk his hand away, Frank didn't realize he'd been holding a plate under water so hot that his skin was red and beginning to puff up. "You know what you said about how kids deal with grief."

Claudia said nothing for so long Frank was sure that she'd walk out. Instead, she went back to Ian.

"And there's your brother!"

"Colin," Ian said.

"Who was in the car in the flood when Dad came?"

"Yes."

"Oh. Well, Colin went into the water. No one knows where Colin is. Do you think he got hurt? I think maybe he got hurt."

"Yes."

"Maybe Colin is even dead. I said that. It was a very bad flood."

Ian began to laugh. Frank's guts squeezed like wet towels. Why was he laughing, about the boy who had forsworn his own salvation to push Ian through the window, telling Frank that Ian was "important"?

"What's so funny, Eeny?" Claudia asked, and even her voice wobbled.

"Because he's not *dead*."

"How do you know?"

"Colin isn't *dead*. He would *say* if he was dead. My mom died. I had another dad and he died. I don't remember. My dad now is doing the dishes."

SIXTEEN

CLAUDIA CLAIMED THAT there was no way of knowing what a child meant when he said his parents were dead.

"He means his parents are dead," Frank said. They were huddled in the back of Pro's cushy recovery stall, just after Hope had left to drive Ian to school. It felt as though they were hiding from the headmaster. They spoke in whispers.

"He has no real understanding of their deaths . . ."

"He's almost four, Claudia. He's not a newborn."

"That's only forty-eight months old, Frank. Whatever happened to Ian happened at a good time for Ian. It's called the latency period, and it's a very stable time of life that starts maybe just about when you start school and ends at about puberty. You're not a baby, and you have deep feelings, but some people think that this is when a child is able to have a sort of amnesia about the earliest traumatic or evil memories. So we go nuts when we hear about somebody raping a two-year-old but for the two-year-old, it's actually easier to recover from sexual abuse and adapt to live a pretty normal life, if she gets the chance, because of being little." She paused. "Still . . . bad guys?" She regarded her nails. "Are you in trouble, Frank? Who were those men in the black car?"

"Claudia, I have no idea. Nobody like those guys ever came up this driveway before. Maybe I just overreacted."

"If you overreacted, why didn't you ever talk about it? You expected it."

"I don't know. Maybe I don't want to think anything's out of the ordinary. At least not until I have to. Claudia, let me tell you. I don't believe in ghosts. I don't believe in predicting the future. I probably don't believe in anything. Whatever I did believe in once, that probably hit the ground with the very first call I went out on, the three-year-old little girl her own father pushed off the fifth-floor balcony one sunny morning right after church. I remember driving up there with my partner Elena and this little girl was just on the grass like a doll, in her little yellow dress. No blood. Just like a little doll. The mom? The mom is upstairs crying with her arms around the dad and telling Elena it's a big misunderstanding, that he really loved his little girl, and that he was possessed, and did we really have to arrest him? If I did believe in the woo-woo, I'd be standing outside the 7-Eleven every Saturday night at ten minutes to twelve to buy my Powerball. Visions, faith healing, God. It's all the fucking Easter Bunny. But what Ian does, I can *see*. It's like the scientific method. Try it, test it, try it again. I'm not the first person who ever saw it." He told Claudia about the gladiators at McDonald's. "So if I'm not the first person, who else has? When he puts bad guys together with his mother and father, I think, What if somebody's looking for Ian? What if I interrupted certain plans? You think they'd be okay with that?"

"Let's try to be pragmatic. He's never said that anyone used—"

"Fuck pragmatic. I am being pragmatic. You tell me. What if somebody got hold of your Mrs. Madrigal? What if she started brokering peace treaties, like Hope said? Yeah, sure, the hope of the world, huh? But it wouldn't be. Tell me the profit in peace on earth and goodwill toward all men. I think Mrs. Madrigal was smart. If everybody knew about her, somebody would want to make money off her. And after somebody wanted to make money off her, somebody would want to stop her. What if what Ian *wanted* was the wrong thing?"

"That's a fair point. Not that I think Ian would ever want the wrong thing. But I'm surprised at it coming from you."

"Surprised? Why?"

"These were cousins of your wife. Cousins, right?" In his haste, Frank had tripped over his own lie, knocking over a pole. He bent to retie his boot, rationalizations snapping through his mind like the flip-books you thumbed to make moving images, little books he found in cereal boxes when he was a kid—somehow so much more magical than actual animation.

"Just . . . it was more . . . her brother who knew them. At least knew them well."

"But still, Ian is probably explaining this symbolically. Bad guys means something to him. The storm, maybe. He's not only a relative by marriage. You love Ian."

"I didn't know what a father's love really was, Claudia. When I agreed to adopt Ian, I didn't know the extent of how he was."

"Would it have stopped you?"

"No! But what I do know, from seeing them at their worst, is how people act, Claudia. Even people who would describe themselves as good parents . . . Take something that doesn't even matter. Fucking beauty pageants! Child abuse for a trophy some shill bought for a hundred bucks the gross. Ribbon that went for fifty cents a thousand. Maybe the family gets a check for a hundred bucks, for the five thousand they spent."

"You could say that about jumping horses. That's what I mean."

"You could say that, and half the time I do! But at least there's something going on there, some athleticism, some work-to-success ratio, something . . . anyway, that has nothing to do with it. I'm just going to have to talk to Ian about it. About why he thinks his mother was killed by bad guys. And about what he's feeling when he does what he does. And about how it's not a great idea for people to know."

Claudia said, "Or I will."

Patrick brought Glory Bee out of her stall and began to warm her up, and Claudia, who would be leaving midweek for an event in Saratoga, New York, was drawn away. Frank stood leaning against Prospero's neck, left alone with the vivid snapshot, never fully realized but ineradicable, of the older boy's face when he caught sight of the navy boat arriving, there in the car filling with brackish water. Even conjuring with the idea that Ian had some way of knowing that his brother had survived was, he would have agreed with Claudia, silly—no matter what gifts Ian had. Ian and . . . well, Colin, were not identical twins. The brother was older by at least three years, maybe four. Frank had sat up late scanning the Web for Etry Castle, Aintree Castle, Atterbury Castle, but Australia was short on castles, so Frank expanded his search. He found an Etry Castle, which looked like a glorified mansion on Lake Michigan, in Annet-sur-Marne, in France. There was no online description of the place—who had built it or why, who owned it now, or what function it fulfilled, domestic or ceremonial. Was it a park or a museum? A private home? Was it one of those places owned by some Asian or Eastern European billionaire whose own name was virtually unknown and whose wealth inhabited numbered bank accounts and bullion caches in neutral nations and island hermitages around the globe? Could Ian have been born in France? He had no trace of an accent except his lazy, flat Australian nasality that was beginning to fade. Some moneyed thug. That was the kind of man, or being (why could it not be a woman?) Frank imagined having an interest in Ian. He'd mentioned bad guys. It was paranoid in the extreme—the stuff of airport reading at its sleazy bubbling—to invest in a preschool child's worldview. But something about Ian's reluctance to give up the merest details of his life before the tsunami, as well as how tight-lipped he'd remained about the identity of the woman in the van, how the information seemed to burst forth suddenly from a broken seam, stoked Frank's sense that what Ian said was genuine, so far as Ian understood it. Frank also had the strong sense that Ian had decided to repair that seam of confiding as quickly as it opened, and had not told half of what he knew. And this person was forty-eight months old. Ian's general grace in the world, the more Frank knew of what the boy may have endured, was staggering.

Frank went out to the ring and watched as Patrick reconfigured the jumps. Claudia sidled Glory Bee closer to the fence.

"I want you to concentrate on what you're doing," he said to Claudia. "You shouldn't even be involved with me when you've set yourself this kind of job."

"Sue Smith trained a Grand National winner, and her husband was an Olympic show jumper. Don't you think they ever fucked, up there in the Yorkshire moors?" Claudia said. "Do you think it frightened the horses?"

"If Patrick overhears this, I'll end you," Frank said in a whisper, struggling not to laugh. Were all doctors so bawdy? Natalie was possessed of the same vinegar. Was that the source of Frank's attraction? Was he trying to fill in the outlines left by his dead wife? And what if he was? A man could do a great deal worse. "I meant, don't worry about Ian. I'll handle that. I don't want you involved."

"You should have told me that before you involved me."

Frank went into the house and made himself his obligatory grilled cheese. He made another and ate it with leftover potato wedges from the fridge. Because food was something he could take or leave, his mother noticed his indulgence. "Did you forget breakfast? What's with all the comfort food?"

"Comfort."

She said, "Are you worried about Ian?"

"News travels fast."

"I could say that you wouldn't be in this state if you hadn't done what you did in the first place."

"But you wouldn't say that because it reeks of self-righteousness."

"That's right. But also, I love Ian, and deplore as I may however he got here to us, I'm not sure that wherever he was before wasn't worse." She paused in her reading and said, "What does Claudia know?"

"Just that I adopted a kid whose parents were killed, a shirttail relative of Claudia's. Like Eden."

"Except Eden and Marty think he was the son of one of Natalie's brothers. Your nephew by marriage. Although Eden doesn't believe it."

"Jesus, Mom. What am I supposed to do, host a family meeting and confess all?"

"Yes, that's exactly what you should do."

"Has he said things to you, Mom?"

Hope sat down. "Give me one of those potatoes," she said. Frank liberally salted and peppered a thick wedge and handed it to Hope in a paper towel.

"Do you want ketchup?"

"Vinegar."

Frank brought the malt vinegar down from the spice cupboard, and Hope thoughtfully cut up and relished her potato for a while. "Sadly, there is no such thing as a bad potato," she said. "He's said a couple of things. I didn't tell you because I thought he was just being a little kid. When you were four or five, you said you saw a spaceship the size of a basketball that glowed green like a glow stick landing in the big pasture."

Frank said, "Well, that happens to be true. I did."

"Ian said he ran away with Cora in the night."

"Cora was the woman in the van, the one we tried to rescue. The woman who looked Filipino or Indonesian. Did he tell you about the castle?"

"No, he didn't say anything about a castle."

"I hope he doesn't say anything at school."

"I don't think you have to worry about that, Frank. He's so self-possessed, it's . . . it's eerie. It seems . . . somehow . . ."

"Learned, right?"

"Exactly."

"So where are they?"

"Who?"

"Whoever lived in the castle, Mom. Or whatever it was. His mother and father. Or his guardians?" Frank carefully cut his potato into slices. "I read the Brisbane papers every week, cover to cover. I read the updates on people who were reunited and found. I read about the missing. There's no one, no one at all, who corresponds to Ian, or his older brother, or that woman. Not one person."

Claudia came in to announce that she was taking off. She was getting together with some former students in Chicago and would be spending the night there. Before she left, she kissed Frank lightly and gave Hope a light shoulder hug.

Chummy.

Hope didn't even roll her eyes at Frank, but closed them in the pleasure of the gesture.

Advantage, Claudia.

But also, good for Claudia. She handled things well, appropriately, neither Victorian nor postmodern, assuming but not presuming.

On Tuesday night, just before she left for New York, Claudia and Frank and Ian planned to load up the trailer for the horse auction in Baraboo, hoping to come home with Ian's birthday present in tow. Frank and Ian had spent an hour looking at photographs of horse breeds in his father's books, and later, on the Internet. Persistently, Ian came back to Arabians, although he didn't like the light-colored ones. Frank didn't subscribe to the myth that Arabians were any spookier than other horses; he liked them for their strength and solid carriage, and he didn't want a forty-pound child mounted on a horse whose shoulder was even with Frank's head.

They arrived early, to be close enough to the bottom of the small amphitheater. The auction had begun promptly at seven, on the third Tuesday of every month, for forty years, run without interruption by Cyrus Young, who claimed to be descended from the great pitcher, a Wisconsin-born Chippewa. Many of the first horses were draft horses, sold by and purchased by what seemed to be identical pairs of Amish men. There were several young paint mares, a nice buckskin quarter horse about ten years old, and a pretty paint and Morgan cross that Frank tried to direct Ian toward, but Ian sat patiently, saying nothing for an hour, then an hour and a half.

"Do you think he's just not into it?" Frank said to Claudia.

"I don't know. Most kids would have wanted every one of them."

The dark gray Arabian mare was led by a college girl who could have been the same college girl as the one he remembered from a long time ago—same oversized sweater and undersized jeans—the one who walked away when her horse didn't sell. But this one had at least the decency to have cried all the way here. You could see it in her swollen face. Some horses had to be sold; he'd sold his own gelding, Pywackit, but to a neighbor, when he'd gone to college, and he still thought about him. Next to him, he felt Ian sit up straight. The horse's name was Sultana, and she was eight years old, owned by Tracy Hollander of Lansing, Michigan, for the past three years, part of the University of Wisconsin Madison's precision color guard and the University of Wisconsin Madison's equestrian team.

"Now, this is a beautiful horse, a beautiful horse," Cy said. "And she is gentle as a kitten. Would do anything this little girl here wanted. Now, if she does not find a buyer tonight, she will be donated, by her owner's family, to Bright Gateway. That's how easy she goes. Sound as a nut, been vetted regular. But a horse like this, she should belong to one person . . ."

"Dad!" Ian said urgently.

"Be still now," Frank told him. He waited. He saw the Kesselberg brothers a few rows up, Galen and Tommy. They would flip her after she threw a foal or two, but by then, she'd be broody, and not as well disposed to the cooperation of horse and rider.

"Let's start the bidding at two hundred," Cy said. "Which is a crime, really. Okay, Galen. I see three. Up there, three fifty. Welcome. Welcome. Tommy? You're going to bet against your own brother?"

"I'm fixing my hat, Cy."

"We have three fifty. Who's going to take this pretty girl home? Four hundred? Galen? Thank you very much. Now, oops! Yes, four fifty. Now, this is more like it. Horse like this, in Chicago, would sell for sixteen hundred dollars, two thousand, five thousand dollars."

"We're in Baraboo tonight, though, Cy!" somebody called out.

"We have four fifty. Do I hear five hundred? Sir? Galen? Well, four fifty once, four-fifty—"

"Dad!" Ian cried. "That's *my* horse!"

"Five hundred!" Claudia called out. Frank stared at her. "What!" she said. "Were you going to sit there?"

"I was just about to say something."

"Five fifty? Do I hear five fifty? Five hundred once, five hundred twice . . . sold to the pretty lady in the blue shirt! Please see Erin down there, we offer delivery for a very minimal charge. A very minimal charge." Cy turned. "These are a matched pair of Morgans, driving horses, shiny as a chestnut. Look at the move."

"Dad! Where are they going with my horse?" Rough-handed farmers turned to smile.

"Come on," Frank said, hauling Ian up onto his shoulder. As they stepped out into the sawdust surrounding the auction barn, Frank said to Claudia, "I'll write you a check."

"I can afford it," Claudia said.

"You already got him a saddle!"

"Now there's a horse to go under it."

"What am I going to get him?" Frank said. "He's my son!"

Claudia said, "A bike."

"A bike?" Ian's face shined.

Frank gave the college girl time to say her goodbyes. "She'll be yours?" the girl said to Claudia.

"I have a horse. It's for him."

"A little boy?" The girl glanced down at Ian. "She's gentle but she can spook."

"Any horse can spook," Frank said.

"Dad, lift me up! Dad! Lift me up!" Ian said. Frank bent to pick Ian up.

"No, don't!" the girl said. "She's never been ridden bareback!"

Ian leaned forward onto Sultana's neck, as if he were about to fall asleep. The horse whickered softly. Ian said, "Come on. Time to go home."

"She spooks when she's loaded. I have a bandana . . . he's really little to be so good at this."

"He's good with animals," Frank said.

"He's not afraid. When I was his age, I was afraid of a Welsh pony."

"I'd be afraid of a Welsh pony, too," Frank said. "I'm sorry to take her away from you."

"She's a good girl. I have her sister. But I'm going to law school in Seattle. I tried for months to sell her. No one wanted her." ·

"He really wants her," Claudia said. "He picked her out in his dreams."

They threaded out carefully, around the vans and trailers. Claudia said, "I feel sorry for that girl. She was sweet." Quietly, alone under one of the lights, the girl who'd owned the horse was scrubbing her eyes with the heels of her hands.

"Can I get in the back?" said Ian. "The horse is lonely."

"If you go to sleep for a while," Frank told him. "Then you can." As if Ian could will himself asleep, as he had in the airport, he was out in thirty seconds. Even when they bumped into the driveway, he didn't wake. Hope came out, and Frank suddenly noticed that every light in the house was on.

Frank called, "Hey, Mom. Well, Ian got his horse. He knew just the one he wanted. She's a really nice little Arabian—"

"Someone came here, Frank. Earlier tonight, just after dark."

"Who?"

"I don't know. A car came up the driveway, rolling very slowly, and then just parked between the back door and the barn. I walked out there. There were two men in the car. I couldn't see their faces. I called to them, Can I help you? They didn't get out, and they didn't speak to me."

"What did you do?"

"I went back in the house and locked the door."

"What happened?" Frank said.

"Nothing. The car just sat there. For fifteen minutes, with the lights on. Then the driver turned it around and drove back down the driveway, very slowly."

"Were you afraid?"

Hope said, "I almost called the police. It was as if they were just brazening it out, coming up to my door, showing me they could."

Frank said nothing; Ian woke up and began chattering about Sultana. Hope held her arms out to him. Claudia said quietly, "Why didn't you call the police?"

With a murderous look at Frank, Hope said, "I couldn't find my phone. I couldn't find the house phone either."

Frank made no move to get out of the truck. Finally, he said, "I own a farm."

"I see that. Congratulations, Farmer Mercy," said Claudia.

"Not this farm. Another farm. A farm in England that Tura left to me, that she bequeathed to me, when she died."

Claudia didn't argue with him. "I see what you're getting at. It wouldn't be hard to find you here. But would it be hard to find you there either?"

"Well, here, after three generations? You could ask the first person you met. Sally the border collie could do it. Anyone who could use a telephone or a computer could do it."

"Would you take him away from here? To somewhere? To there?" Claudia said.

Frank hadn't considered it until tonight. He thought of himself now, the lonely laird, up in all what he imagined from the pictures to be clefted, purple-carpeted vastness, vastness that nevertheless would be a few miles up the track from some smoky, shitty little factory city. And where would the track finally end? He shrugged. Quietly, Claudia kissed him on the cheek and slid out of the cab, got into her own car, and departed.

SEVENTEEN

ONE MORNING IN early September, Frank was in his bathroom, shaving naked at the sink, when Ian pounded at the door and finally nearly fell in. Ian asked, "Why's your penis so big? Why's it got hair on it? Are you sick?"

"That happens when you grow up," Frank said, reaching for his pajama bottoms. He'd obviously never seen a grown man naked. So much for his beloved father. "It'll happen to you, too."

"No. I'm pretty sure I don't want it to."

"Well, it happens anyhow."

"Did it happen to Claudia? Is she sick?"

Sweet Christ. Wasn't this talk supposed to come later? Like at age fifteen?

"Women don't have penises. They have vaginas."

"That's . . . like . . . what?"

"Like a hole sort of."

"Like your butt? Girls have to pee out their butts?"

"Nope. They have two holes. One for, well, for being their vagina where a baby comes out when they have a baby."

"A real baby could come out your *butt*?"

"No, honey. It's different. It's like . . . stretchy. Anyhow, they grow up and they get a little hair there, too. Under their arms, too. Men and women."

"Do you think it happened to Colin?" Ian asked.

His brother.

"Not yet. Colin would only be . . . how old was Colin when the flood came?"

"Eight."

Frank would have guessed six, but it had been only moments, pulled taut by anxiety and exhaustion; there had been no time for a good look. How light Ian had felt that morning, in his arms, like a bundle of sticks. Ian must have gained ten pounds since Christmas.

"So he'd be almost nine now."

"Hmm," Ian said. "Are you pretty old, Dad?"

The jocular affirmative answer, something about older than mud, sprang to Frank's lips, but he quelled it. Children with lost parents were extremely serious about death, and he didn't need a psychiatrist to tell him that. The margin between death and their parents concerned them, particularly if they'd experienced loss. "No, I'm not that old. Look at old Grandpa Jack. I could get that old. My father died, when he was my age, but it was in an accident. He got caught in a big accident. I'm pretty good."

"I hope you don't get old like Jack," Ian said. "Jack is very, very, very sad."

"But Grandma's happy, and she's old, in a way. She's not going to die."

"Is Claudia pretty old?"

"Claudia's only the same age as Eden. She's not even a little old."

"What about Glory Bee?" Ian said. "She could die. I don't think Sultana would die."

"She could die."

"Would you be sad?"

"Yes."

"I mean about Claudia."

Frank's head felt cold, the way it had when he was a child and slugged down a second tumbler of lemonade with ginger—cold so intense it was an ache that seemed it would never abate.

"I would be sad."

"Would you shoot a bad guy if he was killing her?"

"I don't know. Probably yes."

"Would you shoot a bad guy killing your old people?" Frank knew that Ian meant Cedric and Tura. "I know a bad guy killed your old people. I liked them."

"I would have. Cedric and Tura were very good. They were very good to me and to you. I wish I had been there."

"If you were there, maybe they would still kill them. And you, too."

"I don't think so."

"They're very bad," Ian said. "Those bad guys are really bad. Colin says they are."

"Did he know them?"

Frank slipped his pajama bottoms back on, trying not to make too big a deal of it, as Ian leaned over the sink, studiously squeezing a whorl of toothpaste around the edge of the drain.

"Yes."

"Yes what?"

"Yes. Colin knew the bad guys," said Ian. "You're not Peter Parker."

"Who's Peter Parker?"

"Uh, *Spider*-Man?"

"Sorry. That's a silly name. Peter Parker. Especially for a superhero."

"He wants it to be silly. It's a secret. Do you want to go bowling tonight? You can bring Claudia."

"It's a school night. I don't think we can. Now go run. You're late for school." Ian dawdled so much over breakfast that he nearly invariably missed the bus, but Hope didn't mind driving him.

Frank heard the car's initial crunch on the gravel die away to the sound of the rain sticks they'd built as children with rice and paper towels. He turned to some papers. The hours melted. It seemed only minutes later, but the sun at the window told him hours, that Patrick yelled up the stairs, "Frank! Gent to see you." Frank looked down from the bedroom window and saw, instead of the usual pickup truck that had seen better days, a car—nondescript, the kind of car a child would draw if asked to draw a car. It was perfectly clean, as if newly waxed. Acting on a signal from the lizard brain, Frank went into his room, pulled on his clothes, and then, carefully closing the door and turning the old key lock, he walked into the closet. Reaching up to one side, he moved the indistinguishable false panel of breadboard that hid a combination safe set flush in the wall of the shelf. His Glock was clean and loaded, as he kept it always. With it stuck in the waistband of the back of his Levi's, under his bomber jacket, he jogged down the stairs and stepped behind the open door to glance out at the man Patrick was talking to—a relaxed, slender, healthy-looking man who could have been fifty or sixty, with his hands in the pockets of what Frank could tell was a very costly suede coat. After a minute, Frank made a noise and stepped outside.

"Hello, Frank," the man said, extending his hand.

"Hello. How are you today?"

"I'm very well, thanks. You look good."

"Thanks, but I don't remember if we've met." Frank was comfortably aware of the weight of the gun at his waist.

"We haven't met that you would remember. But I knew your father as a young man, and your grandfather, your mother as well."

"She's off driving my son to school."

"You have a son? A fourth generation?"

He didn't ask if Frank had a wife. Frank's fingertips tingled, the way people's forearms do after they've narrowly avoided being creamed in a car smashup. Something about the way the visitor stood was telltale, the way a tennis pro might stand, at the ready to move left or right. An athlete. A soldier.

A cop.

"I'm a widower. My wife died nearly a year ago."

"I'm sorry for your loss. I am a widower as well."

Was this guy police? The phrase was so earnestly spoken, yet seemed to glide so effortlessly from the guy's lips, without even a shift in posture, that there was history behind it. Frank said, "Are you on the job?"

"I'm retired. You?"

"Once upon a time. Long time ago. How can I help you?"

"I came to see a man about a horse actually. My daughter was at the Mistingay in Chicago in July and she got her heart set on a horse she said you owned. A horse named Glory Bee."

"That's my horse, but the truth is, she's not for sale," Frank said.

"I can offer a very nice price. As a matter of fact, isn't that the horse?" Claudia was leading Glory Bee down from the arena. Frank wanted to signal her, *Go back!* Instead, he put himself between the horse and the man's line of vision. "Were you there?"

"I wasn't. We live north of the city. She's a grown woman, but still her dad's little girl. And she's looking for a horse. My daughter described a tall, entirely black mare about five years old. First event and she all but walked away with it, Lynette said. That never happens."

"It never happens. There was some luck involved."

"Not according to Lynette. She was very impressed with the horse's presence."

The pale girl whom Patrick paid to rub Glory Bee down and watch her overnight. The tiny girl from the jockey school. Not Lynette.

Linnet, like the bird.

Frank experienced the sensation police psychiatrists sometimes called flooding, a cascade of perceptions that refused to be categorized, all pertinent and all in no order. People he had known described this kind of event to shrinks almost like a kind of breakdown, when they went in for mandatory visits after a shooting, or an accidental death in custody. Who was the girl? If he called the jockey school where Patrick had gone to speak, would there be a student of that name? How could an ex-cop afford a horse that would cost several hundred grand, easy? Why would a girl bent on flat racing suddenly decide she wanted a jumper? Unless his wife left him loaded, but even then. Frank said, "Patrick, go help Claudia rub Glory Bee down, would you?"

"She's okay. She's still got half her workout to do."

"I want her to rest for today, okay?" Frank turned back to the friendly father. "My friend Patrick likes her, your daughter. I think he's visited her school. I know they were together at the Mistingay." He didn't say he had himself met Linnet, like the bird, at the Mistingay.

"Really?"

"Long drive from here. To her school. For Patrick. Long drive for you."

"Yep."

"Do you go see her much?"

"We do sometimes."

"You and your wife?"

"Hmm. She's an only child."

"Must be difficult, having only one and her in Kentucky. Kentucky, right?"

"Kentucky, yes. You get used to it."

"Well, unless you want to talk about something else, Glory Bee's not for sale. She's training right now with a rider for the U.S. team."

"She's that good. Mind if I watch?"

Frank bared his teeth and made huffing noises he hoped resembled a laugh. "Oh, well, if you know much about show jumping, you know we can't afford to let out those trade secrets, can we?" He said then, "You like Volvos?"

The man said, "They're the best. Lynette calls it a grandma car. But I get a new one every three years."

Linnet. Like the bird. Clearly, neither name was her real name.

"I might get one."

"Sure," the man said, in a hurry now, his voice just a quarter note flatter, like an iron bell struck while someone was holding the side of it with one hand. "I'll be going, then."

How bad a bad guy could he be and be this shitty stupid? He dressed very well, too. On the other hand, Frank had met some really ignorant bad guys who did very well for themselves.

Without further ado, or any handshakes, the man got into his spotless car and took off.

"Pat!" Frank called. "Did you ever actually see that girl Linnet ride a horse?"

"No," Patrick said. "She didn't come to the talks I gave because she said it was her practice time and they were very tight about that."

"And the college was in Indiana, Patrick, not Kentucky. Right?"

"All those flats run over each other for me, guv. But I would have remembered Kentucky. I used to look at the pictures of the farms when I was a lad. Indiana sounds right."

"Did you know she was coming to Chicago?"

Patrick blushed. "I never asked her to. I just saw her at the school until then. How I found out about her school, I wrote a letter once, I was a kid, twelve, to 'the Jockey,' a fanboy sort of a thing. They had a story about schools. So I asked, could I come see the place? Place to work if this didn't work out here maybe. Which it did, Frank."

"And?"

"And she was a pretty little bird." For a moment, Frank thought Patrick was referring to a bird, to the girl's name. Then he recognized old Brit slang.

"So you . . ."

"A bit. Then she showed up inside by the barns in Chicago. That's her dad, huh? Toff."

Frank said, "A bit."

Almost idly, Frank called in the tags on the car. Minnesota plates. Memorizing plate numbers was a skill he'd mastered long ago.

The guy who looked up the plates was Eden's age. His name was Shane Baker, and their mothers were acquainted.

"This is unremarkable, Frank," he said, after they exchanged pleasantries, and Shane offered Frank condolences for the loss of his wife, and congratulations for the marriage of his sister. "This car is registered to Patricia Roe, of Minnetonka, Minnesota. No arrests, no violations, not even a parking ticket."

"She didn't live in Chicago?"

"No. Nothing here seems to suggest anything such as that. She was an ordinary citizen, according to these records. An exemplary citizen."

Frank wanted to laugh. Like many people without much of an education, Shane Baker spoke with a formality that verged on parody. It reminded Frank of the horse race gamblers in *Guys and Dolls*. He glanced down at his watch. Ian's bus would come soon. The guy in the black car hadn't been gone for two full minutes. What if the guy simply waited, out of sight, as Ian descended from the bus? That's all he would need to do. Sally, who could hear Ian's school bus two miles off, gave up herding Hope's newest project, five milking goats, and began racing toward the end of the drive, where she would lie in wait for Ian with her muzzle on her paws. As Frank watched, she then followed Ian, running out and then back to circle Ian's legs as he made his slow, digressive journey up the drive—stopping to pick up stones and examine them for veins of gold, to prod coyote scat with a stick to find mouse skeletons, to search the gully where he'd once found, and proudly left untouched, a nest of tawny-flecked quail eggs. He was still so small and skinny, his favorite green necktie askew, blond hair spangling red strands in the bright sun.

When he got to the dooryard, Frank lifted him up. "Would you like to move to England?" he said.

"I don't know," Ian told him, warily. "Where is it? I'd like to go bowling."

Ian had his birthday party planned. It would be all bowling, including the cake. He and Frank had scouted the location. Ian had gone over the guest list. He'd written down the triplets, a quiet little boy named Ted, and a talkative girl named Mai Lin.

"Can you help me put the saddle on Sultana?"

"You look beat today, buddy."

"She likes a ride every day. Just a little ride."

"Okay, son. Here we go." Frank brushed Sultana and laid her red saddle pad across her back, and then buckled her into her saddle, finally setting Ian astride her. As he did, Ian reached out and brushed the back of Frank's neck with his small hand, a tiny gesture between a pat and a hug.

Frank thought, I would shoot them. I would shoot them all.

As Ian circled the paddock, Frank heard his phone buzzing. Shane Baker was calling back.

He said, "About that car. This is rather interesting, Frank. Patricia Roe is deceased. She had not committed a crime, but it may be that she was the victim of one. She died two years ago, of a fall, in her house. She simply fell down a staircase. But there was an investigation. There was a suspicion of foul play, for some things were missing from her house. Some jewelry. An expensive oil painting of museum quality."

"Not this car?"

"No, that car is not a stolen vehicle. The registration is current."

"Who has it? Who are her relatives? Her children?"

"She had no relatives, no children or spouse. She was a marathon runner. Her possessions went to the library in her town and to a scholarship fund for female athletes."

"But who has the car? It's a new car. Newer. Two years old."

"Well, Frank, it says here that she does," Shane said. "I'm going to pass this along."

Frank was willing to bet that the driver of that crisp Volvo had already decided on an early trade-in.

EIGHTEEN

FOR ONE OF the two psychology classes he took in college, Frank had to submit to experiments devised by professors and carried out by graduate students. One was built on the scaffolding of the old conundrum: I have some good news and some bad news, which would you like first? Like almost everyone else—eighty percent of people—Frank wanted the bad news first. The bitter pill was easier to sweeten. Frank also learned that the huge majority of people had a stubborn belief that a cycle of bad tidings would be followed by a cycle of good luck, and half of those thought that the break meant that happy days were here again for good. This was notwithstanding all past evidence to the contrary, whether they suffered under corrupt government leaders or suffered chronic migraines or their children were addicted to drugs or they ran a Korean grocery that was robbed every three months like clockwork or thugs in nice clothes who didn't know their daughters' own names and drove cars registered to dead people pulled up to their houses. Human beings were hardwired to be optimistic.

So when Brian Donovan called, Frank expected bad news. Receiving news that was instead not only good but miraculous, he could not, he later thought, blame himself for believing that the clouds had rolled away and that days thereafter would be fair.

Frank came in one night late, after waiting while the vet cleaned up a cut on the little paint's hock.

Hope said, "Your . . . your brother-in-law called. Brian Donovan. He asked if you'd gotten an envelope from him. You did. It's in your room. He also said to call him back, that it was urgent you call him the minute you got it."

"I will," Frank said.

"He said *the minute*," Hope repeated.

Frank dawdled. He called Claudia, who was at her apartment, preparing for an interview the next morning that could lead to a lucrative, prestigious series of lectures the following year. "How bad could it be?" Frank said. "Everything bad has already happened."

"The answer's in the question, Frank," Claudia said, sounding distracted to the point of impatience. "Maybe it's good news about his brother and the wife who were never found."

Just a week before, Frank received the copy of the documentary special Brian had made, *We Were the Donovans*, that had aired across Australia and other parts of the world. Dutifully, Frank had popped it into the international player he still had, but the third or fourth image was Natalie throwing her cap into the air at her college graduation, and Frank couldn't watch anymore. Was that what this urgent call was about?

Was it more likely that someone who'd seen the documentary had been in touch with Brian—someone who'd nearly given up hope, who'd been desperately searching for a child?

Frank ripped the thick parcel open at the back.

Legal papers with little pink Post-it notes attached marking places to sign tumbled out. When he was able to settle his heart's thudding, he saw that these were documents pertaining to his and Natalie's will, drawn up just when she'd learned she was pregnant, mere weeks before she died— a million five each on each other, hers now augmented because of the accidental death provision. Her directives included a small bequest for each of her brothers, and half was to be kept in trust for her minor children, should they outlive her. Frank signed the documents and put them back in the big stamped envelope. There was another, separate envelope— the check with the payout on the destruction of his house. He'd got the value out of the condominium they'd owned, and was glad, if you could be glad about such a thing, that they'd purchased flood insurance when they moved to Carson Place. There was a third envelope—little, with a waxy coating, the kind parents made kids use to write thank-you notes.

Who knew how long Brian had held on to these documents or, for that matter, how long they'd taken to reach Brian? Frank left Brisbane leaving no forwarding address but this one, and Brian, it seemed, had been consumed for a long while with his documentary. Sadly, Frank wondered what would fill Brian's hours now.

He slit open the little envelope, and out fell a folded single sheet, a couple of newspaper clippings, both old, one with a headline about a child called "Moses" . . . and a photo of Ian. Except . . . it wasn't Ian. The child in the picture, squinting into the sun, was older, thinner, taller, with a square chin. Frank grabbed up the newspaper page. It was the picture of him carrying a child crushed against him.

The white sheet was a letter from Brian.

Dear Frank,

This is a picture I took last week, after I visited a convent that houses a Red Cross foundling center near Byron Bay. The telephone number of Sister Elizabeth Gray, the nun who called me, is written on the back of this letter. She said the boy lives there with a dozen other children who have no families and that he saw the documentary I made, which you have by now, We Were the Donovans. *The boy spoke to her the next day and showed her the newspaper picture of you. I went to visit him last week. He's a likely boy, and I don't remember the looks of the boy you adopted, but he insists this is his brother. His name is Colin McTeague. He seems convinced that you have his brother, Ian. She would like you to call her, but perhaps call me first. I'm a bit at loose ends.*

With best regards,
Brian Donovan

Frank read no more.

It was 5:23 a.m. in Brisbane.

He picked up the telephone.

"God grant you peace, and good morning," said the soft voice.

"I need to speak with Sister Elizabeth Gray."

"Mother."

"Mother Elizabeth Gray."

"She's at her prayers. I can take your number and ask her to call you back after breakfast. No more than an hour or two."

"Could I wait?"

"I don't know."

"It's urgent. It's about a child. It's about Colin."

"I'll go get her now," the soft voice replied.

A minute passed, then two and then three. Twice, Frank heard the clicking of shoes approaching the phone and the soft birdsong of voices, but they died away. Five minutes. Six.

"This is Elizabeth Gray."

"Hello. This is Frank Mercy. I'm calling from the United States. I apologize for the hour."

"It's quite all right. We are up early."

"I heard about a boy called Colin, and I thought, I hoped that perhaps it was the same Colin."

"Ah. Good morning. This is the American uncle?"

"Yes."

"You left Australia." There was the slightest hint of accusation.

"I saw the car go over, Sister. I saw it disappear under the floodwater. I didn't believe he could have survived. I followed up, diligently. I checked the shelters and the newspapers."

"Not diligently enough. For here he is, asleep upstairs." There was an ancientness of Irish in her speech. She paused. "But never mind. This has happened a hundred times since that night, all over Queensland."

"Is he badly . . . is he disabled?"

"He's quite well. Not much use for reading, but sound as a house otherwise. He longs for his brother. For Ian."

How could Colin have known what Frank called him?

"He asks for his brother . . . Ian?"

"What else? He says they have no parents. Only you."

"Of course," Frank said.

"But yours is not the name on their birth certificates."

"I'm related on the mother's side, so of course . . . Mary was my cousin."

Mary. It was as if someone had spoken in his ear.

"Yes, Mary," said the sister.

Frank exhaled in a painful wheeze. He had pulled the name Mary out of his ass, and was ready to say that Mary was the nickname for Rita or Monica, who hated her name, even though she was called after their sainted grandmother.

"The boy carried a waterproof pouch, sewn into a backpack. There's a little slit on the inside. Colin Weldon McTeague. Ian Weldon McTeague. Now the parents were American, living in England; but I'm sorry to say, Mary Weldon McTeague, deceased, Jakarta. James Bell McTeague . . . but you know this."

"Of course."

"So will you come for him? Or shall we put him on the plane with our sister Ursula Shriver, who has to travel to New York in a week's time . . ."

"I'll be happy to pay for her transport and his, and if anyone else is coming, hers, too."

"That's very kind. We will accept your paying for the two, one way. The other way won't be necessary," said Mother Elizabeth. "I must say that he will be very happy. He's a good lad."

"He is," Frank said, his own voice near to breaking.

"I'll call you with the details."

"Good night, then."

"Good morning. God grant you peace."

"And you also," Frank said.

He had to sit down.

Ian was his real name.

*   ⋆   ⋆

Hours later, Frank and Ian squeezed together side by side on Ian's bed, the man and the boy against a headboard maybe thirty-six inches long.

Ian's lids literally drooped, but he would not give up without his reading. Soapy smelling in the way only a kid too young to have hormones can be, Ian was tucked up in fresh pajamas, the waffle top red, the short waffle bottoms orange, for Ian would still brook no matching ensembles.

Go, Dog, Go and *Knuffle Bunny* lay on Ian's pillow: they were favorites, so two readings of each one counted for the requisite four books.

Frank could tell that Ian knew something was up.

Would Frank ever be able to figure out if Ian really *knew* that Colin was alive? Colin's photo was in Frank's shirt pocket, and he would introduce the topic before he left the room, and explain the arrival of Ian's presumed-dead brother, in less than a week.

Frank read.

"Do you like my hat?" Ian asked.

"No, I do not like your hat," Frank answered.

"Goodbye."

"Goodbye."

Ian cracked up. Something about this exchange struck him so funny that he could not give up the book, and had committed every word to memory, even though he was now reading tiny chapter books about Father mowing the lawn and chewing up Owen's rubber dinosaurs. Hope had given Ian so many books that Claudia called Ian's room the Carnegie-Ian Library.

The books completed, Frank had to break the news.

As he suspected, Brian had received papers from the lawyer months before and had done nothing with them. He had found them a few weeks before under a jumble of photos and papers he'd used for the film. Part of that work took place in a care facility where his leg slowly healed, and Frank winced about letting the poor man languish there. Then Brian went home, to his house that still smelled of his girls and his wife, and took an indefinite leave from work, for nothing seemed to fit or make sense. The visit to the convent and the lonely, determined little boy had been among the first decisive things he'd done for months. It had been the first time Brian had driven his own car.

"Won't you come to see us?" Frank had asked, but Brian demurred, promising he would come, another time, when he was stronger. Brian's perpetual twilight was in this sense a boon. To Frank's relief, Brian didn't even question Frank's connection to Colin. By the same preposterous logic that made Frank responsible for Ian, he also was responsible for Colin. A call to one of Charley Wilder's friends, an adoption attorney in Milwaukee, confirmed that a six-month period of foster placement with Frank, Ian's adoptive dad, and the published search for known relatives could quite readily lead to Frank's adopting the nearly nine-year-old Colin as a single parent. Frank asked, "What relatives?" Relatives in Brisbane? Or in Indonesia? The parents, he explained, had apparently died in Indonesia, but the boys were born in England. Well, then, the attorney said, it would be necessary to publish in all those places.

Great. That was great. Fucking great.

Here he was, the genial kidnapper father, the warmhearted capital criminal who spent time trying to think of ways that Ian could put the equivalent of a funny rubber nose on his superpowers, and this woman was suggesting a "published search" for known relatives on several continents. It wrung Frank's neck muscles until he had the sensation that someone was slowly pulling his head back by the hair. Perhaps something would change. Sure. Fuck yes. Perhaps he'd wake up one morning and a big black helicopter would be sitting in the high pasture, or a motorcade of feds would arrive in the driveway. He'd been reduced to sentiments like the ones his mother's batty friend Arabella often expressed, among Frank's favorites being exactly what he now absurdly could not help but feel, *Well, things can only get better . . .*

"I have to tell you something, honey," Frank finally told Ian.

"I'm not going to Catholic school," said Ian. "It's not really better. Grandma's friend Johnny is daft."

Johnny was a sweet guy, gayer than Christmas and about forty years younger than Hope. He'd taken over her job at the high school library and they gossiped and cooked together with more vigor than anything Hope did with her book club or her lifetime sidekicks, Arabella and Janet. Johnny was a very big advocate of the Catholic school, which Frank and his friends, growing up, called Our Lady of Perpetual Misery.

"He's not daft. He just has his opinion. But no, you don't have to go to Catholic school."

"I'm not getting a different horse. I can train Sultana myself. She doesn't like Patrick."

"It's not about Sultana." Sultana did not, in fact, like Patrick. "It's about Colin."

Ian, who had attached long pieces of tape to his toes and was pretending to drive the pony cart, sat up. "Is he here?"

"Not yet. But he is alive. He lived after the flood. And he's coming here. And we're going to the airport in New York City to get him."

"Well, that's good," Ian said with a sigh, lying back and rearranging the tapes on his toes.

No shock.

No tears.

No nothing but acceptance, as if the other shoe had dropped.

"Was your name Ian before the flood?"

From the universal gesture palette of childhood, Ian selected the head duck and eye roll that meant, duh.

"How could I know, Ian? You didn't talk!"

"Well, you called me Ian."

"I just liked the name."

"Because . . . It. Was. My. Name."

"Are you excited to see Colin?"

"Yes." Ian carefully removed his tapes, stowing them on the headboard. "Is Cora dead?"

"I don't know. We can ask Colin."

"I think she's dead. Like Natalie," Ian said, and proffered the books. They finished one, and then Ian said, "Do you know what, Dad?"

"What?"

"We might need an ark, too, for floods."

"Hmmmmm," Frank replied, half asleep, for the reading worked better on him than on Ian. "I don't know how to make an ark that would float. We could build a little one."

Ian said, "Not good enough."

"There's no reason to worry. Go to sleep."

"I'm not tired. Could we get Colin now?"

"In a few sleeps. Six sleeps. I'll make you a calendar, with the one from the bank. The sooner you sleep, the sooner we go." He kissed Ian's forehead, and then his eyes.

Downstairs, he found Hope, who offered him some of the tea she'd just made. Frank said, "Where's Claudia?"

"She went home. That girl is a nervous wreck, Frank."

"Mom, I'm a nervous wreck."

Perhaps Claudia was only tired. Tomorrow was a training day in the indoor arena: two events, one in Florida and one in the Netherlands, were on the horizon.

That was it. Claudia was tired. And other hallucinations. Life was hurling events at the two of them like a pitching machine stuck on fastball. Claudia was at her limit.

"I hope you know what you're getting into, Frank, with this other little boy," Hope said suddenly.

Frank poured his tea, sat down, and bit his lip. Hope was in all things a patient and open-minded woman, her love for Ian immense and her temperament generally a region where the month was always May. When she said things like this, rarely enough, Frank wanted to pick up the cups one by one and smash each of them against the fireplace brick. He had no idea if this desire was triggered by his own impossible pickle, or the inherent tension of being a grown man living in his mother's house, or because he simply couldn't fathom why anyone as smart as Hope would say something so ludicrous. What could Frank do? Turn away Ian's brother, who had, impossibly, made it to safety from that buried van after the tsunami? Lived in an orphanage? Had the ingenuity to understand that the man holding his little brother in the photo was somehow linked to the things he heard in a television program? If Frank wanted to, how could he even presume to deny Colin, who, in the teetering van with that filthy water swamping the bow of the powerboat, had looked clear-eyed at Frank and said, take my brother first, he's important? If Frank did end up going to prison, at least it would take years to extricate Colin and Ian from Tenacity Farms, from Claudia, who would fight to keep them, who would deny she ever knew about any wrongdoing, from Marty and Eden, who would do the same thing, from Hope herself.

At least, once Colin got here, he would be . . . something like home.

"I have no idea what I'm getting into," Frank said. "The nuns said he's a good boy. Natalie's brother Brian went out there and said he seems very nice."

"How is Natalie's brother?"

Who knew when Brian would work full-time again? Just before they hung up, Brian haltingly—as if abashed by bringing it up at all—described the bequest that Natalie had left to each of her brothers. Hugh, of course, was not legally dead. Brian apologized for glancing at Frank's private papers. Frank decided to send a check that combined the portions for all the brothers, the next day. Brian was not only struggling financially, but barely respiring emotionally. If he'd had Natalie or any of his brothers, or his parents, or his wife. He had no one.

By contrast, the Donovans were tight, always, close in age, mates as well as siblings, as likely to call each other to get up to fishing or bashing a ball around as to call a friend. As short a time as he'd known them, Frank admired their comradeship, Natalie just the same as one of the brothers, and had thought this might be the family he would have one day. A corner of consciousness lifted like a hat brim in a stiff breeze and, for an instant, Frank saw a thought, that he might still have . . . such a family.

He might still pull this off. There was a chance. Trauma could never be outlived, but it could be survived.

He would ask Claudia more about trauma.

"You know I have to bring him home, Mom," Frank said. "And if I didn't want to, I still would. Nothing else is possible."

"Of course," Hope said, lightly touching Frank's shoulder. "I just worry for you. So much, in such a short time."

"It's not as if it makes it worse. It somehow makes it better. If anyone ever finds out what I did . . . Whatever comes, I know you'll vouch for how well we looked after them . . ."

"Don't say such things, Frank. I know that you love Ian more than you have ever loved anyone."

"I think he's bewitched me."

"What if he has? He wants you to be happy so he's happy. It's what the world could use more of." Hope began to clear the teacups. "What I meant was . . . another child. You've only had this child less than a year. Colin is not . . . like that, is he?"

"No, Mom. He's just an ordinary kid."

NINETEEN

OW HE WOULD lose Claudia.

Frank had nothing but contempt for guys who said, Gee, I never realized how much she meant to me until she was gone.

Saps.

Or cops.

"Ode to My First Ex" was the police brotherhood theme song. Now he would be one of them. If someone had asked him even just a month before what he felt about Claudia, he would have said she was just great. She was great, and they had a great time. What a fool he was. To have thought he really believed that it was only a great time. He would tell Claudia the truth, and she would cringe away from him, like a normal person. He would beg her not to do more, although her doctor's oath, he presumed, extended to crimes against children. She would leave him, and the place she left would throb with his pulse like a bruise. It would grow less. But so would he. He had lied to Claudia. Had he lied to her because he loved her? It didn't matter.

He had to stop this now, whatever happened.

From an envelope in a manila folder in the back of his desk, he retrieved one of the copies of the newspaper page with his picture on it, carrying Ian.

When Claudia came inside after her ride, he summoned her up to his room and spread the page out on the desk.

"Frank," she said, raking her fingers through her sweaty hair. "That's you. I knew you participated in the rescue. But that little child, it looks like Ian."

"It is Ian."

"How was he hurt? You never told me." Already, there was the slight tang of resentment. *There can be no secrets.*

"No."

"Why is he soaking wet?"

"I found him in a van that was sinking in the second wave. After my wife died. He and this boy, his brother, I know now, were in the van with a woman. I couldn't get either of them out. The other boy or the woman. The van just went end over end, and it was gone, swept away."

"I don't understand," Claudia said. "Why was *Ian* in someone else's van?"

"That's how I got Ian, Claudia. He's not the child of a relative of Natalie's. He's not the child of anyone I ever knew. He's a child I found when I was on rescue patrol, the morning after the tsunami, the morning after Natalie died, last Christmas . . ."

"Then how did you adopt him?"

"I didn't." Claudia sat down hard on the padded bench, lips parted on a sigh. "I just took him. I got a friend to make up dummy papers. I should have given him to the Red Cross workers the first day, but I didn't." Claudia spread her hands and seemed to study them. "Claudia, I don't know why I did it."

"I'm sure Ian knows why," Claudia said. Then, in a moment, she seemed to grow smaller in the chair. Claudia was strong, as physically strong as any woman he had known—stronger than Natalie had been. When she was tired, or angry or sad, though, she folded into herself, like the morning glories Hope planted in summer around the stone pillars at Tenacity, which closed into tiny pale umbrellas at night. Frank lifted her loosely fisted hand and kissed her knuckles.

"I know you'll leave me now. And if you hesitate, I should make you leave me."

"You can't *make* me do anything, Frank. I hate you for thinking you can just dismiss me when you decide to drop the big bombshell."

"No one's dismissing you. Now that Colin is coming—"

"Colin is probably going to be afraid of abandonment because he never knew if anyone would ever find him. He probably thought he'd have to go looking for Ian when he was finally eighteen. And Ian? Ian could make one wrong turn and end up actually going to a bank and asking the teller nicely to give him ten thousand dollars . . . All those bad things could happen. That's the worst that could happen. What about the best?"

"You're the best that could happen, Claudia. You and I together with them, that's what's best. But what if I'm putting you in danger just because I don't want to lose you? I don't want to be melodramatic about it, but you know it's entirely possible that people are after Ian. I know that sounds like a bad movie. It's true, though."

"You can protect him better alone than both of us can?"

Frank got up and laid his hands against the frame of the big window. "No."

"And you'd protect them better if you lost me? Is this what this little boy Colin deserves? A father mourning again for someone he loved and who left him? Well, maybe I flatter myself."

"Claudia, you know I love you."

"You never said the words."

"I love you, Claudia. If I had a life I could plan, I'd want that life to be with you."

"But you only have this life. What are you going to do with this life?"

She stood up and kissed him and he tasted the tears and sweat on her mouth. They lay down on his bed, and shrugged and tugged until all their clothes were rolled around their feet like children's beach towels, and then, though they were in a house where other people were wandering around downstairs, they made love without thought of intrusion or conclusion.

"We forgot to use anything," Frank said suddenly.

"It doesn't matter," Claudia said. "The chance that I could get pregnant right now is pretty small. I'm a doctor. I know."

"But it could happen! What if it did?"

Claudia sat up and rummaged in Frank's bureau for one of his ten identical pairs of navy-blue sweatpants. She took these and a tee shirt into the shower and hummed old John Barry movie themes as she rinsed her hair and scrubbed her body. When she came out, turbaned in a towel, wearing the sweatpants and shirt, she next unfurled her quilt, which made Frank a nervous wreck. He was always thinking he'd roll over in bed and put his foot through one of the soft-as-tissue quilts stitched in Italy by Claudia's great-grandmother Campo. Although Claudia believed heartily in using things that were old, she also grieved every popped thread and was always paying extravagant sums to have the Fancy Dance or Rosewood Border reinforced. Once cocooned in it, she said, "What if I did get pregnant? Big deal. I could take care of a child on my own. After all, you do, with only the help of your mother and me, and Patrick, and the whole village." Claudia wrinkled her nose to take the sting out of her words. "I could get a job in North Carolina, where my father and my sisters live."

"North Carolina?"

"People raise children there all the time, when they're not eating possum and having sex with close relatives."

"I mean, you'd leave here? Away from me?"

"Do you want children, Frank?"

"I have children."

"I mean, children with me?"

"Claudia, this isn't . . ."

"Well, I don't mean tomorrow. It's nine months until the World Cup, and then the Olympic team is chosen. By then I'll be thirty-four. I mean after. If I do have children, I want to have them then."

"And I'll be forty-five then."

"So what? You're forty-two now, so this boy, Colin, was born when you were my age. Ian was born when you were thirty-nine. Natalie was forty and pregnant for the first time. That's not extraordinary on the age charts for postmillennial parenting."

"Aren't you worried about it being too late? Biologically?"

"Weren't you with Natalie?"

"She was a doctor."

"As am I. Frank. Why do people think that psychiatrists aren't real doctors?"

"A woman's fertility declines . . ."

"Frank, I just said this twice. I'm a *doctor*. I know what the propaganda is. Yeah, women miscarry more as they get closer to forty and a lot of those are early miscarriages because there's something wrong with the fetus, maybe a birth defect. By then, there'll be a simple blood test for chromosomal abnormalities, probably by the second month. Even without that, when you put it all together, if you had a seventy or a seventy-five percent chance that Glory Bee would take a silver medal, would you think those were good or bad odds?"

Frank shrugged. "I'd say those were good odds."

"Those are about the odds we would have a healthy kid. And I'm an Italian girl, Frank, and I want to have a baby. End of story. End of our story maybe because—"

"Claudia, let me catch up. Let me take one thing at a time. I'm a widower for nine months here!"

"And?"

"And . . ." Frank didn't honestly know *and what*. How had he mourned Natalie? In an hour at the morgue? On his knees next to his mother's sofa, in the barn, stabbing at forkfuls of hay? That was what work was for. Hard work burned the muscles, tired the brain. Work trumped mourning. But the truth was, Ian trumped mourning. Frank had mourned, and he had healed, through Ian, balm of the lost. Now would come Colin, rescued from the flood, carried safe to this place. Who knew what this kid would be like? But to find out, and to help this boy, already certainly so marked by loss, Frank would need . . . Claudia. Not some woman. Not a helpmate. Claudia, herself.

That was the truth.

He looked at Claudia now, her wet hair spiking out in back as she toweled it, her skin rosy from her shower, and saw that his life without Claudia would be a round of days, of the challenges of fatherhood, brotherhood, manhood, farmerhood, without the flavor these past few months had taught him to take for granted. She was a doctor, a curious and learned woman, tough and game. She was his friend, his playmate, his physical equal, and the fun they had in bed still dumbfounded him. Like no other woman ever would, she understood Ian. Only a man as anointed with good luck as with bad could happen across two such remarkable women in one life of not even vaguely trying, and only a fool with shit for brains would release a woman like this woman.

"Did you ever suspect anything?" Frank asked her.

"No," she said. "And I know when people are lying. Maybe it's because you're not really lying. You don't believe you did anything wrong." She got up and began to painstakingly separate the strands of her hair. "Frank, when I was a resident, I had to do marriage counseling. Couples in trouble always say, But . . . we've been through so much together. And I told them, That is the worst reason to hang on! Like digging a hole to fill a hole. I would ask them, what if you substituted the phrase 'because he refused to work' instead of 'You've gone through so much together'? Would you think that justified holding on?"

"What do you mean?"

"Well, now I feel like that. You and I have been through so much in a very short time, really since the day we met. Of course I feel as though I have known you forever. Everyone feels that. And while I don't want you to think I condone this . . ."

"I don't want you to think that I do."

"Some things are more important . . ."

That's just a legal thing, surely.

Frank said, "Wait, Claudia. Cops use that line of logic all the time, and they call it a higher law, when they want to justify doing something wrong."

"Do you think Ian is better off with you?"

"Absolutely. I don't think there's anywhere else Ian could be on earth. And if I did the so-called right thing, and took them back . . ."

"You know what would happen. A foster family. And then maybe an adoption, a changed name. They would be unhappy for a long time," Claudia said. "Missing us."

"You're right," Frank said. He stood and let the winter sun gild his arms and hands. The case clock in the hall clucked patiently.

Slowly then, he said, "Claudia, I don't know how it all comes out. We've done everything like an avalanche. We became a family almost before we became a couple. And sure, 'family' is another word that people use to cover up a multitude of sins. They say, 'He's family,' like those patients of yours who had been through so much together." Frank put his hands under Claudia's elbows and pulled her up to face him. "And as for love? We ignore the facts. Like the sun. We know that the sun is just a dying star, Claudia, a ball of gas. We know it for a fact. We know the sun can be dangerous. But we think of the sun as something generous and magical, that lets us have baseball and sweet corn and turns trees after an ice storm into these wizard's wands of pure glass. We feel like it's a privilege just to wake up to the sight of the sun. So maybe that's how it is with love. We ignore what we know. We know everybody feels it. People use the word 'love' to push people around. Love can make people cruel. Love can make people weak. Love doesn't always stay the same. And sometimes it goes dark, like a star that gets extinguished and just leaves the memory of its light. But how I feel, it's a privilege just to wake up and remember how lucky I am. If you left me right now, the memory of this . . . well, light, I would still be way luckier than I deserve. The facts are, it's too soon, and it's too much of a risk, and it's too complicated, and it could even be dangerous. It's all that. And still, our love makes me alive. Maybe we don't get a long past. Maybe we just get a future. Maybe this isn't the first time in my life I've loved anyone this much. It might be. But I know for sure that it's the last time." Claudia let one of her hands drift across her eyes, and then looked up at Frank. "So you have to ignore the facts, Claudia. You have to say yes. Will you marry me?"

"How could I say no? That must be the largest number of sentences you've ever said to me."

"It's the largest number I've ever said, period. So say yes. I want to hear you say yes."

"Yes, Frank. Yes. I can't wait to marry you."

They all stood at the Qantas arrivals door, behind the railing, Ian holding the poster that said, in block letters twelve inches high, *COLIN*.

In the end, not only Claudia but Hope had come along to New York. They'd come on the Thursday, with Frank and Claudia spending two days alone at the W, in celebration of their engagement, and Hope wandering happily around the city with Ian, up to the top of the Empire State Building, then to a matinee of *The Lion King*, which Ian loved mightily. The next day, Hope, nearly seventy-four, took Ian on a four-mile forced march through Central Park, stopping for hotdogs and the zoo. Only when he was tired did they go to FAO Schwarz, where they dropped four hundred dollars on toys for Colin, including a game system that Ian knew his brother would love, although, up to this point, the only video game Ian had ever played was something called a MobiGo at Henry, Oliver, and Abe's house. Hope drew Frank's credit card like a gun, despite understanding now that, in the part of her mind that was being steered by a four-year-old, she had no idea of the value of money.

Every few hours, Ian asked Hope, "Is Colin at the airplane yet?"

On the day of the arrival, just before they left for Kennedy, they all moved over to a couple of rooms at the Giraffe, because it was smaller and funny, and Frank wanted Colin to have a chance to put his feet on the ground for a day before they returned to Wisconsin. He needed his own feet on the ground, in honesty.

They got to the airport hours early, and took walks up and down the main terminal until everyone had gotten "the kinks" out of their legs—Hope's euphemistic term, although no one had done much except

246 ∾ JACQUELYN MITCHARD

walk for the past three days. Ian was fascinated by the electronic vending machine and Frank had taken out his card to buy a mini iPod before he realized that it wasn't his idea. Denied a music player, Ian then scowled about die-cast airplanes and jellybeans ("He's going to have to have all his teeth removed by the time he's thirty," said Claudia). Denied the jellybeans, Ian ate so many bags of potato chips that he threw up in the bathroom. Frank bought him a toothbrush, and Ian insisted on buying one for Colin as well. Claudia confessed that she felt like throwing up, too. Frank said he would also buy her a toothbrush.

Summoning up all his years of experience at imposing calm on the agitated, Frank had no more effect on any of them than an obnoxious used-car salesman.

I'm scared, said a voice.

"Don't be scared. It's fine," Frank told Ian.

Ian said, "What? I'm not scared."

Frank rocked up and down on his toes. Even his clothing felt funny, as if sewn from broken-down cardboard boxes. Every few minutes, the doors from the European flights would burst open and people would push against the barriers. People were generally too demonstrative in public. He turned to glare at some particularly boisterous groups; but they noticed him no more than they noticed the anemic music on its endless loop.

When he saw the big plane with its triangulated kangaroo in red, he said nothing at all. Behind him, rather more sternly than was her usual, Hope was telling Ian to stop running between the rows of seats. He'd already knocked over one girl's huge hobo bag, scattering lipgloss, candy, and tampons, and while she assured Hope that no harm was done, her face said that she would happily have set Ian on fire.

And then the door opened and a woman perhaps ten years younger than Hope strode out of the customs area. She was unmistakably a nun, dressed in a coarse knit suit so unfashionable it had to be deliberate, holding a little boy by the hand. He was only a little boy, small for his age, unmistakably the boy from the van. Frank saw his face that morning, determined, terrified, his chin lifted against the water that rose to his armpits. *Take my brother . . .*

What had Frank expected, a preteen?

He had.

But Colin was just a second grader, in khakis that were too long for him, a red shirt, and a navy-blue blazer. The coat he and Hope had purchased would be big enough for both boys.

Ian stopped careening. He turned, ran a few steps toward the woman and the boy, and stopped again. He was about to duck under the railing, when Frank stepped forward to quiet him. Frank watched Colin's face, an ineffable alloy of pity and relief. Colin came around the barrier and said quietly, "Hullo, Ian. It's okay. It's me."

Ian wrapped his arms so hard around Colin's waist he nearly knocked the good sister over. Hope got to them first, amazing Frank, as she always did, with the agility that let her crouch down and take both Colin's hands, once Ian let him go. "I'm Hope, the grandmother," she said. "Everything is okay." Claudia covered her face with both hands and sat down hard, in a chair. Frank wanted to say, *Mom, what happened to Frank, I hope you know what you're getting into with this other little boy . . .*

Hope stood and offered her hand to the nun, who took it a little reluctantly.

"Where is the uncle?" she said.

"I'm Frank Mercy and this is . . . my fiancée, Claudia. And you've met Ian."

"Our Colin was rather upset on the airplane," the nun said. "I'm glad we're here now." A group of stolid people, equally drab, was approaching in a throng.

"Sister!" one called, and the old woman's face split in what appeared to be an unaccustomed smile.

"I'll leave you now," she said. "Good luck, Colin. There's a lad."

"Goodbye, Sister Ursula."

"His luggage," Claudia said. "Will it be downstairs?"

"He has no luggage. That backpack is all. He won't let that go. He slept with it."

"Let's go back to the hotel," Hope said. "You're going to like New York. It's the second biggest city in the world. I think."

The two groups turned to leave each other, but Colin hesitated.

"You can," Ian said. Colin reached up and took Hope's free hand.

Frank stopped, his feet solider than his knees, which threatened to give out. "You were scared in the airplane, weren't you?" he said to Colin. "And you were bored a few days ago . . . you told me, didn't you? And you called me with your mind, and told me you weren't dead. Didn't you?" Colin nodded. "What do you call that?"

Colin shrugged. "Nothing. Talking without my mouth."

"You told me . . . Why didn't you talk to my mother and my . . . Claudia?"

As if he were twenty instead of eight, Colin jerked his chin at Claudia and Hope. "I didn't even know they existed, did I?"

"What is this about?" Hope asked.

"We can discuss it later."

That night, with boxes of clothes and toys opened and strewn around the room where Ian lay nearly on top of Colin on a two-foot-wide section of the queen-sized bed, Frank quietly told Claudia and Hope what Colin could do.

"What is that called? Telepathy? It doesn't exist. The Duke experiments were equivocal . . ." said Claudia. "But yeah. Those Duke researchers, they never met Ian."

"He's been talking to me for weeks," Frank said. "I thought I was hallucinating."

"You said he didn't have . . . this thing," Hope pleaded. "You said he was just like any other little boy."

"Mom, I didn't know! And Ian's just like every other little boy," Frank said. "I don't know if this is that thing or another thing, but I guess it exists or we're all nuts."

"It could be both," Claudia said, and sighed.

After Hope went to bed, they opened the backpack, both leery of invading Colin's privacy, both rationalizing that he was eight years old and needed protecting. If Frank hadn't known from Mother Elizabeth that it was there, he would never have seen the slit that held the documents in their thick waterproof envelope. Frank didn't disturb them. The newspaper clipping with Frank's picture was soft as flannel now, ruptured along the folds from being opened and refolded so many times. The one Brian sent must have been another copy. There was his passport, some rocks and shells and pencil nubs of the kind boys seem to need, and a small stack of ruled papers, torn from notebooks, letters written in pencil and never finished.

Dear Mr. Mercy,

Hello from me. Blessings to you in Christ. Please come get me. I am in Australia. Weetabix puts sun in your day. I am not

Dear Frank,

This is Colin. Cora died. She went with Jesus. It can be kind to let me come

Dear Mr. Mercy,

This is Colin. Ian is my little brother. I would have courage. Do it for your loved ones. I would come where

Dear Mr. Frank Mercy,

Hello. This is Colin McTeague. How are you? I am alive. I do good things. The sisters feed me. One time I was in a van after the sunami. I pushed Ian out. Ian is my brother. He is three. I did not drawn. I hit my head. I have a scar. I broke a half of my neck. Do it for your loved ones. Jesus is a loving father. Can you be gentle. Send

"The language," Claudia said. "It's so odd. I know what! He was copying what people were saying around him, and what he saw in books at the convent."

Frank nodded, barely able to answer, a picture in his mind of Colin working hard, trying to get the words just right.

Abruptly, he got up and left Claudia.

Frank had cried more in the past year than in the previous ten, but only for a moment in the morgue as he watched the attendant towel the dirty floodwater from Natalie's sweet face. To his surprise, he felt that upside-down wedge crowd his throat now. He walked into the bathroom and shut the door, closed the lid on the toilet, and rested his chin on his hands. After a while, hiccuping, he unspooled toilet paper and blew his nose. Breathing began to hurt. He blew his nose again. Frank thought he might never stop crying.

What if he had not found Colin?

What if good-hearted Brian had never done his documentary and this young boy had not taken on the equivalent of an adult earning a master's degree—in finding Frank?

The great, hot bale of guilt over the taking of Ian that pressed customarily on Frank rolled away, and into its place rolled one even hotter, wetter, heavier: he had saved one child at another's expense. Pressing the heels of his hands against his eyes, he imagined a Colin ten years on—tall, muscled by work, certainly furious, perhaps feral, left to die for his own valor—standing at Frank's door, finally to find the little brother.

A small sound tapped, apart from the ordinary whooshes and snaps of hotel atmosphere. Colin was standing in the doorway.

"Do you need to use the bathroom?"

"No."

"Are you sick?"

"No."

"What's wrong?"

"I'm not a baby."

"I know that," Frank said. "I'm not a baby either. I'm just kind of sad you had to wait so long for us."

"I talked to Ian."

"So you knew Ian was alive, somewhere."

"No, I didn't."

"You said you talked to him."

"I said I talked to him. He can't talk back."

"Oh," said Frank. It was like a radio with only a receiver on the other end, and no transmitter. "Do you have to be close to the person?" Colin looked as though he might laugh.

"No," he said. "I never tried to talk to anybody who was in the space station or something. I suppose I could, though." Colin regarded his too-large socks. "I was only a little afraid."

"You don't have to be a baby to be really afraid. When I was a policeman, I was scared lots of times."

"You were a policeman?"

"Yes, for a long time. Just until a few years ago."

Mother Elizabeth said say thank you.

Colin said, "Thank you."

"You don't have to thank us, Colin. You belong here." Frank got up and led Colin to the chair in the bedroom where Claudia lay asleep on the second large bed. "Can you hear what I say, too?"

This time he did laugh. "No!" His face sobered then, and he glanced around the room, which was done all in black and white. One wall was striped, one wall dotted, the bedsheets satiny black as crow's wings, the coverlets white, and everywhere—on little shelves, high on the top of the curtain rods that looked down over the toy-town sparkle of Park Avenue, the great dark sea of the park beyond—were those little mime dolls, pierrots, Frank thought they were called. They were creepy. Hope's room was done up as a French open-air market, a great deal more restful. Colin said then, "My mum could hear everybody, unless she turned it off on purpose. She took drugs because it drove her crazy."

She died.

"How did she die?"

"She took too many drugs one night and she just fell asleep. My dad said it didn't hurt."

"I'm sure it didn't," Frank said, thinking, This . . . and the tsunami, too? Life owed this kid an apology.

"Was Ian always able to . . . Did he always get people to be nice and do what he wanted?"

Colin said, "He could make them be the way he wanted them to be. He's mostly nice, so nice, sure. And give him stuff."

"What about you?"

"I knew people could hear me talk to them when I wanted to, from little." Colin said, "I don't think the drugs made her happy, like my dad said. I think she just wanted it to be quiet."

"Do you remember her very much?"

"In my dreaming, I do. Not really."

"I think you'll be happy here."

"Well, I have to look after Ian, don't I?"

"No," said Frank. "You don't. We do that. We're the grownups. You just have to have fun and go to school."

Colin held out his right hand. At first, Frank thought he was going to try to help him up out of the low chair. But the boy was offering to shake hands. Scrubbing at his face once more with one more wad of tissue, Frank held out his own hand, and they shook gravely. Frank then led Colin back to the bed. He put the blanket around his shoulders and Ian's. "Go to sleep." Frank went back to the chair and got out his book, flipping on the small pin reading light.

"Will you stay awake?"

"Does it bother you?"

"No. The whole window's like a light anyhow. Like a Christmas tree. Which we never had one."

"We have one now. We have two, in fact."

"That'd be good, I guess," the boy said.

"Well, okay. I guess I'll stay awake and read for now."

"Until it's morning? I don't care. I just want to know."

"Yes, until then."

TWENTY

COLIN ATTRACTED AN immediate circle of third-grade buddies. And even fourth-grade buddies. Most of them were card-carrying members of the young psychopaths' union. Colin could score off anybody at soccer. There was no wall too high for him to jump off, no tree too high for him to climb, no car too fast for him to try to dodge, no teacher too august for him to impersonate. Hope still had plenty of friends who were teachers—and one man at Linda Jean Williams Elementary said that since Colin arrived, the third-grade team met each morning to light candles in supplication that the days until Thanksgiving would fly past like the falling maple leaves.

Colin did get good grades. Everyone at home was delighted to see him so eager to get up and jump on the bus each morning, for he had never been to school before and loved everything about it, including the gruesome food. Yet Colin was also a half-broke horse. His deferential period of exploration of life at Tenacity lasted about a week. Then he grew louder and louder, and rowdier and rowdier, and rougher and rougher. A few times, he tripped Ian as they ran up the drive, once leaving Ian sobbing with a chunk of stone lodged deep in his knee. Hope saw it happen, and knew it wasn't a mistake. She hated to reprimand him so soon, with all he had been through, but it was impossible to see him be unkind to Ian, who adored him with doglike devotion. Frank and Claudia made do with frowns until the first time Colin told Ian not to be "such a fucking drongo."

Claudia lowered the boom. Honoring traditions of boyhood hardened in the fire of time, Colin sulked and objected that it was only a word. "And it just means being a dummy."

"'Drongo' was not the word I meant."

"Yeah. So?"

"Kids don't use it," said Claudia. "Even if they know it. And nice adults don't even use it much."

"Patrick does."

Glaring at Frank, Claudia said, "He shouldn't, and he's not a kid."

"They'll say I'm a sissy."

"Did boys at the convent say that?"

"When I wouldn't fight, yeah."

"You're not a sissy. Aren't you the fastest runner in your class?"

"Yes."

"And aren't you better at football, well, at soccer, than anybody?"

"Yes."

"Colin, I don't have boys of my own . . ." Claudia said, and Frank heard Colin's silent sigh and wondered if she could have put it a little less bluntly. "But I know this much. Only a fool gets in a fight for nothing. Why would you want to mess up that face? You have a face like a movie star. Tell them to shut their mouths and tell them—"

"They look like drongos," Frank put in.

"Gee, thanks, Frank. Just don't make your mouth dirty. Colin, do you want Ian to say 'fuck'?"

"Ian's a baby."

"And are you so grown-up? Are you even ten yet, Colin?"

Colin blushed. Claudia knew perfectly well that Colin was going on nine. "You can have a birthday party in a couple of months, and you can invite nine guys from your soccer team and school, and we can have a hayride, and put Saratoga and Bobbie on the hay wagon, and you can have a fire outside for hotdogs and cake. And . . . Dad Frank even has fireworks he thinks I don't know about . . ."

"You always have fireworks on New Year's in Brisbane, and in Australia, too!" Colin said.

"But if you swear again, I'll call every one of those boys and tell every single one of them that you can't have a party or presents until . . . until you're eleven. Is that fair?"

"Yes," Colin said, not like a child, but with the air of someone who was used to doing what he agreed to do, however grim.

"Good." Claudia lifted her chin at Frank and almost preened.

Then Colin said, "It's kind of not fair."

"What?"

"I never said 'fuck' in Brisbane and I never got to have a birthday party anyhow."

Against her will, Claudia laughed. On the superhighway of instant almost-motherhood, she had blown a tire.

Then, one day, she asked Colin to go for a run with her. She'd checked with her doctor, and had gotten clearance. Since her riding accident, so long ago, she'd favored stretching, yoga, dance, low-impact pursuits. She was, however, starting to notice that her pure aerobic fitness was not what she wanted it to be. "I'm going to be slow as a snail," she warned Colin.

"It's okay," he said, proud to be doing something that didn't involve a little kid, like Ian. "If I have to go ahead of you, I'll loop back, okay?"

She later told Frank that they set off across the fields, and when they got to the top of Penny Hill, Claudia said, "I'm going to have a heart attack. Let me sit down for a minute. Oh, hell, am I out of shape."

Colin said, "The van was all filled with mud and Cora was dead."

"It's too warm for November," Claudia answered carefully, because it was best to stay low and oblique. "The air smells like metal. That means it might snow tonight. At least that's what my dad used to say."

"Where's your dad?"

"Down in the South. In North Carolina. But he grew up in New York. It snows there all the time."

"She was brave," Colin said.

"Cora?"

"Yes, she was pretty brave. She was hurting my head to hold my face up where there was air. Then the water covered her up."

Claudia told Frank that her heart began to slap against her ribs at this matter-of-fact recitation of witness to a heroic death.

"Did you know Cora very long?"

"She was my mum's nanny. Not granny . . . nanny. When my mom was little."

"When she was little in Australia?"

Colin laughed. "My mum wasn't little in Australia! She was little in Leeds!"

"That's in England," Claudia said.

"Too right. Except I don't know where it is. They have football there. My dad listened to it on the radio."

It didn't seem that Colin would want to back off the subject of soccer and his own certainty that he was destined for the big-kid team because of his prowess, although Claudia assured him that he would probably be placed by age rather than greatness.

"I want to be a professional football player," he said.

"You don't mean American football?"

"No. That's for fat wankers. Real football. Soccer." He stood up. "I'm still sad Cora died."

"Are you sure she died?"

"I saw her."

Claudia and Colin began to run, slowly. Colin said that he woke with his nose filled with mud, his face pressed against the roof of the truck by Cora's dead hands. With his own small hands, he showed Claudia the size of the space, maybe three inches. He had to put his face in the muddy water to push his way out through a window that was stuck half-way down, but it was okay because, one day in the amethyst sea near the

Tree Castle—Etry Castle, Claudia thought—Cora had taught both him and Ian to hold their breath and bubble, and then to swim.

Colin swam for a few feet. He floated but the water stank around him, so he swam for a few more feet, until he could grab a piece of a metal roof. Then he climbed over that and swam a little more. At last, there was ground under his feet.

He crawled up toward a road, slipping and falling back into the water so many times he said he would have let go if he didn't make it the last time. When he did make it, he blew the mud out of his nose and wiped it on some leaves. Then he put his backpack under him and slept in the shade of a big rhododendron, and when he woke up, he tried to go back to sleep because he was so thirsty he was afraid he would die of thirst and he didn't want to die while he was awake. Even at eight years old, he knew he could not drink the floodwater. The next time he woke up, he thought he was dead then because he heard buzzing, like a million angry bees. It was a motorbike. A boy and a girl on a motorbike found this little kid covered entirely in mud. They said to the lady they took him to that they couldn't even tell what race he was. The girl held him on her lap, and they took him to a church. The minister was there, and he had a wife. The wife brought Colin to a hospital, where he was treated for what sounded to Claudia like dehydration, a fracture of his neck (Claudia assumed that this was his collarbone), and cuts and bruises.

The minister's wife sat beside him for two days.

Her name was Helen, and once, she was reading the newspaper, a special newspaper about the tsunami; Colin saw the big picture and recognized the fireman and his brother. When Helen was done, Colin didn't know if he should tell her that the boy in the picture was Ian.

"Were you afraid someone would find Ian?" Claudia asked.

"Yes."

"Didn't you want your mother and father?"

"Already dead," Colin said. Claudia wished she had a thumb drive for her own memory so that she could recall all this exactly. She told Frank later she had the feeling it would not be something that Colin would recite again—at least in so much detail.

"So, I told Frank, our mummy said it drove her mad, because she could hear when people were thinking. Not like me. Other people can hear me thinking, but only if I want to. My dad said, Mary, Mary, please no more drugs but she said shut up, go see the man with the lightning tattoo on his head, and the Hula man. Go now. She said, go now. But she was a good mummy except for those times."

"Hula man?"

"He was from Hawaii. He told Cora he could do the hula like a hula bug."

"What does that mean?"

"I don't know. But I talked to him when I was in the convent."

"He came there?"

"No," Colin said. "I talked to him like I do. I pretended I was crying. I told him that Ian was drowned and he was dead."

"So they wouldn't look for Ian."

"Too right."

Claudia said she wanted to hug him then, but knew that he could be as amiable as an oyster, so she said they had better go home, it was getting cold. The sun was setting, early, the way it did that time of year, and the temperature dropping fast. Claudia was soaked through and clammy with the chill, although Colin didn't seem bothered. She figured they had two miles to run back—she hadn't meant to come so far. "I thought I should call you to pick us up, but I didn't want to stop him talking," she told Frank later. "I also didn't want him to keep talking."

And Colin kept on talking, fearful as Claudia was that he'd blow himself out and clam up for good. As they tromped along, he told Claudia, "When I saw that newspaper, I knew it was Ian but he looked like dead."

Colin put the page under the mattress, and then, later, when he was alone, slid it inside the rubber envelope that Cora had given him a long time ago—the one that she stole from the people. In the rubber envelope was another paper envelope, and in that were all "our papers," Colin explained. He had never learned to read. His parents hadn't taught them to read. From what Colin described, they sounded like a pair of harmless hippie travelers who should never have had children. Colin described staying on "farms not like this farm," where his father fed animals and did raking and his mother slept and cried and ate pills.

They always left in the night.

Ian got them cars. Their father would take them to car-selling places and Ian would ask the car people to be nice and do that hand thing, or not even have to ask them, and they would give him a car. His father broke the cars a couple of times. They would go to another farm. Once, by a place where there were big boats with tons of people, they met the Hula man and a red-haired girl who said "fuck" all the time.

"Do you talk to her?"

"I don't," Colin said. "Never."

They were home by then.

"Are you starving?" Claudia said. "I'm starving." She added, "I want to hear more but I'm too starving. Aren't you?"

Colin went inside and yelled back, "It's Glory Bee beef stew! They've cut up the horse." That made Ian cry.

Late into the night, Frank lay awake, scoring his leg with the heel of his hand, imagining the poor addled druggie mother, who must have been so very young. The next night, Claudia and Frank took refuge at her apartment, the only place they now felt even remotely comfortable making love or talking about anything that involved the boys and their past.

"I never thought I was taking Ian from anybody," Frank told Claudia. "I would never have done that."

"How could you have known?" Claudia said.

"I should have known because Colin would have talked to me with his mind like he did when he was at the convent."

"Was your name on that photo in the newspaper?"

Frank thought. "No. But the man at the airport recognized me. And I'm not distinctive-looking." Claudia didn't disagree, and Frank was stung. Pulling out her computer, Claudia propped it on her naked belly and pulled up the *Brisbane Standard*'s special issue of images from the tsunami. "There's no name. It says an American firefighter," she told him, pointing out the picture. "How did they even know that?"

"Someone could have told them. People on my crew. Or even me. I don't remember. I don't remember whole parts of those days, or whole days, for that matter. All I really remember is calling the guy who was the head of the navy rescue, this was weeks before I left for the United States, and saying I was getting out of Brisbane the next day."

"Why did you do that?"

"I didn't want them to call me up again. I wanted to be thought of as gone."

TWENTY-ONE

THERE WOULD BE no formal engagement, Claudia said, waxing traditional, until Frank met her father and her sisters. Although he grumbled that they were grownups and he hardly had to ask for her hand, she pointed out righteously that she practically lived with his family. She did not, in fact, want Hope and the others to know that their wedding was impending until after her family was informed.

"We could go for Thanksgiving," Claudia said.

"I can't just up and leave the farm for days and days," Frank said.

"You up and left the farm for years and years," Claudia reminded him. "Patrick will look after it. We'll bring the boys and make a long weekend of it."

"Fine," Frank said, admitting to himself that he was a little rueful about showing up—the gimpy farmer and ex-cop and his two little blond jackaroos with their nasal drawls—to marry the doctor's daughter.

"My dad will like you," Claudia insisted.

"Even if you knew he'd hate me on sight, you'd have to say that, wouldn't you?"

Two weeks before Thanksgiving, Frank noticed a flyer in the Firefly Coffee Shop. It was for youth hockey, classes and leagues forming this week. Standing there in the store, he phoned to see if there were still places left for kids Colin and Ian's age, and there were, although only a couple. Hockey, Frank thought. It was difficult. It was aggressive. It was the kind of sport played by men with hair on their teeth. It would be perfect for Colin. Ian, neither aggressive nor particularly coordinated, could just learn to skate.

That Thursday night, Frank loaded up the approximate metric ton of pads and skates and sticks and helmets (could he return all this stuff if they hated hockey or were hopeless at it?) and found room in the truck for Ian's car seat and the booster the law required Colin to sit in until he hit eighty pounds. With Ian chattering away and Colin in aggrieved silence, they drove to Spring Green Ice Sports, a modest building faced in white brick, the rest of it a tin pole barn.

"Here we are!" Frank said heartily.

"Do you have to come in with me?" Colin asked. "I'm used to being on my own."

"Get unused to it."

"I know a guy in my class who's here. I bet he doesn't have a minder come with him. And I hate sitting in this baby pram back here."

"It's the law, bud," said Frank. "You're only sixty pounds. I don't know if you'll ever weigh eighty."

Colin leveled a gaze of purest contempt at Frank. "My real dad wasn't very big, but he was a lot stronger than you are. I think you're kind of a sissy."

"Me, too," Frank said, pulling out the duffels that held the skates and sticks. "You'd be a sissy, too, if you had to shoot bad guys to death in cold blood. I had to do that for twenty years."

Colin's brows arched. He was only a kid, and that wasn't fair.

"That's what you did," he said. "Claudia said that. I said, sure, I bet."

"He's a police!" Ian said. "Aren't you, Dad? Everybody has to do what he said. His big horse chased bad guys down into the woods and the horse backed them up against the fence, and Dad didn't even have to take his gun out, and the horse one time . . . What was his name, Dad?"

"Tarmac. Because he was the color of the runway at the airport, not quite gray and not quite black."

"Tarmac shoved the bad guys and Dad jumped off and tied them all up."

"He's little," Colin said. "He would believe any scary crap."

"It's true. I don't tell him the real scary crap because he's only little," Frank said.

He had, in fact, chased down an armed rapist and his wannabe slasher buddy after the buddy cut open his pregnant girlfriend's belly. Both mother and baby survived. But that had been one incident out of one. The truly grisly TV-cop-opera incidents in Frank's career he could count on one hand.

But the stakes were high here with Colin. Frank aimed to impress.

"I hate it here," Colin said.

"Worse than the nuns?"

"Maybe. This thing with skates is for wankers. My dad took us to Gabba once . . . and now, they were sports." This was Wooloongabba, the Brisbane cricket ground.

"Yep," said Frank. "Cricket. The sport of the titans. They stop the game so their mommies can bring them cookies. Look, why'd you even want to come here?"

"Somebody had to see to Ian!" Colin said, hacking at the ground with the hockey stick Frank had bought that afternoon. "It looked like fun, like Disney and those mountains with the guys skiing. But all you do here is work and sleep and ride stupid horses. The old lady is okay, but your Claudia, she's yabber yabber about how do you feel . . . just leave a guy alone! What a wowser. And the school's all for babies. I could do all that stuff when I was three."

"Collie, Claudia's good," said Ian. "She's like a good mom."

"Not mine, thanks!"

"I don't like you to be mean on Claudia. She took you running."

"She couldn't even keep up," Colin muttered.

Frank broke in: "Well, you need something to do besides watching TV and reading and poking people in school with pencils. Soccer . . . ah, football, soccer, starts in the spring. And you only just got here. Give it a chance."

"Reading! Who wants to sit and read about a bunch of fairies with horses?"

"That's a stupid thing to say. We don't call people fairies," Frank said.

"Dad, they *are* fairies. It's the *Green Fairy Book*," Ian put in. "Don't they like people to call them fairies? Do they get mad? Do you call them little people?"

Frank's mind sputtered. "A guy needs a sport. Let's go in. Or, are you scared?"

He hated himself for saying that. This little desperado was fifty-three inches tall. Colin would never have seen ice, much less tried to stand up on it. He might be hell with a soccer ball, but hockey was a complex skill set that meant the ability to control two exacting disciplines, the reason people played field hockey. If Colin failed, he'd fall deeper into the bitterness that seemed to be his default position, despite his confiding moments with Claudia.

To Frank's surprise, the first thing he heard was his own name called. Bellowed. "Frank Mercy! You sonofabitch!" (Colin smiled triumphantly.) "I thought you went back to the beach babies and the kangaroos! Somebody said you left town."

Billy Stokes (he was still called "Billy") was part of Frank's high school circle, to the extent that Frank had one. They'd played American Legion baseball together—Billy at shortstop, Frank at first—and during junior year, for a while, in some kind of bemused way, Frank went out with Billy's sister Katie. On their second date, Katie suggested that they both take advantage of the fact that they were healthy, young, and knew each other well enough to know that neither one of them was a junkie, to lose their virginity. This had seemed like a fabulous option to Frank at the time, despite his being in love with another girl—also, disconcertingly, called Kate. Now it gave him pause, when he met Billy as the U-11 hockey coach for the district, and wondered if his sister had ever told him that story.

"Bill!" Frank said. "How have you been? What has it been, ten years?"

"I see your mom and Edie all the time in town . . . they told me you got married a couple of years ago . . . Who's this?"

"How's Katie?"

"Oh, big as a house. Must weight a hundred and seventy-five. She and Ray Shawcross had five in eight years. All boys! He's a school principal in Rockford!"

"Well, this is Colin. Colin is . . . my son. Through adoption . . . well, in the process. This is Ian, his brother. Their family was killed in the tsunami in Brisbane, and my wife and her whole family were killed also . . ."

"I heard that, Frank. Hoped it was a mistake." Billy hunched down to greet Colin. "You like to skate?"

"Well, I never did. Where I live, it's hot all the time."

"Is it always hot in Australia?" Billy asked Frank. "I never knew that."

Colin sighed loudly. "That's why they call it the *southern* hemisphere—"

Frank interrupted. "Go on. I'll be right over there. And I'll come back as soon as Ian's sorted. If you yell, I can hear you."

"I'm not going to *yell*, for Christ's sake," said Colin.

Billy's eyes went wide and he shrugged. "I'm sorry," Frank said, and he heard, distinctly, *Fuck you.* "Cut that out right now, Colin."

Ian said, "I'm changing my mind. I don't really want to fall. But Colin loves it."

"He's just said it was for wankers. How do you know he loves it?"

"You shouldn't say 'wanker,' Dad. It's like a swear. It has penis in it."

"Okay, but how do you know?"

"He's saying he loves it."

Frank glanced around the partition: Colin was flying across the ice, bobbing and crossing at the corners.

"You can't tell me that kid never skated," Billy said. "He's better than my son. And Jeremy started skating when he was two."

Just then, one of the group of guys in navy-blue SGIS jackets—like grown-up septuplets, all about the same height, the same coloring, the tamped-down Zamboni caps—motioned to Billy. "Frank, your mother called! There's a fire at the farm. Now, I'm sure it's fine, Frank. Terry Jovovich's wife is on the fire department and she said the trucks were already there . . ."

"Was my mom okay? I'll get the boys . . ."

"No, no. Just go, Frank. Leave them here with me. I don't have another group until ten. Let me work a little with Colin. Maybe Ian, too. They don't need to see that."

"What happened?"

"They say the old man's pipe was what started it."

"What old man? What pipe?"

"Your grandfather. Jack. They say that he dropped the pipe he was smoking."

"He's never smoked. Not once in his life."

Frank laid on the horn all the way back so no one would even suspect that he might stop at any lights. As he turned onto Sun Valley Road, ashes flew toward him like black snow. An ambulance shot past him, running lights, as he made the driveway. Who was hurt? Patrick's low cabin was adjacent to the house, but set back from the corner where the old wing of the house almost met the old stable, a ruin Frank used as a cursory roof for protecting baled hay and a bench he had set up for mending tack. The only horse in there was Prospero, in the hospital stall Frank and Patrick had knocked together for him, to isolate him from getting kicked or overexcited. The big square stall accommodated Prospero's walking ramp and the shiny mobiles of exercise equipment the veterinary physical therapist brought in. The vet could back her van up to the wide mouth of the makeshift stall on the days she loaded Prospero to take him for X-rays and heat therapy.

It had crossed Frank's mind that the corner of the old barn where the roof was sturdiest, where he stored hay, was probably too close to the corner of the house, or at least to one edge of the broad covered porch that encircled the house. That would all be corrected when Pro was better and Frank knocked the whole thing down for good. But when he thought about that proximity, it was the possibility of rats getting into the house that he worried over—not fire.

As he wheeled up the drive, the last froth of flames was already sinking to black steam, but the smell that came toward him on the wind was cloying and unmistakable, and it was not fire.

Not Glory Bee, Frank selfishly prayed. Not Sultana. Not Saratoga.

In their thickest coats, Eden and his mother huddled halfway down the drive as Marty and Patrick led the horses up to the high pasture. The dog, Sally, slunk quaking and whining at their feet. Frank urged them all into the truck as he began to leg it up the road. Marty came back, and caught up with him in a few strides.

"Is Edie okay? And the baby?"

"She's fine," Marty said, but he looked miserable.

Patrick came past and nodded to Frank. "Have a care, guv. I'll see to the horses," he said, and Frank turned back to his brother-in-law.

"What's wrong, Marty? That old stable was nothing but a rat condo anyhow."

"The old man is dead, Frank. Your mom's a basket case."

Jack, Frank thought, and a portrait shivered for a moment in his mind, of Jack running up and down in the low pasture—his favorite horse, Rough Magic—chasing him like a puppy, although both man and horse were old then, Jack well into his seventies and Rough Magic nearly thirty.

Marty said, "He somehow walked out from that porch behind the old barn, and Jesus, Frank, we don't even know how. I didn't think Jack could walk on his own. The fire department said he was smoking his pipe and dropped it . . ."

Frank said, "Jack didn't smoke."

"Even when he was young? He must have taken it up again."

"No, he couldn't have. He was a beast on the subject of smoking, a real monster. He never had a cigarette in his life. When I was a kid, there was a guy who worked here. I remember his name was Nate Stead, because he called himself N. Stead. He'd walk all the way up to the top of Penny Hill to have a smoke, but Jack caught him. He hit that guy right across the back with a quirt, and I thought my dad was going to kill Jack if N. Stead didn't kill him first."

"Frank, the firefighters didn't even have to search. They found a pouch of tobacco and smoking stuff near that old rocker on the back porch—"

"Where was Jack?"

"He apparently walked over to the barn and dropped the pipe in the hay."

"He didn't smoke. Marty. Ever. And where would Jack have found a pipe and tobacco? How did he stroll over from the porch to the barn? He could barely walk, and never in the dark. Why would he be outside on a cold night, out having a smoke? Did my mom see him leave?"

"Your mom was with Eden at Annabelle's . . . is that her name?"

"At Arabella's."

"They were giving Edie a little baby shower, the older ladies. And I was upstairs reading. I just ran outside because I heard the horses. I never heard a sound like that. They were screaming, Frank."

"They're scared of it. And they were confined."

"Pat and I had a helluva time getting them out. We had to cover Glory Bee's eyes, and Pro . . . we couldn't . . . help Pro."

"Pro's dead?"

"We couldn't get him out, and we couldn't reach the stall. I'm sorry, Frank. We had to get the others."

Frank said, "Shit. Did you call Claudia?"

"She had some event in the city."

"Well, I should see to Mom. It's okay, Marty. The house is barely touched, and Jack was ninety-six . . ."

Then, clearly, Frank heard, *Help, Dad. Help.*

"I don't think that they're even going to investigate," Marty went on. "As to arson."

Dad! Help!

Without bothering even to speak to Marty, Frank turned and beat it back to the truck. As he got close, he yelled, "Get out, Mom. Get out, Eden. I'm sorry. I need the truck."

"Frank!" Hope cried. "What?"

"I have to get the boys."

"Why didn't you bring them back? Are they still at the skating rink? I need you to be here. Your grandfather—"

"Mom, get out of the truck!" he shouted, no louder than he meant to. Frank put his arms under Eden's and lifted her down, while Hope, indignant, braced and slid herself down from the tall running board. Frank wheeled the truck down into the gully next to the drive and back up again, hitting seventy as he gained the road, laying on the horn a second time through the two stoplights in town, hoping that whoever was out patrolling would follow him, and would try to stop him . . . He would welcome police. He would explain that his nine-year-old kid communicated with him telepathically and if they would just find him, then they could take Frank to the hospital for the mentally ill at Mendota, and he'd go willingly.

The rink was quiet, but a light was on deep within, and when Frank blasted through the door, the only ones left on the ice were Billy's older private-pay students preparing for college tryouts.

"Where are my boys?" Frank yelled from the door.

"What do you mean?"

"Where are they?"

"They went with Patrick. He came in to get them."

"I just saw Patrick . . . Billy, how do you know Patrick?"

"The little short guy? Works at Tenacity? Got an English accent? Red hair? Sure. When your mom called . . ."

Frank turned away from Billy and ran out into the empty parking lot. Who had called? A few minutes before, he'd been grimly grateful that there would be no arson investigation, despite the fact that this surely was a set fire, because Frank knew that an investigation of any kind could lead to the spurious identity of Ian Not-Donovan Not-Mercy. Now he would call the FBI if he had to. The fucking Marines. A fire caused by old Jack's . . . pipe! Frank knew now he should have never left the boys, or gone back for them the moment he heard about the spurious *pipe*! An old man's life, the destruction of a pregnant woman, a whole family—a family and their home, their horses—these were just small expediencies if they could get to the boy. He dug in his pocket for his phone, fumbled, dropped it, watched in horror as the glass shattered. When he scraped it up, it still functioned, but Claudia's number went over to voicemail. Frank limped off down the street, in the direction of the pool building, but then turned back toward the truck. What could he do on foot?

His phone chimed and Claudia said, "I already know. I know. I heard Colin."

"Where are you?"

"It was a while ago. He said help. He said, *Help*."

"Claudia, where are you?"

"I went to the farm, after your mother called me . . . but now I'm in town . . . in Spring Green."

"So am I."

"He's not saying anything. If he can't call us, he's unconscious," Claudia said. "There wouldn't be anything Ian could do."

"He could make them stop. He could make them let him go."

"Only if he can reach them, Frank. They wouldn't send someone to take them if it was someone he could get to. Who has human feelings. They must be smart enough to know he can only have the Ian effect on someone who has—"

"Claudia, not very many bad guys are very smart. And not many people are truly psychopaths," Frank said. "I'm calling the police. Hang up."

Frank heard the officer answer, "Spring Green Police . . ." before he realized he was standing directly in front of the police station, nearly under the upended cone of light that spilled out over the steps of the miniature municipal building, where small bridges with iron-lace fencing with metal weavings representing black-eyed Susan and scarlet catch-fly connected the library with the fire department, the department of public works, and the police.

"I'm calling to report that my two boys are missing . . ."

"Is this Frank Mercy?

Struck still, Frank finally said, "Yes."

"Frank, I think it's fine. This is Shane. Shane Baker. We had a report about fifteen minutes ago from a man walking his dog, an older guy who declined to leave his name, about two little boys trying to break a window at the pool building. I think there were three boys, a teenager with them at first, but he drove away when they hid under the steps. Maybe they're hiding because they think they're going to get a spanking. We sent a car over there just now, but the officer didn't see them right away—"

Frank heard Claudia scream, "Frank! Over here."

She came stumbling through the park, past the little band shell where Eden and his mother set up a cardboard stand for three summers and sold hotdogs and bloated, greasy cream puffs for a fund to make those little bridges between the buildings. Claudia came out of the darkness into the false, orange Arizona of the sodium-vapor sunlight. She was staggering, carrying Colin, whose eyes were shut, his mouth slack, and his pale hair, his white waffle jersey, and even his gray sweatpants were black with blood.

There was no sign of Ian.

TWENTY-TWO

I s HE CONSCIOUS?" Frank said, and stopped. Fear had made him foolish. "Is he breathing?

"He's fine," Claudia said. "It's . . . he says it's not his blood."

"Colin, where's your brother?"

"He's on the steps at the pool," Colin said. "He's outside. He has the skates and the hockey sticks. We have to go back. They could come back." He held out his arms to Frank and started to cry. "I thought she was gone, but she came back."

Claudia turned and ran back across the park. Frank's phone was still lying in the grass where he had left it.

It was still speaking, as though Frank had never left it.

"You were right! Hiding!" Frank said when he reached down with one hand and picked it up. "What a night for us." He pressed the bar to disconnect. "It's okay, Collie. It's okay. I've got you. Claudia will get Ian."

Slowly, carrying Colin, Frank walked through the deserted streets.

"Will you still keep me?" Colin said softly. "I don't really hate her."

"Keep you? Of course we'll keep you. There was never any thought that we wouldn't keep you. You're our kid."

"I'm pretty bad. My mum—"

"Your mum said that? You were bad? You're not bad. You just have a wild streak. That's all. Like Glory Bee."

"She didn't say I was bad. But she took drugs."

"That doesn't have anything to do with you."

"It does kind of."

"No," said Frank. "It never does. It never has anything to do with your kid."

They walked on, a few more steps, Colin's crying quieting enough so that he could catch breaths. Frank said, "I know you love Ian. I love Ian. I can help you take care of him. We'll take care of both of you. Claudia and me. Grandma and Eden and Marty. Patrick even. We don't just love Ian. We want to love you, too."

"My dad said take care of Ian, when my dad was sick."

"He meant take care of him in the big brother way, like, make sure other boys don't beat him up."

Colin said, "No, he didn't. He meant the other."

Frank could see Claudia approaching by then, bent over under the weight of the two big hockey bags, holding Ian's hand. He thought he would shout from love of her. Who had they sent—if Billy believed it was Patrick? Who was little like that? Who walked in bold enough . . . The kids didn't think it was Patrick?

"Did Patrick pick you up?" he asked Colin quickly.

Colin began to cry again, going heavy in Frank's arms, shuddering like a hooked fish. "No, no. He said it was Patrick."

"Who did?"

"The man, the coach said go ahead, it's okay. Patrick went back out to move the truck and it looked like the truck for a minute and I don't know the names of trucks from America, like Ford, and it was dark where he put it. Then a guy come down the walk and says, hi, Patrick, like a cobber, and Patrick had on this big long anorak. He picks up Ian and puts him in the middle of the front seat and then puts me on the side by the door and I knew Patrick wouldn't do that. He says sit there, all pommy. He jumps in the other side and pulled off the cap. I saw her hair and it was her."

"It was her?"

"That girl, the girl with the red hair. She said Don't you fucking move. I didn't mean to swear."

"It's okay," Claudia said.

That was exactly what Billy had said, describing Patrick. Surely, Billy was not to blame; Billy may have seen Patrick twice in his life, probably in the sour murk of Raise the Bar, the tavern where the better cut of his townspeople watered—the others driving just north to the Country Scholar, a curiously decorous name for a bar fight with four walls around it. Patrick's hair was thick, dark brown, like Frank's own.

Frank said, "Then what?" Colin cried harder, so hard that he began to choke, and leaned out of Frank's arms to throw up an evil jet of soda pop.

"I think that's enough for him now," Claudia said. "He needs to go home and have a rest. Nothing will change by talking about this right now."

"Should we . . . should we take them to a hotel or something? The house will stink of fire, and . . ." He did not say it, but Claudia would know he meant that this, on top of Jack's death and everything else, would be too much for the stunned family back at Tenacity. Even more, he was sure that Claudia didn't yet know that Prospero was dead.

She said, "I think home is best, no matter how it smells or looks. The house wasn't damaged. Just that old porch on the back of the old barn. And your grandfather. I'm so sorry, Frank."

"What?" said Ian. "Why are we being sorry?"

"There was a fire at the farm. At Tenacity. That's why I left the skating rink, but I will never leave the skating rink again. Ever. And old Grandpa Jack died in the fire. He was very old, and he couldn't get away and no one could save him."

"Oh," said Ian. "That's sad. Is Grandma okay? Is Sally okay? Is Glory Bee okay? Is Sultana okay? Is Edie okay?"

"They're okay. Let's go home," Frank said. "Let me get a blanket out of the truck."

Claudia and the boys sat side by side on a bench in the dark, chilly park as the wind plucked and tousled the leaves above their heads. Frank came back and shook out the blanket preparatory to winding Colin in it, but Colin stood up and screamed. They were twenty feet from the front of the police station, with a screaming child. An officer going up the stairs paused; Frank waved at him, and the man waved back and kept going. *We're just going to finish raping and abducting this kid and then stuff him in these big black bags* . . . Frank was glad the guy hadn't checked on them, but also felt alone at the end of a long promontory in dark water. Colin screamed again.

"Colin, what?" Claudia said.

"You'll push it against me with that blanket!"

"What?"

"The blood! I have to take these off! I don't want this shirt anymore!" He didn't even want his new shoes. Using the toe of one on the heel of the other, he kicked and shoved, trying to force his sturdy high-top off his foot.

"We'll throw them out," Claudia said. "It's okay. Right here. We'll put them in this old sack that's on the backseat and throw them out."

Frank thought, Not yet.

"We'll burn them," he said. But if the blood wasn't Colin's, Frank would keep at least the shirt and bring it to someone at the state hygiene lab, or ask Claudia to find an acquaintance to type and match it and run DNA. But why? They were ghosties. There would be no match in any criminal database. Frank extracted his pocketknife and, carefully, with the tenderest of unhurried movements, cut open the back of Colin's shirt and pants, and helped him out of his socks and shoes. Claudia unwound her white scarf and used it to wipe the blood from Colin's hair and face.

"There's a fountain over there, Frank. Wet this," she said. Turning to Colin: "When you get home, you can have a bath."

"Collie killed her," Ian said. "He had to. He had to kind of kill her. Almost."

"You saved yourself and your brother," Claudia said. "You are a hero."

Weak with crying, Colin sagged against Frank. Frank draped the blanket and over Colin's slight shoulders and then crossed one flap under the other, papoosing the boy. He pulled Colin down across his legs.

"She was going very fast," Colin said. "I had my skates over my shoulder. So I took off the rubber thing and I hit her with the rubber thing on the eyes and she put her hands up on her face and she tried to grab me, but the car went up over the side of the street, the bump there. She had to let go. Then she got out and said You are going in the back, you little buster."

"You opened the door . . ." Frank said.

"*She* opened the door and I hit her head with my skate blade and she fell down and I jumped out and I pulled on Ian. He fell out with the bags. She couldn't see. We hit her with the sticks. This man come with his dog and he said, You there . . . ! The dog started to run around and around. We ran away to the pool. I said, Ian, bash in the window. We both tried to break the window and we heard her truck and then somebody grabbed my neck but it was Claudia."

"Good job, Colin," Claudia said. "Okay, let me wipe off your face now . . ." She dabbed at Colin's face with the wet scarf—cashmere, Frank noticed—and showed Colin the stain. "Boy! This is coming off. Good. It's almost all gone. And when we get home, you'll have a bath and I'll help you scrub if you don't mind. You can wear your swimming trunks."

"Okay, but with bubble stuff," Colin moaned.

TWENTY-THREE

THAT SATURDAY, IAN followed Frank outside and, unasked, as he always did, began to help him muck out the stalls and feed the horses. A few minutes later, Colin—as he never did—followed.

"I'll do it, Ian," he said. "You go play with Sultana."

Freed, Ian skipped away. Frank wondered if Sultana would be able to keep her coat for the remainder of her life or if she would go bald in spots from being curried so relentlessly.

"Sultana," Ian sang to her as he brushed. "You are my orange and my banana. I like you as much as Grandma, rama lama lama lama . . ."

Although Colin didn't like the horses, he was competent with them, and, just as cats liked Frank—who could not stand cats—they responded to Colin with respect and affection. In this, Colin reminded Frank of himself. He did not adore horses either, but horses made themselves his.

"You don't have to do this, Colin. I got it," Frank said.

"I should help."

"You do help."

"I'm sorry I called Claudia a wowser."

"You shouldn't have," Frank said. "But she forgives you."

Colin said, "I'm sorry that your grandpa died."

"My mother heard you telling her that. In her head at church. I'm going to go plant a little tree on his grave. Do you want to come with me?"

Colin said, "Okay."

For the next hour, working quietly, Colin was a different child. It was as though the hell-raiser rheostat on Colin's personality had been turned down to dim. Lately, he was polite even with his mind. Hope sometimes heard him speak to her: *I'm sorry, but I don't like mashed potatoes because they make me gag.* So did Ian. *Ian, you can be the deadliest pirate if you want.* In a sitcom, Hope would have been taking his temperature. Time would tell whether this was Colin's personality or the aftermath of fear.

When Claudia knelt at the mound of dirt under the biggest hickory tree on Penny Hill and wept like a little girl for Prospero, Colin as well as Ian knelt on either side of her, each holding one of her hands.

"Pro was a very nice horse," Colin said. "Ian is good to the horses. More than me. But Pro was very, very nice to me."

"He liked you," Claudia said. "He could tell you cared about people, horse people, too, even though he was sick."

Claudia told Frank later that Colin said then, "Come on, Claudia. I can see Frank all the way down there. He's knocking that porch down that burned up. The barn bits, too."

"That's good," Claudia said. "It's dangerous, with all those old nails."

"He's got a magnet picks them up," said Colin. "Did you ever see it?"

Colin was telling her, Claudia said, that life goes on.

Colin and Ian took a long time choosing the little evergreen that would grow near Jack Mercy's grave. Frank explained that it couldn't get too big, because they needed to respect the graves where other old people were buried, so they would have to look at all the trees around the one they chose and make sure they weren't too big. They chose a juniper that might get to be five feet tall, and Frank then drove them over the hill to the cemetery, with the tree in a bucket of fragrant dried manure.

"Are they all old people up here?" Colin asked.

Frank thought, Oh no.

"Not every one of them."

Ian said, "Look, Dad! This one was only one years!"

Frank thought, Oh no.

He said, "Long ago, doctors didn't know how to make babies get better if they got sick . . ."

"This girl was only one, two, six, ten, sixteen!" Ian yelled. "Look, you can see her picture!"

"Let's plant Jack's tree," Frank said. "Most people grow up."

"Our dad died from being sick," Colin said.

Nearly flinching, Frank asked, "Did you see him when he was dead?"

"No, but I saw him when he was sick. He was in the bed. I heard people talking about him being dead soon, he would die pretty soon."

"What did they say?"

"What if those boys find out they were dead this whole time? What if it messes Ian up? Then the old guy said, oh well, boo-hoo. We will unmess him up."

"What about your granny?"

"She was a nanny."

"I don't mean Cora."

"I didn't have a granny. My dad said, Mary, you and the kids are my only family I have. That was when he wanted to stop taking drugs."

"When was that?"

Colin thought hard. "It was a long time ago. Maybe I was seven. Maybe. It was before we lived in the tree."

"What tree? This would be just right before the flood. Right?"

Colin shrugged. For what did years mean to a child? The time before Christmas was the same as the time before dinner, the time that Ian found the sea turtle's shell was the same as the time Ian got a cold coin for making the red horse win the race, and the time when they had a swimming pool was the same as the time as when they lived in a tree. They weren't real memories but collages cut from shadows and circlets of memories and photos and murmurs overheard.

On the subject of his father's death, however, Colin was firm and detailed.

"He had stripes in this throat. They didn't let him go to a doctor because he would tell about Mum and us. He got very sleepy and even more sleepy. Then one morning I woke up and he wasn't there. Then Cora took us to the place with the pool."

"I know!" Ian shrieked, raising his hand. "I had a burn."

"Did you have to go to a hospital?" Frank asked.

"It was just a sunburn!" Colin said. "He got a sunburn right before we left the island with the tree castle."

"What was it?"

"A tree castle."

Not *Etry Castle. A tree castle*. They really did live in a tree house.

"What was that like?"

"It was really, really big. It was built with all these pretty walls with different grass baskets for shelves. It had ten rooms but not a fridge. It had beds but not a real roof. You could run on the swingy sidewalks."

"I know!" Ian cried out again. "You had to go in the boat to the town. We had cookies and ice cream in town. I never had ice cream!"

At night, they took the ladder down and left them up there with Cora. "It was four hundred feet," said Ian.

Colin said, "Like high as the racehorse spinner on the barn."

Colin meant the weather vane. So thirty or forty feet up, perhaps more. The red-haired girl, the same one Colin hit with his skate blade, came one morning to bring their food and unlocked the door to the stairs and let the stairs fall down from the tree house. She turned her back when they climbed down the stairs.

"Did Ian make her do it?"

Colin nodded. He didn't know why that day and not another day.

Cora drove them to the airport in a Jeep she found on the street. He didn't know why.

They met a lady who gave them the purple van and gave Cora money and bought them backpacks and shorts. He didn't know why.

They went shopping and had corn and ice cream. Then Cora was crying and pushed them in the purple van. The man who wore soft shirts was chasing them in a car. He didn't know why.

They drove too fast, and Cora wasn't a very good driver, and she drove off the road, right down into the flood.

Colin didn't remember very much of his first few days in the hospital, except that he always felt like he was just about to wake up or just about to go to sleep.

Then a woman came, with a tape recorder the size of Colin's smallest finger. Another woman took pictures. She talked to Colin and asked him where he lived and what his mommy and daddy's names were. Colin didn't answer. Then two men came from the TV station, calling him "Moses."

Colin said nothing to them either. He knew that his parents would not come, but he was afraid that the girl with the red hair would. She didn't. Neither did the tall black man with lightning tats on his head, or Hula man, or the man with the sharp nose who wore soft shirts. No one came, despite newspaper pictures, and stories on the telly and police searches.

Colin never told anyone about his family, or the house in the tree, not even the nurses or the doctors.

After a while, he got better and went home with Helen, wearing what he described as a big scarf around one arm, which Frank interpreted to mean a sling. Helen had cut out the stories about him, and put them into a folder from the church that had a big blue-and-gold cross on it. She got him a new backpack and offered to clean the rubber-coated envelope. Colin liked the new backpack, a big North Face Borealis, orange and blue, but he would not give up the brown envelope even to be cleaned. She might steal it. Once, he woke from sleeping in the church house and heard the minister and Helen having a fight. Helen was begging to keep Colin, and the minister was saying that his flock were their children, although at the time Colin didn't know that the minister meant people and not sheep.

Colin heard her crying, "Robert, it's as if God Himself sent him to us."

But the minister said, "I'm sorry to see you this way, Helen. Maybe you are suffering from division."

The wife said, "It's not a case of division to want a child! All women want a child."

"God didn't give us a child, so there must be a divine raisin. It's up to you to find the raisin in this."

The minister's wife had a sister who was a nun, Sister Mary Francis de Sales. The minister said he would drive Colin to the convent if Helen didn't.

One day, Helen drove him to the convent, and hugged him goodbye, still crying, as she had for days, pretty much all the time—but her sister did not. Helen smelled of pears and face powder, and she was a little too old and sad to be a mother. Still, he would have rather stayed with Helen and the minister than with the nuns.

The nuns were even older, and they liked the seven girls but not any of the boys, except the littlest, who was only two. They ate the same food every day—porridge for breakfast, toast and potato soup for lunch, carrots and eggs for dinner, and on Sundays some nasty fish and more potato soup. There was a box of dominoes and a box of checkers, but so many pieces were lost there was no way to make up proper sides for a game. After a couple of months, some ladies brought other things, writing and drawing paper and pens for everyone, and puzzles with a thousand pieces, and a race car set. The older boys took the race car set and wouldn't let the boys Colin's age or younger ever touch it. But Colin got writing paper and pens and hid them in his backpack. For months, he slept and played in a long room high up in the nuns' house, with the seven other boys bigger and littler than him. The big ones farted all night. The little ones cried for their mummies and the big ones cried, too, but just when it was dark. The littlest boy cried until he was sick on the floor about once a week. The biggest one punched Colin's face and pinched and pulled on his willy, and told other boys to do the same but only one did. The boy said he'd say Colin tried to grab his butt in the shower if he told.

So he didn't tell, but he thought all the time about Ian and he asked if he could help the nuns in the kitchen. They said he could. He washed potatoes, and then he could hear the telly and the radio without them knowing. He watched the lines on the TV so he could make out some words, because he still couldn't read or write. After a while, he started to recognize lots of words. He found words in a book of fairy tales and more in a book of children's prayers.

He started writing his letters to Frank, although he knew him only as "the Fireman."

Colin was sure that when he completed one, the nuns would find a way to send it. He would talk to them, without talking, and they would. He didn't give them any of the letters, though. He wanted to wait until he was sure of the best one, the one named Mary Dominic, who always gave him sweets that her younger sister sent to her, little sugar half-moons that tasted like oranges and strawberries. He told her he didn't know nuns had real sisters, and Mary Dominic started to cry.

Colin took action.

"She's sad," Colin told Mother Elizabeth Gray. "She wants to go home to her real sisters."

"She's not really sad, Colin," said Mother Elizabeth Gray. "She's just going through the hard time people go through when they have a vacation."

One day in the late afternoon, he overheard the program that Brian Donovan made about his family. He saw the picture. He heard the name of the firefighter, Frank Mercy, whom the TV guy called "my gallant brother-in-law." He would have to change the name on all the letters!

Sister Agatha said, "Sister, please turn that off. There's a young one here who has had enough of—"

But then Colin screamed, first with this mind and then with his mouth, "No!"

All the nuns came running, from all over the building. Even the ones out in the garden heard him scream, in their minds.

"What, child?" Mother Elizabeth Gray said.

"That little boy! That is my gallant brother," Colin said.

All the nuns clustered around.

Which picture had his brother in it? Could Colin tell if the brother was alive? Colin wasn't sure; Ian couldn't talk to him, but he had a notion that he would know if Ian had died. After all, he told Frank, just a few seconds before he hit his head and passed out, "I saw you grab Ian, Dad."

Frank could tell that Colin didn't want him to react to the use of the word *Dad*, so he simply nodded.

The big man from the telly showed up three days later. He walked with a stick but he was kind. He said he had two girls who died in the flood. He took Colin out for lunch, for a huge lunch of shrimp and chips. He took pictures of Colin with a camera that made the pictures right there before your eyes, and gave Colin one and promised he would send the other one to Frank Mercy.

Six sleeps later (Colin counted every night by making a little mark on the wall with his toothbrush), Mother Elizabeth Gray came to tell him to make sure he had a good shower and wore the clothes given to him by the women from the committee, because he was going to the United States the next day.

"Jesus Christ!" Colin said.

"Don't swear, lad," the nun told him.

Colin told the mother nun that he was praying. "Why am I going?" he asked her.

"Someone there is sending for you. Someone who has your brother. You have an uncle there."

"Were you excited?" Frank asked. "About leaving?"

"No, scared."

"Of course, you didn't know me."

"I thought you could be a bad guy. You could work for them. You still could work for them."

And why not? They'd been little children living with what sounded like rather bemused hippie parents. Their mother died. Their father died. Except for Cora, the people they were left with treated Ian like a tool. They made Ian do things that Colin knew were stealing. They went on planes to cities. Sometimes they slept on the airplanes. Ian asked people to give him pictures from the walls in big white buildings that only had pictures and jewelry from locked stores with buzzers to let you in. The man in the soft clothes and the red-haired girl always took them, not the Hula man or anyone else.

Always those two. They dressed differently every time, in hats and wigs. The man made his hair blond.

"There would have been cameras in the walls at those places," Frank told Colin. "They take pictures of those paintings because they're very valuable."

Not very good cameras, he thought.

But Frank didn't know where the museums were, or what had happened to any of the security systems before the pair brought in their risk-free, blood-free, hassle-free theft device.

"She took us to this place once where they had little dolls that were God," Colin said. "Little dolls made out of rocks. They took us to the racetrack a lot. That's why Ian likes horses so much."

Wherever they went, they saw people who were friends of theirs and Ian made them give things to them.

"Did you ever tell the people you didn't want to be with the man or the red-haired girl?"

Colin's eyes saucered. "No!"

"Were you scared to?"

"She said Shut the fuck up or I will fucking kill you."

How colorful.

"So you thought I might have fooled Mother Elizabeth? Did you tell her you were afraid?"

"I was afraid more to stay there. It would have made me mental."

"I'm surprised he isn't mental anyhow," Claudia said to Frank, later. "He might never trust anyone." She paused. "At least, like I said, it didn't happen when he was older."

"Can you be grateful for something awful that happened," Frank asked her, "just because it didn't happen later?"

TWENTY-FOUR

T HEY HAD DECIDED to arrive at Dr. Campo's on the earliest flight, the morning of Thanksgiving day, leaving on the Saturday night. Frank was happy about that. In and out. Not too much scrutiny from Claudia's sisters. Albert Campo was the second generation of Campo physicians, his mother a doctor in the United States Air Force, and Claudia was, she said, her father's favorite, the one who'd followed in his footsteps.

Then she brought up Julia Madrigal.

That was another story.

Frank had forgotten about the woman Claudia had met when she was a medical student. The woman who was like Ian, who was the reason that Claudia hadn't run from him like he was on fire, back on Edie's wedding day when she saw Ian stop the neighborhood horse thief in his tracks. He didn't suspect a setup. But when Claudia suggested that they visit her, being, as it were, in the neighborhood, Frank felt queasy. It all seemed too southern and gothic. There was nothing he wanted to do less than climb up to some tumbledown cabin to encounter an eccentric who shot squirrels with an old and unreliable rifle. Frank was, irrationally, he admitted, deeply suspicious of anyone who lived south of Peoria, Illinois.

"I don't know if I want them to meet her," Frank said, when they were on the plane. It was nine in the morning and the boys had fallen instantly to sleep. Claudia had already called the woman, and made an appointment to drop by for a cup of tea on Friday. Frank hadn't objected—which was not, to him, the same as agreeing.

"What? Why didn't you say something?"

"I didn't want to be rude. And you just sort of bulled ahead with it . . ."

"I did not bull ahead with it, Frank. I asked you if it was okay, and you shrugged your shoulders. That's the same as an oration from you!"

"I did not say yes."

"Well, what are you scared of? She's not a goblin. She has more experience with this than Ian and Colin put together, too. They've lived it, but she's lived it longer. What if she has some insight about how to help them manage?"

"She won't."

"What if she does?"

"She won't."

"If only you weren't so truculent!" Claudia told him. People in the airplane glanced up from their newspapers.

"I'm not . . . what?" Frank said. He knew perfectly well what *truculent* meant.

"Silent to the point of irritability. Unforthcoming. An asshole."

"I'm not in the least silent, Claudia. I just don't emote, like you do. I'm betting she'll say, Well, everyone's different. And she'd be right. Big deal."

"But how has this affected her life? I think I remember that she kept to herself. Do we want the boys to"—she made quote marks in the air with her fingertips—"keep to themselves?"

Frank didn't answer at first. He had begun counting out his life in incident-free increments, bundles of days. It had been weeks since the fire and Linnet-like-the-bird's attempt on the boys. In Frank's ordinary life, the one he'd planned to have, any one of a dozen incidents in the past five months would have been the signal event of a *decade*. In this reconstructed life, an ordinary day was rare and treasured. Why not just be happy? The teacher scrawled radiant praise all over Colin's homework papers. There were no more mutterings of mayhem. Ian was the sunny center of his class. (Ian also got excellent grades, at whatever kindergartners got grades for, although Frank couldn't be sure that Ian wasn't putting the moves on the teacher's brain through some kind of sweet-natured necromancy.) The mother of the satanic triplets now brought them to Tenacity Farms in the way a pilgrim would approach a shrine. Eden's pregnancy was blossoming. Hope's health was good.

Why ask any questions at all?

Still, he knew that this fragile bubble would burst, in a way that Frank hoped would not be threatening or grotesque. He knew full well that these people—nameless, but so described by Colin that Frank felt sure he could pick them out of a lineup—weren't going to give up. Linnet and her not-real-father and the man with the lightning tattoo, the Hula man, the fireman, whoever else there was, they wanted Ian back as much as Frank wanted to keep him—for reasons exactly antithetical in the universe of reasons.

How would anyone manage a long life with those kinds of stresses? Why even think about them? Claudia, meanwhile, waited for him to answer her, her temper visibly escalating. Was he afraid? Was he afraid of seeing what Ian and Colin could become?

Frank changed the subject. He said, "Do you think Ian is too nice?"

"I think it's the way he is."

"Nobody could blame Colin for being so mad he wanted to kill somebody, the way he was when he came. But Ian's nice to everyone. He's almost supernaturally, what would you say, caring. He really cares. He hardly ever has a tantrum . . ."

"There's no reason to have a tantrum if you think, I want manicotti and you get manicotti. I'm surprised we don't have it every night," Claudia said.

"There are kids who run their parents like that without any particular powers except their parents are too tired."

"Somebody might say it was reaction formation," Claudia said. "He's so nice because in reality, he's so mad he wants to kill somebody, too . . ."

"Thank you, Dr. Freud."

"I'm not the one saying that. Some people would say that."

"It's farfetched."

"But maybe that exaggerated sympathy is what people—"

"And dogs. And horses—"

"Beings. Creatures. They could be responding to that overly nice—"

"I think that's nuts."

"I think you're nuts," Claudia said. "You're the world's youngest grouchy old man." She finished her ginger ale and asked, "Do you think about Natalie all the time these days? And that you would have been a father by now?"

Frank's breath hitched. The baby . . . his son . . . would have been five months old. He'd have recognized Frank's voice. Kids smiled by five months, maybe they sat up or something. Grief seized his gut like a cramp. The truth was, he thought of Natalie all the time, but he did not think of the baby.

He was a father. He had a boy. Ian. Colin.

"Are you nervous about me meeting your dad? Because I'm not a doctor? Because I'm just an ex-cop with a dirt farm?"

"It's better than last time."

"Wow!" Frank said. "What last time? Is it that the air is thin up here or what? More headlines in the last hour than in the last month!"

"I meant, the last time I took a man to meet my dad. And Becca and Miranda, and all my nieces. We all got married the same year, and only one princess got a shoe that didn't fit."

"Which one?" Claudia smiled and lifted the dregs of her ginger ale in the parody of a toast. Frank said, "Wait! You were *married*?"

"For a stupid, really stupid, not even agonizing, just stupid eleven months."

"You never even said . . ."

"It wasn't worth even saying. I got my lab partner confused with my life partner. I had this idea that I had to get married and have a baby or I never would. And I was twenty-five when I was thinking this. Then, one night, we were at a party and I caught him making out with this first-year, and I have no idea why, I was humiliated, and I threw a punch, and—"

"He hit you?"

"The girl hit me. The first-year! And she knocked me flat on my ass. I got a bruise on my eye like a plum. So I ran home to my mama and daddy. I never even picked up my clothes. He never tried to call me, and I never tried to call him. He had money, so I sold my big old engagement ring, and I packed up Prospero and I moved to Madison, and do you know what? I have no idea whatever happened to Prentice Allen. I have no idea where he is now."

"I promise I won't let anyone punch you in the eye," Frank said.

Dr. Campo lived in a four-story log home girded with as many decks as there were doors. Each deck was equipped with wooden rockers that invited the occupants to look out upon mountain views so absurdly spectacular that Frank kept expecting someone to turn off the projector. Handed a camera, a blind man could have pointed it in any direction and created a calendar. To the east, notched into the chin of a taller hill, was a waterfall that spilled down into the open skirt of a river hole. The older man had earlier wrapped a bundle of egg sandwiches with slices of onion, and taken Ian and Claudia's niece to fish until he had to go in to work, a brief round of visits to his patients at the medical center at Claudia's alma mater, Duke. Dr. Campo—who said to Frank, "I know I should say, call me Al, but nobody calls me Al. I'm Albert"—specialized in cardiopulmonary bypass surgery. "It's just like plumbing, Frank. Exactly like plumbing. You have a clog, you replace the pipes, tell him use some fiber now, Drano, keep those pipes open." Albert quickly took the boys down to fish for trout, along with the youngest sister's little girl, Ray, short for Ramona. "I'm not a fan of turkey, really," Albert said. "Are you, Ray?"

"I love turkey, Grandpa," she said. "I would eat it every day."

"It's bland, Ray. It's not the Italian part of you that likes turkey. That's why we're having pheasant, Ray! It's a nobler bird. And Cornish hens! Like having a little chicken all to yourself. The Italian part of you knows that all that's better than turkey."

"But all the other parts of me don't know that," she said.

The other girls, the older sister's daughters, Angela and Mary, dressed Ian up in an old gypsy dance costume that had belonged to Claudia's mother. All the sisters teared up. Colin held back.

"What's wrong, buddy?" Frank asked him.

"They're like . . . half-wits," Colin said, sounding so grown up and weary of women that Frank couldn't help but grin. "Can I go in there where the big TV is and watch hockey?" Billy, who still had no idea of what had really happened the night of the fire, said that next year, whatever age he was, Colin would have to move up a class.

"I'm so sorry about your wife," said Becca. Her husband had yet to arrive, delayed at work, like Miranda's husband, Mark, who was a private caterer. Frank smiled briefly in acknowledgment. People always told him that they couldn't imagine the tsunami, and, since they were correct—even if they had seen videos, they really couldn't imagine it—he never elaborated. Not long after, they sat down to dinner, Colin by then awake and ravenous, Ian content to watch this celebration of gluttony, a holiday he had never seen.

"Rad says to go on ahead without him," Becca told everyone. Rad was her husband. They sat down. But when he was served a Cornish hen with wild-rice dressing, Ian, who ate everything, refused to even try it. He said it was creepy.

"Picky eater?" Becca said. "I had one of them. Got to cure him. Tabbouleh for a week."

"No, really not. He loves food," Frank told her. "What's up, buddy?" Ian flushed. Frank might not have noticed it if Becca hadn't leaned over at that moment to light the candles, eight of them in two small and one big candelabra. Darkness pressed close against the windows, having fallen, as it sometimes does, rather than slipped down slowly. Frank could still see a halo of fading purple crown the crest of the tallest visible mountain.

"They're babies," Ian said. "I don't want to eat a baby."

Colin had come back. "They're grown up, Ian. They're just little. Little tiny chicken legs."

"That makes me gag, Collie."

Everyone laughed, and Ian, still wearing the gypsy shirt and a spangled kerchief, got up. As if he'd seen leaves turn over and clouds begin to pile, Frank sensed a storm. Not now, Ian, not in front of . . . He stopped himself, realizing he'd been about to think, family. But Ian simply walked away, muttering "excuse me," and went to the nearest bedroom, a small room that seemed to be in part used as a library, and lay down on the daybed, his face pressed into Frank's light jacket. Frank swallowed the three bites it took to consume his whole meal, and then got up, intending to check on Ian. With his mind, Colin said, He's a baby. He's spoiled. Frank ignored Colin.

Not that anyone would have heard him.

But he was distracted in his progress by Claudia and Becca, arguing loudly about the likelihood and feasibility of a woman president while Miranda tried vainly to call a truce. "I just don't think the country's ready," Becca said.

"You mean your husband, Supercoach Rad Cartwright, isn't ready," said Claudia. "And maybe you aren't either. It might lead to a shortage of cheerleaders with their pointy toes and their pointy boobs."

"They're third in the nation in their division, Claude." Becca was a cheerleading coach—this, like football, was one of the Stations of the Cross in North Carolina.

Claudia flapped the towel at Becca. Then she nudged Frank and whispered, "Hey!" It meant, Frank, do we tell them now? Frank nodded, gesturing that first he would check on Ian. He did.

"Are you sick? Is that why you didn't want to eat that little chicken? It was a grown-up chicken," Frank said.

"It icked me," Ian told him simply. "I didn't like the slimy berries either and the rice had yellow stuff in it."

"That was curry. You like curry," said Frank.

Ian actually shuddered.

Claudia came in and said, "Eeny, are you better?"

Ian put the pillow over his face. "I'd be better if everyone would leave me alone but Dad." If he had said this to Frank, Frank would have slunk away hurt, but Claudia, equable creature, just rolled her eyes and made jazz hands at Ian's fretful form. "I just want to go to sleep, Cloudy." It was a massive admission for a kid in a house full of kids.

"Let me tuck you up," Claudia said. "You don't have to brush your teeth."

From down the hall, Frank heard Colin say soundlessly, *He doesn't have to brush his teeth?*

"If he's sick, we'd just have to throw the toothbrush out anyhow. Bet you didn't brush all the time in the tree castle," Claudia said, knowing Colin would hear. "And no, I am not spoiling him."

Being able to sass with your mind had its advantages. As Frank watched Claudia tuck Ian in, he could not help but admire how capable she was—how she had gone from a presumably preening, pretty, pampered, and accomplished young academic darling to a loving and beloved . . . well, mother, in such a short space of time.

"Claudia," he said.

"Hmm?"

"I love you."

Colin telegraphed to both of them, *UGH.*

"So, okay, if you stop talking. Cloudy, why don't you take Colin and go play with your sisters?" Ian sounded just like an impatient adult who wanted a moment's peace, telling a child to go upstairs and work on his puzzles. Whiny wasn't like Ian.

"I'll do that," Claudia said.

Colin came in and said, "I think you're faking." Mean-to-Ian wasn't like him either. Something was in the air.

Frank told Ian, "I can't stay in here all night. We're visiting Claudia's dad and that means they made all that nice food, which you wouldn't eat, for us. I have to go back and talk to them, because we're guests. But

I'll be with them, right out there . . . okay?" With one hand, Ian was making a circling motion that plainly said, *blah, blah, blah.*

"Just talk to me about something, okay?"

"For a few minutes."

"About your gun," Ian said.

"What about it?"

"Do you still have your police gun?"

"Yep."

"Are you sure?"

"Yes, I'm sure. I have two guns."

Ian sighed. "Good." He said, "So, are you sure you never shot anybody?"

"I'm sure."

"What would make you shoot somebody?"

"I guess, if somebody tried to take you."

"Somebody might try to take me."

"Who?"

"A bad guy. You took me."

Frank's stomach rolled. He didn't always reckon on Ian remembering
his deliverance. This was the first time he'd ever spoken of it.

"Yes. That was wrong, too, Ian. I don't know why I did that."

"You wanted me."

"You don't just take what you want."

"*Did* you want me?"

"I wanted to help you," Frank said.

"You didn't want me, to be your boy?"

"Yes, I did. But I don't know why I thought I could just take you."

"Was it wrong for Collie, too?"

Frank said slowly, "If I really thought so, I guess I'd give you back to
somebody who was related to your—"

Ian sat up, and began crying. "You'd give us to someone?"

"No, no, no. Didn't I just say no?"

"Promise. Never."

"Never. Not ever. I promise."

Despite his pallor, Ian then seemed energized. "Don't they have any PBJ here?"

"Yes. How about just some cornbread and a little turkey instead?"

"How about no. Can we get a PBJ? Or some Brie and jelly like Claudia makes?"

"Sure," Frank said. "Those guys. How could they make you go with them to get things, Ian?"

"What things?"

"Things the bad guys wanted, like money or to win a race."

"They would say Get up or I'll kill Colin or Cora."

"Why didn't you . . . make them be nice?"

"I did, lots of times."

"What happened?"

"The guy who was nice, another guy shot him . . . Can we *please* have food?"

"Aren't you sick anymore?"

"I wasn't sick. I was mad. I don't want to go see that lady Cloudy knows."

"Cloudy says she's really nice."

"They will for sure kill her, then."

"Huh." Frank couldn't swallow. He stood up.

"Plus, Colin says someone is thinking some goddamn bad things," Ian added.

What a hallucinatory quality life had. Frank walked out into the dining room. "Ian, yeah . . . he wants to know if you have any peanut butter and—"

"Picky eater," Becca said.

"He's tired, is all."

"Let him go to sleep hungry once . . ."

Frank said, "No." Becca widened her eyes.

Claudia got up and began cutting slices of the thick bread.

"Would he rather have Brie and jam?"

"He would, actually."

Miranda said, "We should go soon. I thought Mark would be here! We're cooking out tomorrow night, right, Dad? No baby chickens?"

"Just trout. And steak," said Dr. Campo. "You know, Frank, Claudia's been fishing all her life."

Just then, Becca's husband, Rad, hipped his way in, a case of Buried Hatchet ale under one arm. Hellos rippled around the room, and Claudia gave him a kiss, and teased him, "I hear congratulations are in order. Another championship season."

"Fingers crossed," Rad said.

What had Claudia told Frank about this guy? They got married when they were both twenty years old? In college? No, that was Miranda, the younger sister, the chef's wife. Becca's husband was a coach, but he'd been an all-American Tar Heel. They got married the day after graduation, because Becca was pregnant with Angela. Kind of an asshole, Claudia said, who still blamed Becca because he hadn't gone all the way to the pros. Frank pointed out that other guys with kids had done that. "Could he really have done it?"

"I don't know that much about football. He was a running back. He didn't have that much size or that much speed. Good, but not *that* good. Good enough for a full ride. Smart enough to stay in. But he's one of those guys who's still living the dream of that championship season when he was a freshman at UNC. So now he's a math teacher, coach at St. Michael's, where we all went. And Becca feels guilty, so he's got that going for him, too."

"They always do."

Now Frank made his own assessment. A drunk. Though he was younger than Frank by a few years, Rad's nose and cheeks already had the stamp of the drinker, like the tiny lines on a map that symbolized rivers. Whatever looks he'd had were roughened, maybe by the outdoors, maybe by the booze. Before he stowed the cans in the iced cooler, he popped open a brew for himself.

Albert began pouring sweet after-dinner wine into ornate miniature glasses.

"Hold on to those for a moment, Dad," Claudia said, taking Frank's hand. "Rad, come to the table. Let's give some thanks. Frank and I have something to tell you."

"No way!" said Becca.

"Oh, Sissy!" said Miranda. "That's why you're so shiny and pearly!"

"I didn't even say anything yet," Claudia said, pretending to pout.

"I'm a lucky man," Frank said, summoning up the nerve to make the equivalent of a speech in front of strangers. "This terrific woman says she'll put up with the likes of me."

The sisters applauded. Dr. Campo said, "That's good news, Claudia. When is the big day?"

"We're not going to have a big wedding. I'm training, you know. But soon. In a few months. Then, in the spring, you'll all come to the farm and we'll have a huge party."

"I've never been that far north," Becca said. "What's it like?"

"People eat roots from the ground they dig up with their teeth," Claudia said. "You never came to see me, that's right. And you've never been even to Chicago? Not even for a competition?"

"As far north as Kentucky," Becca said.

"Well, you will love Frank's farm, and his sister and her husband, and their mom, Hope . . . "

"She's a widow, Albert," Frank said, and the sisters applauded again. "And she's got multiple graduate degrees."

They all lifted their glasses, and when Frank caught Colin's eye, Colin was smiling. He let himself nurture a spear of hope. They would never be the kind of family made from the usual materials; but they would be a family. To look at them now, they already were. For a while then, Frank nearly dozed, as Becca and Rad, and to a lesser degree, Albert, watched two teams from somewhere south of Peoria bash away at each other.

"So you're Claudia's latest?" Rad said. It took Frank a moment to wake up and realize that the man was really expecting a reply.

"And greatest," Frank answered. "I don't get the impression that I'm part of a long tradition of boyfriends, not that we talk about it much."

"Last one was a doctor, though."

"I'm just a farmer."

"But you train those horses like hers."

"The riders, too."

Rad hunched forward in his chair, one hand entirely encircling the can of ale sweating into his thick, denim-skinned thigh. "If I was a psychiatrist, I'm saying, and making good money like she makes, would I take two years off to try to dress up in white pants and one of those sissy coats and be in the Olympics? You bet no, sir, I would not. And what if she don't make it? There's two years and your pay right down the shitter." Rad sat back with an approving nod, as though that were that.

"She's on a sabbatical year, this year, for starters, so she gets paid, and I guess it's what she always wanted. She wanted to do it before—"

"And she broke her damn neck! What if she kills herself this time? That old man can't take care of a disabled daughter, and she's got no husband."

"If she killed herself," Frank said, as unable to resist what came next as he was sure he should keep his mouth shut, "nobody would have to take care of her. And you heard what she said. It won't be long before she has a husband."

"You know what I mean."

"I know you're concerned, sure. Horses fall, sure. Riders fall. It has its risks. And now that her horse got hurt, the young horse she's riding is pretty spooky. She's a game horse but she needs a lot of rider. I would worry more if it was any rider but Claudia."

"You put her on a wild horse?"

Frank felt his knee bite him; it was like what he'd heard people describe as the aura they saw before a migraine, lightning flashes from the corners of their eyes. His leg was just heralding a storm, which he hoped would blow itself out tonight so they could get back to Wisconsin, which suddenly seemed like the end point of a pilgrimage. But the sharp pain was an alert; it felt like a gut reaction to Rad's challenge. Slowly, Frank said, "I didn't put her on anything. Look, you've known Claudia longer than I have. She does what she wants."

"Becca does what I want."

"Hmmmm."

"So you make a good dollar training horses? And women?"

Desperate now, Frank glanced around for an exit plan. Dr. Campo was snoring, and Colin was pitching fly balls to Angela, and Ian was nowhere in sight. Just getting up would be downright un-southern-hospitable, although maybe the guy would think that Frank was going outside to smoke or something. Not once in his life had he ever provoked a confrontation.

"So, your team is doing well," Frank said, imploring Claudia to come to his side. But Miranda's husband, Mark, had just come in, and exchanged an exhausted greeting with Frank in the full minute before Claudia commandeered him to discuss a wedding cake, gold, like a medal, and blue flowers, five layers, but nothing tacky . . .

"You weed out the pussies who're afraid to hurt their little fingers . . ."

"Dad," Ian said, appearing, his hair as wet from running as if he'd taken a shower. "We were playing under the porch, and, Dad, I'm not making this up, you can ask Ray, we saw a bear! I know it was a bear, because it was black. Ray said to yell, 'Go away, bear!' because they wouldn't hurt you, they're actually, actually scared of you, but the grandfather guy has binoculars down there, and we got them out . . ." Ian went still.

"Who's this?" Rad asked.

"My son, Ian. Say hi, Ian. Shake hands."

"You married, too? On top of everything else?"

"Widower. My wife died a year ago. Ian, this is Rad, Mary and Angela's daddy."

"You don't have to hit Cloudy's sister," Ian said. "Be nice."

Rad's hand closed around the still-half-filled can, nearly crushing it.

"Be nice. Be happy. It makes her sad because it hurts." Ian turned to Frank. "Dad, do you want to see if we can look out the top floor and maybe see more bears?"

"Sure," Frank said, and to Rad, he shrugged, in what he hoped was the universal sign for *What can you do with kids?*

Rad's mouth squirmed. "Your kid here, you should teach him some manners. If he was my son?"

"But he isn't."

"Whatever a man does with his wife—"

"Is probably private unless he hits her and then it's not private, it's public. A few years ago, I met a whole lot of big boys like you who liked to tie one on and then knock their wives around. You might have friends who look the other way, but they're not as good friends as you think they are."

"This from a volunteer fireman?"

"Yes," said Frank.

"You don't talk like a fireman."

"Well, Rad, for twenty years, I was a cop. And you know, a lot of guys, they feared domestic disputes, the way you fear going in a yard where some asshole has trained the dog to attack because he thinks it makes him have a bigger dick. But I loved bringing those guys out. I loved it. I bet I could still do it."

"Be nice," Ian said.

"You're right," Rad said suddenly, and Frank gasped. He breathed heavily, like a man after a run, or a fight. "I never laid a hand on Rebecca before. But she can't take the . . ." He lifted the can and shrugged. "The booze. This stuff. She hates it with a passion."

"Quit," said Frank. "People do."

Rad's already fuddled eyes watered. He stood and held the can in his hand. He said, "I'm afraid to try. But she's going to take my girls and leave me."

"You wouldn't want your girls to be afraid."

"No."

"So try."

"Okay," Rad said.

Later, Claudia, Frank, and Ian lay in the little bed that had belonged to Claudia's mother, with Colin on the floor, on a pile of pillows covered by sheets. There were plenty of bedrooms, but neither of the boys was interested in being alone. After the excruciatingly long time she spent every night brushing her teeth (Frank was surprised that her gums weren't bloody rags), Claudia came into the bedroom, as fetching as a child in black buttoned-up pajamas with polka dots. Abruptly, still smiling at her, Frank fell asleep. And then he woke. There was a knock at the door of the bedroom. He glanced at the clock. It wasn't even ten. Why did it feel like a quarter to next week?

"Claudia?" said a deep voice.

"Dad?"

"I'm sorry to bother you."

"Are you okay, Dad?" She got up, snapping on the low bedroom lamp, and Frank could hear her mentally rummaging for a stethoscope, as if her dad was clutching his left arm in pain.

"Claudia, there just wasn't time to speak to you two about this earlier, and it wasn't something I wanted to do in front of everyone."

"Are you sick, Dad?"

"I'm as good as living forever, Claudia. I have something I'd like to give you, if you two want it." Sitting down in the low sewing rocker, Albert opened a small ornate carved box.

Claudia said, "Those are Mom's rings."

"Well, I wanted to know if perhaps you'd like to be married with your mother's wedding ring."

"Dad, won't it hurt Rebecca? She's the oldest. And why . . . Dad, I was married before and you didn't offer me this."

"Well, I had a feeling about that adventure," Albert said. "Let's leave it at that. And I have a feeling about this one as well."

Claudia kneeled next to her father's chair. Painfully swinging his aching leg over the side, Frank sat up in his sweats and Albert placed the yellow-gold basket-weave setting with the big old-fashioned pear-shaped stone in his hand. Frank said, "You're the one kneeling, Claudia."

Shyly, she sat next to him on the bed while he slipped the ring onto her finger. She hugged her father, and Frank shook Albert's hand. "Those are very nice boys," Albert said. "I apologize for Rebecca's husband . . ."

"No need."

"But you handled it admirably. And so did Ian."

Together, without words, Frank and Claudia lay with the boys tumbled around them, admiring the dusky majesty of the old ring. Then Claudia got up and lay down on the other side of Ian, scooching her body close to his, adjusting the light-blocking mask she said that she would need if she lived in an underground cave, then doing the thing that endeared her to Frank in a way that almost nothing else did, not her smarts, or her riding, not even her sexy. Claudia wasn't like other women, who needed to be draped in someone's arms as they slept. But she needed a little touch. What she did was straighten both her arms and tuck her hands under Frank's back as she prepared to sleep. Now Ian, Frank had noticed, did the same thing on those nights he slept next to Colin.

Frank lay awake, listening to some chuffing and coughing noise in the near distance that was certainly too big to be anything but a bear. Somewhere out there was the nutty old woman they would go to see tomorrow, stirring a pot filled with eyeballs and dried frogs, who Claudia seemed to think might hold the key to their future. Frank was sure she had the key to nothing. What else was out there?

He never wanted to get out of the soft bed, which felt like an old refuge where two hardheaded people guarded two kids who were not only small and vulnerable, but who knew it. If only there were just bears, or wolves or sharks, or anything with simple reasons for their rampages.

TWENTY-FIVE

THE SIGN READ, *Please Park Here Wildflowers.*

"Is that a signature? Or a reference to the flora and fauna?" Frank said.

"I don't remember it this way," Claudia said, taking Ian's hand. Frank took Colin's hand. Colin shook him off, and then, glancing up, repented. Ian counted each of the two hundred and fifty-six steps that led up to what they all assumed would be a house, although nothing was visible from the stairs except a dark crowd of fir and maples, second-growth trees huddled along the jaw of a ridge. When they got to the top, even Claudia, who now regularly ran three or four miles around Lake Monona or at the farm, was pulling her soaked linen shirt away from her breast and gasping. Frank's bad leg and his lungs were burning flaps.

Ian was spent.

Colin was fine.

As they drew closer, they saw the house, which to Frank looked so little he could scarcely believe it was inhabited by humans and not elves, but it was sturdy, the yard so colorful it was almost a sound. Instead of the traditional southern wraparound porch, there was a sort of squared-off widow's walk with high railings on top, which Frank imagined must give a killer view of the valley and the hills beyond, this afternoon cloaked in the blue clouds that gave the range its name.

"Do you think she's here?" Claudia said. "I sent her a note, just as I was supposed to do. Do you think we have the right time?"

Some heightened sense of his own made Frank turn around, so quickly he almost elbowed the tall, dark-haired woman standing so close behind him she could have cut his throat with the large set of garden shears that lay in the flat basket she held. She smiled, a smile that burst up into her all but black eyes like a small sunrise. Not pretty . . . the word that came to Frank was *arresting*. Her hair was very long, and though Frank couldn't tell how old she was because her face was fair and unlined, she was probably past the age when his own mother said that women needed to cut their hair so as not to seem to be pretending to be the girls they were once. "I think we're looking for your mother," Frank said.

"You'd have to go all the way to Tampa for that," the woman said. "It's me you're looking for." She set the basket on the ground and held out her hand. "Hello, Claudia. It's been a long time, but you look just the same."

Claudia said, "You recognize me?"

"Not that many medical students come to see me. In the thirty years I've lived here, you make a grand total of two," said the woman. "I think the other one was my kinsman, your professor. I must have seemed so old to you then."

How long could she have lived here, alone on this mountaintop? Frank studied the woman's face. If she was forty, that would have made her less than thirty when Claudia first visited this place. She had to be older than that. The thick mink-colored hair was not graying, however, and although she was dressed for the outdoors, it was in modern and expensive clothes, tapered gray pants and a long black sweater that hugged her thighs. She wore silver filigreed earrings and a touch of expertly applied makeup.

"Do you have children?" Frank asked.

"Have we been introduced?" she said, with a disarming smile.

"I'm so sorry. I had the feeling that we had been. I'm Frank Mercy, and these are my sons, Colin and Ian."

"And I'm Julia Madrigal. There are dozen of Madrigals all over this county. I do have children. I have one son. His name is Hale. His name is Hale Winslow, though. His dad's name. He's at basketball right now. Colin, you don't have to be bored. Go up there behind the house. There are about six tire swings."

"You heard him?" Frank said.

Julia said, "Sure."

"That was rude, Colin," Claudia said.

"Well, he is bored."

Colin glanced at Frank and then took off.

"Telepathy is pretty useful and amazing. I think I know about thirty senders and that many receivers, about ten who are both."

"Their mother, before us, was both," Frank said.

"Ian, you're about four or five, right?" Julia said. "Do you watch TV too much?" Ian nodded. "Hale does, too. But not on school nights." She gestured toward her door. "I built this house myself. You won't believe that, but I'm very handy. Our old house was much bigger, on this very site, but not nearly so energy efficient. You know, Claudia, I am still a kindergarten teacher. Do y'all have Saturday kindergarten? We're thinking of starting it here. I've just been picking in my kitchen garden and puttering around until you came." Julia Madrigal smiled, displayed a full set of very straight and well-kept teeth.

Not one element of her appearance or demeanor conformed with what Frank had envisioned. She lived in a Spartan cabin. She had herbs in her basket—but they were parsley and oregano. She looked like an Eddie Bauer model. Something about all that ordinariness made Frank wonder if she was an authentic . . . what? They'd never figured out a name for it. Should they call Ian a healer? A medium or some goddamned thing?

Opening the unlocked door, Julia invited them in.

The house was little, but gave the effect of spaciousness because it was so spare and studded all around with cut-glass windows. The table and benches were built into one wall, as were two benches that snapped flush when they weren't in use, and two chairs that could be pulled up to little shelflike desks: Frank imagined the young Hale, who had feet the size of a teenager judging from the rubber muck boots stationed on a sisal rug at the door, doing his homework. There was a galley tightly fitted with almost miniature kitchen appliances. The ceiling, crowded with three big triangular skylights, went straight up to the peak of the house. A small spiral staircase probably led to the top deck. Loft railings jutted out on three sides—the two bedrooms, Julia explained, and the room that jumbled together a library, TV area, and playroom for Hale, as well as spillover sleeping for guests.

"My husband, Cato, he just loved the old house. But you could have pushed a rat through the holes in the walls, and when I saw the state of that cellar after I tore it down, I reckon that plenty of rats had done just that. Cato died when Hale was just five, in an accident . . ."

"You couldn't warn him?" Claudia asked, and then, embarrassed, put a hand up to shield her eyes.

"I'm not a psychic," said Julia Madrigal. "I can't do what Colin does, send messages or speech telepathically. I can't see the future, honey. There was a logging truck and its brakes failed. Cato was just pulling out of the grocery store. That trucker came down Canaan Road like a freight train and the poor driver was killed as well."

"You must have been happy together," Claudia said. "You and Cato. Imagine being able to get your husband out of a bad mood just by being around him."

"We were happy. I never met anyone else I enjoyed talking to as much as Cato. We could sit and talk for eight hours, and, when Hale was a baby, sometimes we did. Cato built furniture. Yeah, I know. That seems just like what you'd have to do if you live in the Smoky Mountains, but he was from Brooklyn, and we met in college. He taught me to build and do woodwork. He studied graphic design, but he never did that."

Claudia said, "What did you major in?"

Julia smiled at Ian. "Witchcraft," she said. "No. Elementary education, since here I am, showing kids that if you pour a half a cup of water with yellow food coloring and a half a cup of water with red food coloring, you get a whole cup of orange. What I'm like, what there is about me . . . what I can *do*, if you want to say that, is not learned."

"Can everyone in your family do it? Because you all should be working for the diplomatic corps, don't you think?" Claudia said. She never said "you all," or lapsed into any other southernisms, in Madison, but her speech had stretched out like taffy since she set foot in North Carolina.

"Nobody else in my family can do this. Nobody even wants to know about it. And as for diplomacy, that's the last thing our government would want—or any other government either. Too evolved for them." What Frank had fussed around with for so long, picking at pieces and edges, suddenly merged: this woman was entirely correct. There was no money in peaceful coexistence. Someone who could foster it was as perilous as a nuclear weapon. *Be happy.* Hell no!

They will for sure kill her, then.

Julia was brewing coffee, slowly slicing a small loaf of banana bread. Colin came in, sweaty. Julia asked the boys if they liked Legos "because Hale has about seven thousand five hundred and eighty-two Legos up there, if you want to play." Ian glanced at Colin, then Frank, then Julia. "Does he have the Death Star?" She nodded. Colin asked, "Could we have some of that bread first?" They did, and then disappeared. "Hale will be sorry he missed them. Not too many boys his age right near here."

"What protects you?" Frank asked, when his boys were gone.

"I used to think about that, being kidnapped by people who wanted to make twenty billion dollar corporate mergers between paranoid corporate leaders. That never happened. No one pays attention to me."

"Claudia said you helped people. Couples. Others. People who got drunk and hit their wives. Who hit their kids. They stopped doing that." Julia nodded and Frank went on, "Can you stop them from being drunks? Like with my grandfather, who's dead now. He had dementia. Ian couldn't make my grandfather well, but he made him stop smacking my mother with his cane and throwing his food at the wall. So, what if they go back to drinking—"

"Most of them never stop."

"What's to keep them from just blabbing in the local bar about what you can do?"

"Nothing. I don't think about it."

"What, you just have faith? In God or something?"

"Or something."

Frustrated, Frank got up and shoved his hands into his pockets, sighing as he gazed out the window. "Why don't you get on a plane and go to, well, Brooklyn and ask someone to give you ten thousand dollars, and then fly to Los Angeles and go to a bank and ask someone to give you ten thousand dollars, and then fly to the Emirates and tell someone to be nice and give you a million dollars . . . ?"

"I'm not set up like that. When I was twelve, I did it with mascara, though. My parents weren't unaware of this. They made it clear that there were appropriate and inappropriate uses for all extraordinary things, just as you will do with your boys. Colin could tell other kids the answers to all the tests, if he knew them, right?"

"Yes."

"Does he?"

"I don't think so."

"He's not wired to do that."

"What does the sign mean that says wildflowers?" Frank asked.

"I don't want people tromping up the low side of the hill and wrecking the wildflowers. They aren't really wild. I sowed rue anemone and hepatica and cohosh and dwarf crested iris just how I want. It should say, 'Beware the owner of the wildflowers.'"

Julia stood up.

"I would guess you all are thinking now, Why does she sit up there with a kid, waiting for someone who wants to use her badly? The practical reason is, this is my home, and where would I go that anyone couldn't follow? People I help out are grateful. They're resourceful and supportive, and protective. Some of them are in law enforcement. Others pitched in to help build the house. Some are clergy. They don't tell, except maybe others who might need me, too." She unselfconsciously began to braid her hair, then to loosen it again. "There's also the fact that anyone who came here with . . . well, bad motives would be affected by me, unless they were crazy. Or missing something."

"What is it that they would be missing?" Frank asked her.

"A human soul, for want of a better term."

"That is exactly who would come," Frank said. "I used to be . . . never mind. People don't go out to kill somebody because they think, Hey, there's this lady making the world a little too safe around Durham, unless they're stone thugs. Irredeemable. You have to find a real fine citizen, a piece of meat, to kill a lady and a kid because they're supposed to."

Claudia was staring at him. She wasn't used to Frank speaking out, especially to strangers. But he couldn't stop himself.

Julia said, "I can't do anything about that . . ."

"Move, or put in a machine-gun turret, or an alarm system. Get a guard dog or a moat. Or something."

"That person you describe wouldn't be deterred by any of that."

"Frank," Claudia said. "You're really worried about them, I know, but what she's saying—"

"Of course I am!"

"We're here to learn from Julia before any of that becomes an issue for us."

It already was an issue, Frank thought, but he said nothing.

"You know, Frank," Julia said, in the voice she would use to tell her kindergartners it was time to clean up their paints, "I don't know anyone else like me. So, can I spend some time with Ian?"

She climbed up, and Colin came down, now clearly close to hostility from enforced hanging around.

"My neck hurts," he said.

"Like a sore throat?" said Claudia.

"No, like . . . something else. I'm just so bored. Can you drive me back to the grandfather's place so I can go fishing and you can stand here and talk all day? I'd rather be back with those girls than be up here."

"Let's climb up to the roof porch," Frank suggested.

Colin said, "Fine."

Frank and Claudia climbed up to the little square porch, where they stood looking out over the ancient furred folds of the mountains. The watery sun and the constant breeze made Claudia sleepy, so they went back down, just as Julia came out onto the landing, beaming.

"What a great kid. What an instrument he has."

Instrument, thought Frank. Like a cello. Like a scalpel.

"And you, Colin, do you have any questions?" Julia asked. "Other than, when can we leave?" She said to Claudia, "Your teacher, back then, called me an empath. But I'm not an empath. An empath is just someone who feels deeply, sometimes to extremes, and who feels called to nurture and give emotionally. You're probably an empath. Many good therapists are. But Ian is different. Ian is an empath and he also has a tremendous, maybe unprecedented ability to exercise what you would call mind control. I am different in that way, too. He can change things and behaviors. Discord hurts him, physically, and makes him feel sick, like he was telling me about your sister's divorce—"

"My sister isn't divorced."

"Ian said your sister is divorced."

"Ian never met my sisters until yesterday. Which sister?"

"He didn't say that, honey," Julia went on. "If he only just met them, I'm sure he doesn't know. He's four. He wants people to feel better. Of course, he's a kid, so part of the reason he wants people to be happy is so it doesn't bug *him*. Or torment *him*." Julia turned to Frank. "But he is also very afraid of bad guys. I think maybe you're putting that idea in his head." Julia Madrigal stood. "I'm sorry to be rude. But now I have to go get Hale. It was so good to meet you all."

She held out her hand.

Frank shook it, feeling her confidence, wishing he could feel anything like it, knowing that wasn't his portion.

By the time they returned, Albert Campo had fished out the stream.

"Look at these trout!" he crowed. "Fresh as if they were still in the stream."

"I can't eat them," Ian said. "They look like not dead. Can I just have corn? Just corn. Just corn and bread," he said.

Claudia said, "Let him have the full-starch option, Dad."

The rest of the evening passed peacefully, and Frank would later be grateful that the first time he'd spent with Claudia's family, all together, which would also be the last time, was so pleasant for both of them. A year later, Becca's husband, Rad, would be killed by one of his best friends in a hunting accident, and by then, Claudia lived so far away that she couldn't even come home to these mountains to comfort her big sister. As a token, for Frank, that weekend was pure and good, a memory he would keep in his hip pocket like his first wedding, a photograph that never got old. Years later, standing alone on some canted hillside, shivering with sweat as he tried to wedge rocks into a makeshift wall, clouds like dirty sheep crowded overhead, Frank would think of the amber evening light in Dr. Campo's kitchen, and watching Claudia so young and so content with all she did, solicitous of her dad, girl-giggling or gossiping with her sisters, deeply compelled by Julia Madrigal, and so tenderly proud of the sweet dependency of the two young boys so newly in her life.

In a few quiet sentences, late that night, Frank told her what had transpired with Rad Cartwright, making only the slightest allusion to the abuse. Claudia's voice bristled. "I don't know if even Ian or Julia could ever change what a jerk he is, but Rebecca didn't seem to mind that he had to be the big, swaggering jock until . . . he started . . . until . . ."

"Until he slapped her around? That's what made Ian sick the first night. He wanted Becca to be happy."

Claudia, who seemed to have prepared remarks for every occasion, could only say, "Wow," followed by "She's getting a divorce? Is that what Ian meant, what he said to Julia? Becca said he hit her once, by accident."

"She's ashamed," Frank said. "For every incident of domestic violence reported, the stats say seven more are never reported. I'd bet that's more like ten or twenty."

"But in my own family."

Frank considered how rich he would be if he had a nickel for every time he'd heard that particular remark. Claudia might be a psychiatrist, but when the planks were in their own eyes, he guessed, they were probably as vulnerable as any other Joe. Even at four, Ian clearly could not ignore what needed doing. He couldn't go through the world easing every dispute. Frank imagined Ian on a street corner in Chicago, with two business harangues, one hostage situation, four phone spats, a breakdown, and a breakup, all unfurling simultaneously within the range of his hearing.

He said, "I hope he helped Rad and Becca. But Julia's right. Ian has to grow into all this."

"Julia seems pretty serene."

"Julia lives on a mountaintop covered with flowers. She's worked at it. She's somehow learned to confine it to when she needs it." He thought of the last thing Julia had said, as they stood at the foot of her hill before driving off, that as she grew older she knew, instinctively, where she could go, where she could not go. She seemed to suggest that the knowingness went with the gift, and that it grew with the gift, and with the person.

Frank had to remind himself again of Ian the adult. If he really was theirs now, someday he would not be. Between any parent and any child, a series of ruptures happened in a natural way, as a child moved out of the parent's boundaries and tested their new freedoms. And when those ruptures healed, they left their breaches, wider each time, the easier for the child to slip through the next time adventure beckoned. The next misadventure. Although Frank understood all this, simply from having lived, there was no way to take comfort in any of it. Ian was still as light in his arms as one of Julia Madrigal's flat reed baskets, filled with nothing but bright leaves, and this thing that pulled Ian along was big, stronger than Ian, stronger than Frank, too much for this little . . . for his little boy.

When Glory Bee was bothered by flies, her whole body cascaded shuddering muscle. Frank now felt his own flesh in such a waterfall of shivers. In Frank's mind, Ian was perpetually a child. But in a dozen years, he'd be grown. He would go to college and get a job and fall in love. He would want to know about his background, or he wouldn't. As Frank had, he would want to put as much distance as possible between himself and Tenacity Farms . . . or, as Frank had, he would want to come back. Someday, Ian would be . . . what? A divorce lawyer? Nobody would ever get divorced. A judge? ("Please. Be happy . . .") A diplomat in the highest realms of dominion? Or would he be a mail carrier, a bricklayer, a bus driver, anything to keep anyone from ever noticing the Ian effect?

Someone would, though.

"She's adjusted," Claudia said. "She hasn't always lived on a hill. She's been around. Ian will do all the things people do, and he'll adjust. He'll learn to do what she does, to confine this to when he needs it. She said she's never met anyone else like her."

"She said that Ian is more than her."

"If he is, well . . . he'll still learn. I don't know how to tell him when it's appropriate. I mean, is it ever inappropriate? It sort of came close to crossing that line with my sister and her husband."

"It turned out okay, though," said Frank, who remembered Rad's congested face and how close he had come to putting his fist in it.

"When I was a little girl, my parents were really careful to say that no one should ever tell a kid not to tell secrets."

"That's how you turned out way too mentally healthy," Frank said, smiling in the darkness.

"But they did tell us that some things were *I-T-H*, and that meant 'in the house.' Private things that were just for our family. So, do we tell him that this is like that?"

"I guess. At least for now."

Frank kissed Claudia's outstretched hand, happy again that they had come to these mountains, when he noticed again the unaccustomed ring on her finger. He thought of the lamplight on her father's thick pelt of silver hair, his thick nose and peasant hands, like Claudia's hands, so unlike the hands of the surgeon Albert was. A good old man, happy for his daughter. But even stoking that feeling, he couldn't shake the chill that swept over him: Julia somehow knew that no one was after her. Ian just as clearly knew that someone was.

TWENTY-SIX

WHEN THEY GOT BACK, the farm, to Frank's consternation, was not even remotely a shambles. If anything, Patrick had done it up so well Frank felt like he'd walked onto a movie set. In honor of the coming season, he'd strung the entire small pasture and the peak of the barn with white lights, and Hope said he'd gone scouting for Christmas trees just the day before. A new bin with a snug hinged and handled lid ran along one wall, and the untidy lower stack of hay bales was surrounded by a slender slatted cage. The horses looked to have been polished. Glory Bee's coat shined like a crow's wing.

The next day, Claudia at work, the boys full of yawns but back in school, Frank called Brian Donovan again. The reverse of a man asking for the daughter's hand, Frank felt it must only be meet and right that he should tell his late wife's brother that he would be married again. A sign of respect. A sign that Frank still considered Brian his kin. It was about four in the afternoon in Brisbane, and the phone rang for so long Frank thought he'd have to leave a message. At last, though, Brian answered, sounding as though he'd been asleep. Frank's worry about Brian spiked anew. "I don't work today," Brian explained. "I was up late reading, and I fell asleep."

"You sound just beat."

"I am, Frank. Every day is harder with the anniversary coming."

This was the worst time to share his news. Frank felt guilty for the joy that underlay the occasional searing remembrance of Christmas past. He thought of a line from Carl Sandburg: *So far? So early? So soon?*

"Really, this is why I called, Brian. There's something I need to tell you; not about the boy, that's all under control. It's that I'm getting married."

So far? So early? So soon?

"Why, that's wonderful, Frank. I wish you only good luck."

"She's very like Natalie. Not to see. In some other ways. Her sense of humor is like Natalie's. Of course, it's not the same. It couldn't be. You only have one first love." In his abashed state, Frank didn't want to back himself into dismissing Claudia as though she was the local tavern keeper and it was just easier to screw her at his house than in the room above the bar. "Her name is Claudia Campo. She's a doctor. A psychiatrist."

"Did you go to see her after your bereavement?"

"She's one of my brother-in-law's professors." Jesus Christ. "My sister's husband, that is. I met her because she's training for the World Cup. Jumping."

"You're still on that?"

"I didn't expect to be, but yes."

"Well, I hope you find contentment and joy, Frank. You deserve it. And it's good for boys to have a mother. She's fine about the boys, is she?"

Frank murmured agreement. He said then, "Brian? Do you ever think that someday you . . ."

"My children died, Frank."

"Of course," Frank said.

"I wish I had, too."

"Brian, come to us for Christmas. My gift to you, please. Everyone would love to see you. A change of scene. It's been years since you've been in the United States. You loved New York. Meet us there . . ."

"I can't, Frank. Lovely of you to ask. I'll let you get on with your day . . . well, your evening now," Brian said. "Have a good night. And a happy Christmas to you." Frank was possessed with the belief that Brian Donovan would take his own life. There was nothing he could do.

Sensing his mood, Claudia came home late, after the boys were asleep, ate a few bites of something from the refrigerator, and sat quietly in the kitchen. Then also quietly, with Claudia carefully dressing in modest flannel pajamas striped in pink and black, she and Frank propped themselves up on pillows, turned on their reading lamps, read their books, and went to sleep.

There should have been champagne and exhausting passion on their engagement night.

But it was no ordinary engagement.

They were no ordinary couple.

Between them swung the weight of sorrows and secrets, the private words and deeds that bound them now, and would never go away. So, in a sense, they were already mated, each the bearer of the other's seal.

The following morning, since Claudia didn't have classes, they'd already decided to treat themselves to the fun of telling everyone else the good news. Frank wouldn't get up at five for chores, and Claudia wouldn't get up at five to take a run and get ready for classes. They would act all crazy, and sleep until seven, like the rest of the household.

Claudia woke first, and tiptoed down to get a cup of tea. The smell of the first day's coffee was like reveille at Tenacity and would get everyone up. When she returned, with two fragrant mugs, she said, "I'm not even sure that Ian knows that was why we went to see my dad."

"Of course he knows."

"He doesn't usually pay any attention to most adult stuff unless somebody's in trouble. That way he's like any other kid."

As if summoned, Ian came in first, fuddled and puzzled that Frank hadn't woken him for chores and his mostly milk coffee before the school bus.

"I'll drive you to school," Frank said. But Ian was distracted by then, by the unfamiliar sight of Claudia in her candy-striped pajamas. "Cloudy, you had a sleepover."

"She can have sleepovers now. We're getting married," Frank said.

"You are?"

"We said so about a hundred times at the grandfather's house."

"I was sick in bed. I was sick from those sickening dead bird babies."

"Yes, of course, I forgot," said Frank. "We have to remember never to cook baby birds for you. No four and twenty blackbirds baked in a pie."

"Did people really do that?" Ian asked.

"No," Frank lied. He knew very well people had, and starved the birds first, so they wouldn't crap as the oven's heat climbed to intolerable levels. He steered the subject away. "Will you let Claudia be your mom?"

"Can I still call her 'Cloudy'?"

"No," Claudia said. "You can call me 'Cloudy' for fun, and I can call you 'Eeny' for fun, but you'll have to call me 'Mommy.'"

"Well, okay." With a small, secret smile, he climbed into Frank's bed between them. "What about Colin? Will he be jealous if I call you 'Mommy'?"

"I'll be his mommy, too, of course," Claudia said.

Colin came into the room. "You stayed over! Does Hope know?"

"I'm going to move in," said Claudia. "We're going to get married."

"I thought that was what you said to all those people when we were having dinner. But I didn't know because at first, I thought you were married already and you just lived someplace else because you were maybe getting a divorce." Frank thought, What a swell job we did of explaining Colin's new life to him.

"Ha! Nope," Claudia said. "There will be some big changes around here, buddy. Like, you have to mind me."

"I already mind you. I'm a mind reader," Colin said, and punched Claudia lightly. She pulled him down and kissed him, and he allowed it.

Hope hurried past, hearing voices, and determined, with purposeful grace, not to notice Claudia in Frank's bed.

"Mom, wait!" Frank called. "Come back." Sighing audibly, Hope did. "We're getting married."

"You're getting married?"

"You're getting married?" Marty said, passing the door in his Badger sweatpants. "Welcome to the fam, Professor Campo."

"*You* are getting married?" Eden said. "You. Frank Mercy?"

"What does that mean, Edie? I was married before. Not so long ago at all."

"You're such an old bachelor. I thought that Natalie must be an enchantress to have broken your will." She leaned back against the wall, her big tummy stretched low against her long nightshirt. "Crabby old men who own six identical shirts must be the thing for beautiful doctors now."

Frank gestured around him, at Ian now somersaulting off the end of the bed. "Edie, you're my sister, so you can't appreciate what a stud bomb I am to other women." Colin laughed until he had to run and blow his nose. "I think good wishes are in order."

"I think good *luck* is the wish—for Claudia anyhow."

"Clearly, cranky Irish girls with big mouths are all the thing for upcoming young Jewish doctors now." Marty made a whipcrack sound with his tongue.

They all stopped as they heard Patrick open the back door and begin to make coffee, grumbling and whistling through his teeth. "Pat!" Marty called. "Frank's getting married."

"Ah, shit," Patrick said. "Does Claudia know?"

TWENTY-SEVEN

J UST HOME FROM early Mass on Christmas Eve with Hope, Ian asked to lead the prayer at the table that included Hope's friend Johnny, the new librarian, and Johnny's beloved, Blake. The food wasn't even on the table when Ian took up his solemn stance at the head: Marty and Claudia were still ferrying steaming platters from the kitchen, where both stoves and both ovens had been working double time since before dawn. In the middle of the living room, between the leather couches that usually faced the fish tank, stood the tree, a blue spruce twelve feet tall and comically rotund, set in a giant galvanized bucket of sand. With the boys, Patrick had made a Yorkshire Christmas tree: they'd folded and strung multifaceted stars from aluminum foil and pierced them with thread. They dipped pinecones in glue and rolled them in glitter. They strung red ribbons from branch to branch, and wrapped the core in white lights. With Hope's small favorites, made by her children, and the handblown glass icicles of many colors that Claudia carried home one summer from Italy, the result was a quiet country fantasy out of Dickens, a kindly and humble tree.

Since the doors from the bedrooms at Tenacity opened out onto a wide hallway balcony with balustrades, Frank and Claudia had taken the precaution of hiding not just the children's Santa presents but everyone else's under the fitted rubber cover on the back of Tenacity's big pickup truck—a tarp tightened down with fasteners that required a tool to open. Even if the boys thought of the hiding place, the adults were reasonably sure they'd never be able to breach it alone. However, Johnny and Blake carried in piles of gifts, Blake wearing a quilted foolscap and a cape in motley colors.

Toasting and prayers, Johnny and Blake insisted, had to wait until after gift giving.

When they handed Colin three wrapped packages, he said, "Thank you, but you don't have to give these to me. You don't even know me."

"But you're Hope's grandson . . ."

"*She* doesn't even know me!"

"We think you must be a good kid," Blake told him. "We think Ian is great, and you're like Ian, but older, so you must be smarter. It's okay to accept presents from friends of your family, and this is your family now."

Ian said, "Be nice now. Let's all eat and pray."

Ian had taken to religion with gusto—and now was part crypto-Catholic and part devout pagan.

He began, "Let's pray for Natalie, because she died at Christmas with no presents."

"Okay," Claudia said, and they did.

"Let's pray for those old people at the farm where Glory Bee lived, and Patrick's sainted mother . . ."

They did that, also.

Ian next ordered a prayer for Grandma to live for a long time, for Ian to be given the power of invisibility, and—Claudia misted up—for Prospero to have wings.

"This is a lot of praying," Frank said. "Can we be done?"

"Just one more," Ian said. "God, please show us how to make an ark."

Frank said, "A what?"

"So we can get out of town in the flood."

"There's not going to be a flood in Spring Green," Frank said.

Then why, Ian wanted to know, had the Sunday school teacher in this very town told them the story of the ark with two cats, two geese, two cows, two pigeons, two zebras, two wombats, two polar bears, two spiders, two monitor lizards, two fruit bats . . .

Frank thought, Why indeed?

"Amen!" Colin said.

Ian crossed himself in several different ways—including one that looked like head, shoulders, knees and toes, knees and toes, and everyone fell upon the platters of turkey, ham, venison, extravagances of potatoes scalloped, mashed, and twice-baked, dressing with apples and walnuts, cranberry relish with orange peels, and breads in the shape of petals and pinwheels and pretzels.

Later, they played games, like charades, that were old to everyone except Ian and Colin—who both had to be taken aside and warned against using any funny stuff in aid of their respective teams. They held a baby-naming contest for Eden and Marty's child. Claudia and Eden were certain it was a girl (Eden favored her grandmother's name, Philippa). Everyone else insisted it was a boy—whom Marty wanted to name after *his* grandfather, Saul, a pronouncement that invariably drew ire from Eden ("Why not Shlomo? Why not Yehuda?"), an outburst that Marty quite righteously found baffling. Eden admitted to being the world's snarkiest pregnant lady, and said they should have let the doctor tell them the baby's gender at the ultrasound instead of being coy about it.

"You could find out now," Hope suggested.

"Oh, it's too late now," said Eden. "Now it would just be weird." She apologized, and went off to bed, Marty following, and calling down, "Well, *shavua tov*, everybody."

Hope, Blake, and Johnny were playing cutthroat Scrabble when Frank turned in.

But he slept uneasily.

Frank imagined he would dream of Natalie, and he did, but not the sweet angel dream of a husband greeting his first true love across the star-strewn gulf of eternity. Natalie came into the room, blue-lipped and naked, her hair wet and slicked back, the morgue sheet slipping from around her hips, trampled under her feet, where puddles formed. In her arms was her unborn baby. *So soon, Frank? Do you think of me, Frank? Be careful, Frank.* A foot from the bedside, Natalie thrust the half-formed baby at Frank. He jerked awake, drenched in sweat, and stumbled from the bed to the protective yellow glow of the bathroom light, shivering as he pulled off his shirt and sweats and slipped into the clean ones he always set out the night before.

What else did he expect from a mind wrung with guilt by the joy he had so indecorously embraced?

Sleep was over. He made coffee in the dark, grabbing a cup, then collecting the things he kept on a low shelf—his water bottle, his flashlight, and his phone. For a moment, emotion flickering between affection and poignancy, he noticed Ian and Colin's small flashlights lined up beside his, at the exact angle.

When he stepped out the back door, it wasn't quite four. More than a foot of snow had quietly fallen: Colin and Ian would be wild with joy, for until now there had been only a dusting. The fall was wet and heavy, and Frank came awake as his muscles engaged, shoveling hard, a path to the stable. The goddamn motion light was out again, but Frank could feel his way. Then he quickly set to a cursory mucking out of the five big boxes, and made sure the troughs were clean and flowing. He stroked the horses' necks as he gave them their measures and filled their mangers with the clean hay he and Patrick had put up last summer.

Still, he couldn't shake the dream. He had worked his way to the end, where the little roan quarter horse they boarded waited impatiently, and prepared to go back up the other side, where the rest of the boarding horses stood. That was when he saw the dark hump of the small car nearly hidden by the wall of the indoor riding ring.

Did Patrick have a girl there? On Christmas? Without the quick blink of moonlight on the bumper, he would not have seen it at all. For a moment, as the moon closed her eye again, he thought he might have imagined it. The blunt shove of something hard above the waistband of his Carhartts . . . he didn't imagine that.

"Where is he?" said a small voice.

"Let me turn around." Without asking to, he did. It didn't matter if he saw Linnet's face, for she would shoot him in any case, as whoever was with her would methodically help her kill everyone in the house. They would slit the rubber top on the truck, and take the laptop that he and Claudia had wrapped for Hope, the golden cuff links of an upraised closed fist, facing back—the ASL sign for "Hold On," their gift to Patrick. They would rummage over the toys, pull out drawers, and mess things up. A robbery on Christmas Eve, people would say. No one around. That poor family . . . all of them . . . so much heartache . . . and the son, the one with the limp, didn't he lose his wife in some big tropical storm? That's the one, he did.

"Go and bring him down. Put something on him. I'll leave the rest of you alone."

"How do you know he's upstairs?"

"A retard could walk right into that house. As if I haven't before. Some supercop you must have been. Go get him and I'll leave the rest of them alone. I can't tell which one is him."

"You won't leave the rest of us alone," Frank said. "My mother will wake up. And my fiancée. You'll shoot them, too. You have somebody in there now, telling them they'll all be fine if they're quiet and nobody makes any fast moves, let's just put this rope around your chair."

"Your precious mother!" she sneered, pushing back the black watch cap to reveal a sweaty frill of red hair and a scar livid on her otherwise perfect face. "Their *mother*, their real mother, took a big handful of baby blues with a glass of gin. She was dead before she dropped the glass."

"Why are you involved in this? You're just a kid. Who's with you?"

"Nobody's with me, you fuck. Why would I bring somebody with me? Nobody who knows about those kids stays alive. Me. And Louis. That's all."

"Who's Louis?"

"You met him. Here."

"How can you be sure of Louis?"

"I know Louis. He raised me from little. Best schools. Nannies. Travel. He trained me."

"Like Oliver Twist."

"Shut up."

"How do you know Patrick?"

"You can find anybody, asshole. People don't bother to hide their tracks. The professor says watching people move around on the Internet, it's like watching ants on an ant farm. You know where they fly, and where they live."

"Who's the professor?"

"What?"

"You said the professor. Who's that? You can't have access to flight manifests unless you're government."

"You fucking fool. You can have anything you want."

"How'd you find Patrick?"

"Sent a letter to the college, telling them to ask him, as part of a student committee. The student club would pay. Sent a letter to him, asking him to come. Put up a flyer and found a place outside he could talk to kids. That took real genius. I gave him the check. You listen to me now. You just tell all your pals here in Mayberry that you found his parents, or just his dad, and he could only take the one boy. Tell them whatever you want. I can take the older one, too, but I'll just kill him. Or maybe not. Maybe Louis will want to keep him to make Ian happy. If you tell people that somebody came here and got them, then somebody will come back and kill your new bitch and your sister. How's that?" She poked Frank, hard, with the gun, a Glock 9mm with a sound suppressor.

"Leave now and I won't say anything," Frank told her, carefully keeping his voice even, uneasy with pleading. The wind groaned in the aspens with the sound of rain. "It's to both our advantages."

"Go get him."

"Leave now and I won't say anything. Look, I don't even know what to say. I don't know who you are and I'm betting that car isn't one your daddy bought you."

"I'm getting tired of this. They're going to find you in the snow out there behind your fancy barn."

Suddenly a small flashlight beam hit them, a dim beam. A toy.

"Be nice," Ian said. "Be happy."

The girl didn't move. She raised her gun and shoved it hard against Frank's chest.

Ian said louder, "Be nice. Please."

Frank could feel the gun shaking.

"Put the gun away. Be nice. That's my dad," Ian said.

He shined the flashlight in her face. Frank could see him, in his mountains-and-trains pajamas, his hat and boots. Slowly, visibly quaking, Linnet began to lower the gun. Striding past Frank, Ian came close enough to touch her—the slim ugly gun in her hand pointed at his little downturned mouth. Inch by inch, the girl reached inside her jacket and began to stick the gun into the waistband of her pants. Then Frank caught her under the chin with his fist, stunning her and knocking her to her knees.

The gun went off with a sickening thump.

Ian screamed.

Blood bloomed from the girl's leg, soaking the cream-colored jeans she wore. She fell sideways and Frank had to skip back to avoid the spurt. Her femoral artery. If he had a tourniquet and a fast car, he might have been able to get her to town in time.

"Someone will always come," Frank said harshly. The girl nodded, unable to speak. "Where's Louis?"

"I don't know."

"Where is he?"

"I don't know. Nobody knows."

"Do you want me to call someone? Anyone for you?"

The girl didn't answer. Her eyes were already stiffening, fixed on a point over Frank's head. A rectangle of orange light pillared on the snow, and Patrick stepped out, the rifle over his shoulder.

Ian screamed, and then screamed again.

Patrick said, "Jesus, have mercy on her." Patrick carried Ian back toward the house while Ian wept into his shoulder.

"Dad," he moaned. "Patrick. Dad, please."

Frank didn't touch the girl. He got a horse blanket off the top of a clean stack of them and threw it over her. Leaning against Glory Bee's stall, he called Claudia.

"There's an intruder," he said. "Claudia, I'll explain later. Will you do me a favor and get Colin and Ian dressed and ask my mom to come with you to the Glass Lamp Inn on Hamilton Street?"

"A hotel? On Christmas morning?"

"They can't be here. I'll follow with the presents and then I have to come back out here for a short while. Don't worry too much."

Frank heard the door open and now Ian was screaming for Claudia.

"Oh my God," she said. "Well, sure, why would I worry?"

Frank called the Glass Lamp, noticing, too late, that it was five in the morning. Sleepily, the innkeeper mumbled, "Merry Christmas."

"It's Frank Mercy, the police officer, from Chicago, who—"

"Of course, Frank," the woman said. "What's up?"

"We've had an accident out here. I don't suppose you're open on Christmas."

"We are, in fact. Not fully. We have two guests from Dublin visiting family."

"We need four rooms, Mrs. Gentry. It's an emergency and I'm sorry to impose. I've adopted two little boys whose parents were victims of the tsunami in Brisbane. This is their first Christmas in America, and the anniversary of the deaths, and there was a hunting accident at our farm. A trespasser. Not someone in our family . . ."

"Well, Frank, of course. That's fine. Give me . . . twenty minutes. You can have the honeymoon floor for the cost of a regular room and two others side by side the next floor down. Will you want a breakfast?"

"Of course, if you can manage. I can't thank you enough," he said.

Frank walked back toward the car, an old black Toyota with a scabrous roof and no plates. There was a blanket on the backseat. Folding it over his hands, for even his gloves would have traces of sweat from his horses, he started the car and drove it several times around the barn, trying to decide what to do with it. Finally, he simply parked it in the woods. Every farm in south-central Wisconsin had several random disabled cars, why not his? He then folded the blanket and placed it in the middle of a stack of twenty filthy horse blankets set out for the industrial laundry service. Then he crossed back to the house up the driveway.

Ian was waiting with Patrick at the kitchen table. He ran to Frank. "Dad! Is that lady gone?"

"She's gone. She's badly hurt and had to go for a doctor. What I want you to do is go with Cloudy and Grandma and Colin to this special Christmas place where we're going to stay until we find out if the lady was another one of those horse stealers . . ."

"Well, she's not."

"Why?"

"She's the same one that came to the ice skating and said she was Patrick, Dad! Collie cut her face with his skate."

Patrick sighed mightily and pillowed his head on his arms. What would he feel, Frank thought, to be a man who had kissed the thighs and breasts of a pretty, fragile woman so feral she would come roaring back to get what she wanted a month after having her face slashed with a skate blade? How would he feel if he had been the tunnel through which the same girl walked into all their lives—or thought he was?

"Pat, when you gave those lectures, how did you set them up?"

"Guv, I never did. They called me, didn't they?"

"You didn't think that was unusual? Why you? You're here, what? A few months? You gave up racing two, three years ago . . ."

"I didn't care, is the truth. They had money and they gave it."

"But you didn't see her in the classes. Only after, she came to you. Maybe that was to get you away from here."

"Frank, I never knew," Patrick said.

"No one could."

Claudia came down, leading Colin and carrying Frank's old leather suitcase. Hope followed her and said to Frank, "I'm turned out of my own home on Christmas Day."

"Mom, you know I'm sorry."

"How long will this—"

"Mom, this once, without being disrespectful, can you go with Claudia and ask me later? I will explain, and I will talk about what's possible and impossible."

Frank followed the van with the truck.

Mrs. Gentry had laid out a feast of cream-cheese-stuffed French toast with cranberry syrup, bacon, and cinnamon rolls. The adults insisted on food and coffee before they revealed what Santa (the canny rascal) had left under Mr. and Mrs. Gentry's astonishing tree—a monster pine with ornaments so new they were techno and so old that they came from the 1939 World's Fair, but all of them silver.

After breakfast, and after hearing Colin sigh and say, "No way . . ." when he saw the presents, Frank admitted his headache was so commanding that even the skin of his face hurt to the touch. Claudia said, "Lie down for a while, sweetheart. We're going to put together the Gamma Earth Defending Fighting Wing here."

"The Red Five X Wing Starfighter," Ian said.

"Why does it seem that all the Lego parts are white?" Claudia asked Colin.

"You have to follow the *book*," Colin said, with a sigh.

"I may take a nap," Frank said, "but then I have to help Patrick."

"It can wait. Patrick said he was going to call his sister and rest a bit. I'll ask Mrs. Gentry if you can take him a plate."

Frank let his mind roam out over the afternoon pasture and what Patrick was really doing. Plowing to cover car tracks. Moving a body.

"Can we go sledding?" Colin said.

Claudia said, "I brought your snow pants. But we don't have sleds."

Mrs. Gentry put in, "We have plenty of sleds, and the hill they call Cabin Creek is just two blocks away, and kids slide out right onto the lake." Colin looked about to enter a state of rapture.

"I'll take you later," Claudia said. "Are Marty and Eden coming out here?"

Frank shrugged. He needed to talk to Eden and Marty, but now he needed oblivion. He went to lie down, borrowing Claudia's sleep mask for an hour. It turned out to be three.

When he came back into the living room area, Claudia and the children had gone sledding, so he took the time to go back out to Tenacity.

"I tried to call you," Patrick told him.

"I'm sorry, Pat. Did I even look at my phone for a text? I didn't. I slept like the dead. Come inside, Pat. There are gifts for you from us, and a nice breakfast . . ."

"The body's gone."

"What do you mean?"

Patrick said, "I mean the girl's body's gone. But I didn't go to sleep. I plowed around some. I had a coffee. Then I came out to try to think through what should be done. And there's nothing there but a rectangle in the snow as if something hot was set there. No blood. And there was blood even on the outside of the stable walls."

"I'm sure if somebody got luminol and a light, there would be blood. But there's no spatter to see . . ."

"Nothing."

Frank said, "Do you have brandy?"

"I don't drink, Frank."

"You don't . . . *You* don't drink."

"I haven't had a drink since June. The last I had was in Chicago, when Glory Bee won."

"That's terrific. It's also too bad. I could use one."

"Your mum drinks a tot of brandy in her coffee. Look under Shakespeare."

"Shakespeare?"

"*The Collected Works.* In the bookshelf."

Frank made himself a mug of coffee, splashed in a measure of Martell Cordon Bleu, and watched a tot of half-and-half bleed into the surface. Then he went out to survey the crime scene, wearing the new lined Muck Boots that Claudia had given him. The temperature had dropped, and a stiff wind shoved the heel of its hand through the sere remnants of the summer's alfalfa.

Mentally triangulating the place where he had stood and where Linnet had stood relative to the wall of Glory Bee's stall, he walked carefully around the deep rectangle sliced with near-geometric precision into the snow. Up the grade toward Penny Hill, the car still sat among the trees, but Frank could see that Patrick had cleaned it as though it were the queen's Bentley. About ten feet beyond the car, the tire tracks began. Someone had carried Linnet to a vehicle, perhaps on a stretcher or tarp. That someone didn't arrive at Tenacity by coming up the driveway or through the stableyard. The tire tracks went up Penny Hill, Frank following them for a while, panting in the deep, wet snow.

He then went back, put a clean blanket on Saratoga, climbed on her back from the fence, and walked her up the hill. Snow was falling by then, fast and thick, at least an additional two inches already down. If he kept going, it would lead over the hill onto Sam and Katie Batchelder's farm. Following the track a little farther, he saw where a very small vehicle had arced off along the lane that divided Tenacity from the Batchelder's land, and then headed out to the highway.

He draped Saratoga's reins over a branch, although she wouldn't run, walked out into a clearing, and sat on one of the log seats that squared into a fire pit Frank's father had made for him—what, thirty-five years ago? Someone had been using it for a campfire—the Mercys were generally casual about the careful use of the farm—and the split straight walnut logs were brushed clean. Frank had a memory of his mother enraged at his dad when that straight black walnut behind the house keeled over in a storm like a soda straw to a breath, the roots coming right up out of the ground. It had been big, more than fifty feet tall, with a flawless trunk, probably worth thousands of dollars. But Frank's father was too impatient to wait for a sawyer to come and have a look at it. After a few hours of staring at the fallen tree, he took a chain saw to it, and was soon chaining up the logs to drag them out here with the tractor.

For years, Frank and his friends slept out here on summer nights, first roasting marshmallows, then smoking pilfered Marlboros, and, finally, smoking other things.

Sometime, he would bring Colin and Ian out here for a fire.

As Frank sat there now, he was aware of a waiting silence. It reminded him of the moments before the wave. There was no birdsong, and no breeze (Frank could remember his mother saying to the child Eden, "The wind is always blowing, even if you can't feel it . . ."). The few bright amber leaves that spiraled down seemed to wrestle themselves free without benefit of a push, weary of holding on. Rossetti, he thought, wrote about how falling leaves made death seem a comely thing. Funny what you remembered from college. Funny when you remembered it.

She was gone without a trace.

What would he have done if she had been there? Called the police? Would he have tried to bury the girl, breaking a machine blade in ground frozen hard as a church floor? Would he simply have moved her to a ravine and let her lie there until bow hunters found her or spring came?

It didn't matter. They'd come for her. They had taken care of their own, their sacrificial creature, only after she was sacrificed.

TWENTY-EIGHT

F RANK WENT TO the farm alone, on the day after Christmas. After he looked after the horses, he decided to take a turn through the house. He could hear the phone ringing before he pushed open the door.

It was Brian Donovan.

To his shame, then, Frank realized he had not called Brian on the anniversary of his own wife Natalie's death, on the anniversary of Brian's whole family's death—Frank, the only other survivor and witness, had not called his brother-in-law. Brian must think he had already consigned him to the past.

There was no way to explain, so Frank simply apologized. "This must have been the hardest day of your life, Brian."

"I spent it with my father's sister, a good old soul. Yes, though. A year without them. I want to call them and say, Enough now, you can all come back. Even my da still had good years ahead." Brian added, "It's not all real to me. I got your card with the photo. She's lovely, Frank."

A week earlier, at Claudia's insistence, they'd had a portrait taken to announce their engagement in the *Raleigh-Durham News and Observer*.

"Yes," Frank said.

"You, too."

"Why, thanks, Brian," said Frank, his abortive laugh a cough.

"You must have been so busy with the children, with the day . . ." *No,* Frank wanted to shout into the phone. *I was not waylaid by joy. Not even close.* He said, "Actually, Brian, I would have called earlier. There was what appeared to be a hunting accident on a hill on the farm. Someone died. It took hours to put it right."

"I see."

"It's been a year of bad events, in some ways."

"Yes."

"Do you hear from your wife's relatives, Brian? Is there any other news since the documentary you made?"

"Only word of the boy. My aunties and I walked to the graves today. It's a small, pretty place now, with a few houses now, and lanes."

For the good are always the merry, save by an evil chance . . .

"I miss her, Brian," Frank said. "I don't want you to believe that my going on means I don't. I will say this. I think if I were to lose these boys, though they have been mine for such a short time, I would feel not the way you do, but close to it. I understand now how a father's love is different."

"It's all in all."

"It is. Brian, what can I do?"

"Nothing, Frank."

"Well, good New Year, Brian. Do try to think of a way to come to us."

"I will, Frank."

They all came home from the inn two days later. As Ian explained to the owner of the inn, the fish needed them.

Frank supposed it would be years before he would stop thinking about Linnet's lonely death. His powerlessness infuriated him.

When he was on the job, there had been things he'd despised. One, the way people had looked at him. They swore at him and let their kids spit on the tires of his car, even when he was trying to help them. It made his gut burn when fear on their faces curdled into hatred after he said he had to ask just a few questions. When he and Elena were rookies, working together on the near north side, Elena could back down a

Cuban guy the size of a sequoia with a machine-gun barrage of Spanish, but Frank's Spanish was halting; he could tell that the *hermanos* thought Elena was the one with a dick.

What he had loved about being on the job was that he could know everything that civilians couldn't know. Driving home some nights, past windows where the lights were going on for dinner, past the dim blue eyes of TV screens, he actually felt pity for regular people watching things on the news that he knew all about—who the bad guy was, and where he was, and how soon they could turn his girlfriend.

Even so, he did not truly feel the satisfaction of a proper fit until he joined the mounted patrol unit. From then until the accident, he thought he must be as happy as a man could be in his work, and not only because people looked up to him, literally as well as figuratively. A surplus of imagination, Frank knew, was not his gift. Unlike his father and his grandfather, he had not, having felt it once brush his hands, chased the contrail of a dream of glory. Until Natalie, and Claudia, and especially the boys, he had simply done things that he knew how to do, handling horses, generally handling people, solving problems not slowly, but slower than some, generally to the best effect.

He was just a civilian now.

He didn't know more than anyone else, or how to find out more.

Even if he called Elena, what would he say? For fun, he looked her up, Elena Vasquez. *Captain Elena Vasquez. Mija, I've been back here for a year, and I haven't even bothered to push a button and call you, but now I have this dead woman in my woods, and I have the feeling she's the girl from nowhere.*

What made a person grow up to be Linnet? What made a person into a thing? Who did that to her? Frank had to admit he didn't ask himself the same questions about the little street kids he ran into back in Chicago days whose mothers swore at them viciously, hit them with their fists, gave them beer in their baby bottles. Linnet didn't look like what she was. At some point, someone must have cradled her, told her that she was pretty, given her a sense of fun, put books into her hands, taught her to be well mannered and well spoken, to fix her hair, to smile up in a quaint way, to make her hands sure and cause horses to trust her. And so, Linnet looked and sounded like an entire person. Nothing about her set off Frank's bullshit detector, not a single thing, until the fake dad showed up in the fake Volvo. Like that Olympic runner from Madison who lived a double life as a high-priced call girl, Linnet projected a welcoming sweetness, her voice pealing with vowels like small bells, an invitation to mirth. He'd left her with Glory Bee and felt easy about it.

That same voice with the small bells under it told him not to fucking talk, the same thing she had told his boys when they were trapped in the truck.

Yet she left nothing. No purse, not one unopened bottle of mineral water. Not a thing in the trunk. Under the passenger seat, Patrick found a single earring, a silver hoop, and a card for Tenacity Farms on which someone, in neither Patrick's handwriting nor Frank's, had written the words *BIG GATE*.

That was it.

Linnet meant nothing to anyone. She knew that she meant nothing to anyone. Frank's work had not brought him in contact with very many killers, and none who were not the parents or siblings of their victims. He had probably met more than one psychopath but didn't know it, since that was their gift.

Yet, undeniably, Linnet had felt the Ian effect when Ian faced off with her. She stood down, and Colin said she had relented once before—on the night that she allowed them to escape with Cora. Did this mean, then, that the girl was not really evil? Did this mean that he had essentially murdered a girl who still had human feelings? If Ian could find the finest fissure in any personality, then that fissure had to exist.

Frank had changed all the locks, on the buildings and on the house, but if there was anything police knew, it was that if they were coming in, they were coming in. But Sally was a better alarm system than any air horn that would go off next to the Sauk County sheriff's head if anyone so much as opened a window from the outside at Frank's farm.

He had no answers, but he owed them all an explanation.

No one worked on December 27, and Frank knew he violated every law of God and nature at eight in the morning by waking people who had planned a luxurious sleep.

Marty said, "Is this some other brutal Christian rite? This is not civilized. This is why Jews worship at night."

They all sat down, having parked Ian and Colin in front of a movie.

"Someone came to the farm the other morning," Frank said.

"You don't mean a guest. That's twice in six months," Hope said, removing a tray of cranberry muffins from the oven. "What's this town coming to? Did you chase him away?"

"It was a her, and yes, I did," Frank said. "But there's way more to it than that."

Patrick arrived then, late, with boxes of his own Christmas gifts for everyone. There were long mufflers, brightly colored and neatly made, that he'd knit himself from merino wool. "You did not make these!" Claudia teased him, modeling hers, a deep russet orange. "You did not!"

"It helped stop me drinking," Patrick said. "There were times I knit so long I couldn't close my hands in the morning." He said to Frank, "You told them?"

"He hasn't told them," said Eden. "And if he doesn't tell them, I'm going back to bed."

"Just, can you all sit down at the table for a moment? If you want something more to eat or drink, bring it over. Edie, there's still half a turkey in there . . ."

"Frank, I've gained exactly twelve pounds with this pregnancy . . ."

"It only shows because you were such a slender wraith to begin with, Edie . . ."

"Shut up! You're not even pregnant and I can see you let your belt out a notch since last year. That could just be natural aging, though. What are you, fifty now?"

"Come on, much as I'd love to continue, this is serious," Frank said.

He really would have loved to continue it, to stretch out this last moment of life that even passed for ordinary—teasing Edie, the smell of freshly brewed coffee and the primeval home-bringing scent of warmed spices a sneer against the winter outside the window. So they brought their mugs to the table, and Hope put out her platters. Within moments, everyone had eaten two of everything, because they were there, because they were nervous. "Okay," Frank began. "Edie, Marty: Mom knows this. There's something I have to tell you about the boys."

"They're okay," Edie said tensely. "Right? Nothing's wrong?"

"They're fine."

"Then what?"

"Well, I'm going to just say it. I never told you how it was that I came to adopt Ian and Colin. They really aren't my relatives through marriage. In fact, I never saw Ian before in my life until I pulled him out of a van the morning after Natalie died, the morning of the tsunami, when I was out on rescue patrol."

"We all know that, Frank," Eden said. "Or something like it."

"What? How?"

"Your widowed brother comes home with a little kid. Even he can't figure out how his wife was really related to this little kid, so he tells you three or four different things. You think, your brother doesn't really have a gift for lying, so he must have lost his mind. Or something else is up."

"Why didn't you say anything?"

"What would we say?" Marty said gently. "Clearly, Ian loves you. You love him. There must be an organizing principle, if he has no one else."

"I feel like an idiot," said Frank.

Eden said then, "And we know the rest of it, too. Mom decides she's going to buy an aquarium the size of Lake Mendota one day. And a bag of every kind of candy at Miller's Market. Sure, maybe this is all Mom wanting a grandkid, sure, but Mom is a stern woman. She gave us grapes and said they were candy. And then . . . just wham! She buys all the Lego Star Wars sets there are. Sets that cost fifty bucks, a hundred bucks. This is the same mom who used to try to get Tupperware small enough that she could save two teaspoons full of peas, because who knows when you might need two teaspoons full of peas, right? She's driving to *Chicago* because Brookfield Zoo is better than Dane County Zoo. I didn't even know they had a zoo in Chicago until I was in high school. One day I say, that kid is going to get rickets, because Ian's eating a corn dog for breakfast and a corn dog for lunch. She says, well, Eden, that's what he wants. And she sounds a little like the Children of the Corn. So I asked Mom about . . . how Ian is. And she told me. And, wait up, Frank, if she hadn't, we would still have known. We have our own eyes and brains."

At least that was in the family, Frank thought. This was turning out easier than he'd thought it would be. No expressions of disbelief or disapproval had come forth, and who cared if Ian had something to do with making everyone be nice? He turned to Claudia. "And you haven't told anyone else, have you?"

"Yes, I have," Claudia said. "Of course."

"What?"

"Well, I told people what he did on Eden's wedding day, of course."

Frank was incredulous. "Why would you do that?"

"What do you do if something amazing happens right in front of your own eyes? You tell people, right?"

"Wrong," said Eden. "He wouldn't tell anyone, and not because he's a former cop, because . . ."

Claudia ignored her. "How was I to know that I'd train with you? How was I to know that I'd know you more than that one day? All I knew is that I'd seen this little kid do something I only ever heard of once before in my life. I wanted to ask you if I could observe him, but then I came here, and I began to care about Ian, and about you . . ."

Marty went into the kitchen to brew more coffee. He said, "Be fair to Dr.—to Claudia, Frank. She didn't have any responsibility to keep what she saw a secret."

"You *told* people?" Frank bored in, still staring at Claudia.

Claudia shrugged. "I didn't give a lecture. But yes, some friends. And some colleagues. And later, I called my former professor, the one who introduced me to Julia Madrigal . . ."

"No wonder the whole fucking world knows."

"It's not because of me!" Claudia shouted, jumping up from the table. She pointed to Patrick. "You think that asshole kid who was trying to steal Glory Bee didn't blab to his buddies? And what about Patrick here, the cockney Romeo of southern Wisconsin?"

Patrick said quietly, "That's hard, Claudia. And it's unfair. I never said a word about Ian since the day on the plane. Not once."

Claudia began to cry. "I'm sorry, Pat. I'm sorry. I'm scared. What a bitch."

"There, never mind," Patrick said. "Never mind. You're on edge."

"Do you know what the consequences of this are?" Frank said. "Does anyone think how these boys might be prized for their gifts? Does anyone know that was the first reason why I wanted them with me?"

Claudia whirled to face Frank. "Don't make yourself out like the big self-sacrificing hero, Frank. Yes, you rescued Ian. But you wanted Ian because you wanted Ian. You wanted Ian because he wanted you to take him. He was the one who knew that you were the right dad for him."

"If it weren't for Frank, the boys would be dead," Hope chided her gently.

"I know," Claudia said, and cried harder.

"This has to be contained!" Frank said. A voice in his head said, *We're starving, Dad. We want pancakes.*

"Well, it can't be, Frank. These kids go to school. We live in the world . . ."

"But . . ."

Hope spoke up. Even when she panicked, Frank and Eden had rarely heard her raise her voice, and she didn't raise her voice now. There was, instead, a magnificent stillness about her that brought all their rustlings and whisperings to a halt. "Frank, Eden is right. You can do whatever you want to make sure that this stays in the family until the boys are older. But you can't contain it. Whoever came here, or whatever he did or she did, maybe that wasn't even because of Ian and Colin. Maybe it was. You haven't told us that. But if it was, it started a long time ago. And not because a few people talked to their friends," Hope said. "Anyone who really wants to know where someone is, even a child, has a vast net of resources, a multilayered buffet of information spread like a three-dimensional net of dots to connect. You really wouldn't need a detective to find someone who'd been living a normal life, doing normal things, just as Eden said, going to school, going to the dentist, for example. All you'd need would be a librarian with a computer."

"So *what happened with this person who came here?*" Eden asked. "My back is killing me, and no, I'm not in labor."

Quietly then, knowing his mother was right, Frank told them everything, from the moments with the animals in the cargo hold of the airplane coming to the United States to the horror of the Christmas morning visit. Marty breathed in sharply.

"You killed a woman?" he said.

"Marty, shut up," Eden said.

"No, I didn't. She did it herself accidentally. But I would have, Marty," Frank told him.

"Where is she?" Marty asked.

"She's gone, someone took her, hand to God," Patrick said.

Marty said, "Claudia, maybe Ian would be safer in a lab setting, living in a nice, secure house on a campus where he can be tested because this is big, this could be very, very big . . ."

"He's my son," Frank said. "He's our son. I wouldn't let that happen if he were a chimp."

"Nor would I. Nor would anybody who cares about chimps," Claudia said. Marty looked downcast. "And what about Colin? The effect of what Colin can do is not so, well, dramatic, but the fact that he does it, and their mother could, suggests inheritance. But, Marty, none of these kinds of abilities have ever been clinically proven even to exist, in trials that can be duplicated, by anyone, anywhere, ever."

Suddenly Colin appeared.

"Do you mind?" Everyone's heads swiveled to stare at him as if he was a burglar. "I would really like some . . . anything that's food. I can get it myself, but you're all in here yelling. You never gave us breakfast. And you never gave us lunch either." He was dazed and jangled by a continuous loop of television. "But you guys are just sitting there eating all the muffins yourself."

"I'll make you some sandwiches and then you should go outside and play," Hope said.

They all stopped, listening, as if for thunder. There had never been a time that anyone thought of the boys being unsafe on this land.

Frank said, "You see that? We can't stay here." To Claudia, he said, "I had already been thinking. What if we just got out of Wisconsin? I think about that place Tura left me. An adventure."

"Whoa! Wait, Frank. We've had adventures enough," Claudia said. "Anyhow, I'm not so sure I could pry you off this land."

"With a chopstick," Frank said. "At least now."

"And this is something you discuss, not something you announce. We haven't discussed this at all. There are other considerations . . ."

"What if we don't have time to discuss it?"

Hope got up and slapped together fat turkey sandwiches for the boys and told them to play right where the adults could see them from the windows. Then they all got out plates and began to consume leftovers. Patrick reminded Frank that he'd promised to visit Tura's childhood home, the farm she'd left to Frank.

"It's mine now, after all," Patrick said. As an extra precaution, Frank, just days before, had transferred the title to Stone Pastures a second time, into the name of the laird Patrick Walsh, who purchased it for the sum of one United States dollar.

But how did any of that matter? Frank thought.

After they ate, Marty and Eden slipped away to watch a movie and Patrick to make a phone call. Frank stayed at the table with his mother and Claudia. For a long while, he spun a globe in his mind. In his mind, it lit up, everywhere he turned: no ports, no big cities . . . how could he have been in so much denial? How little any of his little precautions mattered, and how had he thought any of them would? It was the work of a keystroke to unmask any of it. Safety, or the illusion of it, was not the reason they should leave here, if it ever had been. They should go—or stay—for their own health. Their psychological health. Their health as a family. If they couldn't disappear, they could still reincarnate. Many times, the Batchelders had offered to lease or buy, especially since the house and arena were updated. They would do that now.

"I still think it could be a fresh start," Frank told Claudia. "People do that when they get married. It's not like I want to. This land has been in my family for four generations, starting with old Jack's father. I never thought I'd leave."

Claudia rubbed the palms of her hands, with their tiny calluses that she massaged each night with coconut oil, sometimes slathering them and wearing cotton gloves to sleep. "Coming back here was Natalie's idea," she said.

"But Australia was always a temporary thing, an escape. Of course, I didn't count on Natalie." He let out a breath. "When I came back, I knew this was home. I couldn't imagine not feeling safe here, right here." There was so much he would never have imagined. Frank turned to his mother.

"Marty and Eden will have their own life, but would you want to live here, on your own, Mom?"

"Not really, Frank."

"In town?"

Claudia said, "If we were to go anywhere, and I'm not saying we are, we'd love it if you would come, too, Hope. I think you're the only one who could make some farm at the end of the world seem like home."

Frank said, "But, Mom, you leaving Spring Green? After fifty years? Your friends? Your church? It's hard to see you anywhere else."

"That's not accurate, Frank. My life has changed, too. I think, perhaps, I would welcome the opportunity to live in England," Hope said. "Not that you've actually invited me. I'd have my own place, of course. England is a librarian's literary amusement park, and I've been there twice, and been drawn there all my life. I wouldn't like to think of seeing Eden only once every few years . . ."

"It would be more than that, Mom. You could come back every year at least once. I'm sure Eden and Marty would welcome you, for as long as you wanted."

"I'd love to help raise the boys. I'd love to have that adventure you talked about, at my age."

When Patrick returned, Frank told him the substance of the discussion.

Patrick said, "I like the USA, myself. I'll live here one day, maybe teach at that college that . . . well, that the girl tried to give out that she went to. Maybe have my own spread like this one. Maybe this one itself if I can afford it. But I'd just as soon go with you now, for I don't want to give up on Glory Bee . . ."

"You'd have to ride her, then," Claudia said. Seeing Patrick's mouth, and Frank's, fall open in consternation, she said, "No, Pat, Frank. Listen. I've been thinking as I've been sitting here. Frank, you just threw all this at me. It's too much to train and compete and handle everything . . ." She waved her hand around her head like a small cyclone. "The boys could be uprooted yet again. Frank and I are just starting out. The children are going to need me. It's not a good time for me to try to give that dream what it deserves. Or to give Glory Bee what she deserves. My heart just would not be in it."

"What's this, then? You're the rider, Claudia," said Pat. "All your life. That dream."

"Dreams don't always come true," Claudia said.

"Yours can," Patrick said.

"Claudia, where's this coming from?" Frank wanted to know.

"It's logic, Frank. Maybe there's still time for this dream. An equestrienne can compete for a long time, until she's fifty. Maybe I'll end up on Glory Bee's foal, down the road. Or maybe I won't. Either way, it's not the primary consideration."

"If this is going to ruin everything you've dreamed of, we shouldn't even consider this move," said Frank.

"So I'd be responsible for something bad happening to Ian, then?"

"I didn't mean that," Frank said.

"Claudia, you never said a word," Patrick went on. "You have your career. Your own family. You're okay with this? This move?"

"Pat, no one has asked a single thing about me," said Claudia, and walked out the back door.

Hope got up, shaking her head ruefully. Patrick stared at Frank, who couldn't deny any of it. He'd thought of everything, except his best girl. How had he taken her so for granted? Claudia was a professor with tenure, a minor wunderkind. She had a life for which she'd worked exceedingly hard, friends, a community, and respect. In exchange, Frank offered her isolation, uncertainty, a staff job at some dinky hospital, and the surrender of her own hopes as an athlete.

Frank got up and followed Claudia, who was pacing in the dooryard.

"I'm a knob," he said.

"There you go, being easy on yourself again."

"I'm an asshole."

"It's not just that you don't take my feelings or even my life into consideration. That's bad enough. Why is here any worse than anywhere else? It's probably better. Remember what Julia Madrigal's priest said about a community that would always protect her?"

"Julia doesn't have a past with a network of thugs. A thug didn't come after Julia Madrigal and try to burn down her little house on the wildflower hill. No one was murdered there."

"I can't take it all in now. We'll talk about it later. You just presented this as if you were saying, Okay, troops, let's mount up and ride!"

That evening, Claudia's bedtime drill was particularly military. "Teeth. Ears. Story. Yes, prayers, Ian. In you go. I'm telling a story tonight. No. Don't complain. It's a good one. It's about a tree that was really a ghost . . ."

Frank stayed below, still sitting at the table, as though he'd been drilled and filled with lead. Around him swirled ordinary people who'd had satisfying and dependable lives until everything they counted on as real was shaken up and dumped out like a jar of marbles—by his choices.

Frank had been given the chance to bring Ian into the huge community center gym and give him over to the genial Red Cross volunteer. Even if he hadn't known what was to come, or where Ian had been before, could he have given him up? Back then?

He could not have.

If Frank had learned nothing else about the essence of parenthood—in the six months that amounted to six minutes of his life—it was that parenthood was not composed of bikes with playing cards in the spokes and tooth fairy pillows, tenpin bowling and extra ketchup, plaster handprint plaques and Nerf footballs, soccer shoes and bike helmets, bedtime books and clapping games. All these bright things guarded its primitive essence. After a certain span of years, a man who has no family of his own becomes if not dangerous, then impervious. The covenants that bound Frank's life now might easily have missed him by a narrow margin. He could have been another man. Except for them.

His life was Ian's now. His death was Ian's. And now Colin's as well. And so was Claudia's.

Frank woke, with an electrical spark of terror along his arms, first uncertain where he was or who was behind him. He jumped up, then slowly reassured himself that he'd only fallen asleep at the kitchen table. Quickly, he glanced at the clock. It was nine, and he'd forgotten all about the horses. He shrugged into his barn coat and boots, but everything was quiet in the stalls. Patrick had seen to all of them. Inside again, Frank went into the boys' room, tucked the comforter around Colin's shoulders, then went back to his own room, sitting down on the padded bench in his room, watching Claudia sleep, trying to anticipate the consequences of dismembering a family, a place, a life, simultaneously admitting that he had no way of dealing with the consequences if he could anticipate them. Earlier, he'd finally decided that the best reason he felt so called to leave was that, if anyone did follow them, it would at least assure that his sister and her family were safe.

But that had not worked with Tura and Cedric.

He had barely fallen asleep when the sound of Claudia stirring awakened him. She pressed her body close to him, hungrily, and exhausted as he was from working his brain like a circular saw, Frank reached eagerly for her, fumbling with the buttons on her nightshirt to free her breasts, handling and suckling them, until he tasted the salty wetness on her neck.

"What's the matter? Claudia. Sweetheart?"

"I don't know if I can do this, Frank," she said softly.

"We don't have to," he said.

"I don't mean sex. I mean, I don't know if I can leave." Frank knew that he should say the right words. He also knew that if there were such words, he didn't know them. "It's not because I don't love you and the boys. You're the reason I'd give up competing. It's not because of my job. I don't mind practicing privately. I'm not in love with teaching."

"Then why?"

"What if there's never a place to stop?" Claudia wrapped her legs around Frank's and fitted her hips to his. "What if that story on Christmas morning had a different ending?" She pushed away but Frank wouldn't let her go, wanting to pull her clothes off roughly, his selfish body aching and swelling for her. "Frank, no, wait. Why does it have to be only one way—go, and go now? You don't give a good goddamn that I was invited to give a lecture series that is very prestigious, and very lucrative, that people twice my age would kill to do . . ."

"Claudia, I don't even know about this. You didn't tell me."

"Would it matter if I had?"

"Ian's not more important than you . . ."

Claudia said, "Yes, he is. I believe that, too."

Frank sat up and settled himself against the headboard, wrapping his arms around his knees. Why did it have to be go, and go now? Why did it all seem so urgent? He was not an impulsive man. Until Christmas morning, he had been content to wait and to watch. Then he saw Linnet, her face heartbroken at the end, surprised, and the dark stain under her small body spreading on the snow, the stain Frank would always see, even if it were to be washed away by a dozen seasons of rain and sun and wind and snow. But if it were to be him alone, he could live around it. But for Ian, who imbibed every emotion and assimilated it into himself?

"I don't think that Ian can forget and just be a kid here. He made a girl put down her gun to save me. And she shot herself in front of him, Claudia."

She closed her eyes and rocked, gently back and forth. Finally, she said, "Yes. He can forget. He's outlived other memories, Frank. There will always be the memory of the tsunami for him."

"That wasn't his home."

Claudia sat still for a long time. Then she reached up and placed her hands firmly on either side of Frank's face. "But, Frank? Do you feel that somehow nothing will ever happen again? That he'll never see anything again that's horrible, wherever we go?"

"He . . . he'll get older. And when he's older . . ."

"It won't get easier, Frank. You don't think that, do you?"

Frank said, "I hope it. But no, I don't think that."

Claudia turned to him tenderly. "At least you're not fooling yourself about that."

TWENTY-NINE

THEY WERE MARRIED on New Year's Eve.

Marty and Patrick were Frank's witnesses; and Claudia's were Hope, Eden, and Claudia's sister Miranda, who, as Frank's wedding surprise, met them on the steps of the courthouse, with their dad. The ceremony lasted exactly six minutes. Even Frank found it cursory. But his bride's beauty and demeanor compensated. In a cream-colored 1940s suit she'd found in some antiques store, carrying calla lilies and white roses, Claudia looked like Grace Kelly. When Claudia made the ancient promises, she surprised Frank when her eyes filled. She had glanced around proudly at the small group and put out her hand to Ian and Colin, pulling their hands between hers and Frank's as Frank placed the ring on her finger.

"Pronounce us, please," Claudia asked prettily. "Husband and wife, and parents and children."

Not many women would have taken him on, Frank thought, and almost none would have taken all three of them. When people spoke of emotional baggage, they rarely meant a virtual mud wagon of wet rocks and manure. But so she had. With the help of a social worker Claudia knew well, the paperwork for a stepparent adoption was already under way, and the home study and interviews with Colin would begin as soon as January.

As Claudia arched her back to toss her flowers, Frank spoke to Natalie, his own eyes stinging. Wish me well, my sweetheart, my generous girl.

Protect us.

After the wedding and a lunch at Old Anthony's, an Italian place they both loved, they all went back to Tenacity Farms. It was a mild day for the last day of the year, and Claudia changed out of her wedding dress, surely the only bride who celebrated her wedding day by putting her horse through a small exhibition. Her father, the other Dr. Campo, said to Frank, "She's something, isn't she? I didn't know how she'd recover from Pro."

"Claudia's gifted, and she trusts me, and Glory Bee trusts her. I would have never imagined either one of those things happening."

"Can she go all the way?"

Frank couldn't imagine tamping down the old man's pride by revealing Claudia's decision. Since there was a hope, slim but real, of another time, Frank played along. "Nothing's certain, but she's already come further than most. I feel good about it."

"You've made her happy," Miranda said.

"I don't quite know how all this happened," Frank said, laughing. "But I'll take it. I'm the one who's lucky. Claudia's too good to be true."

"Wait until you get a taste of her temper," said her dad.

"I have and I'm sticking to it. She's too good to be true."

The following week, Frank began the process of dissolving Tenacity. Tearfully, Eden decided to give Saratoga to her best friend from childhood. Frank obtained passage for Glory Bee, Sultana, and Bobbie Champion. Finally, on a bitter January day, he chose to walk past the lower corrals, around the indoor ring, and up Penny Hill to hand over the lease on Tenacity to the Batchelders. They could exercise the option to buy after two years unless Frank and his family returned.

When he came back, he was freezing, and quickly slipped through the outer and inner doors to take refuge by the fire in one of the leather chairs that wasn't new—an old high-backed oxblood-colored thing that had belonged to his father. How many times had he sat in this very chair, removing his gloves and liners, holding his fingers out to the fire, trying to pick out the bouquets of spices—turmeric or cumin or oregano—that described the dinner to come. He sat back and looked up at the rubbed hardwoods of the wide stairs, the marks on the wall beside the downstairs bath that signaled the incremental growth of Eden Constable Mercy, the great half-moon window at the end of the living room that showed the rise to Penny Hill and, each night, showcased the sunset. How many other Mercys before him had done the same thing?

As they began to pack, and to separate out what they would sell before the move, Hope grew pensive and, on occasion, weepy. She looked at things she certainly would not need—an ancient set of embroidered towels, a nest of cast-iron cake-baking mugs, outdated art unearthed from closets, a thousand hardcover books—and treasured them unreasonably. For the first time Frank could remember, she seemed querulous. One day, as she and Eden prepared tags for the auction to come, she said, "It's not these things. It's what I see as I sort them. I fed my babies in this kitchen. It may be fixed up, but it's still my kitchen. I still see the same trees and fields and hills from my windows. I roasted a hundred turkeys, and sat up late at this table doing the bills after Francis died, waiting for Eden to come home from a date, doing the dishes while a thunderstorm rolled up over those hills. I'm leaving the thousands of mornings I started my day in this room, taking my coffee and my newspaper to that big red leather chair. I leave the sound of Frank calling my name when he came home from overseas with the medal, and the doorway he carried me through when I was a twenty-year-old bride. The phone call telling me that you and Natalie were going to be married, and that my husband was dead. All the sun and shadows of a life."

Together, for a moment, they listened to Ian, who was murmuring to the fish, something he did often, calling them by name, and lately, encouraging them not to forget him. All of the grownups had explained to Ian that their new house might one day have a place for an aquarium, maybe even an aquarium as big as this one, but they couldn't take these very fish or this very aquarium. Frank warned Ian that if they started feeling pretty sure they wanted to do it even when they knew they couldn't, they would know it was Ian working on their brains and Ian would get a consequence for that: it was hard enough for all of them to move and Ian didn't need to make it harder.

Knowing he sounded like a child, Frank said, "You'll make new memories, Mom."

"No, I won't. But I'll try to keep these dear. I always imagined that I would be the grandmother in this house and this would be where my grandchildren would come for summer weeks."

Frank said, "I'm sorry." He added, "You could get married again. Plenty of people in their seventies get married."

"Plenty of people in their seventies die, Frank, and a few people in their seventies get married. I've had about five dates since your father died, period."

Frank had no idea there had been so many.

"But if you went now, and Eden and Marty went, given everything that's happened, it wouldn't be the same. It's as if I'm not leaving home, Frank, it's leaving me."

THIRTY

I N THE VILLAGE of Stead, Jane Eyre might easily have just disappeared around the corner, her arm crooked through the hoop of a shopping basket. In the truck still lettered *Tenacity*, Frank and the boys arrived on a dove-colored afternoon, driving over an arched stone bridge into a half-cobbled village thoroughfare that couldn't decide if it wanted to be in the nineteenth or twentieth century—there being no question of the twenty-first. As they paused, a green April mist that seemed equal parts liquid and vegetal shimmered in the air, and then, for a minute, rain fell in earnest.

"The people live out in the street," Ian said.

It seemed that way. Houses and stores bumped up against the thoroughfare, with no front yard or parkway except a scrap of tufty grass tucked behind ancient dry stone walls—their slabs stacked like shrunken books. At the back of buildings that clustered together like a toy village, there were small yards, with play structures, tumbles of wild roses and balls of shrub, that rose up to the curved and clefted hills, where old packhorse tracks and winding lanes slipped through a verdant quilt of new green, a burnished brown, and a child's Easter purple. Frank couldn't deny the view's extravagance, but he worried about the austerity of the splendor. Small beings in small places clung to the side of an indifferent landscape. This was not, he thought, a settling place for those who lacked the kind of work that occupied their hands and hearts.

In front of a bow-fronted bakery that promised cream teas sat a bright red ragtop Packard that might have been eighty years old. It gleamed like the day it was made.

"Now, look at *that* car," said Colin, at nine already a gearhead. He shouted aloud when the door of the antique car swung open and Patrick Walsh got out, waving his arms and then pulling off his hat to wave that, too. "Dad! It's Patrick!" Colin nearly crawled out of the window when Frank explained briefly that the car had been Tura's father's, and was now theirs.

"I'll do anything for that car," Colin said simply. "I have five years until I'm fourteen."

"You can't drive until you're grown up," Ian said.

"What could I do, Dad? I can muck stalls every night. I could get all A's. I'll do the dishes. I'll be Ian's tutor."

"I read better than you," Ian said murderously.

Frank pulled Colin back down as both boys swarmed toward Patrick and freedom. "Wait up," Frank said. "Let's do this sensibly." The truck's rubber tarp was stretched taut over carefully wedged mounds of luggage, and he'd agonized all the way from the airport that at any minute a corner might open and spew their life, from winter socks to electric shavers, in a confetti of trash. What kind of man shipped a not very new or useful truck to *England*? Where its steering wheel was on the wrong side? And planned to have the steering wheel altered? Well . . . Frank. pulled the truck into what looked like a car park, although there were no signs. "Just let me lock up, and I'll walk you over." It was like holding back a team of sled dogs in full cry. Then they were on top of Pat, nearly bowling him over while Frank dug his fingers deep into the declivity of his hip to try to coax out the pain that had taken up lair there on the flight from Chicago.

Since the end of January, Pat had been living at a small guesthouse called Mrs. West's ("She asks me when I'll be in at night and do I want hot towels left in the covered bin. I feel like I'm living some old lady's mystery story . . ."). He'd spent most of his time supervising work on Stone Pastures, sending reports of a new fence and new pipes, of the horses passing through quarantine, finding the vet who would see to them all and be ready to deliver Glory Bee at the end of her pregnancy.

Since they were living in England, and since so much had changed, Patrick had decided that he would not take Glory Bee's competition further. As he told Frank, he was sick about it, but he was young, a young man, with much to do and see, and he had determined long ago that he would own and raise a colt of Glory Bee's. To try to ease everyone's disappointment at the anticlimax, Frank gave his consent to breed Glory Bee sooner rather than later. For some reason, Frank wanted this to happen at Tenacity, where Twelfth Night had been bred, but he wanted to involve Tura's horses, too. A single vial of chilled sperm from the German owner of Rodin, the Hanoverian stallion that had been Tura and Cedric's, did the trick. It was Frank's sentiment about the provenance of the horse that made the choice for him, although Rodin's status on the 2009 Irish Equestrian Eventing Team and the eight splendid foals to his credit were on the plus side of the ledger as well.

At Stone Pastures, the manager, was similarly taking down the breeding operation. It had dwindled to a slice of its former bounty after the Bellinghams' death, after Kate sold Tura Farms. Under her direction, the two younger stud horses were sold. The manager wrote to Frank telling him that the remaining stud, Demetrius, was a friend to him and he would like him to spend his later time with the people he comprehended as his family. Perhaps Demetrius had a last foal in him, and what did Frank think was a good price for the horse? Horrified, Frank insisted that the manager have the stallion outright, prompting a blustering telephone exchange. Frank ultimately prevailed, although making Frank feel beholden, as though it was him being given a gift. The manager kept one broodmare as well, supervising the sale of the others to farms around. He insisted that he would help Frank when he and Patrick came out to put the farm to rights. The manager had not lived in the house, although Tura had offered it. He had his own snug place in the village, above the yarn shop his wife owned, and they had only a single child, a daughter of twelve.

Now there was nothing to do but to go.

They would put aside regrets, "and past glories," Patrick said, at least for the moment. They would make their life quietly and slowly, saving their champions for the future when the crackling current of menace that propelled them was a memory like gunfire from a border town. Transporting a spooky, pregnant young mare also was the very definition of gambling, but something about the hormones surging through her seemed to have solaced Glory Bee, and she crossed the sea in relative serenity, as did Sultana and the aging Bobbie Champion, this time in a proper conveyance.

After the horses were in order, Patrick had hired a very capable, and very pretty, groom, and an assistant, a local boy who came in four times a week, and turned over the daily routines of care and exercise. He set about overseeing droves of sturdy workers who cobbled up sturdy fences that would keep the horses safe without dislodging those old walls of stones wedged and balanced like irregular plates centuries ago, for dry stone walls were held together by nothing but skill and gravity. Tradesmen renovated the water and heating systems. A family crew raised a high barn, as well as a good, solid stable that fed into a riding ring designed deftly to sit half indoors and half out. The cottage that would be Pat's own home grew steadily up from the ruins of a gamekeeper's small lodgings just over a rise from the main house: he would have two small bedrooms and a bath up a low staircase and a common room with a dab of a kitchen below. It would be a tidy place soon. The family's home was another matter.

"However bad you think it is when you get there, guv, it's not as bad as it was," Patrick said. "Mrs. Bellingham, she never lied. It was clean as a pin and tucked up tight. Even the windows, what they had, were washed. But the water smelled like it came from a bog and it took all the juice in the house to turn on a light the size of a mushroom."

"And now?" Frank said, not quite sure he wanted to know.

"Now there's a fine well, the big fireplace that burns logs is working, and there's another one with gas up in the big bedroom." Water filled the new troughs and ten acres were in seed. And yet, Patrick admitted, strong work lay ahead on what he called "the living bits" of the house. "The guy you had draw the downstairs plan, with the half-moon windows and such, he took off, leaving those not finished. A girl in town who's still at university finished the plans and showed me how to save some energy and space. With a little luck, you can be in style by the time you light the bonfires. And there's phone and wireless operating in case you have to call for help."

Patrick referred to the ancient and not-altogether-innocent June rites of midsummer, called, mostly as an excuse for well-aled revels, the Feast of St. John the Baptist. Claudia's first planned visit would be for a month at the end of May, with Hope, who was coming to stay. Hope had lived with her friend Arabella, to help out with Eden and Marty's baby—a boy born in February named for both their grandfathers' middle names—Daniel James Mercy Fisher. If all went well, Frank would go back to the States in September to hear Claudia's last Hillerand Lecture, this one in Chicago. Before she left Madison for her father's house in North Carolina, where she would stay for the duration, she kept up a breezy front, cuffing and cuddling the boys and saying, "Now you're part of me. And we Campo women are tough. We'll all be fine." When she and Frank spoke, she described herself as diligent and joyous, staying up late and reading like a single girl, enjoying dinners and day trips with her sisters and relishing her last bit of freedom before coming to what she still called the farm at the end of the world. Later, he would learn that Claudia's last carefree single days were as much fun for her as a short stint in the Rock County Jail, that the days collapsing to bring her nearer him and the boys were the only thing that smartened her resolve. Without them, Claudia's emotions skittered around like a colt on ice: she felt foolish for yielding so readily, doubtful for letting her emotions overwhelm her good sense. He would admire her for embroidering the time they spent apart as an idyll and concealing an ambivalence he should have known she would experience even more than he did—for she had so much more to lose. She saw him off teasing and untrammeled, to do what Frank did best—stir his worry into work, until it bled like cream into tea and was scarcely noticeable.

When he arrived in Stead, finally, Frank mentally rubbed his hands together. Patrick had warned him the farm was in rum shape, half hope, half ruin. Frank hoped it was worse. Then there would be more to do, more sweat, more tired muscles—more dreamless nights. Frank wanted to leave for the farm the minute Pat greeted him and the boys.

Before they actually saw that farm, Patrick said he needed to get them some tea. Or did Frank want to go to a pub? Frank could have stood a strong coffee infused with whiskey, but Patrick still didn't drink, a summit that Patrick seemed to tread tentatively. They settled for a big bag of raisin buns and apples from the store with cups of strong, sweet black tea for him and Frank, the boys' cups half filled with milk. They carried all of it to a wooden table with a shot umbrella that canted crazily out like a beckoning arm. The local grocer, Harry, seemed to be Patrick's new best friend. But the boys were restless, and soon after restless came perverse. After consuming the buns in a few sticky chomps, they began to kick the bag around like a soccer ball and, when it was shredded, made a game of jumping on and off the seats of the picnic table, finally knocking over Patrick's tea. "Settle down!" Frank shouted at them. He had aspirin in his small carry-on bag, but the gnawing in his hip and thigh admonished him even against the thought of going to get it. He kneaded his temples for a moment—surreptitiously, he hoped. But Patrick saw, and stood.

"Are you ready to head out to the new God's country?" Patrick said. "Follow on. It's barely two kee from here." Ian jumped back into the truck, and Patrick, with a flourish, opened the door of the Packard to admit Colin. They drove for just minutes. Then, as if glimpsing something from a recurring dream, Frank recognized Stone Pastures from the road. It was much more imposing than the photos conveyed. The house was primitive in shape, walls straight up and squared off, the ells that ran away from it low and rambling. But it was massive, set back from the road by a circle drive with sentinel yews, with a stone fence a little higher than most flanking an arch for several hundred feet in either direction. They got out and the boys burst through the unlocked front door, using their combined weight to shove it open.

Frank walked slowly through the first floor, satisfied that the rooms were commodious and every corner met neatly the corner beside it.

"When do you want to get started?" Patrick said. "Next week? You'll want to get the boys enrolled at school."

"They're not going the rest of the year," Frank told him as Colin and Ian silently did a dance of joy. "I'm homeschooling. That is to say, nobody's homeschooling. Ian's reading all the Laura Ingalls Wilder books and Colin's got *The Hitchhiker's Guide to the Galaxy*."

"What about their math? And their citizenship or what have you?" Patrick said.

"They'll help us measure pieces of wood. That's math, and they're good citizens already. They'll learn history. The truth is, I don't need one more thing to worry about. I don't need conferences and bus routes."

"You could have just left them there with your mum," Patrick said. "They could have stayed with their friends . . ."

"Tenacity's being taken apart. And this place is being put together as a home. It seemed best for them to be on the front end instead of saying goodbye. I could be wrong. That wouldn't be any surprise."

That night, Frank lay on a mattress, for not all of the bedrooms—how many were there?—had bedsteads yet. He imagined the house, and the farm around and above it, circling like a domestic animal, its heartbeat slowing as it lay down. The stillness against the hills seemed to fall then, benign and absolute. He rested.

The next day, they were no longer tourists, and they unpacked their clothes and toothbrushes.

Because Frank kept forgetting to do a thorough marketing—there must have been a time in his adult life when he'd moved into a place that had no sugar or salt or coffee or butter, but he could not remember it—the boys ate cheese-and-pickle sandwiches from Harry's shop three times a day. "I'm an addict," Colin said. "I only ever want cheese-and-pickle sandwiches." They washed cream buns down with fizzy orange. Neither of them was ever seen without an open bag of crisps. Patrick hitched Bobbie Champion to their mother's old pony cart and though

Colin had never driven, after a few times around the driveway (and substantial encouragement from the horse), they were trotting up and down the road, then up and down the hill tracks. Frank felt as though he could actually *see* round-bellied Bobbie Champion losing weight. Because the boys read at night before they fell asleep, at least for ten minutes, and helped the pretty groom see to all the stable chores, Frank decided not to notice that they had gone native.

Proud of himself, about a week later, he remembered to make them take baths before the family journeyed to Manchester. From a list provided by Hope and Claudia, they went to good stores, and picked out tables and bed frames and the right kind of appliances. Then the boys caught sight of a pair of bright red down-filled sofas with green accent chairs, each the approximate girth of a humpback whale.

"That's a bit much," Patrick said. "Claudia fancies the toff beige stuff."

"We'll buy all these throw pillows to soften it up," Frank said. "There's a beige pillow right here."

They purchased ten pillows in colors that the boys thought went very well with red—black and bright blue as well as beige.

"It looks like the bloody circus," said Patrick.

"They're very comfortable," Ian told him. "I can't wait for them to be in the house. Can we get the fish tank next?"

"No," Frank and Patrick said together.

Freed again from domestic obligations, the boys ran in and out of the doors, sometimes wearing their dirty parkas or jean jackets or ski hats, just as often not even wearing their shoes, as burly men with hand trucks hefted heavy beds up the stairs and uncrated a double oven, a double refrigerator, and double bathroom sinks, along with miles of colored-glass bathroom countertop that Claudia insisted was the newest and sturdiest thing. "Can we keep the boxes, Dad?" Ian begged.

"No! They're full of nails!"

Frank later spotted the long plywood fort the boys had built outside from those very boxes, after Pat slipped the deliverymen some cash to flatten the nails. Frank sighed.

Yet, since they were eating fruit twice a day and brushing their teeth at least at night, Frank decided not to care.

When Patrick and Frank set to work on an earnest finishing of the remodeling, the boys drove the pony cart up and down, dropping in on neighbors who would either be charmed or hate them, depending on the local character.

Frank sighed.

One day, a woman who went six feet and two twenty easily showed up at the gate. "I'm Grace Gerrick," she said, with a grip that nearly brought Frank to his knees. Frank regarded the amazon warily until she said, "I'm great friends with your Colin and your Ian, and I've brought you some bits because they've said they haven't a mother."

Colin's voice in Frank's head explained, *I didn't say we didn't have a mother. I said we didn't have our mother here yet.* Frank smiled and thanked Grace Gerrick, who said her sons would help out if Frank liked. The bits included four meat pies, two fruit pies, two quarts of home-canned peaches, and Mrs. Gerrick's specialty, homemade ketchup.

"When everyone else in the county thinks you guys are orphans and outlaws, we'll remember that Mrs. Gerrick said you have perfect manners," Frank told the boys. They were eating the pies from flattened pizza boxes using plastic forks from Curry Corner. No one had the nerve to unpack the crates of Hope's pearl-colored wedding china, twenty place settings that had endured fifty-one Thanksgivings and Christmases without a single chip.

The remodeling went forward. Feeling like a laird, Frank helped a chimney sweep rout the nest of what he said must have been the unusual roost of a great gray owl. Patrick and Frank seven-times-sealed the thick planked floors, and concentrated on the upstairs.

Back came the plumbers, to parcel off one of the five bedrooms into a smaller sleeping space and a third big bathroom. There were no closets at all, but in his rambles Patrick had come across a contractor tearing down an old house for a new one twice its size and scored eight rough-hewn armoires the man was discarding. These they bolted to the walls. Both of them puzzled over a small, doorless depression in the wall near the chimney, kettle-shaped, about eight feet deep and eight feet wide, until Patrick figured that this had once been the house chapel, and the worn plaster niches in the walls must once have been shrines. Frank decided that this would serve as his office—for the luck of the lapsed Irish Catholic. From the back wall of that office, a tiny iron stairway ascended to a trapdoor and a flat porch on the roof that reminded Frank of the deck on Julia Madrigal's house. Up there, a person could see the whole countryside laid out like a child's farm set, the river valleys, the distant shrouded hills, and far off, the winking canals of the Pennine watershed.

A couple of wet weeks kept Ian and Colin bundled up and indoors. The children consented to do their reading only after Frank thundered at them that they would end up ignorant laughingstocks among the much-brighter British children ("It's not true, Dad. You just think they're smarter because they have accents," said Colin). Later the same day, the boys unpacked their own building equipment. They constructed a Lego metropolis, comprising many styles and time periods, along sixteen feet of shelving in their room. It ranged from a medieval marketplace complete with spitted pigs to the Lego Star Wars Death Star ship. Chronological history evidently did not preclude Princess Leia from shopping for pears in the twelfth century or flying back to her own digs in a modern American medevac helicopter.

Then, that bored them as well.

Finally, the days began to come up windy and fair, and the boys ran out to explore the old farm buildings, finding handmade wooden pegs burned black in some ancient fire, a drinking tankard pounded out of metal, a gigantic old sleigh in better shape than the shack it stood up in, and enough spearheads to start their own museum. Now able to hitch Bobbie Champion up without help from any adult, they went collecting farther afield, dutifully wearing helmets, and they brought back everything—an iron box containing medals from World War I, a piece of rock with real prehistoric figures cut on it, the handle of an old sword, seashells from a place that had seen no sea in millennia, a crushed hawk's nest, and a crumbling shredded leather bag green with age and with some kind of broken earthenware vessel inside it. Each night, they displayed their booty while Frank and Patrick murmured their stunned appreciation.

The boys now introduced themselves to neighbors from farther away. They ended up well fed.

Beyond the amiable Gerricks lived a German couple with a girl Ian's age, as well as the Lashes and the Shepsons. Ian and Colin first had to go miles to turn the cart around in the village square, as they weren't allowed to cross the road without an adult. However, it didn't take them long to find adults so taken with the two little boys in the cart that they would stand in the road to stop traffic for them. Directly across was another American—a man writing a novel, and his girlfriend—and next to them, a married couple, husband and wife just seventeen years old with a newborn baby girl.

Frank was glad that he could consider them safe—at least according to the shopkeeper Harry—to explore even the next town beyond Stead. To his relief, he thought that they would never get bored with exploring. To his amazement, they did.

One night at dinner, Ian said, "We should build something ourselves on this house."

"We need a fire escape," Colin said. "There is no back door."

"Right you are, mate," said Patrick. Frank conceded the point.

This being heavy work, they recruited the help of Grace Gerrick's massive twenty-year-old twin sons, who said such a thing could be built with nothing but what was right at hand in the field. The Gerrick boys were six five and six eight, making their mother and their older brothers look dainty. Starting with a wide base beneath the boys' bedroom window, they made their own dry stone wall from field remnants, a three-dimensional jigsaw puzzle they knocked into eternal fit with rock hammers. After not too many hours, they had a pyramid with indentations at irregular intervals. On each of these indentations, they fitted lozenge-shaped paving stones, hoisting the midlevel stones with a makeshift pulley hung from the bucket of the Gerricks' huge John Deere tractor, the twins lowering the last two from the bedroom window with straps fashioned of old horse tack. From the fields, the staircase looked like some sort of artful chimney, but Colin could swing his feet out the bedroom window and be safely on the ground within seconds. It became his favorite place to depart for his morning run. The first run he had ever taken was with Claudia, but he'd kept it up and found the activity soothing and strengthening. These days and nights, he grew serious about it, going out at least three times a week if not more. Cautious about hypothermia, Frank made sure he had a flexible bottle of hot tea in his little backpack.

"Run with me, Dad," Colin urged, nudging Frank, who had fallen asleep with his napkin in his lap, a plate of rice and beans and bread untouched before him. "If you ran, maybe your leg would get better."

"My leg can't ever get better," Frank said. "I'm lucky I still have it attached to my body. You think I'm lazy?"

"I think you're a little fat but not that much. And I don't see why you won't try."

Frank laughed. He had worked hard in his life, but never so hard as this, and was feeling pretty much like the architect of the domestic world. But a father who couldn't run was something a kid simply didn't choose to see. How had Frank lived forty and more years of life without ever knowing . . . anything . . . and figured himself a real student of human nature? In human years, Frank calculated that he'd come home from Australia at about twenty-six, and had grown into his true age like a plant in time-lapse photography over the course of a couple of seasons.

"I want to be able to run," he said, lying. "Maybe I'll try someday. Right now all I want to do is get this joint ready for Grandma coming home and Mom's visit."

All of Hope's things were installed in the suite of rooms to the left of the entrance to the main house, along with a shiny new black desk and a sleek maroon sofa to match the old maroon chair from the kitchen at Tenacity. Even the dishes were gingerly placed in a china cabinet. For Hope and Claudia, there would have to be flowers in jugs everywhere.

There would have to be new sheets for those new beds, and shiny kettle made right here in West Yorkshire.

Finally, the women of the house made their entrance.

Hope had mailed her clothing. She filled her suitcases with American schoolbooks, peanut butter, maple syrup, chocolate chips, and Frank's Hot Sauce, which Eden and Frank had grown up calling "No Relation." One of Claudia's silly, heavy leather suitcases was packed plump with presents—vapor guns, giant sketchbooks and tempura paints in sticks, e-readers with games, and new running shoes ("They're called *trainers*," Colin said, and Claudia replied, "I know. I speak British.").

With Colin proudly driving the pony cart, the boys took their new mother and grandmother—new to them and new to the neighborhood—to meet every single shop owner in Stead, including the postal clerk. They visited every neighbor they'd met, and Claudia brought each one a card with her name and a small wrapped wedge of Wisconsin cheese. A few days later, they were buried in pork pies and shepherd's pies and currant buns and scones—more than any family of six—counting Patrick—could ever have consumed. The groom and local workers toiling away at the barn and house were delighted. They spoke gently of "the missus." Claudia praised them lavishly in turn, especially in awe of the gleaming countertops, the well-measured risers on the stairs, the artful fire escape. Hope crooned over the kitchen.

Like a boy of eighteen impressing his mom and his girl, Frank felt the ego strokes literally drawing him up in bravura straight-spined pride. He delighted in simply driving to Stead and sharing a coffee with Claudia in the morning. Life had never seemed so perfectly measured and tender, like an aspic to be slowly consumed. One morning, just as it grew light, he heard a horse come down over the closest arm of the miles-long outcropping called Whitsunday Crag, against which this part of the county nestled, like a kitten against a recumbent cat. It was Claudia, astride Sultana.

"Where were you?"

"I wanted to see the dawn from up there," she told him. "It's such an old beauty. It doesn't care if we're here or not."

"Fortunately, it seems that most of the people do."

They did. Lavishly. Some of the older women, Hope's age, remembered Tura from her girlhood, when Tura wanted to "read" for veterinary medicine and her gruff old father wanted to herd her into marriage. They remembered riding Tura's horses up to picnics by the waterfall and trudging all together to the school building that was now the village arts center.

Walking with Ian, Claudia met the author's wife-to-be, a doctor who had been a biathlete in the 2010 Winter Olympics. One night, when she and Frank joined them for pasta with leeks and peas, they said that they had rented the house for a year, but often thought they might never leave. In Stead, Claudia spent several hours with Harry's wife. Their older daughter had Down syndrome and had begun to exhibit violent behavior as she entered her thirties. She visited the small psychiatric hospital called Hope of the Moor, where she might one day hope to find a job. On the two weekends, they went to York and took the train to Edinburgh.

Then the month was over, and it was time for Claudia to prepare for her fourth lecture.

At the airport, Colin clung to her, begging her not to leave. She clung to him also.

"This was a terrible mistake," she said to Frank. "I need to be here. I need to be with my family."

"It's only two more months," Frank said. "And I'll come in September."

"Remember how tough you said you were?" Colin reminded her, although drops hung on his lashes. "Just like me?"

"Lots of tough women are done in by a handsome guy," said Claudia, taking Colin's chin in one of her hands.

Then, one late afternoon six weeks or so later, Frank came down from the barn to find a taxi in the driveway. The wedge in his throat dissolved at the sight of the full set of Claudia's old, unwheeled caramel leather luggage sitting on the steps. Then Claudia got out, filling the cabbie's hands with pounds sterling.

"I'm home!" she said. "I'm home to stay!"

When the cab left, without a word, Frank picked her up and carried her over the threshold, in his best imitation of a bridegroom. He kissed her, and he didn't ask why.

By the time Ian finished his riding lesson with Patrick, and Colin came in from his run, a small lorry had arrived, and the owners brought in the few things Claudia had decided to keep. Beyond her clothing and her medical books, there was an antique writing desk that family legend said had belonged to Louisa May Alcott's sister Abigail, her pillow-topped space-foam mattress, her grotesque multiplicity of pillows, and trunks filled with all those dozens of paper-thin embroidered quilts. There was also a huge box with what looked like dozens of rods and armatures that fit into canvas loops. It was called a Kelso Speedster.

Claudia asked the boys to put the contraption together.

"This is for good, then," Frank finally said. "And you're fine."

"It is," Claudia told him. "And I am."

"The lectures . . ."

"Were wonderful," she said. "I'm going to finish the last two next year. I met with the committee after it became clear that I needed a dispensation for medical reasons, as I kept having the persistent wish to barf all over the podium. In fact, I have that persistent wish still."

"Medical reasons."

"Ordinary ones," she said with a smile.

"Are you expecting, Claudia?"

"I am," Claudia said. "Hooray!"

Frank gasped, as elated, frightened, thrilled, and disbelieving as any father-to-be.

"I can't believe it," he said. "Are you okay? Is the baby okay?" He put his arms around her, leaving a full six inches between their bodies, gently hugging her shoulders.

"Frank!" Claudia tugged him into a close embrace. "You know better. I could probably bounce down a black-diamond ski run and not have a miscarriage at this point. You went through this before." A minor note plucked, distantly. Natalie. *So far? So early? So soon?* As she recognized her gaffe, she compressed her lips and turned to the children, who had set out the dozen bags of screws and bolts and the lengths of aluminum pipe on the floor around them. "How about that, boys? What do you think of another girl around here? A little bitty one?" she said. Ian and Colin smiled politely. "Just three months, and all systems are go, despite my very advanced age."

Ian patted her flat belly. He said, "You'll be like Glory Bee. She's having a baby, too!"

"As soon as I can quit throwing up, I'll eat more than she does," Claudia said. "I dream in scones now."

Vaguely annoyed, Colin said, "You really are having a baby. This thing is a baby stroller! It's not a scooter."

"Alas, not everything is for you," Claudia told him. "But I saw these Razor scooters in New York that have motors. I think there might be a couple of them stashed in the truck with the rest of my stuff. And maybe if you're very good—"

"Are you sure it's a girl?" Ian asked.

"I am sure it's a girl," Claudia replied. There was no way of knowing.

"Well, I want to name her Guinevere," said Ian.

Frank and Claudia stared at him.

"What? It's a nice name," Ian told them, trying to see if he could fit in the seat of the Kelso Speedster and propel it with his feet.

Life turned another page.

Frank asked which of the rooms Claudia wanted for a nursery, and she told him none, thank you, the baby would sleep in their room until she was ready to sleep in a bed. "There's never been a proven case of SIDS for a child sleeping in bed with the parents. All those stories about people who rolled over on their babies and suffocated them, well, either those people were drunk or they suffocated the baby on purpose. I don't approve of cribs. Maybe a little cradle for naps."

"Okay, then," Frank said, and went back to working on the new barn.

A few weeks later, they went to the Keighley Clinic for an ultrasound. Not having been to a doctor in the area, Frank expected something quaint and thatched, out of James Herriot, but the clinic was all cliffed verges of granite and glass, with vertiginous floor-to-ceiling windows in the examining rooms.

"Guinevere appears to be Arthur," Claudia said as the incontrovertible image swam into view under the ultrasound technician's expert pressure. The technician gave them pictures, but she let Frank hold them. She let Frank make the next appointment and spun the door, and was gone. When he caught up with her outside, Claudia was sitting on an ornate wrought-iron bench, sobbing. Thinking himself wise and prescient, Frank veered slightly away to an outdoor stall, where he purchased a big cup of tea with extra sugar and a plain biscuit for Claudia. It always worked in BBC movies. By the time he got there, however, she was nearly inconsolable, shaking—way past the cup-of-tea-dear stage.

"Sweetheart!" Frank sat down, spilling the tea all over his knee.

"I needed that tea!" she wailed. Frank practically ran, hobbling, back to get another, this one with a lid.

When he returned, he said softly, "Claudia, are you in pain?"

"No!"

"Do you not want the baby? Are you so disappointed? That you had to give up the honor of the Hillerand . . ."

"Of course not, Frank!"

What was wrong with her? She tried to take small swallows of the tea, but only cried harder. Finally, Frank hit on it.

"You wanted a girl. Claudia, I'm so sorry. That's it."

"I did want a girl!"

"But there'll be another time. We don't need to stop at three. The baby is healthy and, Claudia, I'm so happy . . ."

Her face swollen, she glanced up at him for the first time since they'd left the echoing clinic lobby. "Are you? Are you really happy? Do you mind?"

"Mind?"

"It's all so sad and broken. You can still love him, even though your first baby was a boy, and he died?"

Frank set the tea on the bench and used his fingers to brush back the sweaty curls from Claudia's cheeks. The day was shirtsleeve warm and bright as a shout, and all around them, there seemed to gather a sudden flash 'mob of parents strolling with children in push chairs and prams, curly-headed blond babies, babies with hair dark and straight as feathers, babies with a comic red frill sticking out of a cap. He could reach back, into the fastnesses of the dark, and wish he could hold the babe that was swept away before he could see the sky, but to let that shadow stand between them and the sun now would be a betrayal. He would betray Claudia, and, Frank now realized, himself, and everyone standing on the sturdy bridge they had built between them, trusting the soundness of the structure, of the future. "Claudia," he said. "I can see why you wonder. But I love our boys, even though my first son died. And I love the baby. I'll love our little girl, someday, even if she's a boy, too. And if we have another child, and she's a boy, too. That will also be fine. I'm in . . . I'm in awe."

She hugged his neck then, uncharacteristically yielding, letting herself be pulled close to him, his arms around her shoulders, her occasional catch of breath a sough against his chest.

"Awe," she said. "That is the word. I've never been pregnant. Not even a scare. I can't believe how enormous this is. He's just so real to me. He's a person."

On the way back, as promised, Frank phoned Hope. Then he and Claudia lingered for an hour over a big lunch of red curry and pad thai—Claudia noting that since her life roiled with ironies, this was the least nauseated she'd felt in weeks. When they pulled into the drive at Stone Pastures, the boys ran out. Hope trailed behind them and sat in the shade of the old chestnut, where Pat had built a wide plank seat encircling the trunk. Behind the boys' backs, she gestured to her son and daughter-in-law, little warning motions that included placing two fingers across her lips.

"You didn't really want a girl, Cloudy, did you?" Ian said. "They're not as good. You already have us and you know how to be a boy's mom."

"They've made you something," Hope added then, motioning Claudia and Frank to a large tray set down on the outdoor wooden trestle table where they sometimes ate their dinner.

The cookies were the pastry embodiment of paper dolls—the man huge, the woman curvaceous with frosting hair as luxuriant as a mermaid's. The mother's snow woman's arms wrapped around a baby with golden balls for eyes and chocolate hair, a baby made in exactly the shape of a figure eight. Then there was a tall woman with a dab of white frosting for hair, and the children, three identical-sized vanilla males.

"These are great. These are stellar," said Frank, and Claudia was off again on another rolling breaker of tears.

Frank said, "But who is that third boy? That one is you, there's Collie, and then Arthur . . ."

Claudia said, "I want to point out that we're not really naming him Arthur."

"That one is Patrick, of course," Colin said.

Crimson with suppressed mirth, Hope headed for the car. She had an appointment for tea at the nicer of the two small restaurants in Stead. Just a couple of weeks after Hope had visited the local Anglican church, the two-years-widowed priest, a few years younger, asked her to go to a local string quartet concert. Frank persisted in calling this a date. Hope persisted in telling him that he would have to think of other ways to get her to move out. One night, Colin told all of them that in service of the Packard that would soon be his own, he had decided to become an auto mechanic. He added, "Ian will just be a farmer. So there's no reason we have to go back to school at all."

All the adults, Patrick included, disabused them of that fact, and as September came and the weather at night occasionally swept the hills like a stiff broom, they took the bus to the consolidated school in Wherry. Colin joined the football team, part of the school's structure even for fifth formers, and when he was found to be just as certainly an ace by British standards as he'd been in the United States, his dance card filled with suppers at friends' houses and football matches. "It's in my blood," he told Frank solemnly.

"It's not in my blood," Ian said happily. "I hate games. I just like horses and TV." His best friend, an Indian boy named Sanjay, brought a different tin of homemade cookies every time he came to play. They ate two dozen, every time, and still their ankles and wrists were as delicate as links of a lady's fine chain, their ribs little xylophones, their knees belled out at the bottom of their flute-sized thighs.

Claudia began working part-time at Hope of the Moor, the plan to take up full-time duties a couple of months after the baby arrived. Although at first she assumed an air of slightly aggrieved sacrifice, Claudia quickly grew to love the power that came simply with listening to her neighbors' travails—William's drink, Janet's spells of sadness, everyone's fear that Alex's attachment to the boy he met at the public school was more than a friendship. The questions that could only be answered by wait, accept, or walk away helped Claudia pick apart her own web of options. An academic, trained in nuance, she felt comforted, as the fall lengthened, knowing that she, too, could only wait, accept, or walk away. As it had done with Glory Bee, pregnancy relaxed her fierce grip on perfection. The bigger Arthur grew, the less eager Claudia became about having another go right away. She spoke of how it might be to adopt a little girl from Ethiopia, as a school friend of hers had just done. Frank reminded her how legally shifty they were, and would be until they were dead, or at least grandparents, and suggested it would be better to make a little girl from things they had lying around the house. Claudia protested. The older she was, the likelier she would gain thirty pounds and lose three teeth, Claudia told him. Frank promised her dentures and a girdle.

One night, he stood outside his own door and listened to gales of fifties music gusting out as far as the road and beyond. Hope was teaching Claudia the jive, and Colin was teaching Ian. They had done it, Frank thought, not daring to speak it aloud. They had come safe home.

THIRTY-ONE

ALL I WANT is cheese and onion, on the wheat bread," Frank told Harry Aker. "Cheddar cheese is fine."

Harry shook his head sorrowfully. "You'll want Wensleydale on the dill bread, with a bit of chutney."

"The Wensleydale is fine, but with just onion, Harry."

"And it's breakfast. You'll need a fried egg."

"I can feel my arteries hardening."

"Well, now you say it, Frank, you don't look good, and there's the truth of it."

Frank didn't doubt that at all. He probably looked like death warmed up. He'd been awake for hours, in an agony of concern. He glanced over Harry Aker's shoulder into the wavy greenish mirror, a reflection that would have made a runway model look like a fresh cadaver. His eyes were bloodshot and his beard, two days of it, grizzled with new gray. "I'm beat. Up at two. My young mare, Glory Bee, was suddenly foaling, and . . . what do you know? Twins. The vet never left her side. We couldn't believe it. The foal's born, in twenty minutes. There was the vet cleaning off the little baby girl, and suddenly my son says, 'Dad, there's another baby horse there.' It was all over within an hour, but what an hour."

"Twin foals? I don't think I've heard of that in years, at least ones that weren't conjoined, you know, like Siamese twins. Must have been battle stations, eh?"

"You can imagine. The vet called her assistant, and he came running, and the Shepsons down the road and Thurman Ross from across the road and then all the Gerrick boys. It seemed like half the county showed up, all before the sun rose."

"Be in the newspaper, as far as Leeds."

"Maybe."

"Those are good lads, the Gerricks. You know that Shipley Gerrick has those horses, well, draft horses, and those twins—boys, not horses, of course, but big as draft horses. Those two huge lads, giants, they're twins."

"Arthur and Lance," Frank said. Both men paused for a moment, in mutual sadness over Grace Gerrick's fascination with Camelot. The Gerrick twins, though built on the scale of redwoods, were biddable and bright. Frank had seen Lance heft a two-hundred-pound solid-oak door the way a man would lift a violin. The Gerrick twins did lift violins, in fact, because both were musicians of no small merit. "The foals, Harry. They are beautiful. Black as the mother, with not one white hair. That's unusual in itself. They say healthy twin foals occur in one in ten thousand births. One in ten thousand, Harry."

"You're sure they're okay?"

"Vet says the way they get up and walk and nurse is a better indication than any blood tests or what have you."

"And you had no indication?" Harry said, slicing the dill bread with the precision of a diamond cutter.

"None at all. And we had a sonogram, because she was so big. We were frightened there might be . . . anything. A tumor. She's a big animal, fourteen hundred pounds, eighteen hands tall. The vet only saw the one baby and said, it's all good." Frank sighed. "I can't believe Glory Bee carried two babies for eleven months. A horse isn't made to carry twins, thirty, forty pounds each. And then I thought she'd go berserk. But no, she was cleaning them off and nuzzling them, right away."

"Tired, though."

"We're going to have to bottle-feed them part of the time. The vet's bringing the things now. She did beautifully."

"The horse or the vet?"

"Both. But it was hard. Glory Bee will lose too much flesh trying to nourish both of them. We've got to make sure she takes it easy."

Frank knew he was talking way too much and way too fast, entirely unlike his quotidian self, but he could not believe the magnitude of the morning. He was the only cop he'd ever known who had never seen a birth, animal or human. It was some compensation for Glory Bee's own promising career cut short. He knew he was babbling, but thought he might levitate with euphoria.

"Who's with her?"

"Patrick, the fellow who . . . well, you know Patrick . . . but he had to follow the vet back to get supplies. Claudia's there now, but I need to get back. It's a workday for her. Cheese sandwich with onion. Jesus. I'm tired. I already said that. I sound like Ernest Hemingway."

"He lives here?"

"No, Harry. He's dead."

"What will you call them? The babies?"

Frank sat down in the red chair that Harry kept near the door and bent over to tie his boots. He'd forgotten to do that before he left. "Well, we didn't plan. We knew that the one, the little girl, would be Patrick's. He decided to call her Gloria in Excelsis."

"Is that sacrilege?"

"No," Frank said. "Not without the 'Deo' on it." He took a bite and complimented Harry on the sandwich. Then he went on: "And the male, my son Colin chose All Saints for his name. It's All Saints today, after all, isn't it? November first? Last night was Halloween. The boys went out with their grandmother in the pony cart around about to get treats and they came home and went to bed. Then, a couple of hours later, I went to check on Glory Bee and she was in labor, so I turned the boys out into their Muck Boots." Harry had made a second sandwich, which he handed to Frank, who ate it in three bites, leaning against the counter. "I should have a pound of this cheese, Harry, too. And a gallon of milk. You were right about that bread. Is there a loaf? Any oranges?

We won't have any time today to go to the market. The boys will sleep until noon."

Harry raised his eyebrows. He was eighty but proud to say that he never looked a day over seventy-six, and flirted so strenuously with Hope that she finally told him she was secretly engaged to the widowed pastor. "What about school? That won't do."

"Just this one day. They were up all night, too. They'll want to watch the foals, and they should. It's part of their lives. The vet says to keep checking to make sure they're not jaundiced or weak."

"School of life."

"Sure. See you, Harry."

Harry wrung out a hot cloth and began painstakingly to clean his slicer. Just as the bells signaled the door about to close behind Frank, Harry said quietly, "A fellow asked last week was there a Yank living around here now."

Frank stopped.

"What did you say?"

"I told him yes. There was an American with his wife. A writer working on another book about the Brontës, a novel this one, because Christ knows the world needs yet one more book about those three. Twenty times as many books written about them as they ever wrote themselves."

"You're too hard, Harry. People are fascinated by those women, all alone out here, nothing but sheep and Yorkshire rednecks and their old dad for company, writing about love as well as anybody ever did, even if they never knew too much about it personally. If anybody ever does." Exhaling deeply, Frank said, "Well, thank you, Harry."

"How's the lad?"

"Ian or Colin?"

"The little one Claudia brought to see to our Rosie."

"He's very well. How is Rosie?"

"She'll never be a genius, Frank. You know that. But she's right as rain now. Happy at her school. Happy at home when she's home. Helping her

mother. Doesn't ever run off." It was a relief to hear. After Harry's older daughters married, Rose terrified her parents by running away repeatedly, getting drunk in pubs—where it was quite legal to serve her—but most horribly, appearing naked in the doorway when the food suppliers arrived. When Harry's patient wife tried to bring her in, Rose socked her mother in the belly. "You know she lives at school now, there five days a week. She likes a boy who's . . . like her. Nice lad. Drives a car." Harry added, "And our Flora's husband. He's found a job. Laid off the pot."

Frank turned back into the store, reaching for his pocket. "That's good. I'm worn out, Harry. I just realized I was walking out of here without paying you."

"Those are on the house, Frank."

"Don't be silly. I just stood here and ate six pounds' worth of expensive cheese and bought another pound of it."

"And my girl Flora can pay her light bill now. It's all a great wheel, isn't it?"

"Well," Frank said.

The sun had risen higher, teasing out the wedges of fog in the dales while Frank was stuffing himself with the sandwiches that now literally distended his gut. He was, in fact, getting a gut. There in the cobbled street of Stead, before he climbed into the Rover, Frank vowed never to drive the car or ride one of the horses this mile or so to the pub or the little shops, ever again.

He would walk everywhere, the way an Englishman should.

Colin had never stopped lecturing him: farm work was not exercise. Frank dug up a boulder and shoved it into a wall, and then sat for ten minutes admiring the view. A city cop by choice, a farmer by birth, he had never, until he came to Stone Pastures, really felt the soil. It used to be something to be brushed off. Now he ran his hands over the contours of rocks as though they were skulls from an archaeological dig, and smelled the tang of the dirt rubbed between his fingers. The view still enthralled Frank. Down below, somewhere, there were plenty of sooty cities. But high up, the sheep, the provenance of this excellent cheese, wandered

up lanes where once the only carts had wooden wheels. The old Rover that had belonged to Tura's father still attacked the steep prows of those hills with geriatric vigor. Most of the time, Frank still drove the Tenacity truck. And most of the time, he drove. Gravely, Colin encouraged Frank to consider his heart. "Even you could do yoga or something, Dad. Lots of old people do."

As he said this, he poked Frank gently above the belt. Patrick—who ate his weight in bacon rolls and puddings every day and still went a hundred and five pounds—stumbled off laughing. Colin's small legs, slightly bowed, were now strapped with tiers of muscle, his back straight as a seam. Each afternoon, he set out alone up those sheep tracks, running for an hour before he came home, drenched and depleted. It was Claudia who told Frank to get Colin a good cell phone in a shockproof case and stock it with endless loops of music—both so that he could find solace in the music and so that he was always instantly ready to dial 411 if he should turn an ankle . . . or meet a stranger.

Frank let a shiver pass over him as he threw the packages into the backseat and pulled open his door. Then he stopped. A fox was crossing the road not ten feet in front of the Rover, and after her trotted three sleek kits. No one wanted a fox in a neighborhood filled with chicken coops. But he wasn't going to disturb her fairytale progress this morning.

As he slipped into the front seat and pulled on the door, Frank heard a sound, nearly simultaneous, like an echo of the clapping shut of the car door. He twisted in his seat.

"Hello, Frank. Quite a morning," Louis said.

THIRTY-TWO

WHEN HE COULD BREATHE, Frank said, "Are you Louis?"

"I suppose it doesn't matter. I'll never see you again. People call me that sometimes. But let's not waste precious moments." The man wore an immaculate long-sleeved white shirt with a raised stripe in the same material under a navy blazer with dull silver buttons. The nails on his gun hand were clean and buffed, and his scent was of nothing. Louis said, "Let's make a plan. Here's how I see it. You can stall so that I shoot you, and no one will recognize that sound because this silencer is absolutely state-of-the-art, and I will still go back to the farm and take Ian. Or you can go back with me and make it all easier. You can keep the other kid. I don't want him."

Of course, Louis would not want Colin. Colin would be a liability.

Although Ian couldn't answer Colin with his mind, there would be some kind of sensitivity that would bind them telepathically, and who knew how much Colin would be able to do when he was older? He might grow up to be a GPS straight to Ian, and Louis knew that Frank would never stop searching for them.

"There's nothing on earth you can do to make me give Ian to you."

"I can kill your wife also."

"Why?" Frank asked. "That just creates more havoc. More ways people could see you. Patrick's there now. So is my mother. And the vet. Will you kill everyone?"

"No, they aren't there now." Louis tapped Frank's skull, not gently, with the muzzle of the Colt. "Your mother is at church, the nice one, miles from here, and Patrick is keeping company with the daughter of the fellow who sells horse chow or whatever it is you buy. He stopped there on the way home from the vet's."

"He'll be back any moment. I told him to be."

"He won't. Don't you think we plan things, Frank? Don't you think my good friend makes webs of all you do, and buy, and all the places you go, and for how long, and your taxes and your inheritances and your medical bills? When the older boy came to the United States, we knew what plane he was on, of course. We knew that the hatchet-faced sister wasn't really just visiting, she was leaving religious life forever. Even you didn't know that. She'd made job inquiries. She'd written letters. Do you think those things are really private to anyone who can really use that vast net of information out there?"

"Some things are."

"No things are, Frank. Not if someone is paying attention. That is an illusion. Privacy is an illusion. The professor has paid attention for many months to bring us to this exact moment."

"Who's the professor?"

"Your transfer of the farm, to Claudia and then to Patrick Walsh, it was not effective, but it was quaint—"

"Who is the professor?"

"Shut up. Now, Patrick left quite a little while after you did, hoping to have a short visit with the girl and return before you missed him, but we've timed him, and you don't start to notice his absence, ever, until at least an hour or so after you get home. We don't need anywhere near an hour."

"How long have you known we were here?"

Louis shook his head tolerantly. "You must know that I knew you were here before you came, Frank. We saw every move you made. We encouraged you."

"Why? Why did you wait?"

"Don't you see how much easier this is? How much more private? Out of your comfort zone, away from all your usual support systems? You don't even have your phone with you. You'd have to think twice to recall the number for emergency services. You're not a stupid man, only a foolish one." Louis sighed, and turned his expensive watch so that the band sat directly on the most prominent bone of his wrist. Louis's wrists were delicate, almost childlike. "I do like things to be easy. Your being so happy and so busy didn't do me any harm. Lots of activity with the horses, and how odd that Prospero was lamed, huh? Lots of romance, lots of fun with the boys, all good distractions. The old Frank Mercy would have noticed certain things a long time ago. He would have noticed people who didn't belong where they were, from day one. Right down to this day. The old Frank Mercy would have locked the car, right here in this quaint little road."

"Police cars lock on their own," Frank said, stuttering before he could stop himself. "Some do now."

"Yes, of course," Louis said. "And I should give you proper credit, Frank. You did foil us. A number of times."

"If you think I'm going to drive you to my house to kill my wife . . ."

"Yes, your wife. You asked why. Why would I kill your wife? I don't really want to, and not because I think she's great, and not because I think I would be caught. I've seen the British police in action. No, it's because it would upset Ian. It would make it harder for me if he's distraught. I want him to think he's just coming with me for a short time to do one important thing, and then coming straight back. He can't tell if you're lying. That's not part of his makeup."

"How do you know?"

"I do know, but also, you will reassure him." Louis paused. "If I must, though, if time starts getting short, I will kill her. You know that." He let the gun burrow into the hair at the base of Frank's skull. "Now, let me tell you about the people who really are at your farm. There are two friends I know quite well, and they have radios in their pockets to match the one I have right here." Louis tapped the pocket of his navy blazer. "It's a little James Bond. I admit that! But there is no decent cell-phone signal up here. So all those things you might be thinking of doing, like crashing the car and hoping you'll knock me senseless, or driving through the window of one of those stores to get attention, or rolling out on the ground, don't even bother. Really don't. The minute I touch my pocket, your wife's head is blown up by one of my friends. Both boys will see it."

"Why do you want me there?" Frank asked, and with all his might, he willed Harry—Harry or anybody—to step out into the silent street, to come out for the newspaper, or a delivery, or a breath of air. "What good will I do?"

"It's obvious. I told you. The confidence you inspire. The hope that puts aside the fear. To lessen the chance that the little kid will shut down mentally. You'll promise him that Daddy will come and get him so he won't be afraid."

"He'll be afraid. And you know he can stop you."

"No, he can't stop me."

"Why? Are you not human?"

Louis sat back slightly in his seat, using his right hand to smooth his gray pants, which Frank studied: they were made of a wool so fine that the fabric puckered and draped like silk. If Frank had dared to chance it, that was the moment he would have shoved open the door and dived out, just as Louis prophesied. But even in his reflective posture, Louis's hand on the gun was steady, pointed correctly and directly at the vulnerable lower globe of Frank's head. "If you asked my parents, they would have said no, I was not human. You can't ask them because they're dead, although this isn't a movie, and I had nothing to do with that. There is no Mycroft to my Sherlock, or to my Moriarty . . . if you will. I'm one of a kind. But whatever I am or am not, the boy's ability, powerful as it is, has no effect on me."

"Do you know why?"

"I don't really know. From what I understand of child psychology, children are solipsistic, something you can ask your lovely wife about one day when the two of you are discussing philosophy. I think they believe until a certain age that what they want is also good," Louis said. "It's possible that other people identify with that notion. I can't explain what I've never felt."

"What if he realizes you were asking him to do wrong?"

"Well, he would have to do it anyway."

"It might not work."

"We would explain to him what would happen to Mommy and Daddy and little Colin if he chose not to do what we asked him to. And if he still resisted, well, sadly, then he would be of no use to us anymore, unless we were able work with him as I worked with the young woman you knew as . . . well, I don't know what name you knew her by. But she came to learn that her childhood instinct for self-preservation as the utmost goal was quite correct and she usually acted accordingly."

Linnet.

"But she sometimes failed with people like Ian," Frank said quietly. "There was something left in her."

"Fortunately for me, there seem to be no other people like Ian, but in a word, yes, she failed."

"And you let her die, even though you raised her from a child."

Louis sighed. "That would also be something my parents might have said, but in reference to a dog or a cat. In fact, she was very talented and I did, as you know, give her a second chance, not even a year ago." Louis sighed again, deeply. "This whole business has been a strain. I'm glad it's over, sincerely. I'm ready to get going to your place now . . ."

Frank turned to face him, for a moment disturbing Louis's aim. Someone of lesser mettle, knowing he was up against a larger, younger man who had been police, would have been unnerved. Louis only blinked. "What's so important that you need Ian to get it for you?"

"You are buying time. But I have a little time. What I want is something . . . like me. Like a very good recycled material, I leave a very small carbon footprint. And so do the things I want. In short, they are things you never really see in ordinary life."

"Like?"

"Oh, some mundane things, a magnificent grade of opiate, currency, of course . . ."

"But you could get that other ways."

"That, probably yes. But other things require a delicacy. Perhaps a lesser version of something like van Gogh's *Poppy Flowers*, or a pre-Columbian figure, or the bas-relief face of a Persian king no bigger than your two hands, from the fifth century BC," Louis said. "What do people do with these things that they pay me millions to bring to them? I don't know. I certainly don't care. They would never tell anyone my name even if they knew it. They can't display their prize. Perhaps they look at it occasionally. Perhaps they feel that thrill that can only come from possession of the one thing that is like no other thing. Power. Which brings us to Ian."

"You don't need Ian."

"I don't need the millions of dollars either. I want them. And Ian made my vocation easier, when it could often be difficult, and sometimes dangerous. I was able to work with Ian for such a short time, just a few months. And who knows what lies ahead for him? Who knows what he could cause people to do, with the proper training? With the proper incentives? Perhaps not art objects, but mineral resources. Perhaps governments. But we're getting ahead of ourselves. It's early days yet for Ian."

To Frank's horror, the street was as resolutely quiet as it had been when he'd first approached Harry's. Later, people would stroll out for tea and fresh pastries, a late breakfast, or a bite after church. Now the only people out were farmers, or people going to work at the kind of places that never closed, like hospitals. Claudia would be leaving soon. Well, she would have been leaving soon.

Dad, are you coming home? There are people down there in the garden.

He wished he could answer, and say, *Run, Colin! Run, Colin, and keep going, even if Ian can't keep up.*

His phone chimed. Claudia. It was a text that had not come through, five or ten minutes old. There was no decent reception.

I need to leave for WORK.

Then, seconds later, there came another. *Frank. Come right now.*

Louis said, "Have they relayed the message that you're to come right now?"

"Yes," Frank said.

None of this was a ruse. He should not have expected a ruse.

Louis said, "Oh, there's a bread truck. A *lorry*. Time for us to be off."

Frank started the car and floored it, intending to smack into the front of the bread truck, hard, on Louis's side, but Louis lowered the gun and reached up for his breast pocket. What was in there could have been a business-card case, or a European cigarette pack, but Frank was pretty certain that it was a radio.

"Frank," Louis said. "You persist in thinking I'm trying to run some kind of game here." So Frank drove slowly, but not too slowly. He was not, and had never been, a speedy reactor, though, for twenty years, he had relied on logic and good instincts to keep himself out of mortal trouble while putting himself in its way for the sake of others. If it hadn't been for the radio in Louis's pocket, he would have driven hard, off the road on Louis's side. But the element of surprise was so unlikely that it was not even theoretical. To wonder about it would be like banking on coincidence.

Frank pulled into his own home, his circle drive, and got out with Louis at his side.

His heart squeezed when he heard Sally barking wildly. Then came two gutty whooshing sounds, in quick sequence, and Sally didn't bark anymore, but he heard Claudia crying. A lean, dark-haired man in dark work pants and a windbreaker came around the side of the house and greeted Louis with a nod. Together, they walked up toward the barn and the paddocks.

Wearing her gray flannel work skirt and a long red sweater, Claudia stood next to the small paddock, a huge baby bottle near the toe of her boot where she had dropped it. Another slender young man, this one collegial and natty, leaned on the fence a few feet from Claudia. His was a shotgun that he cradled gently. At the corner where the fences met lay the terribly small, bloodied mat of fur that had been Sally. In a moment of crackling clarity, Frank recognized him as the guy who'd stood outside Gate A-2 in the Brisbane Airport the day he'd taken Ian to the United States, the young man in tortoiseshell glasses. Quickly, Frank averted his face, but before he could, he saw the guy make the same connection. *So far? So early? So soon?*

Claudia said, "Frank, don't let them take Ian." Stepping forward, Frank put his arms around his wife. Peripherally, he could see the boys' small, white faces in the frame of their bedroom window, but he did not look up at them. "Don't let them take Ian."

"We're not going to discuss this, the way people would do in a film," Louis said. "I want you to go into the house and bring Ian down here. Don't bother with any of his clothing unless he has something he specially loves. Then Frank will explain to him that I'm only taking him for today to London, not back to the tree house or anywhere else."

Frank said, "No."

The young English-professor fellow leaned over the fence and fired into the soft ear of the baby colt All Saints, and the little horse crumpled, a window blind with cut strings. Glory Bee and the other colt shrieked and pelted to the other side of the paddock.

Ian was suddenly there, tears all over his dirty face. "Be happy," he said to the professor, who smiled gently and swung the gun back on Claudia. Frank glanced up covertly and prayed that Colin was not on his way down. The other man with Louis turned away, toward the low fence and gate that bounded the house from the road.

Colin, run, Frank thought. Don't look back.

They would all die, he thought, trapped in a foolish vise caused by bad timing on his part and exceedingly good timing by men of bad intent.

If he could let Ian go with Louis, he might save Claudia and Colin. Or the mild young man that had shot down the newborn colt might turn back from the vehicle and pop all of them in parting. Patrick would summon the police, but Louis would have melted away with Ian and the others slipping identically back into the box of human life like a tube of glass alongside many others. Given Louis's disdain for mess and his confidence in his own camouflage, there was a chance they would simply go—or shoot to wound Frank or Claudia and then go. If he gave Ian up to them, Frank could console himself in the untruth that Ian could be found. He would never see Ian again. Ian would be like dead. But he would not be dead. The money was not on misplaced heroics.

Kneeling, Frank said, "I know you're scared of him. But Dad wouldn't let you go unless I could come and get you. You'll only go to London and get one box or some papers for this man, and then he'll leave you . . . Where will you leave him?"

"At Paddington Station in the Rose Cup, at ten tonight," Louis said, as if this all were real. "Like the bear."

"I'll already be there at Paddington Station with Mommy and Colin. You won't see us, but we'll see you. We'll come right to you and we'll catch you up and bring you home."

Ian didn't speak. His lips shut tightly, he studied Frank's face.

Claudia said, "Frank, wait . . ." but the young man in glasses jabbed Claudia fiercely in the side with the stock of his shotgun. She sat down hard in the mud.

"I'm a little scared, Dad," Ian said.

"Don't be scared," Frank told him.

"Do you promise I shouldn't be scared, Dad?"

"I promise."

"He killed the baby horse."

"Yes."

"Is that why you're letting them take me away, Dad?"

"I wouldn't let them take you away for overnight . . ." Frank glanced down at Claudia, then up at the loaf of hill between Stone Pastures and the Gerrick farm, Windward. Distantly, he saw Shipley Gerrick and one of his boys preparing or plowing soil, rumbling along toward him in Gerrick's proudest possession, his nine-thousand-pound John Deere tractor. Someone else drove the smaller tilling machine with its mouth of blades. If only he had a flag. Frank picked Ian up and asked Louis if he could get Ian's booster out of his own Land Rover.

"Of course," Louis said.

Go slow, Dad. Go really slow.

"The belt is stuck," Frank said. "My hands are shaking. Claudia, help me."

Getting up, she walked over to Frank, her shoulder touching his. They pretended to pull at the clasp on the seat belts. "It's too old," Claudia said. "It hasn't got the right kind of releases."

"I'll do it," the young professor said. "I had a kid." Nodding to Louis for permission, he momentarily propped the gun against the side of the Land Rover, and stepped between Claudia and Frank to lean into the backseat. Frank could hear the big tractor now, and the bumping whine of the harvester, and, additionally from behind him, some other kind of heavy, rolling machinery.

Louis glanced up just as four trucks rounded the gate and pulled into the drive, blocking the cars. The dark, lean young man reached for his gun as Ian whispered, "Please, be nice." The man tried to look away. Frank heard the gun hit the gravel.

"What's going on here, Frank?" shouted Tom Ross, who drove the fifth truck. He got out, lightly swinging a mallet. The Gerrick twins piloted the huge tractor around the garage.

Louis, suddenly seeming confused, looked around and shook his head as if an insect bothered him. "What did you say?"

"I said who are you!" It was broad, ruddy Peter Shepson, striding toward Louis like Friar Tuck. "You've no place here." He struck Louis with one broad hand and the older man stumbled. "We got . . . word to come, Frank."

Wiley Mitchell, the American writer, joined them with his girlfriend, who carried her shotgun in the crook of her arm. "We called the police in Wherry, Frank," he said. "They're on the way. Who are these assholes?"

The professor dropped the car seat and skipped into the first few steps of a run. The author's fiancée cocked her gun. "Stop, please," she said to the back of his head. The professor stopped, and raised both hands slowly. "Just get on your knees," she said. "Don't move."

"Were you a police officer?" Frank asked.

She said, "Marine."

As the tall dark-skinned man made a charge in the opposite direction, down the driveway, Shipley Gerrick tripped him, and, when the man sprang back to his feet, hit him across the back with the maul he carried, which must have weighed ten pounds. Shipley spun the mallet in his big hands as another man might have spun an umbrella, and struck the man again. They turned to look when a great, shrieking *whuff* burst from the man, who fell forward into the dirt. He was conscious, but lay still.

With them diverted, Louis took his chance to run. Frank gasped at the agility with which Louis bounded up to the paddock fence and over, fleet-footing it straight for Glory Bee and the remaining colt. Time slowed as Frank wondered what Glory Bee would do. Glory Bee was a prey animal, and, as such, her feelings toward any of them were slight, touch-based, lukewarm compared with the ardent devotion even of Sally the dog. Now, however, Glory Bee had an imperative—her remaining foal, Gloria in Excelsis. Still holding Ian's hand, Frank stepped forward as Louis ran straight toward the big mare waving his arms and yelling, "Gaw! Move, you bitch!"

And she did. Putting herself between Louis and her baby, Glory Bee quivered and twitched, sliding her haunches under her as she cross-stepped, snorting and pawing. Only a fool would be unafraid of the massive black horse, her mouth dripping foam. Louis skipped away, to one side, toward the back gate, but Glory Bee wheeled and faced him there.

"Gaw!" Louis shouted again, and Glory Bee was up and on him, berserk and bellicose, her shod hooves hammering his shoulders, clipping his skull, and when he was laid out flat, his legs and back.

Frank glanced down at Ian, his impulse to shield him from the sight. But Ian was watching intently, making no move to stop Glory Bee, his candle-pale small face motionless, his arms folded tight across his chest. Looking up, he turned and put his face against Frank's rough barn coat.

Then, rattling down the road from the direction of town came a sixth truck, Harry's old panel vehicle, and shuddered to a stop at the front wall. Colin burst from it, running wet as an otter into Claudia's arms. "I told them," he said. "I ran up the hills and behind the houses to town and I told them all to come and help Frank and Claudia at Stone Pastures Farm."

Frank picked Ian up. "You did this, Colin. I couldn't save you."

"You could, Dad. You were fooling," Ian said. "You knew."

Frank thought, Could he? Had he?

"I ran down the stairs me and Patrick made," Colin said, "and then up the hill to the Lashes' house and to Declan's, then over to the Gerricks', and Mrs. Gerrick drove me to town to get Harry, but I called them all the way, I called, Help them. Help Frank and Claudia."

"You're very brave," Claudia said. "You're brave and wise. I love you."

Colin put his arms around Claudia's waist and began to cry. Frank saw how tall he had grown, at nearly ten his head nearly grazing Claudia's shoulder. Setting Ian down, he said, "Go get your sweatshirts. For you and Collie. Everything's okay now."

A moment before the humped dark police car appeared, Patrick jumped out of the truck lettered *Tenacity*. Stopping in the road, not even taking the time to close the door of the truck, he vaulted over the wall. When he saw the dead foal, he laid his boot against the face of the professor, holding him down, apparently gently, in fact increasing the pressure with his heel on the man's throat until his eyes went wide and blank and the police said, There, that was good enough, they'd take it from here, but, turning away, Patrick seemed to stumble, his heel grinding the young man's nose. The woman from across the way kept her gun on both of Louis's men, until the police told her it was good now, to put it away.

It was a while before any of them except Frank noticed All Saints, who lay emptied in the dust like a man's old coat, and at last Louis, splayed crooked in the middle of the paddock. Frank didn't hurry the police along.

All that day and the next, the police took prints and measured and photographed what shoe marks they could find. After Tom Ross and the Gerricks helped Patrick bury Sally and All Saints, the police went over the paddock carefully before they allowed Frank to clean away the blood. Finally, they sent a tow for the car, in which they would later tell Frank they found a single strand of wool fiber and several of Frank Mercy's own hairs.

After the professor's broken nose was bandaged, police questioned him and the dark-skinned man at the central station. Neither of them spoke, except the professor, to ask for a glass of milk. Neither had a criminal record or any identification, not even a change of clothes. They would both be charged with assault and staging a home invasion, and the dark-skinned man with criminal damage to property in the death of the colt.

At Queens Hospital in Leeds, doctors said they would conduct scans to see if Louis's coma was reversible. His cheekbone and four ribs were broken; he had a long, thin crack in his skull. On the third day, he stopped breathing on his own and was placed on a ventilator. The brain scans were inconclusive.

"Did you know these men?" an inspector asked Frank.

"I don't know them," he explained. "I thought I might have seen the older man once before, but I'm not sure."

The officer leaned back roughly in the dark maroon chair that had been Frank's father's. "That's the piss. If it wasn't for that, we might say the man in hospital and two in jail were mistaken and meant to be after someone else here, that it was all a cock-up and they took a family of farmers, and a doctor, of course, for drug runners or somewhat."

"It was a mix-up, I'm sure," Frank said. "What could they have wanted from us? We don't have any jewelry or art or drugs, nothing like that.

They didn't even bring a horse trailer, and that's all we have, our horses, and two little boys."

"They weren't looking for two little boys. Unless they're film stars," said the young constable. "Are they film stars, hiding out up here?"

Frank said, "You guessed it."

THIRTY-THREE

S O MANY THINGS happen when people can't sleep.

Colin sat up late with Claudia not one night, but four in a row. He wanted just one thing—the reason that the yellow-haired man had killed Sally, and especially why he had killed the foal called All Saints, who couldn't make noise or bite him.

"A baby horse isn't dangerous," Colin said.

"He knew that All Saints wasn't dangerous," Claudia told him. "He killed him anyway. He was trying to show us that he would kill people, too."

"I know I can't change that All Saints is dead," Colin said. "But I think Ian should have stopped that man."

"He is evil," Claudia told him. "Ian couldn't stop him. Ian has to have something in the person that's good so he can grab on to it with his mind. It wouldn't have mattered if All Saints was a human baby. He would have killed him anyway."

"I don't get it."

"You're not supposed to get it. It's not something people can ever understand. Because of how that man was, in his head. Ian couldn't stop him. He couldn't stop the other man from killing our dog. I don't know why, but they weren't like other people."

"Ian should have thought of a way," said Colin. "Why didn't Dad kill them with his gun?"

"Dad would have gotten in trouble for that. They would have taken Dad to jail for killing a man who shot a horse by mistake."

"But it wasn't by mistake. It was on purpose."

"They would say it was a mistake and the gun went off because Dad was trying to hurt them. The police might believe that. They might think Dad was the bad one. We're not from around here. They didn't have any proof, Collie."

On the fourth night, Colin got up off the bed and picked up Frank's old iron boot pull. Rearing back, he hurled it across the room, where it stuck in the old wood of the armoire like a hatchet. He stalked out of the room, knocking a deck of books off the shelf onto the floor as he went. Colin was more upset about what had happened to the animals than he was about the threat to all of them.

"Don't go after him," Claudia said. "He needs to be that angry." She got up too quickly to gather the books and winced. Under her long white shirt there was a hot purple bruise under her ribs, thick as the tip of a scythe. The baby was fine. A doctor recommended by her colleague at Hope of the Moor had taken over Claudia's obstetrical care. So Frank was not worried about Arthur, except in hoping that they would soon think of an actual name for him, but he was worried about Colin. Colin was running more than ever, but now he came back not just with a stinking pullover but with swollen eyes. He cried in private, and at home, he raged. Would he always be so angry? A kid did right; he risked himself to prevail, and his own little horse, his just for a few hours, the only animal he'd ever decided to let himself like, was shot like a steer with a bolt gun. Colin had looked up how animals were slaughtered for meat, and announced that he would never eat meat again. You've told him that he probably can't ever understand it, Frank told Claudia, so how do we help him handle that memory? It was as if Colin had removed himself from a world he found too forbidding; he hadn't spoken to any of them in thought since his long run for the help that saved them.

"We bind him to us. Hang close," Claudia told Frank, with something that began with a shrug and ended in a shudder running over her shoulders. "Hang close until something better comes. There isn't anything else we can do. Until he gets on a team. Until he's fourteen and falls in love. There's nothing to make him better yet because how could he be better? We aren't going to feel better for a long time." To her credit, she never mentioned the things she had told Frank, months before, when she said that there were no guarantees the boys wouldn't see something awful again, wherever they alighted on earth.

They went to the zoo in London a week later, on Saturday, a doleful, meek little bunch wandering tentatively as sandpipers under a thrashed sky that fitfully spit rain. Ian didn't sleep well, and neither boy was enchanted by the Thistle Hotel in Kensington Garden or had an appetite for the lush cream tea. Early on Sunday, they came home, creeping onto the farm like ghosts of themselves. Driven by fear into a frenzy of activity, Hope had cooked the kitchen into an aromatic cave that burst with pepper and tomato soup, thick dark bread, and hearty pies. The boys tasted the hearty food, and nodded gently, but their eyes were masked as clouds.

That day, snow fell. Claudia woke the boys to invoke the customary enchantment and again they smiled politely, like adults inhabiting little bodies. Then, just before their late dinner, there came a huge knock at the door. Shipley Gerrick stood in the frame with a caul of snow over his long dark hair and a great covered basket in his arms.

"Come in for some tea," Hope said.

"Oh, I'd love a cup where I stand, Mrs. Mercy. But it's them boys I've come to see. Happy Christmas early, lads," he said to Colin and Ian. "I've not asked your mum and dad if I can gift you because they'd sure say no." Shipley opened one of the sides of the wooden basket and a fat, honey-colored puppy began to squirm out. Ian's face opened; Frank groaned, and Shipley said, "Who can have a farm without a dog? She's a good one, from my own Gentle Annie and my brother's big herding dog, Ring. I guarantee that if you had sheep, she'd keep them humble. She's wormed and I give her a shot, and if you want another just like her, I got another. One for each boy. As it is, I think I hear my good wife calling."

"Well, Shipley, I guess this is where I say thanks," Frank told him as the little pup squatted and placidly squirted on the rug. "I think one puppy is just fine. That will be an outside dog, now, Collie, like Sally was, so we'll make her a basket and a barrier here . . ."

Colin said, "He can take her back, then." And he left the room.

After a moment, Claudia said, "Thanks, Shipley. We'll keep her indoors. A dog inside is a good thing, and this isn't a Beverly Hills Murano glass kind of a house."

That night, after she'd eaten scrambled eggs with cheese, and was tucked into a crate lined with the boys' outgrown summer shirts and made of boxes taped together with thick slits cut in the sides, Jennifer ("Jennifer?" said Claudia) slept like a proverbial baby. At least, she slept until about midnight, when she began squealing so ferociously that Frank leaped out of bed and ran for the boys' room. Ian was already standing on the bed, screaming, "She's dying! She's going to die right now!"

In fact, all that had befallen Jennifer was panic: she'd stuck one paw into a slat in her makeshift crate and couldn't free it. Frank carried her outside, where she peed a river, and then headed back up with the puppy in his arms. When he was halfway up, Claudia called him and asked if he could bring up a glass of water. Frank tucked Jennifer in first and Claudia apologized. "I hate to make you go back down."

"I don't mind."

He brought the glass, and cracked the window. Claudia had one of her ancestral quilts—still paper-fragile, still cherished—gathered up around her breasts. "I just heard Colin scream," she said.

"That was Ian. That was before."

"No, this time it was Colin. He just did, when you were downstairs."

What the Christ now? Frank thought.

"Dad," said Colin. He stood pressed against the stone wall outside their room, shivering in his underwear. "There's a ghost in the yard."

"Oh, that again," said Frank. "Well, I'll check."

He crossed to the window, and caught his breath. Just beneath the window stood what Frank first actually thought was a ghost, but then, switching on his reasoning mind, he understood was a fallow deer. He had never seen one, except in pictures, and would never have believed that the real thing could look so much like a mythical creature—a massive stag with bouldered shoulders and a rack of antlers that would have disgraced an American elk, four or five feet from tip to tip. Pale and motionless as marble, only its eyes and nose alive, it peered up at him like an illustration breathed from an old tapestry.

Her quilt around her like a cape, Claudia came up behind him and whispered, "My God. Is that normal?"

"I don't think they live around here. I think they live in France. Or in a park at some palace."

"But it's real?"

"It's real," said Frank.

"It really is a real ghost!" Colin told Ian. "I'm right. See?"

"Is it coming through the wall?" Ian asked. "Is it coming up the stairs?"

"No. Don't worry. It is real, but it's an animal. It would be scared of us," Frank said. "It's a stag. A father fallow deer. There are lots of fallow deer in some places. One special kind is pure white. They are very rare."

Then Claudia held up her hand. "Listen. What's that?"

The sound was also something Frank had never experienced, but in a moment, he also knew what it was. It was birdsong. Branches filled with blackbirds, from the sound of it, were singing, their liquid five- and seven-note trills sliding up and slipping down, calling and answering.

"Are those singing ghosts?" Ian said.

"They're birds," Frank said.

"Now you're really lying, Dad. It's night," Colin told him. "They're not birds. They're ghosts. Who's playing that noise?"

"They're not ghosts."

"They could be angels," Ian said. "Do you think they're angels?"

"They're birds," Frank said.

"Angels," said Ian. "Maybe angels are coming for All Saints and Sally?"

"You know," Claudia said, elbowing Frank. "Maybe they are."

So they hustled back into their room, carrying Jennifer in her box. Claudia hitched away from her customary spot near the middle of the bed, and Frank made a space for the boys between them, and both of the boys curled in, by now knobby-elbowed figures of frost, for neither of them could abide staying covered. As they settled down, Frank told them that in England, blackbirds often sang all night, and that until he looked it up online, he thought it must be a recording, or the kind of weird reversal of nature, like whales leaping out of the seas, that foretold some great natural disaster overturning the natural order. No sooner had he said this than he cursed himself inwardly, for he could all but hear the boys thinking of a storm, and it was only caution that prevented Colin from sending that thought to Frank. And so he talked on, and told them how local people professed to be annoyed by the sound. "But how could they be? It's so good, isn't it?" Frank said. "It's a good noise." They all murmured sleepily, and Frank nearly closed his eyes, hitched by the sweet sounds to some ancient chain of hopeful repose.

But there was something out of place.

"It can't be happening," said Frank. "That's what it is."

"What can't?" Claudia said.

Blackbirds, the farmers told Frank when he came, would crowd the spring, beginning their night's revels as soon as a warm February. "But they don't sing in the fall or winter. Ever. Blackbirds don't sing at this time of year. It's impossible."

Propping herself up with her arms, Claudia began to laugh. Her hair had burst around her face in ringlets, her inner heat defying the bite of chill in the room. With her unaccustomed fullness, her child's hair gave her the look of a Vermeer. She laughed, so hard that Frank was roused to worry rather than mirth. He knew that pregnant women's emotions swung a wide arc in service of their hormonal drama—not that they needed hormones for drama. He finally said, "Are you okay? What's so funny?"

"There's a giant white stag on the lawn and they only live in France. And there are four-and-twenty blackbirds singing at night in the middle of November."

Frank said, "And so?"

"So maybe they don't know."

"What?"

"That it's all impossible. That deer can't be here. Those birds can't be singing. And still they are. So maybe they don't know it's all impossible."

"What if they did?"

Claudia said softly, "Who knows? They might stop."

Frank turned off the lamps.

As he did, he remembered something Hope used to say when he was a child. She told him that the "heavenly host," so often depicted in Christmas carols and the gospel of St. Luke, was not, the way people thought, a kind of celestial a cappella group. The heavenly host was an army of angels arrayed for battle, summoned to use whenever they had to triumph over Satan. An army of angels, in trucks and tractors, with mallets and pitchforks . . . well, Frank thought. Tucked up compact and secure on their bed, tucked with one of their hands under the next one's back, Frank and his family slid on the square raft of their bed into the night, through its darks and over its deeps, as, with a mighty joy, the choir of birds raised their voices all around them, singing them to sleep and then singing in their dreams, straight through until morning.

Acknowledgments

IF THIS BOOK has any merit at all, it is due to the strong creative influence and intellectual rigor of my beloved agent and friend, Jane Gelfman, and my thoughtful and generous editor, Trish Todd. With high minds and high standards, both gave me their very best. Thanks is due to the four "horse whisperers" who helped me understand the nuances of A-level jumping events, especially Ann and Penny, and to Brisbaner Sally Clark. I must acknowledge with gratitude the MacDowell Colony, the Corporation of Yaddo, and the Ragdale Foundation—where substantial portions of this story were written in 2013 and 2014. To Karen Cooper, publisher of Merit Press, the proud young adult imprint where I am editor in chief, great thanks, and to my colleague Meredith O'Hayre McCarthy, more than you know. For their encouragement, I also thank fellow writers and pals Ann Garvin, Lisa Genova, Hollis Gillespie, Molly Howes. Kathleen O'Brien, Deborah Stetson, Clint McCown, Rebecca Wells, Wiley Cash, and Mitch Wieland. Most of all, eternal debt must always be to Team Jackie—my brother, my sis, my lucky-me best friends—and my children, Rob, Dan, Marty, Francie, Merit, Mia, Will, Marta, and Atticus. You have turned my mourning to dancing.

About the Author

JACQUELYN MITCHARD has written ten novels for adults, including several *New York Times* best sellers and several that have enjoyed critical acclaim and awards, including Great Britain's Talk-about Prize and the Orange Broadband Prize for Fiction long list. She has also written seven young adult novels; five children's books; a memoir, *Mother Less Child*; and a collection of essays, *The Rest of Us: Dispatches from the Mother Ship*. Her essays have been published in newspapers and magazines worldwide, widely anthologized, and incorporated into school curricula. Her reportage on educational issues facing American Indian children won the Hampton and Maggie Awards for Public Service Journalism. Mitchard's work as part of *Shadow Show*, the anthology of short stories honoring her mentor, Ray Bradbury, won the Bram Stoker Award and Shirley Jackson Award, and was short-listed for the Audie Award. She served on the fiction jury for the 2003 National Book Awards, and her first novel, *The Deep End of the Ocean*, was the inaugural selection of the Oprah Winfrey Book Club, later adapted for a feature film starring and produced by Michelle Pfeiffer. Mitchard is the editor in chief and co-creator of Merit Press, a realistic-YA-fiction imprint. She is a distinguished fellow at the Ragdale Foundation in Lake Forest, Illinois, and a DeWitt Walker Reader's Digest fellow at the MacDowell Colony in Peterboro, New Hampshire. She lives on Cape Cod with her husband and their nine children, who range in age from nine to thirty.